BRIGHT ANGELS
& FAMILIARS
CONTEMPORARY MORMON STORIES

BRIGHT ANGELS
& FAMILIARS

CONTEMPORARY MORMON STORIES

EUGENE ENGLAND • EDITOR

Signature Books
Salt Lake City
• 1 9 9 2 •

Cover design by Larry Clarkson.

Interior design by Brent Corcoran.

∞ Printed on acid-free paper.

96   95   94   93   92   6   5   4   3   2   1

LIBRARY OF CONGRESS CATALOGING-IN-PUBLICATION DATA

Bright angels and familiars : contemporary Mormon stories / edited by
     Eugene England.
     ISBN: 1-56085-026-4
     1. Short stories, American—Mormon authors. 2. Mormons—Fiction.
I. England, Eugene.
Ps591.M6B75   1992
813'.010892283—dc20   92-16705
                                                          CIP

FOR

Virginia Sorensen,
1912-91,

and

Maurine Whipple,
1903-92.

THEY TAUGHT US HOW.

CONTENTS

The New Mormon Fiction

EUGENE ENGLAND

Both Mormonism and the short story, as Bruce Jorgensen has noted,[1] were revealed and invented in the same few years, about 1820 to 1835. It may in fact be more than mere coincidence that the short, lyrical form of prose narrative and an extremely practical, personal, and narrative-oriented world religion were both created during the height of the Romantic movement, that watershed in human history whose consequences we are still living out.

The Church of Jesus Christ of Latter-day Saints began with a book, the Book of Mormon, which people who are not LDS consider to be fiction. Many Mormons themselves recognize the personal shaping and influence of point of view on this ancient history as it was edited and translated. However, the first of what could be called Mormon fiction was actually written by Parley P. Pratt in the 1840s. Sections of Pratt's *Autobiography,* though edited by others and published in the 1880s, are personal narratives shaped and self-conscious in precisely the way good fiction is, while his "Dialogue Between Joe Smith and the Devil" (*New York Herald,* 1843) is the first Mormon short story. It is witty, imaginative in setting and dialogue and, though clearly pro-Mormon, aimed at a non-Mormon audience.

Like much other early Mormon literature, it is a combination of apologetic and satire, committed to a perfect Zion and fiercely critical of the perishing Babylon everywhere else.

For the first fifty years of Mormonism, well into the settled Utah period when nationally published novels from classics to popular trash became increasingly available, all fiction was distrusted as at best inferior to "the truth" in history, biography, and sermons. In the 1880s Orson F. Whitney determined to combat the influences of non-Mormon literature and philosophy (especially Christian Science) and spearheaded a movement to produce at home in Utah uplifting fiction and poetry by, for, and in defense of the Saints—what he called "home literature." Josephine Spencer, Susa Young Gates, and Nephi Anderson produced a large quantity of such home-consumed fiction based more in dogma than experience. However, it was often, as Edward Geary has noted, even in its distinctive Mormon characteristics "only skin deep, masking an underlying vision which is as foreign to the gospel as it is to real life."[2]

Of this literature only Anderson's *Added Upon* continued to be read well into the twentieth century. However, works true to the movement's ideals and purposes, and thus also known to Mormon literary scholarship as "home literature," have continued as the mainstay of the most popular Mormon reading: didactic and sentimental stories published in official church publications or by official or semi-official presses.

Beginning with Vardis Fisher's *Children of God* in 1939 and continuing with Maurine Whipple, Virginia Sorensen, Samuel Taylor, and a number of others, a new kind of fiction began to be written by and about Mormons and published and praised nationally. These authors have been identified by Geary as Mormondom's "lost generation."[3] They were similar to the American "lost generation" twenty years earlier in their impatience with their culture and expatriation from their people, and they were largely lost to Mormon audiences and as an influence on Mormon writers.

But not entirely lost. Geary himself remembers as a young student finding Virginia Sorensen on the Mormon fiction shelf of the library at Brigham Young University, being amazed by the first good literature he had read that spoke to his own Mormon and rural Utah experience, and then reading down the shelves through the lost treasure of similar writers of the 1940s and 1950s.

The following collection begins with part of that treasure, short works by Sorensen and Whipple that are among the first Mormon stories that can be called *contemporary*. Sorensen's "Where Nothing Is Long Ago" (a fictionalized murder over water rights) was published in the *New Yorker* in 1953 and is a perfect example of the critical but nostalgic and loving stance of the best of lost generation work. Whipple's "They Did Go Forth," recently discovered along with a number of her other unpublished stories, is, in its affirmative retelling of a "Three Nephite" folktale, closer than either Sorensen's work or Whipple's own *The Giant Joshua* to the spirit of "home literature." But both stories belong in this collection because they reflect the skills of the two most influential among the "lost" pioneers of the Mormon fiction which continues to best challenge and move readers and inspire writers.

Coming about twenty years later, Douglas Thayer and Donald R. Marshall were the pioneers of a second generation. As Jorgensen discovered,[4] there were a number of "late expatriates" besides Sorensen publishing Mormon stories in a variety of national and regional publications from about 1940 to 1965, including Ray B. West, Jr., Wayne Carver, and most notably David L. Wright. Wright produced excellent poetry and drama and published five stories in literary quarterlies before his sudden death at age forty-five in 1967. None of these writers is included here. None gained a Mormon readership or influenced younger Mormon writers as did Thayer and Marshall, mainly because there were no Mormon outlets for the new fiction. Such outlets were provided in the 1960s with the founding of *Brigham Young University Studies* and *Dialogue: A Journal of Mormon Thought*.

Thayer and Marshall benefitted in their pioneering efforts from two separate influences: they studied modern British and American writers, such as Joyce, Hemingway, Porter, and Flannery O'Connor, and they learned new approaches to Mormon history and culture from the nationally published writers of the lost generation.

They also had access to a Mormon audience, critics, and outlets in an expanding intellectual community. They benefitted especially from Clinton Larson, a poet and dramatist who in the 1950s and 1960s became the first Mormon writer to combine excellent contemporary training and natural talent with an informed and passionate faith that he made central to his work.

With *The Rummage Sale* (1973) Marshall produced a collection of stories which took rural Mormon culture for granted as a context for apparently humorous but also deeply serious examinations of religious and moral conflicts. "The Week-end," published here, shows his skill with point-of-view, perhaps the fiction writer's chief formal tool.

Thayer did not publish his first collection, *Under the Cottonwoods,* until 1977, but he started writing his unique Mormon stories earlier than Marshall, in the early 1960s, and his influence on other Mormon writers has been perhaps wider and continued longer. As John Bennion has said, "He was the first to solve the major problem. He taught us how to explore the interior life, with its conflicts of doubt and faith, goodness and evil, of a believing Mormon." Here I have chosen a story from his first collection, "Opening Day," which shows Thayer's characteristic strategy of an extended journey of the mind based on experience in nature.

Jorgensen has shown that Thayer's strategy both follows closely that of the Romantic poets' "Great Odes" and also undermines Romantic assumptions.[5] "Opening Day" and all of the stories in Thayer's recent collection, *Mr. Wahlquist in Yellowstone,* especially "The Redtail Hawk," confront in a uniquely Mormon way the basic Romantic anxiety: their heartfelt attraction to life in, even union with, nature—which conflicts with their moral understanding that pursuing such union is only possible in unconsciousness, loss of language, and even death.[6]

Others were learning from Marshall and Thayer and from the best contemporary American writers. Karen Rosenbaum studied at Stanford University in the 1960s with Wallace Stegner and has regularly published wry, delicate stories of relationships complicated by the quest for faith. Bruce Jorgensen (who uses his middle name,

Wayne, for his fiction) studied at Brigham Young University and Cornell University and has written a few meticulously-crafted stories based firmly in his Mormon experience.

Lewis Horne, raised in Arizona and settled in mid-Canada, began writing stories about his Mormon youth and has been published nationally and honored in *Best American Short Stories, 1974* and *Prize Stories, 1987: The O. Henry Awards.* Eileen Gibbons Kump wrote a connected series of stories about a second-generation pioneer woman (*Bread and Milk,* 1979), which shows remarkable psychological and historical insight. "Sayso or Sense," included here, is perhaps the first Mormon story to deal directly with feminist issues. Meanwhile Gladys Farmer (*Elders and Sisters,* 1977) and Béla Petsco (*Nothing Very Important and Other Stories,* 1979) produced collections of missionary stories, which like Kump's were connected into a longer narrative by common central characters.

In the 1980s these beginnings produced a cascade of individual works and then collections, published through the independent Mormon and regional publications and presses and increasingly through national outlets as well. Among a group of what Jorgensen in 1983 called "Up-and-Comers," Levi S. Peterson achieved the major breakthrough, becoming the first of this second generation of contemporary Mormon writers to publish a collection nationally (*The Canyons of Grace,* in the prestigious University of Illinois short fiction series, 1982). He continued Thayer's work on interior Mormon male landscape and used Thayer's sophisticated first-person narration, which played the moral and spiritual naiveté of the young protagonist against his more mature narrating self, and he also took on major Mormon theological and historical issues. Peterson has continued Marshall's use of rural Mormonism for humor and pathos but, in a story like "The Christianizing of Coburn Heights," took Mormon humor into new realms of pain and despair. In his latest collection, *Night Soil* (1990), Peterson has secured his place as the most prolific author of high-quality contemporary Mormon short fiction.

But he has close competition. In the 1970s a young Mormon

playwright, Orson Scott Card, left the Mormon literary scene to become one of America's most widely read and critically acclaimed science fiction writers. He first won the top two prizes, the Hugo and Nebula, for *Ender's Game* (1985), then made un unprecedented second sweep of the same prizes the next year with *Speaker for the Dead*. Meanwhile he began writing Mormon science fiction stories (collected in *The Folk of the Fringe,* 1989) and Mormon fantasy. His "Alvin Maker" series is based on a figure much like Joseph Smith, growing up to be a prophet in an imaginary alternative America (the first novel's first section, "Hatrack River," was published as a story in 1987 and won the World Fantasy Award).

Pauline Mortensen has used the rural Mormon stereotype to make witty, hip, exquisitely vocalized tales (especially "Woman Talking to a Cow," included here, from *Back Before the World Turned Nasty,* 1989). Neal Chandler (*Benediction,* 1989) writes about Mormon experience *outside* the traditional Wasatch front, which tends to be overshadowed by ghosts of pioneer history and present authority. Like Levi Peterson he has pioneered the use of humor ("Benediction") and folk mythology ("The Last Nephite").

Darrell Spencer, at Brigham Young University, is the contemporary Mormon writer perhaps least focused on Mormon characters and culture. He writes post-modernist, occasionally minimalist, stories, published widely in prestigious "little" magazines and collected in *A Woman Packing a Pistol* (1987). He shows what this approach can do within a Mormon context in "I am Buzz Gaulter, Left-hander." Phyllis Barber has also made her reputation mainly outside Mormon literary circles, with *The School of Love* (1990) and *And the Desert Shall Blossom* (1991). *How I Got Cultured: A Nevada Memoir* won the Associated Writing Programs prize in 1991 and was published by the University of Georgia Press in 1992.

Judith Freeman grew up in Utah and has written stories about female characters who live there, as in *Family Attractions: Stories* (1987) or, as in her novel, *The Chinchilla Farm* (1989), begin their odysseys there. She has a particularly understated, affecting style, evident in her story here and especially in her novel *Set for Life* (1991), which takes place in Southern Idaho. Michael Fillerup has explored in a number of stories (see *Visions and Other Stories,* 1990) the relationship of Mormonism to native American peoples (such as "Lost and Found" in this volume). Linda Sillitoe has tended to focus (in *Windows on the Sea and Other Stories,* 1989) on the interior life of contemporary Mormon women. But Fillerup in "The Renovation of Marsha Fletcher" has written persuasively from a Mormon woman's perspective, and Sillitoe in "Coyote Tracks" has written persuasively of the confrontation of Mormon anglo and native American world views.

Most of the writers included in this collection that I have discussed to this point were born before 1950 and all are now established—by virtue of their influence, their published collections which continue to be read, or their consistent output of contributions to Mormon letters—as part of a developing canon of Mormon fiction. I have also chosen from a younger group in order to show some new directions contemporary Mormon fiction is taking.

One of the youngest, Walter Kirn, has already in his late twenties achieved remarkable success nationally with his first collection, *My Hard Bargain* (1990). A convert to Mormonism, Kirn writes about growing up in the church ("Whole Other Bodies" is based on his family's conversion) and more general stories about life on farms in Wisconsin. Kirn began publishing in national magazines such as *Esquire* (whose editors thought his Mormon stories had to be changed to a Utah setting to be believable). John Bennion, who studied under contemporary masters such as Donald Barthelme at Houston, recently published his first collection, *Breeding Leah and Other Stories* (1991), from which I have chosen "Dust," a story written in a fashionable contemporary style that is also intriguingly Mormon. Margaret Young has published two novels and is beginning to publish stories nationally as well as in the independent Mormon press (her first collection *Elegies and Lovesongs,* from which I have chosen "Outsiders," appeared in 1992).

M. Shayne Bell, much influenced by Orson Scott Card, spent 1991-92 on a National Endowment for the Humanities Grant, writing science fiction stories. Stories such as the one included here, "Dry Niger," are Mormon in no overt way but are recognizably so in their moral values and vision concerning the last days of the earth. Sibyl Johnston has been working, supported by a Fellowship in Literature at Radcliffe's Bunting Institute, on an experimental, nearly autobiographical novel, part of which, "Iris Holmes," was published as a story in the anthology *Hot Type* (1988) and is included here.

So what makes these stories recognizably Mormon as well as contemporary? And what does it matter? It matters, I think, because Mormonism is a new religious tradition with a unique theology and a powerful ethnic identity and mythic vision of the kind that should produce good and characteristic literature. Writers reveal their fundamental values and beliefs, their integrity and compassion or meanness and blindness, as well as their way of seeing the world, in all the decisions, small and large, that go into form and content and finally make the novel or story or essay believable and moving.[7] Flannery O'Connor put the case this way: "It makes a great difference to the look of a novel whether its author believes that the world came late into being and continues to come by a creative act of God, or whether he believes that the world and ourselves are the product of a cosmic accident. It makes a great difference to his novel whether he believes that we are created in God's image, or whether he believes we create God in our own. It makes a great difference whether he believes that our wills are free, or bound like those of the other animals."[8]

I believe authors' beliefs, inevitably affecting the nature and quality of their writing, also make a great deal of difference to readers—to what we are able to get out of a story. So I have chosen stories that are not only valuable because they are skillful, the product of natural gifts, careful training or apprenticeship, and good understanding of the traditions of classic short stories and contemporary innovations. They are also valuable because they are written by people with a recognizably Mormon background which leads them through their stories to express, reveal, develop, and challenge the shape of Mormon beliefs.

Mormonism holds that individual identity is uncreated and indestructible, that free choice is absolutely necessary if we are to develop human potential, and that yielding one's individuality to the sociality of marriage and larger communities is equally essential. Furthermore Mormonism insists that divinity continues to reveal such things to prophets and further understanding of them to all people. One crucial way such insight can come, I believe, is through the telling of stories, and the stories here are such revelations.

How can these stories be revelations, some might ask, if they describe doubt, despair, failure, and sin? Morality—and faith—in fiction are not a matter simply of content nor even a question of whether a matter is presented in a "balanced" way. They have much more to do with the shape of the author's own belief and moral vision, which inevitably show through to a careful reader. The stories I have chosen occasionally describe, in precise and relevant language, troubled thoughts and human frailties which are necessary parts of a whole picture. In each case, that picture is a new vision of life, filtered and energized through a believing, moral intelligence as well as a gifted and disciplined artistic sensibility.

Mormonism integrates an almost materialistic affirmation of worldly realities with a yearning to reach beyond the world. We make our homes here and imagine heaven as much like this place—but constantly sense that our true home is elsewhere. Most of these stories are exceptionally accurate and thorough in describing the surfaces of the world we know. Many also evoke visions and epiphanies which seem related to another world of the spirit. Thus the title reminds us that the best Mormon fiction concerns both bright angels of spiritual reality and the familiar, beautiful world in which we live and create our being.

This collection, of course, is indebted to the pioneering work in Mormon letters of earlier anthologists and critics. In the very first anthology of Mormon literature, A Believing People (1974), editors Richard H. Cracroft and Neal E. Lambert, who had also begun, at Brigham Young University, the first classes in Mormon literature, provided an excellent sampling of nineteenth-century fiction and the best work of the lost generation—as well as samples of the early work of Thayer and Marshall and Kump. That same year they produced a look at the future in Twenty-Two Young Mormon Writers.

Then, just as the explosion of the 1980s was getting under way,

Levi Peterson edited a collection, *Greening Wheat: Fifteen Mormon Stories* (1983), of newly written works that revealed the range that was developing in the second generation—fifteen excellent and mature writers when ten years before there had only been two or three. Now, less than another ten years along, the growth has continued, requiring difficult selection from among dozens of good writers, many of whom are increasingly published nationally as well as in the growing number of selective independent Mormon and regional periodicals like *Brigham Young University Studies, Dialogue: A Journal of Mormon Thought, Exponent II, Sunstone,* and *Wasatch Review International,* which is devoted entirely to Mormon literature; and presses like Aspen Books, Bookcraft, Covenant Communications, Deseret Book, Signature Books, and the University of Utah Press. I regret that all the fine contemporary Mormon story writers could not be included here. Look for them in the list of "Other Notable Mormon Stories" at the end of this book (which Bruce Jorgensen helped to compile) and in future periodicals and press catalogues.

NOTES

1. Bruce W. Jorgensen, "A 'Smaller Canvas' of the Mormon Short Story Since 1950," *Mormon Letters Annual, 1983* (Salt Lake City: Association for Mormon Letters, 1984), 10.

2. Edward Geary, "The Poetics of Provincialism: Mormon Regional Fiction," *Dialogue: A Journal of Mormon Thought* 11 (Summer 1978): 15.

3. Edward Geary, "Mormondom's Lost Generation: The Novelists of the 1940s," *Brigham Young University Studies* 18 (Fall 1977): 89.

4. Jorgensen, "A 'Smaller Canvas,'" 12-14.

5. Bruce W. Jorgensen, "Romantic Lyric Form and Western Mormon Experience in the Stories of Douglas Thayer," *Western American Literature* 22 (May 1987): 43-47.

6. See Eugene England, "Thayer's Ode to the Redtail Hawk," *Mormon Letters Annual, 1983,* 42-53.

7. Bruce W. Jorgensen, "'Herself Moving Beside Herself, Out There Alone': The Shape of Mormon Belief in Virginia Sorensen's *The Evening and the Morning,*" *Dialogue: A Journal of Mormon Thought* 13 (Fall 1980): 45-47.

8. Flannery O'Connor, *Mystery and Manners,* ed. Sally and Robert Fitzgerald (New York: Farrar, Straus, and Giroux, 1969), 156-57.

ONE

Where Nothing Is Long Ago

VIRGINIA SORENSEN

You'll probably remember Brother Tolsen and that awful thing that happened when you were a little girl," my mother wrote me recently. Her fat script traveled the whole way around the photograph and obituary she had clipped from our Mormon newspaper. "The killing wasn't even mentioned at his funeral. All the speakers just said what a good man he always was."

Remember Brother Tolsen? I looked at his square jaw and his steady eyes, and it was as if I had seen him yesterday. Well, I thought, another one is gone; soon there won't be a real Danish accent left in that whole valley. Mormon converts from Denmark came to Utah by the thousands during the second half of the nineteenth century. Now there were only a few survivors. Not long before, it had been old Bishop Petersen himself who had died.

I was with Bishop Petersen, in his garden, the morning the Tolsen trouble happened. My mother thought I had a morbid interest in the affair, and I guess I had. It was the summer I was nine, and I was morbid about almost everything. I was absolutely certain for years afterward that two piles of bloody rabbits' ears I saw on the courthouse lawn at the time of Brother Tolsen's trial had something to do with the killing he was being tried for. They

1

hadn't. They were merely tokens of the fact that the annual county rabbit hunt had gone off according to schedule.

Mother, who loves accuracy, often complains about the peculiar quality of my memories, and likely she's right. The Tolsen case, for instance, tends to get mixed in my mind with other water-thief murders I've heard of. My mother sent me a clipping about one in Utah Valley, near Provo, just last year. This man was killed with a gun, however, instead of a shovel—as Brother Tolsen killed *his* thief—and then the killer turned the gun on himself. Mother wrote on that latest clipping, "Dad and I don't see why he had to shoot himself, too. Do you?"

That's a very Western query. A poem written by Thomas Hornsby Ferril begins: "Here in America nothing is long ago . . ." and that's very Western, too. People out West remember when important things were settled violently, and they remember the wide, dry wastes before the mountain water was captured and put to use. Even now, the dry spaces, where the jack rabbits hop through the brush as thick as mites on a hen, are always there, waiting to take over; dryness hugs the green fields, pushing in, only the irrigation ditches keeping it at bay.

July was when the Tolsen trouble happened. In Utah, that's when the dry heat is most intense. Our whole valley floor is like a spot on a piece of paper when you focus the sun on it through a glass; you feel as if, any second, it is going to brown and then smoke and then burst into flame. Around it there are the quiet mountains, cool and blue, but long, dusty roads and scrubby hills lie between them and the simmering town. The river is the single link, flowing down between dusty-leaved cottonwoods from the mountains to the people in the valley.

Not that I minded heat in those days. There was no need to be hot when, on either side of the wide streets, there was cold water, brought from the river by the town's main ditch and diverted into smaller channels that ran along the sidewalks. It rushed constantly there, between banks lined with mint and grass. Wearing huge black bloomers and white pantywaists with the garters off, I spent most of my summer days in the ditches. Main Ditch was deep and lined with stones; when I skated along it in wintertime, I could hardly see over its banks. The ditches leading from it along the streets were shallow, having perhaps a foot of water in them at the peak of the spring supply.

Each household in town had its own dam—often nothing more than a couple of broad boards with a short handle nailed to them—and its own water turn when the dam was put to use. Set across the streams in the street-side ditches, and packed in with wet turf, these dams were sufficient to turn the water onto lawns and gardens, and nothing short of a calamity could prevent a house-holder from putting in his dam at the proper time. Every spring, the Water Master—an official of great importance in a Utah town—provided each family with a list of Water Turns, carefully worked out. We always kept our list tacked inside the door of the kitchen cupboard.

We children followed the water like pioneers, finding what dams were in and wading in the ditches where the water was highest. We kept ourselves rosy and crisp with it. Sometimes my grandmother would go with us and put her feet into the water to cool off. I recall her saying many times that Brigham Young must have been a true prophet, because he had said that Utah was The Place right in the middle of July, when nobody would think, to look at it without water, that it would ever grow a respectable bean. It was on the twenty-fourth of July that Brigham Young made his historic pronounce-ment, and as far as I know not a drop of rain has ever fallen to spoil the parades, the fireworks, and the pageants that take place every year on that day.

The Tolsen trouble must have been on the twenty-fifth of July, because I remember Mother's saying I couldn't wade in the grass, which was about to be flooded, unless I first collected every burned-out sparkler that had been left on the ground the night before. So, early that morning, I was busily searching the grass for wires when I saw Bishop Petersen, whose dam was in, working with the water in his garden next door. The full stream was running into it, as it would presently run into ours, for our turn followed his. His garden, like every other one in Utah, had a series of shallow furrows between the rows of vegetables, and he was damming them with chunks of turf and opening one or two at a time, so that each, in turn, received the stream. It was beautiful to see the tall green vegetables in precise lines and the moving water twinkling between them.

In half a minute, I was paddling alongside Bishop Petersen. The water in the furrows was warmer than that in the ditches, and it was glorious to feel the soft mud between my toes. And I loved to hear Bishop Petersen tell about Denmark, from which he had come as a young man. I asked him all sorts of questions to keep him talking, for his odd accent and his laughter pleased me. I recall how the robins sang and hopped down into the furrows as water darkened them and lured out long, fat worms.

Bishop Petersen said that to leave the lovely land of Denmark one had to be very certain it was to God's Kingdom he was coming. He himself had been sure of it when he heard about the mountain water, so pure, so shining, so cold, so free. Whenever his turn came to speak at Testimony Meeting, which followed Sunday school on the first Sunday of every month, he spoke about the water. It was to him, next to the Gospel itself, the unmistakable sign of the Kingdom.

That twenty-fifth of July, he talked as usual, his white beard wobbling like an elf's, and now and then I had to turn my back to prevent him from seeing that I was smiling. He thought that, as one descended from Danes myself, I ought to know that the crisp peas I was picking and eating were *ualmindelig god* (unusually good). He wanted me to repeat the phrase, but I couldn't. The very sound of most Danish words made me giggle until I was weak. The language bristled with "g's" and "k's" exactly the way Bishop Petersen bristled with white whiskers. Yet goodness and kindness and excellent husbandry went along with all the things about him that made me laugh. I loved him dearly, as my parents did, and to most of us to be Danish—as to be Mormon—meant to be virtuous, kind, and of good report.

Mother came out to call me for breakfast, and she stood awhile,

4

leaning on the fence, to talk. What she said and what Bishop Petersen replied is lost to me now, but while they talked, I saw Brother Tolsen coming. He ran into the yard with so urgent and desperate a look on his usually cheerful face that even I knew at once that he was in bad trouble. "Come in now," Mother said sharply to me. "The eggs will be cold already."

By suppertime, it was known all over town that Brother Tolsen had killed a man.

"But why did he hit him like that?" Mother asked my father. "It's not like Brother Tolsen to strike anybody. Such a gentle man!"

"Twice he had turned Brother Tolsen's water off his fields in the night. *Twice!*" My father spoke with the patience of a man obliged to explain violence to a woman. "Brother Tolsen says he had no notion of hitting so hard, but he hit him with a shovel, after all. From what I hear, it struck on the edge and went over the forehead, and one eye came—"

"Finish your supper and go out to play," Mother said to me severely, and to my father, "Is it necessary to go into those terrible details in front of the children? It's enough to curdle their souls, the way you men tell it—as if you enjoyed it!"

It may seem an odd thing to remember, but I do remember that I was eating cottage cheese that night. It was made by my mother on the back of the stove and served in great bowls. Cream was poured over it, and there was a great, lovely red blob of jelly in the middle of it, from which one took a little chip of a jewel with every bite, eating one curd of the cheese at a time. It was a common summer supper. I also had a bowl of fresh lettuce, with cream and sugar, and I ate that slowly too, leaf by leaf.

My parents said no more about Brother Tolsen until I had finished and gone outside, but I lingered on the porch in the shadows of the Virginia creepers. I heard my father say how big my ears were—". . . as big as soup ladles. She never misses a thing"—but he laughed when he said it. It was a family joke about me and my big ears, and how I was as deaf as a post when it suited me. Presently, they were talking about the killing again—how the victim's head had been bashed in and he had been found in a pool of blood near Brother Tolsen's dam.

I remember sitting there on the porch and holding my hands up against the setting sun. Sunset was huge and red and terribly intense in July, over the western hills. Against it, I could see my own blood shining red through my skin. Heads were brimful of blood, too—I knew that from nosebleed and from teeth coming out, and from the time I hit a stump and went over the handlebars of my bicycle square onto my skull. The man Brother Tolsen had killed was not very well known to me, probably because, as Grandmother remarked, he had "fallen away from the faith" and didn't often come to church. Now, losing the faith, I knew, was one of the greatest of sins, but murder was worse; it was the greatest sin of them all. And Brother Tolsen I knew very well indeed. He was important in our ward of the church, and I had often heard his testimony at meeting, just as I had heard Bishop Petersen's, and in the same delightful accent. In fact, he was so good a speaker that I had heard him more than once making sermons at funerals.

I liked funerals very much then, and I find them rather stimulating now. The philosophy I learned as a child made death more fascinating than terrible. The first corpse I ever saw was the mother of one of my grade-school friends. She had died in childbirth. I had received fresh cookies from her hands a day or so before, but now she lay exactly like Snow White, like one dreaming in a lovely bed, with an infinitely small and doll-like child in the crook of her arm. I stood and gazed at her with awe and admiration.

After that I went to every funeral remotely connected with anybody I knew. They were never forbidden to me. The corpses of men and women alike were always dressed in pure white, with bright-green aprons cheerfully embroidered to look like the fig leaves of the Garden of Eden. It was perfectly reasonable to me to believe that, as I was assured, they had just stepped "through the veil between earth and heaven." It seemed to me that they were always much handsomer than they had ever been in life, in their common house aprons or in their overalls stained with manure. I pictured them, in their clean new clothes, walking slowly westward with the sun and vanishing in a tremendous scarlet smile of sunset. I had even seen something like that in the movies, so I suspected that the miracle happened not only in Utah but also in California.

When Mother told me I could not go to the funeral of the man Brother Tolsen had killed, I was devastated, especially because there were rumors that Brother Tolsen himself would attend. He had been in jail a few hours and then had been released to attend to his work until the trial. He had a big family and a farm, and goodness only knew, people said, what would happen to them if he had to spend the rest of the summer in the jail.

"But Mother—" I cried, over and over.

"No! Absolutely not!" she said each time. She knew full well, of course, that I had a morbid interest in seeing a corpse with its head bashed in, and also that I wanted to enjoy the spectacle of a man going to the funeral of someone he had knocked headlong "through the veil" with a shovel.

In the end, I was not only forbidden to go, I was even given a neighbor's baby to tend, and in agony of spirit I saw Mother and Dad and Grandmother and just about everybody else in town go marching off to the dead man's house. No sooner were they gone, however, than I bundled the baby into his buggy and pushed him rapidly to that street. There I could at least see all the people standing around in the yard silent and serious, and I thought I might catch a glimpse of Brother Tolsen coming or going. Back and forth I walked, back and forth, pushing the buggy in the heat, envying the people as they filed slowly into the house and slowly out again after viewing the remains.

And then I really did see Brother Tolsen. Walking with his wife and oldest son, he passed so close to me on the sidewalk that he would have brushed against me if I had not drawn the buggy quickly off onto the grass. He nodded to me but did not smile, and I thought he appeared much as he always did when he went to church. People looked down at their shoes as he entered the dead man's gate, but when he moved along the walk toward the house, many stepped forward and greeted him. Between the gate and the porch, he must have stopped to shake hands twenty times. The front door opened and he went inside, and I found myself standing with my stomach pressed against the fence to watch. I could hear a breeze of comment among the people nearest me.

"It won't be easy for him to see Lena today."

"She knows it was an accident."

"But how can she believe her own husband would steal water?"

Presently, Brother Tolsen and his wife and son came out of the house. This time he did not pause to shake the hand of anyone but walked quickly from the yard. Then the door of the house remained closed for a while, and most of the people started toward the church, a few blocks away. When Mother and Dad and Grandmother came out of the yard, I began to push the buggy toward home, but I turned back as soon as they were out of sight. The hearse and a leading car, filled with flowers, were waiting in front of the house, and nobody was going to deny me a sight of the coffin.

I heard someone say "Poor Lena!" and the door opened again. Lena is still, to me, a vision of total sorrow. She leaned forward as she walked after the coffin, doubled over like a person with a violent stomachache. She was dressed in heavy black, with a black veil, and I think now how hot she must have been on that blistering day. After she had been carried off in a car that followed the hearse, the people who were left went away, and the whole house and yard looked empty and bedraggled. I walked back and forth, staring in. On the path, just inside the gate, lay one red rose, but I only looked at it. I wouldn't any more have touched it than I would have stirred my finger in a pool of blood.

Poor Lena! I knew that since her husband had fallen away from the faith she could never get much glory in the next world. Even if he had not been a water-thief, he wouldn't have done her much good in heaven. In the Mormon church, every man can aspire to some sort of ordination—every small boy of any virtue whatever is a Deacon and can go on to be a Priest and an Elder and a Teacher and a High Priest and all sorts of important-sounding things. But a woman has no Priesthood and must depend on her husband to take her to The Highest Degree. I visualized dazzling marble steps stretching up and up to the throne of God himself, with winged people arranged thereon according to their just deserts.

Not once, as I recall, did I think Poor Brother Tolsen! The two figures are clear in my mind. Brother Tolsen had looked sad but very straight and dignified as he walked into the house where the corpse lay, shaking hands with his Brethren as he went. Sister Lena, stooping and wild, had hidden her face in her handkerchief as she was led away. Later, I heard some talk of "poor Lena," who was "young yet, after all" and "should marry a real believer," but after the funeral I never laid eyes on her again, though I often rode my bicycle past her house, and looked and looked.

The next thing I remember about the Tolsen case is walking after school with my best friend, Carol. We went past the court-house, where we knew the jury was being selected, and there were those great piles of bloody rabbits' ears on the courthouse lawn, being counted. The hunters were always divided into two teams, and the losers had to give the winners what was called a Rabbit Supper. I learned later, with relief, that they did not eat the ears, or even the jack rabbits, but had chicken pies at the church, cooked by the women of the Relief Society. Nevertheless, those piles of ears I see to this day.

That night there was talk at our supper table, and on the porch afterward, about how difficult it had been to find jurors "without prejudice." The trial itself lasted only three short afternoons. At home, it was discussed freely, and the talk consisted mostly of repeating what character witnesses had said. There had been no witness to the killing itself, and Brother Tolsen had given up at once to the authorities: first to his bishop, which was entirely proper in all eyes, and then—in company with Bishop Petersen—to the sheriff. As for Lena, she did not come to the trial at all, but was said to have disappeared into that vast place where there were yellow streetcars, blue-coated policemen, a shining capitol building, and a merry-go-round in Liberty Park—Great Salt Lake City.

Almost all that was left to be done after the character witnesses were through was to hear the simple story told by Brother Tolsen himself and repeated in the town with nods of understanding and respect. His friends and neighbors considered him innocent of any real wrongdoing, and in this the jury soon concurred. I remember Dad repeating the words of somebody who had been very important at the trial—probably Brother Tolsen's lawyer. "If a thief enters a man's own house in the night and means to rob him of all he has, all his clothing and all his food, thereby meaning to take the very lives of his wife and his little children—then what shall that householder do? Would his actions be judged as malice aforethought? Is it not true that he who steals water is stealing life itself?"

It was a joyful thing for Brother Tolsen's friends to see him at home again, and they have all been safer because of him. There has been no water-stealing that I have heard of in that valley since.

One other memory remains. I recall an evening, months after the trial was over, when my parents and I were driving along the road where his fields lay and saw Brother Tolsen working with the little streams that were running among his young corn. Dad and Mother waved and called to him. He lifted an arm to answer, and I saw that he held a shovel in the other hand. "I wonder if he bought a new shovel," I said suddenly.

For a minute, the air seemed to have gone dead about us, in the peculiar way it sometimes can, which is so puzzling to a child. Then Mother turned to me angrily. "Don't you ever let me hear you say a thing like that again!" she said. "Brother Tolsen is a good, kind man!"

So until this very hour I never have.

TWO

They Did Go Forth

MAURINE WHIPPLE

Tildy Elizabeth sat by the cradle, Book of Mormon open on her knee. One hand rocked absently while the other traced in painful concentration the small print, dim in the yellow lamplight. Some time ago the bugle had sounded for supper, "Do what is right, let the consequence follow," and the sisters had gone to the dining room. She wanted to memorize the words so that she could think about them even after they got back. Longing to do this ever since the baby took sick, she hadn't had a minute alone before.

Of course, taking turns sitting up, the sisters were only doing their duty and being kind, but she knew they'd disapprove—All right, what if Brother Brigham *had* exhorted against such things as speaking in tongues! Tildy Elizabeth *knew* there were spirits wandering the earth until the Second Coming. Many's the time she had overheard the men whispering about the Gadianton Robbers told about in this same Book of Mormon, that brotherhood of murderers sprung up among the Nephites and the Lamanites in the century before Christ came. She'd heard talk about how they haunted a certain rocky gorge near the Nevada line; how the Dixie freighters, hauling early vegetables to the Nevada mining camps, had been scared out of their wits by huge boulders that missed them by inches; and by the very canyon walls closing up to squeeze them to death. Still, the Dixie freighters were going directly against counsel in trading of their substance with the gentiles, and she knew there were good spirits as well as bad! The sisters might think that in conjuring up the Three Nephites *she* was going against counsel—was even daring God. But it couldn't be helped.

Mostly Tildy didn't pay much mind to what anybody said, so long's she felt all right inside. It was only that she had never felt so alone before. She couldn't stand having folks against her now. It was only that she'd never felt so *desperate* before.

Over and over she had pondered the question: Where had they backslid? How had they displeased him? She and Thomas had joined the church with their families, shipped via the Perpetual Emigration Fund from Liverpool in 1850, endured constant hunger, cold, and sickness all during the long and bitter voyage, and finally walked behind handcarts from May to September for fourteen hundred miles. They had watched parents and brothers and sisters die. Then in 1864 just after their first child was born and Thomas was doing well on his Cottonwood farm, they answered Brother Brigham's call a second time to go five hundred miles into the desert with the Lead Mission. Here on the Muddy, near Las Vegas, they were asked right off by the settlers already there, "Which would you rather have, boards underfoot or overhead? Can't have both!" But nothing would have mattered, neither the harassing Indians nor the eternal wind-fretted sand which mowed down sprouting corn like scythes—if they hadn't lost their baby.

They stuck it out nearly ten years. Even then, when Brother Brigham finally saw that the lead they worked was just too brittle and flaky for bullets and ordered the Muddy Mission another three hundred miles up the river, through even more hair-prickling country, to colonize Long Valley—even then Thomas hadn't grumbled. Even when their second child, Tommy, had gone. Seems like these wildernesses killed children off easier than you could kill flies.

Thomas did not complain. Although it wasn't specific counsel to join, he turned everything he owned into the United Order and worked long and hard to get the coal and fuller's earth from the hillsides. Timber grew tall and close-fisted on the uplands, grasses were nutritious and deep on slope and ravine. The Order vegetable garden and orchard and the farms produced unbelievably; she had her own shanty dwelling in the square of shanties; she had managed to carry a child full-term again, had even been delivered by Ann Rice, forewoman of the midwife department. Life in the fort began to be pleasant. Then the authorities called Thomas on a mission back to England. They said he'd know how to make lots of converts among the miners there. But she wondered inside herself if converts were so important.

Her baby was still nursing when he left; she could still feel the sharp tugging of its gums. It was summer, two years ago, and she had stood in the roadway, dust churning about her ankles, and watched Thomas spring up beside the driver on the high seat of the buckboard, turn and wave to her and the child while the mules clattered off between the soaring green flanks of the valley. Even in memory there was an ache of pride at her heart. Herself, she had cleaned and carded and spun the wool for his jeans, gathered the kinnikinnick bark, and mixed the logwood for dyeing them black. She had knitted his gray socks, sulphur-bleached and braided the straw for his wide-brimmed Enoch hat that was like an official insignia of the Order. Only his carpet bag was not new—that, and the sawed-off shotgun he cradled across his knees. In the bed of the accompanying wagon, the Jolley boys lustily fiddled a parting serenade clear to the point of the mountain, but Tildy Elizabeth twisted the waist-apron of store calico she'd worn for the occasion and knew only bitterness.

Now, brooding over the child, obsessed with thoughts of the Three Nephites, she wondered if that bitterness was the reason for her present trouble: for the first time, trouble she had to bear without Thomas. No use even writing him. In his last letter he had said he was "in flesh and most excellent spirits"; and by the time he could get her bad news, everything would be over, one way or the other.

Tildy Elizabeth lifted her head and listened. She heard the sound of wheels crunching the snow, the blowing of a horse. That would be Brother Allen with the milk wagon. From her pantry recess, she lifted the quart wooden bucket made by Brother Cox in the Order's own cooper shop, shrugged into her shawl, and went out into the zero twilight. Ladling full her bucket from one of the great stone crocks, Brother Allen tried to josh with her. His breath puffed out like smoke in the freezing air. But she hadn't the heart to josh back. Before her the square stretched deep with drifted snow, except for the paths shoveled like wheel spokes from shanties to the dining room crouched impressively behind its flagpole. Now with the sociable goings-on, the dining room bulged with gaiety, its windows dripping lamplight on the whiteness outside. Tildy Elizabeth could hear an occasional burst of laughter, clear in the brittle air. About now the children would be sitting down at the second table. And then the dishes would be cleared, chairs and tables pushed back against the wall, and the Jolley boys would strike up "Old Dan Tucker" on their fiddles. Maybe another hour of grace. If the Nephites were going to come at all!

Brother Allen clucked to his horses, drove on around the square. She stood on the icy planks of the sidewalk a moment longer, staring at the maple and box elder trees etched blackly against the white fire of the stars, at the frozen tumult of the mountains. Even if a doctor better than Priddy Meeks were closer than Salt Lake, four hundred miles away, he'd be snowed out.

Inside once more, she warmed some of the milk, hoping against hope. But the child still lay in her stupor, motionless as death except for the almost imperceptible lifting of the bedclothes.

Tildy Elizabeth heaved another cottonwood log on the grate, and the coals rustled like the sound of leaves, as if memories of spring were stored up in the dried wood.

Once again she lifted her head to listen. Heart thumping, she flung open the door even before the knock came. But it was only one of the junior waitresses, red cheeks bunched in an excited grin. The little girl curtseyed as she'd been taught by Aunty Harmon, forewoman of all the waitresses, and held out a cloth-covered tray.

"Corn-meal mush and johnny cake and a whole firkin of butter!"

babbled the youngster. "And Aunty says she don't know who deserves a glass of honey more'n you, and there's a small bottle of brandy in the commissary, if you want it!"

Tildy Elizabeth thanked the child, then shooed her out of the room. Chattering drove her frantic. Even the sight of food drove her frantic. She put the mush and the butter and the honey away but hesitated with the johnny cake. The baby in the cradle loved fresh-baked johnny cake. Maybe the warm delicious smell might penetrate where sound or sight or touch could not. Quickly she wrapped the loaf in a napkin to keep it fresh, placed it on the bedside chair, and went back to her studying. She had the feeling that if she could just finish this last passage—

The knock this time was loud and authoritative. Sighing, she closed the book. That would be Priddy Meeks.

It had begun to snow again. The air outside was curdled with flakes. Dr. Meeks shut the door, stamped snow from his boots, shook it from his shoulders, and went directly to his patient. It wasn't that Tildy Elizabeth lacked faith in Dr. Meeks. Watching the light pick out his fringe of chin whiskers, his domed forehead, all the strong, kind lines of his face, she told herself again that he was the best doctor on the Thompsonian or botanical system of medicine in the whole territory. Traveling much, a body would be bound to pick up knowledge. And Priddy himself said his father had been "inclined to new countries." As a child Priddy could remember moving from South Carolina to Kentucky; as a man he had emigrated from Indiana to Nauvoo, Illinois (where the Lord had appeared to him one day in the fields and counseled him to "quit a-plowing and go to doctoring"), from Nauvoo to Great Salt Lake City, thence to the Iron Mission at Parowan, to the Cotton Mission at Harrisburg, and finally to the United Order Mission at Orderville. Undoubtedly he knew a lot. Folks said he had "eyes in his fingers."

Tildy Elizabeth watched him complete his examination, then look up from the still child's face to the hovering mother.

"You can't never tell about the green sickness," he muttered, shaking his head. "But 'tany rate, it can't last much longer." He got to his feet, still staring at the baby. "When you can get it down, give

her another good thorough emetic of lobelia. Keep up that poultic-
ing with the charcoal, the hops, and vinegar. Keep the pores of her
skin open with the yellow-dock-and-dandelion rub, and remember
what I told you about cayenne pepper—it's the best stimulant known
in the compass of medicine, 'twill increase the very life of the
system—"

He lowered his voice and glanced significantly about the room.
"Have any strange old women been near her?"

Tildy shook her head.

"Well, there might be a witch about! Yesterday I attended a
woman with foul spirits. You could see the prints of the witch's teeth
where it had bitten her on her belly and arms. A very good practice
for you mothers is to hold out your children to make water in the
fire when convenient, and *a word to the wise is sufficient!*" He
picked up Tildy's Book of Mormon and slipped it under the child's
pillow. "You can't never tell what'll scare a witch!"

After he was gone, Tildy retrieved the book. It would soon be
curfew-time. She hadn't much longer. "And . . . he spake unto his
disciples, one by one, saying unto them: What is it that ye desire of
me, after that I am gone to the Father?" This was in South America
when Jesus appeared to the Nephites there after he had completed
his career in Judea and had arisen from the Holy Sepulchre. Nine
of the Twelve answered him: "We desire that after we have lived
unto the age of man, that . . . we may speedily come unto thee in
thy kingdom." But three were silent. "And . . . he turned himself
unto the three, and said unto them, . . . Behold, I know your
thoughts, and ye have desired . . . that ye might bring the souls of
men unto me, while the world shall stand," and because of this, "Ye
shall not have pain while ye shall dwell in the flesh, neither sorrow
save it be for the sins of the world." And the Three Nephites "were
changed from this body of flesh into an immortal state, that they
could behold the things of God [and] did go forth upon the face of
the land."

Reading aloud, Tildy Elizabeth did not hear the door open. Only
when she sensed the presence of another person in the room, did
she look up. The man was old, with a long beard and snow-white

hair. He did not speak but continued to gaze at her. His eyes had an intent brilliance about them, and the skin of his cheeks was as soft and fresh as a babe's. At a glance Tildy knew that he was from far away. In place of the Order's coarse, buckskin-laced cowhide boots, the stranger wore store-bought overshoes of heavy cloth; in place of a coyote-skin cap with tail down the back, he wore a store-bought black cap with fine fur about the ears; in place of a buckskin jumper, his black overcoat was long and well-fitting and fur-lined. Considering that he must be a traveler, Tildy couldn't understand his immaculate appearance. Not even his overshoes were damp from the snow. And there was something vaguely familiar about that high-bridged nose. She had it! Although much older, of course, he looked like the prophet Joseph.

"Sister Stalworthy?"

Tildy could only nod.

The old man's voice was mellow and fluted as violin music. Then he smiled, and Tildy felt the ice about her heart melting, running out in inexplicable relief.

"You have a sick child, a very sick child." It was not put as a question. The stranger made a statement of fact in that soft sweet voice. "Trust in God and not in the arm of the flesh.' May I have your consecrated oil?" Without further ado he came up to the cradle.

Tildy shut her gaping mouth and scrambled hastily to her feet. Her heart beat like a prisoned thing in her throat.

The old man was kneeling, anointing her baby with the oil, laying on his hands, praying. Never had a prayer seemed so beautiful. Tildy was speechless.

Her visitor lingered a moment longer, then got slowly to his feet. He smiled again. "Your little girl will get well now."

Tildy could only cradle the child with her eyes, fondling the inert hands in an ecstasy of hope. Even as she gazed the baby stirred, looked at her mother, smiled, and said, "I'm hungry."

Blind with tears Tildy turned to find the johnny cake, to bless the old man. He was gone! The johnny cake was gone! In an agony of contrition, she realized that he must have been hungry and she too taken up with her own affairs to offer him even food. Thank heaven he'd taken the johnny cake, even if one of her best napkins had gone with it!

She rushed to the door. She must find him, thank him. But the white world outside was empty, silent except for the merriment still oozing from the dining room. Two ways he might have taken: out the sidewalk, on to the valley and outside, or across the square to the party. But although she snatched time from the child to grab the lamp, hurry into the night, and explore both routes, the freshly fallen snow remained unbroken, innocent of tracks. Mystified and chagrined, Tildy went slowly back into the house. And then suddenly she clapped a hand to her mouth. She *knew!*

At the same time, in England, Elder Thomas Stalworthy and his companion trudged along a black, foggy road. Behind them was the village where Thomas had searched out his relatives—cousins and uncles and aunts. He had brought them the gospel, and they had mocked him, stoned him, driven him out. Both men were cold and very, very hungry.

Suddenly Thomas could stand it no longer. "We're a-doin' the Lord's work, ain't we?"

His companion grunted.

"Well, then, he'll take care of us. 'H'ask and ye shall receive'!"

Without another word he flopped down in the mud and prayed aloud. "H'I don't mean to rebuke Thee," said Thomas, "but mebbe ye need remindin' now and agin like other folks!"

Up on their feet again, the two men felt amazingly refreshed.

"'E is all-powerful," reasoned Thomas. "'E wouldn't 'ave to necessarily feed us through the mouth!"

Suddenly he stumbled, kicked against something in the mud. He stooped, picked the object up. Incredulously he put it to his nose, sniffed. It was a loaf of fresh-baked johnny-cake, wrapped in a napkin!

There was even a drum added to the two fiddles. Tildy was sure not all the 'igh and mighty boasted such music.

Her youngun dancing beside her, Tildy stood in the roadway,

outside the fort, and watched the procession advance up the valley. "Hail the Conq'ring Hero Comes!" shrilled the fiddles, and all about her voices took up the refrain.

Then Thomas was there, in the flesh, waving, coming toward her, lifting them both in his big bear hug. Afterward in the shanty— oh, long afterward!—when their talk had spurted and spurted again and then stopped for sheer inability to swallow the lump in the throat, Tildy collected her senses long enough to unpack his carpetbag. It was thus she found it. The napkin.

"Tom, 'ow did you come by my napkin?" She kept her voice carefully flat.

Thomas looked at her over the head of the child on his knee. "Why, Tildy," he chided. "You must be mistaken. The Lord sent me a loaf of warm 'ome-made johnny cake when I was hungry. That's the Lord's napkin."

Tildy raised her chin. "No it ain't. It's *my* napkin!"

For it unmistakably completed the set of hand-spun Irish linen her mother had cherished all the way from England, across the plains. The same h'original tatted edging—

Sometimes Tildy's daughter, even though she's now an old, old woman herself, climbs up to the attic of *her* daughter's house and rocks the squat wooden cradle made in the Order's own cooper shop. She uses the cradle as a sort of chest, and sometimes she dreams over its treasures one by one. Most precious of all is a certain linen napkin, somewhat yellowed and frayed perhaps but still outlasting time—perhaps outlasting even those Three who "did go forth."

THREE

Opening Day

DOUGLAS THAYER

Doc and my father got up at 4 o'clock to light the fire, heat water on the Coleman stoves for washing, and get the breakfast started, then woke the rest of us. Standing outside of our white tent in the cool darkness, I buckled on my heavy cartridge belt and breathed in deep the smell of wood smoke and sagebrush. I looked down Blind Canyon and then turned to look up at the black silhouette of the ridge under the stars. I knew the bucks would already be out feeding in the draws. The ridge ran east and west, and we hunted the draws on the south and north slopes. I still felt the old excitement of the opening day of the deer hunt, an empty tight feeling as if my whole body were being squeezed. I still wanted to see the big mule-deer bucks jump out of the oak brush ahead of the line, shoot them as they ran. But then I hadn't expected to have absolute control over my emotions just because while I was on my mission in Germany I had decided to stop hunting. When I got married and had sons, I didn't want them to hunt, but I knew that it wouldn't be easy for me to stop killing birds and animals.

Bliss, Dean, and Ken stood by the fire, and Jerry washed in the pan of warm water on the end of the table. The light from the fire and the two Coleman lanterns glared off from their red hats, sweat shirts, and jackets. When they moved, the handles of their hunting knives, aluminum lids of their old GI belt canteens, and the shells in their full cartridge belts glinted.

When the rest of us had washed, Doc asked me to give the morning prayer and blessing on the food; he said that we had to keep the returned missionaries busy. After we ate we got our rifles out of the cases in the tent, saddled Bliss's three horses, and put the lunches and the two walkie-talkies in the saddlebags. We turned off the lanterns, shoveled dirt on the fire, and we were ready, each of us carrying his rifle slung. My father, Doc, and Bliss, who were older and worked on the Union Pacific Railroad together, rode the horses, the rest of us following in single file across the sagebrush flat to the start of the trail at the base of the ridge. Every hundred yards we had to stop to rest, our breath white in the flashlight beams as we sat breathing hard.

I had been home from Germany four days, and while I was gone I had decided to quit hunting. Two years of knowing that I would probably be drafted and sent to Vietnam, hearing the older Germans talk about World War II, and every day preaching the gospel of Christ changed me. I felt guilty because of all the rabbits, pheasants, ducks, geese, and deer I had killed, which were beautiful and had a right to live. All things had been created spiritually before they were physically. Our family ate the meat, but we didn't need it. We weren't pioneers or Indians, and we were commanded to eat meat mostly in time of famine anyway, and then with thanksgiving. The deer herds had to be controlled, but I knew that I hunted because I liked to kill, not because I was a conservationist. A mule-deer buck was a beautiful animal, sleek and grey, powerful, had a being all its own. To kill was to deny the influence of the Holy Ghost, which I wanted to continue to develop.

I had started three letters to my father to tell him how I had changed, but I couldn't make them sound right, and I knew that I would have to wait until I got home to tell him. I had three older married sisters but no brothers, and my father and I had been very close. Even before I was old enough to buy a license for anything or even shoot, he took me hunting. He helped me make my bows and arrows, bought me a BB-gun, my Browning .22, and my Winchester .270. For my birthdays and Christmases he always gave me something for hunting, although I had bought my own knife when I was eight. We built a walnut gun cabinet, a duck boat, and we cleaned and repaired the camping equipment together every year. Every month we read and talked about the stories in *Outdoor Life* and *Field and Stream,* which I saved.

We had even planned my mission so that I would have the deer hunt to look forward to when I got home. When I met my family at the Salt Lake airport, all my father could talk about driving home to Provo was the opening day Saturday and how wonderful it was having me home again to be with him in the deer camp. Upstairs in my room I found my .270, knife, full cartridge belt, and red hunting clothes laid out on my bed. My father had bought me a new red hat, cleaned and oiled my .270, and loaded three boxes of shells for me to use for target practicing. When I went back downstairs, he took me out to see the new sets of antlers he had nailed to the back of the garage the two seasons I was away.

I knew then that I would have to hunt the opening day. I couldn't disappoint my father. We could have Friday night in camp together, and all day Saturday I would drive the draws, help clean the bucks if I had to, pack them on the horses, but I wouldn't kill a buck myself. I would shoot just to stop questions if a buck jumped up and a member of the camp was standing where he could see me, but I would miss. We always came home Saturday night to go to church on Sunday, and I would tell my father Sunday about my decision. I wouldn't hunt during the week or next Saturday, which was the last Saturday. My mother always said that my father should have been born an Indian two hundred years ago so that he could have hunted elk, wolves, buffalo, and grizzly bear, hunted every day.

Climbing up the trail I was the last in line. Ahead of me the flashlights lit up the high oak brush on both sides, and the horses' hooves clicked against the rocks. Doc, Bliss, and my father stayed on the horses when we stopped to rest. Because we knew the ridge, organized our drives, and hunted hard, we always got bucks. A camp needed horses to haul the bucks off the high ridge, so we had little competition. Sitting on the edge of the trail, the sweat cooling on my back, I picked up little white pebbles, flipped them away, thought about Germany.

Although I had sold more Books of Mormon than any other elder in the mission and been assistant to President Wunderlich my last five months, I had baptized only two converts in two years. The younger Germans weren't interested in the gospel, and when the older Germans invited me and my companion in, they often talked about the war. They showed us pictures of their sons that we had killed, and they wanted to know why the American army hadn't joined the German army to fight the Russians. They showed us pictures of whole families of relatives burned alive or buried in the rubble during the great Allied bombing raids on Nuremberg, Hamburg, and Dresden. They called Hitler a madman and asked why the English and French governments didn't stop him before 1939. They wanted to know how there could be a God if he let such terrible things happen, and I told them that it wasn't God that caused wars but men. If all mankind would just live the gospel of Christ there wouldn't be any more wars. I wanted to get a doctorate in sociology so that I could teach at B.Y.U. and help people to live together in peace and harmony.

On the streets in the German towns, older men who had been invalided in the war wore yellow armbands with black circles, a lot of them amputees, but there were no beggars. My first fall in Germany, a German brother took me and my companion on a Saturday out to visit a small German military cemetery near Offenbach. One of the caretakers raking leaves under the oak trees said that most of the soldiers had been killed fighting Americans. I picked up a handful of the leaves. In Utah in the fall I had followed wounded bucks by their blood trails on the leaves under the oak brush. In the places where they lay down, the blood soaked slowly into the pressed leaves.

The trail led onto a little flat, and above us the ridge was still black under the stars. In every direction were ridges, canyons, mountains, but they were still black and indistinct. Points of light flashed where hunters climbed other ridges, and in the bottom of Blind Canyon fires still burned. As a boy at night I dreamed about the ridge. Although a lot of big bucks hid in the short, steep, pine-filled draws on the north slope, I liked the south draws best because I could see the bucks running up through the oak brush, shoot for three and four hundred yards if I were on a good ledge. In my dreams I shot and shot, killed the running bucks, their antlers flashing in the sun like swords, rolled them back down the steep side of the draw. And I dreamed too that we jumped five and six bucks in one bunch, and it was like a battle with all of us shooting, but because we gang-hunted I wanted to fill all of the permits myself. I wanted to feel all of the thrill, cut the throats, the blood spreading out through the leaves, holler up to the others how big the bucks were, how many points on the antlers. If we shot too many bucks, on the way down Blind Canyon going home we always gave the smaller ones to other camps, didn't waste any. One opening day I shot three bucks, but they were all singles.

When we stopped on the trail again to rest, Jerry leaned forward to pour some dextrose tablets into my palm. "Quick energy, Troy," he said. "It takes a while for you returned missionaries to get back into shape." Chewing two of the tablets, I sat and held my .270 between my legs, the barrel cold against the side of my neck, rubbed the stock with the flat of my hand. Up the trail one of the horses stomped.

A Winchester Model 70 mounted with a 3-9x variable scope, the .270 was a present from my father on my sixteenth birthday. The evening I got it, in the sitting position on my bed, left arm tight in the sling, I aimed at the pictures of bears, lions, and deer on my walls, and, later, out the windows at cars and people passing below on our street, centered the cross hairs. Then I broke the .270 down, oiled each metal part, reassembled it, broke it down again. And I kept filling the magazine with shells, worked the bolt over and over to flip them out on my bed. That night after I showered, I got the .270 out of the case again to hold it against my body. I had a .22 pistol, .22 rifle, .22-250 varminter, two shotguns, but my .270 had always been my favorite gun. I had waited for it, knew that my father would give me a deer rifle too when I was sixteen, which was the first year I could buy a buck permit. I liked to take my .270 out of our gun cabinet just to hold it and work the action, wipe it clean with an oiled cloth.

I thought of my guns when I saw the filled-in shrapnel and bullet holes in the old stone German buildings that hadn't been destroyed. If the older German sisters talked long enough about the war, they always cried, and I never asked them about the concentration camps, the SS, or the Gestapo. On a street in Darmstadt after I was transferred from Offenbach, I saw a legless, armless blind man sitting on a padded box singing while another man played a guitar, but there was no cup or dish in front of them and they weren't begging. Some of the older Germans said that they were sorry for the young Americans in Vietnam and asked if my companion and I would have to go too. I knew that if I couldn't get a student deferment and go back to B.Y.U. to start my sophomore year, I would be drafted. It was impossible to get into the Utah National Guard. I would kill other men, shoot them in the jungle or running across the rice paddies, their blood turning the brown water near their bodies red. And I knew also by then that the excitement of killing a man must be a little like that of killing a buck.

When we got to the top of the ridge, we sat and watched the band of white light grow over the east mountains, our red hats, sweat shirts, and jackets almost black in the half-light. Excited, my heart pounding hard even though I was rested, I pulled the cold shells from my belt to load the .270, heard around me shells clicking into magazines. "Good luck, son," my father said when he stood up, shook my hand. "I hope you nail a big one first thing." The others came over to shake my hand and tell me how good it was to have me back on the ridge again. Separating, we spread out along the top of the ridge to take the points we had drawn Friday night.

Ten minutes later, cradling the .270, I stood on my ledge in the half-light looking down into the pine-filled basin at the head of Sheep Draw on the north side of the ridge. Trembling a little, my mouth dry, I watched the clearings for movement. The light grew and the first shots came booming along the ridge. Then below me two does and a little two-point buck stepped out of the pines into a patch of brush. My body tight, blood pounding in my throat, I slowly raised the .270 and centered the cross hairs over the little buck's heart. I fought the desire to ease down into the sitting position, tighten into the sling, squeeze the trigger slowly. I wanted to hear the explosion, feel the .270 kick, see the little two-point hump and drop, feel that satisfaction again. The first season I carried the .270, I had killed a two-point at first light, had been unable to wait for the bigger buck I wanted. Fighting that feeling, I closed my eyes, opened them. Suddenly the three deer tensed, then crossed the clearing and slipped back into the pines as quiet and smooth as gliding birds. Glad I hadn't shot, I lowered the .270.

At 9 o'clock the camp met to drive Porcupine, the first draw on the west end of the south slope, where we always started. Jerry had passed up a small two-point, and Dean missed three shots at a big buck some hunters had pushed up from below. While Doc and Jerry tested the walkie-talkies again, I scoped the draw and the basin. Broken only by ledges and scattered pines, the leafless oak brush and scrub maple were like a smooth low-lying haze. But a dozen bucks could be hiding, waiting. You never knew. Each draw was a surprise. Everything would be quiet, not even a bird moving, then two or three bucks would be running in front of the line, running grey and beautiful, heads up, antlers gleaming in the sun, going for the top and the thick pines on the north slope, and then the shooting would start. It was as if you had waited all year for just that one moment because it was the best time out of the whole year.

I stopped the scope on a patch of scrub maple where I had killed a three-point the season before I left to go on my mission. To the left was the clearing where Jerry had killed the biggest buck ever killed on the ridge, a big eight-point with a forty-inch spread. He had the mounted head in his real estate office. I knew where all of the big bucks had been killed. We cut the legs off the bucks at the knee to load them on the horses, and sometimes I found legs from two and three seasons back. There was always a black stain on the ground where the entrails had lain the year before. In twenty-five years the camp had killed over a hundred and fifty bucks on the ridge.

"Okay," Doc said, "let's get the big ones. There's one down in there for you, Troy, a nice big fourpoint." The clear sky was dark blue, and now the warming sun brought out the dusty smell of brush and dead leaves. Lines of blue ridges and mountains extended to the horizon on every side.

Doc and my father stayed on the rim, and Jerry led the rest of us down into the draw to organize the drive, Bliss riding his horse. We formed the line, each of us a hundred yards apart across the bottom and up both sides, and started slowly back toward the top. Expecting to see a big buck jump up any minute, excited but controlling myself, I walked tense, stopped, checked the openings ahead on both sides, listened for deer running through the brush. Across the draw, Dean and Ken vanished, reappeared, stopped to throw rocks ahead of them, their red hunting clothes bright against the grey leafless brush. Jerry and Bliss were above me where I couldn't see them. I stopped to toe the fresh droppings with my boot, knelt on one knee to look at the fresh tracks in the deer trail I was on. Mouth dry, hands sweaty on the .270, I froze when Ken first jumped seven does and fawns, which I scoped until they vanished over the top, their white rear ends flashing. Shooting echoed from ridge to ridge, some of it coming in sharp bursts like machine-gun fire, and far down the draw four hunters stood together on a knoll. When I was a boy, the shooting from the other ridges always made me jealous.

I had just walked out onto a ledge at the bottom end of the basin topping the draw when Dean yelled, "Buck! Buck! Buck! He's in the bottom!" Dean shot twice, shot again. Warned, my heart pounding in my throat, I half raised the .270. Another rifle started. Then I saw the big buck moving through the high scrub maples, head down, going smooth like a cat, not making the big ten-foot bounding jumps. But when I jammed the .270 into my shoulder, got the cross hairs on him, he was already blundering, crashing into the brush. A round patch of blood widened behind the shoulder on the grey side, and his mouth dripped blood. Lung-shot. Hit again, he came crashing, rolling back down toward the bottom. He got up, shook his head. Hit again, he humped and dropped, lay in a clearing. The whooping started then, and Dean, Ken following him, jogged down through the brush, hollered for directions twice. They hollered up that he was a fat four-point, cut his throat, then got out their cameras to take colored slides before they cleaned him. Breathing deep, I tried to stop trembling.

"Aren't you coming down, Troy?" Bliss asked me when he came past leading his horse through the brush.

"No, I'll stay here. They don't need me."

"I shot but I think Dean got him, unless you did."

"No, I didn't."

"Too bad, looks like a nice buck. Jerry's going to stay put and watch for anything pushed up from the bottom by the other camps."

I sat down on the ledge, laid the .270 on my hat and ate a Hershey bar, rinsed my teeth and drank from my canteen. Dean, Ken, and Bliss bent over the buck. Watching two hawks circle out over the draw, I picked up a dead branch, broke off pieces and flipped them away.

Before I was sixteen and could shoot a buck, using my own knife I cut the throats of my father's bucks and other bucks I got to first. My father taught me how to clean a buck, cut around the genitals, up through the stomach and ribs, reach up into the chest and grab the severed wind pipe to pull everything out together without getting my hands bloody above the wrists. I always cut the heart away from the blue pile of entrails to hold up and see if it had been hit. Afterward my father poured water on my hands from his canteen, and I wiped them clean with handfuls of dry leaves. Yet even with two or three of us shooting, hit several times, a buck still might not go down. A buck with both front legs shot off would still lunge forward, work his antlers through the low limbs, crawl to get away. Following blood trails, I had found pieces of entrails snagged on the oak brush and splinters of bone lying on the leaves.

The limbless blind man made me think about the fantastic pain I caused by just squeezing the trigger of my .270 to send the hundred-and-fifty-grain slug at three thousand feet per second slamming into a buck. I saw the man once more before President Wunderlich made me a zone leader and transferred me from

Darmstadt to Heidelberg. He rode in a big rucksack on his friend's back, just his head showing, bobbing, as if he saw the passing people and into the store windows. His friend carried the guitar and the padded box. When I ate, dressed, showered, I wondered how he did those things. Lying in bed at night I tried to imagine what it would be like for him to be in bed, and I wanted to know if he was married. I knew then that I couldn't go on hunting and killing when I got home and still expect to feel the full influence of the Holy Ghost in my life, be spiritual, which had to be earned. Breaking off the last few pieces of the dead branch, I flipped them over the ledge. Then I got out my clean handkerchief and wiped off the scope and the .270.

Ken, Dean, and Bliss loaded the buck on the horse, and we hunted the basin to the top of the ridge, where they hung the buck from the low limb of a big pine. In Middle Draw, the last drive we always made before lunch and the draw where I had killed the two-point when I was sixteen, Doc and my father both shot three-points as they came up out of the basin over the top. I didn't see either buck but stood cradling the .270, counted the shots, felt empty, then heard Jerry hollering after he talked to Doc on the walkie-talkie. When we got to the top, we helped drag the bucks over to the trail to hang them up. I broke sticks to prop open the stomachs so the bucks would cool faster. We always hung our bucks in the garage to cure for a week before we had them cut up for the freezer. Skinned, the heads cut off, they hung stiff and white upside down, the blunt front legs sticking out, spots of blood on the cement floor.

"Well, Troy," my father said when we all gathered to eat lunch on the ledge above Doc's draw, "I wish that you had been on the rim instead of me. Those two three-points came sneaking up through the brush ahead of you boys in the line just perfect. It couldn't have been prettier."

"No, I guess not," I said. Ken, Jerry, and Dean had black dry deer blood on their red sweat shirts and blue Levis. You couldn't wash the smell of the blood from your hands unless you had hot soap and water, but you could get the blood out from under your fingernails with the point of a sharp hunting knife.

"Oh, we'll get Troy a nice buck today or next Saturday, don't worry about that," Doc said. Doc and Bliss had taken the bridles off the horses and poured some oats for them.

"Sure," Jerry said, unwrapping a piece of cake.

Eating my sandwich, I looked out over the draw toward the lines of blue ridges out past Blind Canyon. Doc had killed three bucks one opening day in the basin as they ran past him at seventy-five yards; after that everybody in camp called it Doc's Draw. Each line of ridges was a different shade of blue. All the shooting had stopped. I was glad that my father had Doc and Bliss to hunt with. They had worked on the Union Pacific together for thirty years. My father had never been on a mission. He had written me long letters about the duck, pheasant, and deer hunts and sent me the best colored slides he had taken. Every month he mailed me his copies of *Outdoor Life* and *Field and Stream*. When I was a boy and my mother made me turn off my bedroom light, I used a flashlight to reread my favorite hunting stories.

After we ate lunch, the others got their red jackets from the saddlebags to use for pillows, pulled their red hats down over their eyes, and lay back on the ledge to doze in the warm sun. Below me nothing moved in the draw. I picked up white chips of rock and flipped them over the ledge. Although I wouldn't hunt I planned to do a lot of back-packing, learn the names of all the Rocky Mountain flora and fauna, and at night study the stars. When I got married and had sons, I wanted them to see the real beauty, design, and completeness of nature, which God had created. I wanted to be as close to my sons as my father had been to me, but without guns and killing. I wouldn't let them carry .22s or varmint rifles to kill the hawks, rabbits, rock chucks, and squirrels they saw, as my father had let me. I wanted them to understand the pioneers and Indians, but they didn't have to hunt to do that. We could start an arrowhead collection and visit all of the historical spots in the state.

A chipmunk came up over the face of the ledge, found a piece of bread. With the shooting stopped, it was very quiet. I flipped a chip of rock. I had read an article by one of the apostles who had visited the Mormon servicemen in Vietnam. He said that in one meeting the men came to the tent carrying their rifles. In the prayers they prayed for the Mormon boys killed the week before, prayed for the spirit of the Lord for themselves. After the testimony meeting some of the soldiers told the apostle that they had met him as missionaries in Europe nine months before when he was touring the missions. In the German magazines I saw pictures of American wounded being carried to helicopters on stretchers, medics running alongside with lifted plasma bottles. Wrapped in their ponchos the American dead lay in rows like packages, but the Viet Cong dead were never covered. I flipped another piece of rock and the chipmunk vanished back over the face of the ledge.

Before we dropped down into Doc's Draw, three hunters on horses from another camp came along the ridge trail. They wanted to know where we got the three nice bucks we had hanging up. "They don't organize and they don't know the country, so all they get are spikes and two-points," Doc said after they left. "They might as well stay in camp as come up on this ridge and ride around."

We jumped one bunch of six does and fawns at the lower end of Doc's Draw, and in the basin Ken, who was across from me, shot a big four-point. Hollering, he directed me to him in the thick brush. One antler dug through the dead leaves into the black dirt, the big buck lay on his side, the four points on each side of the antlers white-tipped, the blood bright red on the leaves. Standing there I wondered if I had scared the buck out to Ken. I didn't pull his head downhill to cut his throat. He was still perfect, the eyes not yet glazed. He still seemed alive, still had that beautiful grey live symmetry as if he might suddenly jump and run. Bending, I ran my hand over the hard antlers, along the neck and onto the heavy shoulders. When Ken and Dean broke through the brush, I told them that I would go and show Bliss the best way to bring the horse down.

"Okay," Ken said. He leaned his rifle against a rock and got out his camera.

"Looks like you really busted a nice one, Ken," Dean said. "Good work."

"Finally."

Climbing up through the brush, I heard them talking. I had actually prayed for a big four-point like Ken's the first morning I had carried the new .270. My father beside me on the ledge overlooking the basin at the top of middle draw, I gripped the Winchester, whispered the prayer to myself, and I would have knelt down too if I had thought that it would do any good. But when in the first light I saw the little two-point standing in the patch of sagebrush with a doe, I moved into the sitting position, tightened into the sling, and killed him with a perfect heart shot, started then to run. When my father got down to me and the little buck, he put his rifle down and hugged me. I cleaned the buck, holding up his shattered heart in my hand to look for pieces of the slug. I had killed a lot of pheasants, ducks, geese, and rabbits before I was sixteen, but I had never felt like that. My father nailed the two-point's antlers over the garage door next to the biggest spread of antlers he had ever taken.

At 2 o'clock we crossed from the south slope of the ridge to the north to hunt the smaller steeper draws full of thick pines. It was cooler there than on the south slope. We jumped bucks, but they were hard to hit running through the pines, and they all got away over the top past Doc and my father. Because the bucks liked to hide in the pines, there was a lot of sign on the deer trails. I saw a beautiful little spike but didn't even raise the .270 to put the scope on him, just watched him until he moved. It made me happy just to watch him. Other years I had found blood trails in the pines from the deer wounded lower on the ridge that sneaked up in the thick cover to die. The second year the scattered bones were white, with hair left only on the legs and skull.

In the next basin, ahead of the others, I sat down against a pine. I cut a Baby Ruth bar in sections with my knife, drank from my canteen, rinsed my teeth, the air cool against my face and throat. Taking off my heavy cartridge belt, I laid it across my knees, began to line the shells up in the loops so that they were all exactly even. I pulled one out and fingered it. The hundred-and-fifty-grain slug with the lead tip and core was built to explode on contact with bone or heavy muscle. In junior high school every fall, I took some of my father's shells with me to class so that I could put my hand in my pocket and feel them. I took my hunting knife one day, but my home-room teacher picked it up and kept it in her desk until school was out in the afternoon. After my father gave me the .270 for my birthday, I loaded my empty brass on his reloading outfit. At night I poured three or four boxes of shells onto my bed just to run my fingers through them. Alone, I dressed in my red hat and shirt, wore my knife and full cartridge belt, cradled the .270 in my left arm to look at myself in the mirror.

Below me in the pines a small bird lit on a dead branch. Everything was in shadow. The German forests seemed always to be in shadow, as if the season were always winter but without snow. The .270 shell I had taken out of the belt was heavy in my palm. One Saturday afternoon a week before President Wunderlich called me to Frankfurt as his assistant, my companion and I rode our bicycles out into the woods near Heidelberg to an area where a German brother said there had been fighting. We walked through the trees until we came to the top of a hill dotted with shallow pits, which I knew must be old shell holes. Some of the pines looked as if they had been hit by lightning a long time ago. Scratching with a stick, my companion found an American hand-grenade pin and three empty rifle shells so corroded that he had to scrape them on a rock to tell if they were American or German. He offered me one of the shells, but I told him no. When we got back to our room, he put his find in a little box to save and take home. Placing the .270 shell back in the belt loop, I took out my handkerchief and wiped off the scope and the rifle.

At 4 o'clock Jerry organized the drive for West Draw. It was the last drive before we went down the ridge to break camp and start the long trip out of Blind Canyon and back to Provo. The shooting from the other ridges had stopped again. The lines of ridges were darker blue now, some of the ledges white like patches of early snow. The Ute Indians buried their dead high in the canyons in the ledges, but I had never found one of the rock-piled graves. I had always wondered if the Indians had hunted the high ridges too or whether they found enough game lower down. As we stood together at the top of the draw, in the afternoon light the hats and sweat shirts seemed darker red. I was glad it was the last drive and we were going home.

Because Jerry wanted to take me out of the line and put me on a point above an opening in the pines called the bowl, Doc held out his walkie-talkie to me. The bowl was the best spot in the basin at the head of West Draw. "No," I said, "I'll go down in the pines and help make the drive. You take the bowl, Bliss. You haven't filled your permit yet."

"Now, Troy," Doc said, "you've hunted hard in that line all day without any luck, and this is your last chance until next Saturday, unless you and your dad get out during the week for a little afternoon hunting. We'd all like to see you get a nice buck."

"No. I don't want to do that."

"Go ahead, Troy," Jerry said. "We all got nice bucks the last two seasons. We're not sweating it."

"Oh no."

"Go on, son," my father said, and Doc put the walkie-talkie into my hand.

"Sure," Jerry said, gripping my shoulder.

Ten minutes later I climbed up to the ledge to the left and nearly to the top of the bowl and sat down. The oak brush was all knee high, stunted, and fallen leaves covered the rocks and bare spots. Because of the timber, none of the others could see me, so I wouldn't even have to shoot if a buck came up through the bowl. I had never killed a buck in West Draw. Sitting there, cradling the .270, I thought about Sunday morning and meeting everybody in church after two years away. I was anxious to tell about all the things that I had learned while I was in Germany on my mission, tell of my experiences, and I wanted to bear my testimony of the truthfulness of the gospel of Christ. I breathed in the cool air full of the smell of pines.

"You ready, Troy?"

I raised the walkie-talkie. "Yes."

"Keep your eyes open. There's an awful lot of tracks and droppings down here on these trails."

Picking up a handful of the wind-blown oak leaves caught in a crack in the ledge, I let them sift through my fingers. Perhaps my father and I could find something else we liked to do together. One of the reasons I wanted to get my doctorate in sociology and teach at B.Y.U. was so that I could live in Provo and raise my family there after I got married. Because my father had given me my .270 for my sixteenth birthday, I would always keep it, but I would get rid of my other guns and my eight-year collection of *Field and Stream* and *Outdoor Life*. I didn't want my sons to get started on them.

"Keep your eyes open, Troy. Something moving out ahead."

I reached down and clicked off the walkie-talkie. Nobody shot. Nothing moved. I waited. Then right at the bottom edge of the bowl, a buck stepped out of the pines. Chest tightening, I slowly lifted the .270 to bring the scope to my eye. A nice three-point. Another buck stepped out, another three-point, moved up to the first. Heart slamming, I scoped them both, when two more moved out of the pines at the same place. They were both four-points, the last one a beautiful big buck with a wide heavy set of antlers.

Bent forward, breathing deep, the blood beginning to pound in my ears, I held the scope to my eye. They were beautiful. I just wanted to watch them, prayed nobody would make it to the edge of the pines in time for a shot. The bucks stopped to look back, started moving again, the big buck leading now. Slipping my arm into the sling, I got into the sitting position to steady my scope. The bucks were nervous but still walking. Beautiful. Biting my lower lip, I shifted the cross hairs back up to the big buck. The antlers were perfectly matched on each side. My pounding blood sounded like rushing water in my ears, louder and louder. Beautiful. I closed my eyes against the feeling, gripped harder, breathless.

The .270 slammed my shoulder, the explosion part of my feeling. Heart-shot, the big buck humped and went down. The other bucks ran now in high leaping bounds, instinct driving them toward the top and me. I shot over the leader, adjusted, got him through the back at seventy-five yards, and he went smashing down. I shot at the first three-point as he came level with me, missed twice. Kneeling, I crammed in more shells, cursed, slammed the bolt home, held the cross hairs on him, saw him come rolling back down the slope. Alone, the last buck was nearly to the top. I shot, missed, stood up, spun him around with a hit in the front leg, got him just as he topped the skyline. He came crashing end-over-end back down the steep slope into the bowl. I found the raised head of the back-shot buck in the scope, shot, and everything was quiet.

"Oh no, no, no," I said, "oh no." Grabbing the short oak brush with my free hand when I slipped, I angled across to the last buck. "No," I said, "no." I laid the .270 down to pull the buck around so that his head was down-hill, then cut his throat. I had to shoot the second buck again to kill him. Whooping and yelling, somebody was climbing toward me up through the brush. "Oh no," I said. I cut the big four-point's throat last, my knife and hands red with blood, his antlers thick at the base where I grabbed them with my sticky hands. "No, no." Still trembling, I knelt down by the big buck's head. His pooled blood started to trickle down through the oak leaves. "Oh, Jesus, Jesus," I whispered.

FOUR

The Week-end

D O N A L D   R .   M A R S H A L L

*W*hen *Thalia Beale's mother died, she knew that a change was in order. That is, Thalia knew. Of course her mother must have known too, for her last words, as she rolled her filmy eyes one final time in their yellow-gray cavities, were "You've been good, Thalia. Always stay—" Thalia was not quite sure what her mother had meant. There was little question about her remaining good. She scarcely had a desire to be otherwise. But "stay"? If her mother's last request had concerned her staying on in the little house in Ephraim, then here indeed was a problem of quite a different sort.*

I guess it was a great loss for Thalia. Her father was killed when the scaffolding gave way back when they were first laying bricks for the Whitney house. She wasn't more than a year and a half old then, and the only brother she might have had in this world died of diphtheria before she was even born. For forty-three years Thalia and her mother (Elvina and Thalia we always called them) lived alone together. Before her mother took ill—but this, mind you, was a long time ago—they did things, the two of them: they went visiting (not, of course, a great deal, but they did like to stop in on Sophora and Pauline and sometimes take a fruitcake or a pint of bullberry jelly down to Walter and his mother), they quilted together (usually over at Reva Willis's house because she had the frames), and they even took the train once to Boulder, Colorado, to attend the Hinckley reunion, only that was the summer that Homer and Ruth got word that Jeddie B. had been killed in Guam and the whole thing had to be called off. For a year or more they came to Relief Society meetings together, but Elvina got her feelings hurt again over the bazaar (some say both of the loaves of bread she baked went for fifty cents apiece and nobody knows what all became of the four bottles of chili sauce and pickle relish) and told Nilene Bolander that that was the last they would ever see of her inside that chapel. Thalia came out to Sunday school fairly regularly before Elvina got so sick, but after that she stayed right at home with her most of the time. There was a time just before that when Thalia seemed to take quite an interest in M.I.A. for a while and was even asked to take a position—Speech and Drama Director was what they wanted her for—but when Elvina got wind that Brother Bettenson had his eye on Thalia for that scoutmaster with five kids whose wife had up and left him, she put a fast stop to that. We didn't see much of Thalia at church at all after that. The visiting teachers, though, they continued to go there and, like as not, the home teachers as well, but Cora Stokes and Idonna both said that it was not likely that Thalia would even step foot in the chapel as long as Elvina was drawing breath.

But it was a great loss for Thalia. I suspect her mother was her whole life. Thalia did have her outside interests. You'd see her taking walks, long walks she'd take clear out to Haney's south pasture and way up to the other end of town past the cemetery and who knows where all. But I guess that's partly what kept her thin, those walks. And she would take a class or two up at the school. You'd see her bringing home a stack of books now and then from the library that she couldn't possibly have read in a year. And then, of course, she had her work. She did it all at home, typing and proofreading. With the college and all, I don't think she ever lacked for work. That and Elvina's relief check kept them going. Heaven knows Thalia must have always eaten like a bird and I doubt if either one of them ever gave two hoots for a new dress. The last time Elvina was out of the house she had on that same black crepe she must have got for Woodruff's funeral and I think she would just as leave have been buried in it. Thalia, she always seemed content in just that little gray sweater of hers and a plain wool skirt a darn sight longer than mine or yours or anybody else's. Most likely her life was always just as full as yours or mine, in its own way. I do know she saved her money and bought a TV set for the two of them. And I suspect that she was just as happy there caring for her mother as she would have been if things had been different for her somehow.

Things were different after her mother died. Thalia sensed this almost immediately. The day after the company left she spent the morning at the cemetery, arranging and rearranging in the cold wind the few wilted flowers that had survived the chill March gusts, and pulling up a few dried weeds stranded among the dingy patches of crusted snow on the Beale plot. But this task occupied only a few minutes; most of the time she walked without plan or purpose between the rows of headstones, under the bare branches of the gray trees, over the frozen and sterile earth. When the gnawing in her empty stomach finally brought her to gather her coat about her and walk down the long road to the little frame house, she began to sense that nothing inside those quiet walls could ever be, had even been, the substance needed to assuage her incessant hunger. One would have thought that the little house with its single straggling brown vine and the vacant spot where the hollyhocks came and went each year would have seemed unbearably empty when she stepped inside, that the hollow stillness of its rooms might have made it seem suddenly almost uncomfortably and unnecessarily large. Yet Thalia was surprised how the house, bereft as it was of fully one half of the life that had wheezed and coughed within it, now seemed different to her for its very smallness and for the uncanny impression of maximum occupancy, not spaciousness, that pervaded the four rooms, pushing at the yellowing papered walls and crowding the dark corners filled with ceramic knick-knacks and tinted photos in their dusty cardboard frames. Thalia sensed this difference as soon as she opened the front door and was met by the almost suffocating hot smell of gray days indoors accumulated upon gray days, days of boiled cabbage and camomile tea, of camphor, Vicks Vapo-Rub, and dark brown cough syrup. What should have been conspicuously missing from the house now suddenly seemed overwhelmingly present. Her hand fluttered at her collar. The stifling warmth from the oil heater almost took her breath; the unending multicolored circles of the braided rug beneath her caused her head to spin. She let herself sink down upon the brown daven-port with its faded afghan and crocheted doilies, taking care, like a visitor, to sit only on the edge rather than giving herself to its sagging and lumpy softness. "I'm a stranger," she heard herself say quietly. The words, heard not without some odd sense of pleasure, even caused her body to tingle a little. "I don't belong here."

She had no business running off like that. If Elvina had lived you can bet she wouldn't have just up and run off one day without so much as a how-do-you-do. What got into her I guess we'll never know. But I suppose that when you get right down to it, it was the grief that drove her. She must have just grieved so after her mother died that she couldn't bear being in that empty house. It's hard on a person, after you've waited hand and foot on someone else, to find yourself alone in the world. Believe me, I know. Anyway, Thalia somehow got it in her head to run off to California. I don't think she told a soul. She must have just woke up one morning with the notion that she had to get away and marched right down and got her a ticket on the bus and away she went. I don't begrudge her a little trip. I suppose she felt she had it coming. But what beats me is what in the world she thought she'd find in California. Velta Lytle asked her if it was relatives or something she went to see, but Thalia just told her no it was not. So there you are. Now Lige and Elouise go down there almost once a year but, good Lord, they've got more folks down there than they've got up here, with Carl and Melba down at Oceanside and Cleora and her family still in Anaheim. But Thalia now had no more business than the man in the moon to go scooting off where she didn't know a living soul. Why on earth she didn't go up to Tremonton with Myrtle Dawn and Nida for a week or two after the funeral—or let Nils and Leona take her back with them to Blanding—sure beats me. Idonna said that as far as she could tell, Thalia just shut up the house one day without a thought as to who was going to feed that cat or water her plants and off she went. And I know for a fact that Elvina had a canary that she wouldn't have parted with for the world, and now who, I ask you, did Thalia think was going to feed that poor bird with the house locked up tighter than a drum and nobody the wiser? Of course the poor thing died. Cora Stokes told me that. And I don't know if Thalia just left the cat in there to die too or if she turned it out to fend for itself. But I suspect she didn't give it a thought one way or another. But then again, who are we to judge? Grief just turned her mind, I guess, and off she went.

Thalia's mind kept turning. "You've been good, Thalia. Always stay—" Stay? She looked around the dark little room until her eyes stopped at the Woolworth card table cramped in the corner, one wobbly leg threatening to collapse under the heavy looseleaf folder, the Smith-Corona in its worn case, the tottering tower of books stacked hastily against the wall the day before the funeral. The books would be due at the library March 23 and would have to be taken back. But there were no classes to hold her. For almost the first time in thirteen years, she had not enrolled in any courses at Snow College. How lucky for her! She had deliberated—"stewed around," her mother had said— going back into Theatre Arts. Oh, not seriously. She would never try out for any of the parts, never let them talk her into being in one of their productions. Just a class or two. And not for credit. She would have just paid her auditing fee again and sat in the back with her notebooks while Dr. Hall talked over the hissing radiator to his class about Marlowe or Chekhov or Ibsen. She had thought too about trying Art one more time, but then she remembered the stack of pale watercolors yellowing secretly under her cot—the still lifes with their lopsided vases and muddy onions cramped between anemic tomatoes, the landscapes with the light-green trees and stiff barns—and Mr. Swanstrom pleading, "Loosen up! Loosen up!" ("Why, I don't think the man's fit to be a painting teacher," her mother had said.) She had tried the course first from Mr. Weedly, then four years later from Mr. Folger, who kept forgetting her name, then twice from Mr. Swanstrom, but she could hear them all, like a Greek chorus, chanting "Don't be afraid to put color in your brush! Let yourself go!" She had not wanted to go into English a third time. Not just yet. If Miss Hibbard taught Wuthering Heights again—or Jane Eyre or Tess of the D'Urbervilles—she would ask permission to audit and sit once more in the corner by the door, but she would not go back to creative writing. "Your work betrays a lack of experience," Dr. Woolley had written on one of her little stories. She had hidden the penciled comment from Mother, but her own sense of humiliation kept her from going back. She longed to write, to open a magazine one day and find her name, in type not too large and maybe not so dark, in some small corner of the page. It almost made her tremble. But not, she quickly reminded herself, until she had had her little adventure, her—again she trembled—"experience."

She moved around in the dim little room. There was nothing to hold her now. Beyond the doorway that led to the quiet kitchen with its sallow oilcloth and linoleum, she could see the bedroom door, slightly ajar, the room's bilious yellow-green hue, consequence of March's light wasting through the dull blinds, oozing infectiously into the remainder of the house. Nothing to hold her back. How fortunate that she had not tried to take a class, that she had contented herself with looking into whatever books had enticed her from their dusty shelves in the library. She looked back at the books on the card table. The Art of Writing Fiction, Fairy Mythology in Shakespeare, Arthurian Legends in Medieval Art, Art as Experience, Wildlife Along the Pacific Trail, Art and Artists in California. *There was little doubt about where she would go if she indeed really dared to go. The beautiful words had called to her each time she saw them written, a far-away whisper of sea and cypress, luring her on: Carmel-by-the-Sea. To say them again to herself made her tremble. Could she really allow herself to go? The books would have to be taken back, she reminded herself. And the fern. Someone would have to water the fern. She could take it to Walter and Maude. Poor Maude would like something green. Her eyes surveyed each item cramped in the dim corners of the room. The cat was gone. No need to worry about Flossie, poor thing. Was it wrong not to have told her mother in those last days that Flossie too had been withering away—distemper, Mr. Stubbs at the drug store had suggested—and was finally buried out back under the plum trees? And Dickie too, as if something contagious, unnoticed under the heavy medicinal smells, had spread through the whole house, poor Dickie too had begun to lose her feathers and stopped her quiet little song. There had still been some of the Hartz seeds in the glass feeder when she found the bird lying stiffly on its back. And Flossie couldn't be blamed—everyone marveled at how they got on together—unless something in Flossie's own illness had caused her to do some-thing to Dickie that she had not known about. But that was not likely. Poor Flossie herself had been beneath the bare trees two days before Dickie was finally laid beside her. Thalia stared at the empty cage dimly lighted by the little window facing the street. Something fluttered briefly in her chest. There was nothing now to hold her.*

But then I suppose there are worse things than letting a canary starve to death in its cage. Lord knows, though, that Thalia was devoted to Elvina and attentive as could be. It makes you wonder sometimes how she could have suddenly been so selfish as to let those animals just wither away while she gallivanted off to some ritzy resort. Lord knows where she stayed or who she thought was going to pay for her whims. It's grief, that's all there is to it. It must have been grief, because it was just not like Thalia to go off and do a thing so completely uncalled for and unnatural.

Listen, do you want to know what she told Nell Lister? Not that Thalia was ever one to tell anyone anything, but Nell has a way of getting things out. Talk about your woman's intuition. Lord, you've never seen a person that's got the knack of reading between the lines Nell's got. Point her out a woman on the street with a suitcase in her hand and she'll tell you the whole story. Just like her Aunt Thule used to be. Thule even read tea leaves until she saw a house in flames in her cup one day and a week later her own son Ned set fire to the seminary building. Be that as it may, here's what Thalia told Nell: she went down there, she said, to have a little adventure for herself. Now your guess is as good as mine what she meant by that. But she told Nell that she had one week-end that she will never forget as long as she lives. Now I want you to keep in mind that Thalia Beale is almost as old as I am. In fact she was in the same class as my younger sister Lila June, but Lila now was always a pretty little thing. Now what business Thalia thought she had going down there around all those artists and poets—and hippies, too, mind you—sure beats me. I can tell you one thing: she never showed her face at church down there any more than here. LaRee Shurtz and her husband are there at Pacific Grove Ward and when Lena wrote and asked them if they ever saw Thalia, LaRee was surprised to even know that Thalia had been down there at all.

Well, anyway, she went down there to this Carmel place until she got good and tired and then she went over to Monterey and stayed there for a while. Monterey, you might recall, is down there where all those soldiers and sailors and I suppose marines and everything else have their bases. Reva's oldest boy Garn was there at the Naval Post Graduate School and I think Delma Lowder's got a boy at Fort Ord right now. Well, Thalia never let on but I've got a hunch there was some man involved. And Thalia Beale forty-three years old. Who knows what all went on. She said she bought her a book that told her a lot of things she's always wanted to know and that she was really beginning to appreciate the wonder of Nature. Nature, my foot. When Nell asked Thalia how she found the people down there, Thalia just sort of hemmed and hawed and finally owned up that there *was* some man she met at the post office that was awfully good to her. Well, she says she had her one week-end, anyway, that she just did everything she had always dreamed about and some things, mind you, she'd never even thought of. I'd like to think she has come back to her senses now, but Nell thinks—and Idonna will tell you the same thing—that Thalia has no regret for whatever she did.

Thalia did not regret that she had chosen Carmel-by-the-Sea. There had been anxious moments when she wanted to ask the bus driver to help her make immediate connections back to Ephraim, Utah. And the absolute incredibility of arriving in Monterey in the almost ethereal nebulosity of an evening fog had made her heart pound in her throat and her skin suddenly feel feverish as she pressed her forehead against the cool dampness of the bus window. But the salty, fishy moistness of the air had at once terrified her and thrilled her as she stepped down into the alien white mist and felt her legs almost buckle when her swollen feet touched the asphalt of this new world. Someone had pointed out the direction in which the ocean—how long she had dreamed of witnessing its dynamic actuality!— might be found, but she had felt better sitting in the corner of the bus station writing a postcard to herself ("I have sailed forbidden seas and landed on barbarous coasts," she wrote with her lavender Flair pen) until 8:35 when another short bus ride through black pines and smoky darkness brought her at last to the dim lights of Carmel's sequestered cottages and hilly lanes. And in her room for $14.00 (she had been too weary to carry her suitcase and her typewriter to more than three motels), still fully dressed in the wrinkled grey tweed, she had fallen asleep on the chenille spread while figuring how long she might stretch the remaining $229.37.

She was afraid to leave the room until the marks, pinkly

visible on the left side of her face until after ten-thirty the next morning, could no longer reveal the secret of her inexperience. Then she left her two pieces of baggage with the woman at the desk, bought an orange at a little market (how it thrilled her to see the fruits and vegetables tucked among the tidy miniature shops clustered along the street that led down to the ocean), and spent the day with a crumpled copy of the weekly Carmel Pine Cone looking for a little room to rent. The village, its twisted trees and creeping vines and tiny lavender-blue flowers almost hiding the quaint houses, left her breathless. The silver-haired men with soft silk ascots, the slender women in their strange boots and gaucho hats leading dogs on long leashes— these made something cry out within her. And once when a bearded gentleman was showing her through the skylighted studio wing of a half-timbered Tudor home for rent, she even stepped back in the cool green shade of the hallway to cry against her white knuckles and then ran down the road to the beach to sob alone in the wind.

By evening, after three people had suggested that she try looking for something more suitable to her needs and pocket-book in one of the surrounding communities, she reluctantly picked up her bags and boarded the bus for Monterey. The place she found—it was "only temporary" she kept telling herself—was a narrow little sleeping room with an electric hot plate and some yellow plastic dishes. It was not in a neighborhood she would have chosen, but it looked less grim by daylight and was only a five-block walk from the public library. It would be only $90 a month the old deaf woman downstairs told her, if she would be careful about the electricity and furnish her own sheets and towels. Thalia stayed the month. For the first week she looked elsewhere, but some areas of the town frightened, her while her own little place on Union Street gradually offered some of the comfort and security of things grown familiar.

Nevertheless, her heart, she had to own, was in Carmel. She went there almost every day by bus, always walking down to watch the blue waves crashing on the sand and, further out, against the rocks. She walked quietly through the tiny galleries, listening inconspicuously to others as they eulogized, in loud and confident voices, paintings she couldn't understand. One day, feeling bold, she even determined to try to merge with the audience at a piano recital she had seen advertised, but her watch must have been slow, for when she walked up the long hill to the church, the doors were already closed and she had to listen to the music from the steps at the side door. At intermission she thought of peeping in to see if there might be a seat near the back, but when the people with their fur stoles and little name cards pinned to their knits and jerseys flittered out on the patio to sip coffee from tiny cups, she pretended she had only been admiring the architecture in passing and hurried, her chest and eyes burning, up the hill to where the 3:30 bus to Monterey was just driving away.

When it rained she spent her afternoons near the big stone fireplace in the library at Carmel, but when the sun was out she tried to devote as much time as possible to exploring the shady little streets without sidewalks, stopping to read the identifying labels—names like Sea Cradle, Journey's End, Harbor Lights— which the neat cottages, with their ornamental doors and oriental gardens, bore instead of numbers. One day after much deliberation, she bought a shiny-covered book—one of two extravagant purchases she permitted herself during that month—that identified for her the trees and plants of the region. Afterwards she took much care to check the colored illustrations against the variety of unique and lovely things she found in her little excursions; memorizing that the blue myrtle was really ceanothus thyrsiflorus, she liked to think, might help her to feel less a stranger to this enchanted region. Her other extravagance came when she let herself buy a pink-orange sweater. She had seen a similar one in the window of a tiny boutique in Carmel—"Italian imports: original creations in melon and coral" the little card had read—at the same time she had noticed in a reflection of herself in the same window that her own gray cardigan would not survive many more washings.

The colors of the sweater in the window both terrified and excited her, and it was only after a long internal debate that she allowed herself to search out something similar, it finally being her fortune to locate the one she bought—luckily marked down on a Discontinued Items Sale—in the Monterey Sprouse-Reitz. The first day she wore it to Carmel she felt everyone's eyes on her. It was ten days before she dared to take it from the drawer and try it again.

The month passed quickly. She had hoped that when April came she might write to someone and say, "Our spring here is lovely! There is so much to see and do!" but, even though it seemed quite true, she was unable to write it and was unable furthermore to even think of who she might write it to. Twice she had gone to the post office in Carmel and asked at the General Delivery counter if there was, by chance, anything for Thalia Beale. There never was—for who even knew where she had gone except Walter and Maude who only knew it was "somewhere out there in Californy"?—but the little man behind the counter had, on both occasions, looked at her sympathetically with his apologetic eyes and once even asked, "Are you just here on a visit?" One Sunday morning, having missed the bus to Carmel, she had walked down Monterey's deserted main street and experienced a sudden longing for the familiar streets and faces of Ephraim. At first she had refused to recognize it, but as it grew stronger she even went to a telephone directory to try to locate the church; she would know no one, she had reasoned, yet perhaps she might feel some sense of belonging. But the nearest church listed had been Pacific Grove; fearing to venture by bus to an area even less familiar to her, she had settled for going back to her room and writing three little poems, all of which she tore up in tears before she fell asleep on her bed at five o'clock.

The idea for the week-end had been growing since the day she discovered her adventure in Carmel-by-the-Sea would have to be primarily the adventure of a daily visitor, of an onlooker, an outsider. It had started that first evening as she waited

disappointedly by the road for the bus to take her back to
Monterey to look for a place to stay. And each day thereafter
as she rode the bus back down the highway through the pines,
she had added mental notes to the original plan. Finally, in
mid-April, she sat in her narrow room and carefully counted the
rewards of her frugality: besides the money required for her
return ticket, $53.15 remained. This time, as she took her bags
and made the twenty-minute trip to Carmel, it seemed as
though tiny wings were flapping wildly inside her breast. Her
own boldness made her tremble. Her little adventure was one
that she wanted no one, and yet, strangely, everyone, to know.

The week-end was going to be beautiful. Yet when she
arrived at the house she had chosen after days of meticulously
studying the Want Ads at the library, the experience was not
without a tinge of disappointment. Its hacienda-appearance
seemed somehow less exotic and more stark than it had that
late sunny afternoon when she had followed tremblingly behind
the boisterous realtor through the tangled garden and throughout its bone-white rooms with their mock-Florentine tapestries
and Moroccan cushions. Yet she was so fortunate to have it at
all, she told herself; it would have been impossible to rent such
a place for three mere days, she had been informed, were it not
that a couple from Honduras had just vacated it and the new
tenants were not due from Connecticut until Monday. It would
be $45 for the three days—half of what she had paid for a month
in Monterey, she worried—yet it was precisely, or at least almost
precisely, what she had come for. And she must have it. She
must not wince, must not falter.

Two things bothered her, however. The street appeared as
quaint as any other, but why, oh why, she asked herself, could
it not have borne a name like the ones running below it—Monte
Verde, Camino Real, Casanova—or even Dolores, the one above
it? Why must it have been called simply Lincoln? And there was
something else, but this she had resolved to do something
about. The house—once she even tremblingly dared to call it
"my hacienda" to herself—had somehow escaped the wonderful

little epithets she had seen tacked on rustic gates and ornate lamp posts elsewhere in the village. Not La Casablanca, not even Wee Hideaway, the house was simply identified, evidently because of its original owner, by a little wooden placard that read Vosbrink. But she had planned ahead here: having found on one of her excursions a piece of driftwood large enough to cover the weathered placard, she had carefully lettered upon it with her watercolors the name—product of much deliberation and many nervous headaches—that she had chosen. For several days she had invented new names, trying them out quietly to herself—Thrushmore, Sea Room, Set Adrift, Linnet's Landing— but she finally settled on something foreign that she had seen on a magazine at the library: BEAU MONDE.

For the three glorious days Thalia's heart ached with inexpressible passion—joy or sadness, she could not be entirely sure which. She wore her new sweater every day, and whenever she left the house she carried with her the looseleaf in which she had jotted down her impressions, the beginnings of poems, even the idea for—the thought made her tremble—a novel, which she had reluctantly promised herself to identify, had anyone ever asked, as her "work in progress." Much of her time she spent walking through the rooms of her house, remarking confidently, if quietly, to the white walls, "This room is especially nice during our rainy season. And here, on the patio, is where I usually spend my afternoons." Twice, indeed, she took a little snack of V-8 juice and Ritz Crackers and went out to sit on the little bench under the gnarled cypress. Although she had jotted down lists of things to do during her little week-end, she found it difficult deciding how to do them. Friday, after she had put things into a drawer and hung up her wool suit in one of the spacious closets, she had gone leisurely about her schedule, even determining that night to sleep as late as she wanted in the big Spanish bed, but when she had opened her eyes at 8:30 on Saturday, she was cross with herself for wasting such valuable time and made certain that every precious moment would have to count throughout the two remaining days. She delighted in being just a five-minute walk away from the shops and galleries on Ocean Avenue, and, each day, on one of her little pilgrimages, she treated herself to something special. This was not counting the three scented candles and the jasmine incense she had bravely bought to burn in her hacienda while she read her new flower book and worked on her poems; these were little surprises that came from the shops she had previously not allowed herself to enter. There was no limit to what she might have, she promised herself, no limit except the diminishing budget she had set aside for these last three beautiful days. One day she chose a Danish pastry at a tiny bakery where the pink-cheeked lady spoke with an accent; on another she had a hot-fudge sundae in the red-and-white-striped candy parlor she had passed so many times; and on the third day, after much vacillation, she went into the Mediterranean Market and emerged with a bottle of marinated artichoke hearts. She was disappointed that she did not particularly like them but contented herself with the knowledge that there were people back in Ephraim who did not even know whether they liked them or not. The thoughts of Ephraim caused her to become suddenly and unexpectedly excited. She wondered if anyone had died, if anyone would look changed, if the hollyhocks could possibly be starting to bloom.

Like I say, you'll see her puttering around out there by her hollyhocks or she'll be passing by here in that little gray sweater of hers on her way out to the edge of town or Lord knows where. With Elvina gone she doesn't like to stay there in the house too much, I suspect. But I guess she's got plenty to do. Lloyd Tenney over at the school is working on his master's (he and Rayona Riggs's boy have both gone up to Utah State almost every summer) and Frieda says that Thalia's typing his thesis for him. It's on breeding sheep and the various diseases they get and I don't know what all. She normally gets twenty-five cents a page but Frieda says she asked her to do it for twenty. I don't know how many she can do an hour, but then, when it gets right down to it, with Elvina gone, what else has she got to do?

I suspect she's glad to be back home here. People are different down there. Nell asked her if she thought she'd ever want to sell the house (Dewey's boy has been looking for a little place just about that size) and go down there to live and Thalia said no, she didn't hardly think she would. She said she didn't really think she would fit in. And, of course, you know as well as I do that it's best if she stays here. Elvina would have wanted that. And too, if she says she had her a week-end she'll never forget, well, I guess she'll always have that to remember. Lord forgive her.

FIVE

The People Who Were Not There

LEWIS HORNE

all
the past lapping them like a
cloak of chaos
—Thom Gunn

Sure, we wanted to move to the country! When Dad asked us—out of the blue of our Arizona sky, as it were—excitement played leapfrog with our surprise. "Fourteen acres," he said, "with an irrigation ditch in front." Seven miles out of town. A new way of life.

But we got used to it quickly. After dark when we went out of doors, as we had to do with the flashlight to get to the outhouse through the trees, a great blackness closed in. No streetlights. No glow from a neighbor's window. On Saturday night we'd hear the Indians rattling home in their wagons to the reservation. Such quiet . . . As my brother Ken and I lay in our beds on the screenporch, dogs yipped one to another across the valley, and a bullfrog sang with dignity on the ditchbank. The only sounds.

During summer days we did our chores. Then with William Conner, a new friend, we swung over the ditch, Tarzan-like, on the branches of an ash tree so monstrous it shaded the whole front yard. Those were the years of World War II, and sparked with a patriotism, fanned to a hot flame by Saturday afternoon movies, we also played commando—in our orchard or among the mesquites in the bottom field or in the orchard of William's grandfather, old Mr. Thorsen. Earlier, living in town, before Pearl Harbor catapulted juvenile energies into the dangers that lay behind German and Japanese lines, we had played at cowboys, stalking about Apache battle grounds.

One day in the second summer we lived on the farm, the two games had a meeting. William, our commando strategist, sent Ken and me crawling in opposite directions through a small gully alongside the road. Mission in mind, faithful and brave, I wriggled through Johnson grass, scratched my knees on rocks, scrambled nose down in earnestness.

This blind earnestness led me directly into the silent horse which might have stepped on me had it been a livelier beast. For even though I cried out, it did not move. Its leg was motionless as a statue as I lifted my head.

Above me seated bareback and peering down with scarcely a smile—or worse, as though I scarcely merited a smile—was an Indian boy a year or so older than me. Not an Apache. Nothing so romantic. Simply a boy from the nearby reservation. The bottoms of his shoes, openings like boils on the worn soles, hit my line of sight, his sock making a downward line from tongue to heel where it disappeared. His smooth brown leg was bare up the calf to the faded khakis he wore.

As I stared up, squatting back on my heels, he took from his mouth a weed he had been chewing and speared it at me. Too light to hold its course, it drifted past my shoulder. But I scrambled backward, crab-like, all the same. Where were Ken and William? This horseman was older than me. He nudged the animal a step forward.

"Stop!"

Arms and legs buckled, raised, bent and stiffened, as I backed away from the plodding horse. The Indian boy smiled.

"Ken! William!"

Where were they? I felt like sobbing as suddenly my arms gave way, elbows collapsing. I flung myself over onto my belly, arms about my head, huddling, waiting. The hoof on my back—I could feel it, injury so unfairly to come. But the sound of the horse brought relief instead, for its movement, frightening at first, took it past me up to the roadside.

Finally I raised my head. The Indian boy, higher yet above me, stared down. William and Ken stood near, looking back at him and then down at me.

Embarrassed to be caught worm-like in the weeds, I rose.

"He was going to ride me down. With that horse."

The Indian boy laughed and rode off bareback down the road.

"He was going to ride me down," I said to Ken and William.

William frowned, watching the horse. "That's Clifford Wellington. He's a mean Indian. His dad irrigates for us."

He was going to ride me down! The thought bucked with my pulse. He was! Or—the next thought after some calm returned—or was he?

"He's 'bout two years behind himself in school. Real mean bastard. Don't ever get in a fight with him."

I didn't get in a fight with him. I never saw anybody get in a fight with him. But after that I seemed to see Clifford again and again, much more often than I wanted. Once, walking home from Ruiz's store with a can of pork and beans for lunch, I saw him ahead of me on his horse, him on one side of the road, me on the other. I tensed, ready to scramble for the ditch, to jump in and splash across fully clothed if I had to. He simply watched me, unsmiling. He knew I was scared. That knowledge seemed to be enough—this time. Later he came into our driveway chasing horses that had run through our open gate into the orchard. On home ground I felt secure. Frequently I saw him on Mr. Thorsen's farm, where his father worked. But there too I felt no threat, for William and Ken were company.

Eventually of course I found myself alone with him again. I was hiding during one of our games. A tent, board floor with a canvas top, stood behind the chicken pen in Mr. Thorsen's yard, and I slipped through an opening to hide from Ken and William. Spy in flight. Shadow of refuge. I settled down, barefoot, my back against a trunk, snuggling in among the boxes near the opening. No one would find me—dusty, dry, hot. Dark corners.

I wouldn't let Ken or William catch me here, I decided. My secret. I would wait until the game was nearly finished and then leave so they wouldn't know where I hid. My sanctuary.

Hard to take one's self away. With Ken, Melissa, Jane—with the family—I felt my life sometimes was too public. I wanted their company, but I wanted privacy too. I couldn't find it in the house on the farm. The rooms, though large, were few. The screenporch, though wide, was crowded with the four bunk beds spread out across it.

But here, in the tent, in the hot shadowy tent, I could hide away.

Twice I saw Ken and William sneak by, hostile enemies, secretive, seeking their enemy. But I, secure, was no one's enemy, no one enemy to me. No friction of relationship. Perspiring, I felt dreamy. I might have been watching the hypnotic spread of a desert, buzzards circling on open wing.

After Ken and William had passed, out of sight and sound, I closed my eyes. The floor was warm under my feet. I wriggled backward, adjusting my position. Shifting, my bottom touched a hand.

Monster in the darkness—snake-like.

I knocked one box off another as I whirled, saw the hand dark in the shadows, flat on the floor as it had been when I felt it.

"What you want?"

Clifford Wellington there, his question bringing out the first words I ever heard him speak. His black hair was shiny, falling straight forward in a kind of bang. His brown face was sweaty, dark eyes alive with a quiet, intense, but strangely unaggressive glow, something subdued and burning in them that did not match the threat in his voice.

"I beat you up," he said.

Maybe he would. Maybe he wouldn't. For me the threat was

half the deed. I stood, wanting to slip out, and Clifford rose, almost a head taller. Easy and strong, easy and lithe.

"Beat you up," he mumbled again.

"Ken! William!" I cried. "Ken!"

I stumbled backward, yelling the whole time, the tied tent flaps reluctant to open. But Clifford didn't move. My cries, like birds released, fluttered away, and I felt foolish standing there. For he didn't move. Would he? Or wouldn't he?

As though to renew performance, he said again, "I beat you up."

But before I could respond, the flaps against which I was leaning came apart, and I fell out onto the ground. Clifford's father stood there and William's grandfather, Mr. Thorsen. William and Ken came running. I picked myself up sheepishly and dusted myself, flipped back the hair out of my eyes.

Clifford stood in the doorway of the tent. He would have smiled at me I'm sure, possibly remembering how I'd risen, craven-like, from the ground earlier by the road, but his father worried him. He spoke to Clifford in a deep voice, broken vowels—a language I could not understand—and pulled him by the arm from the floor of the tent. He spoke again and pointed up the driveway past Mr. Thorsen's barn to the citrus grove. Wordlessly, Clifford walked away. Did not look back. Walked with grace and some kind of inward rhythm. With contained energy, managing, it seemed, his furies, whatever they were.

Clifford's dad told Mr. Thorsen he was sorry his son was where he should not be.

"Don't worry about it, Allan. Just boys."

As Clifford's dad went to the barn, Mr. Thorsen turned to us. "Now what you boys been doing? What were you in the tent for—hah?"

Both Ken and William protested. They weren't in there. They'd never been in there.

Eyes wheeled to me. "I was just—just hiding. From them. And then I found out he—Clifford Wellington—was in there. And I started yelling. That's all I did."

Mr. Thorsen's face, lined and brown, white hair thick and coarse as a brush, did not tell me whether he believed or not.

"Honest," I said. "That's all."

"You're the Phillips boys—yah?"

I nodded. He spoke heavily, as though some of the words were still awkward for his lips and tongue. He had come to this country from Norway as a boy, parents proselytized by Mormon missionaries, and entered the valley by horse and wagon. He never talked to us when we played with William but moved about, rigid and heavy-shouldered and silent, with his own thoughts. In his seventies, manipulating a cane, he walked down the country road to church every Sunday so long as the weather was fine, kept track of the farm he lived on with his widowed daughter and grandson.

He had dignity. But his dignity came from distance—and heaviness—and history. He was far from us.

"Well," he said, "I trust you. Your grandfather was my friend and I trust his grandsons."

The statement frightened me. For my grandfather, dead during the second decade of the century, was a distant and even mythic figure. I wished I could pull back my words to make sure I had cast no shame on his memory.

"You know what is in that tent?"

We all three shook our heads.

He stepped into the opening, pushing himself up with his cane. "Come in," he said. As we hesitated: "Come on."

We helped fold back the door flaps and zip open a window.

"Here," he said, "is my past—yah. William's past, too."

In his heavy and awkward voice, he explained. He kept everything, he said. Deeds, mortgages, second mortgages. Diaries. Photographs and letters. Put away in boxes and trunks, each labeled. Some by year. Some by content. "I am a pack rat," he said with barely a lift of a smile. "My daughter Maud complains." One label read: *Mother & Father*. Something like mute melodies sounded, ghost-songs. Time became quickly tangible and frightening, and I was pushed by a compulsion to track Mr. Thorsen back from his white-haired and bone-hardened age to some imaginable (or unimaginable) babyhood begun in swaddling clothes. But my mind couldn't hold the trail.

I could only smile weakly, when Mr. Thorsen, seeing me look at the words, said, "Yes, *my* father and mother."

In such a holy of holies, Mr. Thorsen was the high priest, Ken and William and I the novitiates.

"I show you something else," he said.

He turned in the heat, pointing a large root-like finger at the labels as he scanned them. Finding a box in the bottom of a pile, he told us to pull it out: *mission.* Opening it, he handed us a small smelly Bible. We couldn't read it.

"That is printed in Samoan," he said. "My mission was to Samoa. Look at this picture."

He showed us six white-suited young men, standing on a beach, palm trees behind. The young men stared, stiff, composed, and steady-eyed.

"That one—" almost covering a face with his wide finger— "that one is me. You believe it?" He almost smiled, and we had to tilt the photograph to the light coming in through the zipped-open window. "And next to me—you know who that is? Hah? That is your grandfather. You didn't know that—hah?"

Before I had time to look at it fully, he took the photograph back.

"I tell you," he said. "This box—you want to look sometime at the pictures, you come and look. You can see your grandfather. You come and look. You should have known your grandfather."

After he left, Ken seemed less concerned about knowing our grandfather than about my trespassing. "Wait'll Mom and Dad find out," he warned.

William said, "Wow, he's never let anybody in there before, Grampa hasn't."

"Just wait'll Mom and Dad find out."

I would have started something at another time. Who's going to tell them? I would have said, taunting, belligerent. But I only said, "So what?" and walked off toward the orchard. For I was caught in a tangle of memories, a net of speculations. The photograph had raised dream figures. Those six white-suited young men. . . . They floated there of a piece. Frozen. Turning slowly in space like clay figures, all six connected. Yet after the photograph was snapped, there in Samoa half a century ago, they had moved. Had taken deep breaths, laughed, talked to each other, turned to watching natives. Had come to life.

But now my imagination hadn't the breath of life to move them.

I walked into the orchard. The ground was wet, for Allan Wellington was irrigating. My feet squashing weeds into the mud, I tried to replace orange trees with palm trees, mud with sand. I tried to people the summer air. But I hadn't seen the picture of my grandfather clearly. With their dark hair and dark eyes, the six all looked alike.

The mud under my feet was the texture of clay. The effort to walk in it pulled me away from Samoan skies. It tugged at my feet, tired my ankles. I turned toward the ditch to wash them and find an easier place to walk. Along the bank was a smoother path.

But at the ditch I came on Clifford Wellington again. Doing what his father had told him to do. He was trying to shut off the opening to the row of trees, the opening through which the water poured, a small torrent, from the ditch. Since the row of trees was fully irrigated, he would shut the opening and break through another one farther up the ditch. But he was having a frustrating time. His energy and anger must have kept him from hearing me. The mud stuck to the shovel. When he finally loosed one shovelful, the swift water washed it away before he could get another in and build up the dam. He was running out of dirt, and the water was not stopped.

I wanted to leave, but I was sure that if I moved he would hear me. Again I was alone with him, Clifford and his anger.

"What you want?"

His voice was low and tense. After he saw that we were alone, the brief smile came back. I was an object he could handle with ease, matter of a situation he could mould. For with me he had time to circle, as it were, to maneuver and plan, gain vantage. Not as in the fight against the endless pouring out of water.

He swung the shovel up over his shoulder. Against the sky it struck a black silhouette. He stood, legs apart, wearing bulky irrigation boots, his body tilted slightly. Mean bastard, William had said. Tall and strong I could see. Also I could sense the harshness of deserts, the arrogance of mountains, hardship and victory, defeat and ignominy. Such flashes made up a photosphere about him. Protective. Like a shield.

Though I sensed the shield, however, even saw it, I saw, too, palm trees and six young men.

He rolled the shovel off his shoulder, held it swinging like a pendulum for a moment before him, then raising it quickly thrust the blade into the mud three or four inches from my toes.

Why didn't I cower? Or yell for help? Clifford expected me to. My pulse clanged. Though afraid, I was ashamed of my cowering and yelling. Besides if Clifford really meant to get me, cowering or yelling would do no good here. Six young men in white suits with dark unblinking eyes hung somewhere above me. A memory from a time out of memory.

"If I held—" my voice quaked— "if I held that board over there for you, held it against the opening, it would cut off the water enough so you could dam it up."

"I can do it," he muttered.

"I can help."

"You get wet. You have to get in the ditch."

"So what?"

I pulled my toes away and picked up the ripped 1-x-8 I saw lying under a tree. I also had to climb in the ditch as Clifford said and get my Levis wet to my hips by the time we finished. But by the time we finished, Clifford had the mud and dirt shoveled in, the water blocked off.

"See you later," I said and walked away, not because I was afraid now (for Clifford no longer scared me) but because it was a kind of pleasure to leave before he could thank me. Would he have done so? Maybe not. But I walked off down the ditchbank anyway, and by the time I got home was almost dry.

When I arrived Ken seemed to have changed his mind about reporting my trespassing in Mr. Thorsen's tent. Without giving preliminary details at supper, I told Dad about the photograph.

"By golly, I'd like to see that," he said. "Your grandfather was never much for souvenirs."

"Mr. Thorsen said we could go in and look at the pictures in the box. He said it was okay."

"I've always liked the old man. Rough old guy. Kind of mean to his kids. But tough. You be respectful when you talk to him, okay? Wouldn't hurt to say 'sir' even. He comes out of another time."

Next day, I opened the flaps of the tent and zipped open the window. The inside no longer felt ominous and secretive as it had the day before but instead mysterious—voices whispering, hands fluttering in the space about. Population of the past.

And also, as I noticed right away, population of the present.

"Hey!" I said. "What are you doing here?"

"You tell?" asked Clifford.

He stood behind a trunk. No threats of beating me up. No smiles of superior leisure. No real victories either, as I came to realize. Clifford had gone about as far in his threats as he could have without being called upon by pride to fulfill them. He did not really want to. I had hit the ground theatrically and often enough to satisfy him and shame myself. So helping him irrigate had come not as a great moment of compromise and brotherhood, not even as the only alternative of action, but simply the most reasonable and easy one. That's why we could be so easy with each other now.

"I won't tell," I said. "But what are you doing here?"

"I like to come in here."

Down on the floor I saw a pad of paper, a box of crayons. "You draw?" I asked.

Rather than answer he asked me again, "What you doing here?"

"Mr. Thorsen said I could. But really—do you draw? Can I see?" He hesitated. So I said, "C'mon. You show me what you have, and I'll show you what Mr. Thorsen showed us yesterday."

It was only a 15-cent pad of paper he held out. He used only a box of eight crayons. But opening the tablet disclosed vistas. Even in the subdued light of the tent, I found a free and bristling world in those colors. My appreciative faculties were no stronger than anyone else's. Yet the designs, the drawings, even the scribblings, pulled a person away, off into a world of wide skies and hot mesas.

My first comment: "Wow!"

The pages gave off drumbeats.

"You really do these? Really, Clifford? Wow!"

He took the pad from me and tossed it on the floor.

"Hey, don't throw it like that!"

"What Mr. Thorsen show you? You tell me now."

How could I expect six white-suited young men to speak to him as they had to me? I don't believe they did. He glanced briefly and handed the photograph back.

"There's supposed to be more in here," I said.

I found two other pictures of a South Sea island—Samoa, it must have been. Looking closely I found my grandfather. In one, two men sat in an open hut apparently at a meal. In the other, the six stood beside a sailing ship cast up on a beach. Behind were uprooted palm trees, the aftermath, it would seem, of a great storm.

"My grandfather," I said to Clifford.

"My grandfather dying."

I stammered at that. "Well—well, mine's dead already. Long time ago. Before I was born."

"He's sick now. Dying."

I tried to explain about my grandfather and Mr. Thorsen, about Samoa. But Clifford turned to leave.

"Is he in the hospital? Your grandfather?"

"At home."

As I watched Clifford walk up the driveway past Mr. Thorsen's chicken pen and Mr. Thorsen's house, I was still unable to tell anything about him. His walk was as smooth as ever. I knew quite well the adobe house on the reservation, the ground barren of grass or weeds around it, standing in the sun, baked through many summers. The Indian horses ran free. Two or three dogs lay in the shade of a single cottonwood. The barren river lay beyond.

Was Clifford's grandfather dying there?

I slipped the two photographs, the meal in the hut and the ship on the beach, back into the box. Outside I saw Mr. Thorsen, leaning on his cane, coming out of the barn.

Courageously—I felt—I asked him about Clifford's grandfather.

He grunted, answered in his clumsy tongue. "He's old. We all get old, boy, don't you know that—hah? He's an old buck, but life's gone out of him. He keeps his hair long—nobody could ever get him to cut it—and eats the Indian foods. How do mesquite beans sound to you—hah? Or sprouts of a cholla? But the old man—he's almost gone."

He died within a few days. It was September, the first week of school. Clifford, to my surprise, though bigger and older, was in my class. He sat behind me, and I felt proud to sit there without fear, for whispers still went about among my schoolmates that he was a mean Indian.

Then not more than three or four days after school had started, Mom and Dad were sitting on the lawn after sundown. Maud Conner had stopped by with William, and we made a small group—the grown-ups in cast-off wicker furniture, Ken and I with William and my sisters sprawled on the grass—waiting for the day's heat to cool. The cows were milked, supper dishes done. Bullfrog time as darkness thickened.

Ken was the first to see the red glow in the sky, exclaiming, "What's that?"

Maud Conner, William's mother, who was both talkative and profane, said, "Something's burning like hell."

We all moved to the front of the yard by the ditch and looked off toward a perceptible horizon marked by mountains and stars. In the earth's darkness was the red glow with perhaps a suggestion of jumping flames.

Dad asked, "Shall we go see?"

In the car we saw first that the fire was on the reservation. Then as we came nearer, Maud, who along with her father knew all the Indians, said, "That's old man Wellington's house."

I stared. The small house was covered with flames. Sparks flew off into the sky, absorbed by the night. The polished dirt around the house was shining, as though it reflected like a sea the fire's glow. Heat reached us where we sat in the car on the road. What made it burn so fiercely?

"I'll be damned," said Maud softly.

In the yard, safely distanced from the house, sat a group of people on benches. Motionless they faced the burning house, silhouettes against the tonguing flames. Women, children, men—figures of clay. They sat watching, either not hearing or not heeding the sound of our car.

As we eased away, Maud said, "I didn't know they ever did that."

"You mean they set it afire?" asked Mom.

Maud said that was right. "I can't remember ever seeing that before. It must be the old people that wanted it."

"But what does the wife do—if they burn the house?"

"It must be the old people, holding to the old ways. I'd bet you Allan Wellington didn't want it that way, but if his mother did—she's old and set in her ways, that old lady is. And she's got a couple of brothers. . . . It's the old people, I bet."

Could I ask Clifford about it? I wondered. So much of the situation puzzled me. He might explain. But I felt it would be a breach of our friendship to question him.

As I lay in bed on the screenporch, I wondered if Clifford had been one of the dark figures watching the fire so quietly. I'd swear he was. Could he keep that experience out of his face and walk, hide it as he did almost everything else? I didn't know.

And I didn't have a chance to find out. Clifford did not return to school. Word came that he was going to an Indian school. Occasionally I saw him after that, but only at widely spaced intervals—in the summer riding a horse with another Indian boy or two, perhaps once during the school year. He looked across me if we met, as though the memory of our acquaintance, of my fear of him and my weak offer of help in Mr. Thorsen's orchard, were, like the experience of the fire, buried far and deep within him.

There was one more fire that I should mention that was more of a loss to me. Mr. Thorsen's tent burned down shortly after Thanksgiving. During a storm, the electricity had gone off, and unknown to Maud the old man took one of the kerosene lanterns out through the rain to the tent. Inside he fell and was barely able to get himself out without burning to death. The wind through the door and partly opened window fanned the flames, protected at the beginning from the rain. The blaze became so strong, got such a start, that it took the whole canvas tent in spite of the storm that had begun to abate. All the boxes were destroyed. A few items were saved in the charred trunks. The pictures, of course, of the young men in Samoa were only ashes.

Memories can make bleak memorials, but pleasanter all the same than more tangible monuments. I can go back today if I wish and look at the farm as it stands on McKennow Road. We had moved there to an area new to us, a stubborn one made less so by our work, tromping through mud with shovel over the shoulder, searching through the bottom field at sunrise and earlier for cows. But the people—they're a different matter. You can't look into them. Mr. Thorsen's boyhood is beyond my sight. What Clifford suggested I can't look at, for he pointed to more distant territories, frontiers lying beyond our own time and space. Distant as Samoa, burned in the fire.

It is said that the Pimas have a word, *Huhugam,* meaning "Those who are gone." *It is sometimes written Ho-ho-kam and is the Pima name for those people who came into our desert country thousands of years ago. No one knows where they came from or what became of them* (Webb, *A Pima Remembers,* 1959, p. 53). So with the mind's desert.

I could find out what became of Clifford, of course, but sometimes it's best not to know. I prefer to leave him walking away up Mr. Thorsen's driveway with his violent and hidden grace, part of the desert country, the Ho-ho-kam.

The plane for Richmond was late. The earlier flight, so late as to overlap my own later one, had just left. But I had been unable to get on. I had been turned away at the gate with the blonde traveling saleswoman sitting beside me. Or rather she had been turned away, having pushed ahead as I came up a minute behind her to hear her, with quiet aggressiveness, ask for a seat. We were both turned away.

"I've found out," she said, "that you've got to make a fuss or you don't get anything. You've got to stand up for yourself. But if the flight's full—" a quick shrug and a friendly smile—"the flight's full. That's all."

So we had come back and found empty seats to sit together in and look out the window from, absorbing the musty smell of wrappers and butts and bodies in the air terminal. To sit and wait.

"Are we going to Richmond for the same reason?" she asked.

I said I thought not. Explained that I was just finishing law school and was going to interview with a Richmond firm. Added that it was my first trip South. Added—for conversation's sake and out of my own feelings of exhilaration—that my wife was in an Ann Arbor hospital with our first child, a daughter born two days before, so it was an uncommon time for us.

"That's lovely," she said.

She spoke quietly. She was a small woman with, I conjectured, a large energy. For a company in a small Massachusetts town she sold spiral notebooks of varying sizes to college bookstores about the country, the college's name and insignia stamped on the covers. She was going to Richmond for a convention, she said. And then—"Your wife and baby are fine?" she asked.

"Oh yes."

"It's an exciting time with a new baby. I remember when I brought my little boy home. My husband was in South Carolina—it was during the war. He was such a big baby."

"Well, I've barely seen our baby. It kind of worries me. You know—how do you hold them, what do you do with them, things like that."

"Oh, you learn. It's wonderful fun."

I had the impression that she laughed infrequently, that her main response was her smile, a quiet but warm acceptance, the smile of one who had absorbed pleasures and experience, made a warm repository of them, a sustaining gospel of memories, private and confidential. She could draw on these without desperation.

"You're lucky you were with your wife while she was in labor. You were there?" she said.

I nodded.

"My husband was away both times—when my little boy was born and when my little girl was born too. He was in Normandy then. I drove myself to the hospital both times."

She didn't speak with any self-pity that I could detect. Time had made the disappointment up to her. We talked about my trip and her business. She always liked to have plenty of time at the airport, she said. Not her boss. He was one of those who preferred to leap from the car and run for the ramp just as it was being wheeled from the plane. Her nerves couldn't tolerate that, she said. "I like to take it easy."

The big sky-storming eagles we saw through the window, the lights beyond, the darkness covering it all—these made up the scene before us. An Army Spec-3 with tired wife and half-awake children wandered by, baby-bag and baby in arms. One terminal was much like another. Willow Run like Washington International. No indication of the particular city from where we sat except for the distant glow.

Our talk lapsed. She smiled sympathetically at the Spec-3's wife with the two children, a boy and a girl, in tow.

"They can sure be a handful," she said.

The darkness held us in, made a kind of sanctuary perhaps, for it was a bitterly cold night out of doors, the harshness of the weather lending a privacy to our *ménage à deux* even among the milling travelers. We all of us, strangers and friends, made a glistening and noisy configuration. The saleswoman I spoke with had opened to me a bit of her life. I had offered her a part of mine. She peopled our talk with the figures of her boss, her children, all a part of her, as my wife and new child and, going back, those figures on McKennow Road were a part of me. Mr. Thorsen. William. Clifford.

To bring them into focus, to make stronger the moment we shared then, I asked further about her children. For it is easier to ask about others than to tell about one's self. The risk of boring is less great.

I said, "Your children must be pretty much self-sufficient by now."

Her answering smile shocked me, a gaunt movement on features suddenly dead, like water fading in a desert. I had seen no smile like it, part resignation, part sorrow—a mask for emptiness. "Both my children," she said, "died when they were very young." I don't know what my face showed. I felt like cowering. "Usually I can mention it," she went on after a moment, "without it hitting back at me this way." I looked away, then back. Her briefcase lay in her lap, her hands clasped on it loosely. What had seemed so vital in her was gone. Acceptance was there—the fact was old, from another time, but it lay exposed, rooted up. She spoke then, as though, exposed, *it* might best be described. I was too dumb to speak, so her comments covered the silence between us like a few stray leaves the ground, the silence beneath the hubbub of the air terminal.

"You expect your parents to die before you," she said, "that's the way of life. But you never think your children will. It's the end . . . the end of the world really. You can have a career. You can work night and day. But no matter how busy you are, nothing makes up for it."

What could I say? I felt as I had, looking up at the threat of Clifford Wellington many summers ago.

"My little girl died of leukemia when she was two and a half. She was brilliant. At two and a half, she told the doctor that she was four, and he believed her. He never knew the difference. My little boy died when he was four. He had a heart condition."

A plane was called. The Spec-3 and his wife gathered together sleepy children and their clutter of belongings and rushed off for the loading gate. The mother kept hurrying the children, who were sleepy and balky.

"My only consolation is that I did everything I could. It wasn't my fault. If they'd smothered or something like that—those things happen, you know—I'd never have been able to live with myself.

But you're right. Had they lived they'd be twenty-three and twenty-four now. Quite self-sufficient."

I wondered about her husband because she said, "I have no family." Was he dead? Killed in the war? Divorced? I felt presumptuous for wondering.

"You spend twenty-five years trying to forget. You work. You engage yourself. You try to forget. And then something like this. . . . "

"I'm sorry."

"It's not your fault. You couldn't have known."

When at last the call for Richmond came, we were sitting silently. My embarrassment kept me dumb. Her children as she had described them had seemed so alive. That they were not. . . .

On the plane, she stood waiting with a kind of compassion and forgiveness, I suspect, for me to sit beside her. We fastened our seat belts, and as the plane banked and we saw the dazzling lights below, rising out of the darkness, she said, "Washington's a beautiful city, isn't it."

The monuments rose, illuminated. Memorial flames. The landscape's decoration flowered out of the dark below, a wrenching, as it were, to the memory. So many monuments burning out of that desert-darkness, all aflame for the people not there. Forgotten often, achingly remembered—a clumsy voice, a smooth walk.

My companion rested her head against the back of the seat, looking out the window until the many lights were gone. Then she turned forward, eyes closed, half smile on her face. Had the hurt receded for a while?

The plane flew on low in the sky towards Richmond. The darkness outside grew deeper and, as it grew deeper, seemed to take on more density, to become populated vastly with shadows. Not forgotten, I don't believe. None of them forgotten. That was the pain of it. Only waiting—like angels—their call.

SIX

Sayso or Sense

EILEEN GIBBONS KUMP

Amy Gordon was to have a new house, and in a frenzy of neighborliness, folks came to tell Israel how to build it. Neighbors who shared work horses and yeast starts freely shared their wisdom. "If I were you, Brother Gordon—"

Too excited and pleased to do otherwise, the Gordons listened well; then after supper they separated the wheat from the chaff and fortified themselves for another day. Israel told Amy, "It's your house, within reason." Reason meant whatever the bank would loan a man with an excellent reputation and fair collateral. She was therefore careful with her dreaming: It would be a simple, strong house with plenty of room and one or two of those up-to-date advantages.

When Israel's father arrived—suitcase in hand—Amy showed him a cot in the children's room. "For as long as you will stay," she said. "Lola begs to sleep on the floor and she will have her wish."

"Thank you, Amy dear."

There were tears in the old man's eyes as Amy kissed him on the cheek. "We need you."

"I thought we would lay foundation today," he said, folding back his shirt cuffs.

Amy smiled and put her arm through his as they walked outside. "Oh, we're not ready for foundation, Grandpa. We've lots to do first." Sixty years experience, she thought. Sixty years head start. She watched him go, thankful in her heart for his strong back and, yes, even for his knowhow. What they did not want of it they could manage a piece at a time. The neighbors had given them plenty of practice.

But what are a few weeks of practice against a lifetime? Amy turned from her sewing and saw Israel and Grandpa, side by side, announcing before she was even aware of their presence that she did not want what she knew she wanted. In Israel's eyes was the zeal of a convert and in Grandpa's the patient kindness a good man shows the child found in error.

"You don't want a basement, Amy dear," said Grandpa.

How could she reply? Despite his size—he was six inches shorter than Israel—Grandpa had in his wide back energy for a full day's labor, in his hands the craftsman's skill. Worse, he had one of those rich, prophetic voices some of the church leaders had, voices that didn't need to shout. And he had an iron gray mustache.

Amy looked at him and at the son who thought his father was Moses and wondered whether to go down fighting.

"Israel says it won't cost much more than an extra room upstairs, Grandpa. I do want a basement."

"Amy, Amy, Amy." Grandpa's voice gradually softened, but it was the softening voice of intensity, not argument. "You don't want one of those—those dugouts on this fine property!" He walked to the window. "What a fine corner lot! My—"

"But it wouldn't be a dugout, Grandpa. We'll have cement. It would be cool—and beautiful!"

"Amy." Grandpa came and put his arm around her shoulders. Still, he was not arguing. Still, his voice did not waver. "Amy, you need to be reminded that your own father—and I've known him all my life—was born in a cave on the side of a hill. I've heard him tell of it, how his pa dug that hole with his own two hands. But your pa never called it a house! It was a place to exist until a house could be built on top of the ground where a house ought to be. Do you think your pa didn't build that house as fast as he could?"

"Grandpa, there are no snakes here!"

He laughed without impatience. "I'm not talking about snakes, my dear. Why, an upstairs is heaven—and closer to heaven, too!" He smiled, his voice jolly and nostalgic at the same time. "My, but the mornings that come back to me out of an attic room with an east window. My, my—"

He was off into thought, as always, absolutely right, absolutely unmovable. But was he right? Amy looked at Israel for an answer but saw only Mosaic adoration.

"You promised me, Israel. We thought about a basement together."

"I know it, and we're not going to do anything you won't allow. But Pa has built a lot of houses."

"And now he's building ours?"

It was an unkind thing to say. No one in southern Utah could build a better. But her basement! She had felt its coolness, imagined the baby asleep there while she canned away August. She had already dug it with her bare hands.

Now Grandpa was rolling his sleeves all the way up, the matter settled. Of course it had been settled when he rode up with his suitcase. Amy would not have her basement. She would not have whatever Grandpa in a lifetime of experience had not found to be good. She could see her house now, just like Grandma Nellie's, with a steaming upstairs and deck porches the width of the house on both floors.

A carpenter came and Amy sent him to join the adversary. She tried to keep away from the window so she would not have to watch them bury forever her undug basement. Could she do as much? Could she bury her anger and never mention basements again as long as she lived? She could try. What did she really know about them anyway? A picture, a comment, things that wouldn't cover the head of a pin beside Grandpa's knowhow. She scolded herself, unselfishly took all the blame for troubling the waters, and hoped for an extended peace, hoped that Lola had not outgrown that old whim of hers about sleeping on the floor.

By the time the foundation was laid and the plans were completed, Amy had given up her ample closets: "Can't you see that they would encourage the foolish acquiring of clothing? Remove temptation. Be frugal and simple, my dear." She had also changed her mind about wanting deeper, more gradual stairs: "A waste of space, daughter. Up is up." But these submissions were trifling. Amy began to suspect male judgment in any form. If Israel said, "Bedtime," she got to looking at the clock, even if she was having difficulty keeping her eyes open. When he called on one of the children to say family prayer—no matter who it was—she knelt there wondering whose turn he had overlooked. But the thing that finally shattered her faith in men, the thing that finally made Grandpa an old man with old-fashioned ideas, was the problem of which direction the house ought to face. Only it was not a problem to Amy. She had never for one second seen it as a matter that needed deciding until she overheard the men talking.

"Will the house look west or south, Brother Gordon?" asked the carpenter.

Grandpa was silent, and silence made Amy uneasy. West. To the main road of course. To the west!

"How fortunate to be on a corner lot and have a choice." Grandpa sounded really grateful. "By all means," he said, "the main entrance should be on the south."

South? Amy looked over at Grandpa and in a tight, slow voice said, "Why don't you put it on the roof?"

"What was that, Amy dear?" asked Grandpa.

"I'm sorry, Grandpa. I was being foolish. I thought I heard you say that the house was to face south."

"By all means."

Amy sat down and picked up her mending, but her trembling hands would not sew. She had been patient. She had been agreeable. Sometimes she had been right. And all those times floated back, giving her strength.

"By *what* means, Grandpa? By *what* means? Why south?" She stood and went to the door. South she saw the cemetery, the narrowing road where it curved into the desert. South she saw one house: the shanty where Watermelon Joe lived.

"Look south! Look!"

"The town is going to grow, Amy. Someday the main part of town will be out there."

"It will?"

"It will."

"But, Grandpa! The school, the church house, the store, the people! They're all north! The whole state is north!" She looked at Israel. "Don't let him!" Back to Grandpa. "What isn't north, Grandpa? Name one thing that isn't north!"

The carpenter filled the silence. "That's just it, Sister Gordon. North is all filled up. North is utilized, fully utilized."

"That's why a south front would be nonsense. Don't you see? Everyone who comes, including our children and ourselves, including you, Grandpa, on your way from Willow Flat, comes from the north." She sat down again. "My garden and kitchen are on the north. Folks will spy the back door and they will come right in. Who will walk clear around the house just to get in right? Everyone will come through my kitchen—the bishop, the Relief Society sisters, the apostles!"

Amy was sure she had been convincing. She would forgive Grandpa his momentary blindness. After all, he had built most of his houses where there were no main streets to consider. She smiled at him and he smiled back.

"This decision is very important. You will live here for the rest of your lives." It was an observation, not a rebuttal.

"That's true, Grandpa."

"You will likely never move again. You ought to be content."

Sometimes she loved that voice.

"Yes, Grandpa. You do see." Perhaps he *was* a Moses.

"And when the town grows south—"

Amy felt her cheeks flame. Had he heard one word?

"When the town grows south, a west entrance will be a daily annoyance, a daily reminder of lack of foresight. When the—"

"When! When! When!" She was sure she would cry. "And when the town does not grow south, I will have a daily annoyance that will drive me out of my mind!" She ran from the room, abandoning the men to their visions. She could see the town through her tears, snuggled against the graveyard, the rattling homestead, the barren fringe of desert. She would *not* submit!

But that night she had a dream. God was conducting priesthood meeting and Grandpa and Israel and the carpenter were on the front row, hanging on every word. God said when they came to earth, men could have their choice—sayso or sense—but they couldn't have both because that wouldn't be fair to the women. He called a vote and Grandpa's hand shot up for sayso before God had finished speaking. Amy awoke, sure the choice had been unanimous. By daylight she had decided that, God approving, she had no alternative but to leave the men to their folly.

After breakfast she made her speech. "The front door should face west, main street. It should be easy and logical to get to from the north. Or the south. My mind is the same as it was last night. However, I gave up my basement, which would have been cool and beautiful, and I gave up my vain closets and wasteful stairway. I will now give up having my front door on the front of the house."

"Amy, Amy, Amy."

"I don't want to talk about it any more."

They left her, their stomachs full, their minds undoubtedly troubled that she did not see. Perhaps Israel reminded his pa that it was Amy's house after all. But Amy never even hoped it. She let herself be mad inside whenever she wanted to, and she watched them build her house the way they wanted to. She never let on what she had dreamed or how much she hurt inside. When they built her a coolroom with several inches of cobble rock underneath the cement floor and with sawdust between the studding in all the walls, she showed them her pleasure. Inwardly she marveled at how the men in her dream could go about building such a fine coolroom without her objections.

But to nurture such sarcasm made Amy uneasy. It was wrong for a woman. When the house was finished, the pictures hung, the rooms moved into, she was pleased, and she longed to have once more her sturdy faith in Israel, that trust that made obedience beautiful. She longed to feel again that the priesthood could actually carry the burdens without throwing the world into chaos.

When it came time to dedicate the new house to the Lord's care, Israel relinquished his right and asked Grandpa to offer the prayer. Amy hid her unsightly wash boiler and such things as usually hang beside a back door, and on Sunday afternoon Grandpa and a radiant band of friends and neighbors filed in through the kitchen. They arranged themselves in the parlor.

As Grandpa began to pray, Amy's heart churned for a miracle. She had to have it! "Father, we dedicate into Thy watchcare and keeping this beautiful home." *Oh Father, it is beautiful, it's beautiful regardless!* "Bless this good family. Thou knowest the intents of their hearts are righteous, Father." *Thou knowest how men are, Father. Help me to take no delight in their folly.* "Bless every comfortable room, bless every child who grows there. Bless the timbers that the elements—" *Bless me never to mention my basement again. Remove bitterness, doubt.* "Within these walls let Thy Holy Spirit abide in peace always, we pray Thee, in Christ's name, Amen." *In peace. In peace. Oh, please! Amen.*

Amy sank into a chair. Not until Grandpa came over and looked into her eyes and took her hands between his own did she realize she was still crying.

"Thank you, Grandpa."

"I'm sorry everybody invaded the woman's realm by tracking through the kitchen, Amy dear, but please don't cry."

She cried harder.

"My, my, Amy. It's only a house," he said.

Amy's eyes were suddenly dry. She looked up at the old man.

"Of course, Amy. A worldly convenience. Trivia is trivia and must remain so in a world of sorrow."

Amy's heart quieted after that. Oh, there were setbacks. The president of the church himself walked through her kitchen once during soap making, and one cold Saturday night the Relief Society sisters almost stumbled over Israel sitting before the oven door in the bathing tub. There may even have been another time or two when Amy came so near telling Israel her dream that she trembled. But she kept it. Trivia is trivia. Besides, how could a dream matter to Israel when it made less and less sense to her.

SEVEN

Hit the Frolicking, Rippling Brooks

KAREN ROSENBAUM

Religion is for women. Says Madeleine, Portuguese-Catholic, chunky in her black pleated skirts, cackling always, nudging God. Women believe it. Women practice it. When pews are filled, they are filled with women. Men eh they sleep and drink beer and mow lawns and fish off the dock instead of going to Mass. Men drop a little money in the priest's pocket and call it a Sunday eh? or men marry off their daughters, there in the center aisle with the organ playing and the priest prating, but religion, the knee-bending, the candle-lighting, the bead-counting, that's for women.

Says Madeleine. Madeleine is sixty-five. Ten years older than Mother. Looks thirty years older. A transplanted New Bedforder, come south when her husband, fireman, died in a two-alarm, come to live with Molly, her daughter, and James, her son-in-law, come to live in the house next door to our flat.

I don't contradict Madeleine. My mother married a Catholic who doesn't even drop money into the priest's pocket, who never chooses to identify himself as a Catholic although somebody there in their fund-raising departments has found out and puts the finger on him every year or so for a hundred bucks. I give to the American Cancer Society, he says and hangs up. Mama now, Mama is a Mormon, like us, no, like Ben maybe, not so much like me, though I am her only daughter, and Ben she didn't acquire until eight months ago when I wooshed off in the dress she made to a ceremony she and Dad couldn't even watch. She was glad she couldn't watch, that I'd done it up right with Ben rather than wrong with that pagan Eddie. Dad wasn't so glad. Dad doesn't drink beer and fish off the docks. He works. Every day. Cassidy's Carpets. He insists his employees, also Mama who does the books, take generous vacations. But himself. He'll die at his coffee cup-cluttered desk.

And Ben will die in his Sunday-go-to-meeting shoes. He does have such shoes. He has his Sunday shoes, his school/play sneakers, and a gorgeous pair of waffle stompers with the waffle hardly stomped. He also has a pair of green leisure slippers that Mama knit him last Christmas. He wore them Christmas morning. It is now June.

Bennion is a good man. Says Madeleine. And my mother. And even my father when he looks up at my brother Arch. I'd introduce him to you but he's out at a meeting. With the Boy Scouts. Ben will be back about ten. Projected scenario.

"Hi." Plops down on the couch, springs shriek.

"How was the meeting?"

"Fine. Starved."

I get up from a heap of final papers I am grading on the floor under our one big-bulbed lamp. "What would you like?"

"Food." He has shed the sneakers and wiggles his grey-socked toes. "But I'll get it." I motion him to stay down. He'd eat the quart of ice cream. I pull out of the refrigerator the chili bean casserole he gobbled part of between 6:45 and 7:00, the only time I recall seeing him today. The casserole dish is the one-quart size. The set included also a one-pint, a one-and-a-half pint and a two-quart. Wedding present. I gave Arch the one-pint and the one-and-a-half pint for his bachelor pad. He eats cereal out of them.

"How's Ronald?" I call into the front room. I'm always interested in Ronald, the cute boy who started a fire down by Enser

Creek and burned all the foliage off a field before the firetruck could get down there.

"He didn't show up. Have you seen my Galbraith? I've got to finish it before I hit the hay."

Hit the hay. I wince. I circle that phrase on English comps. All college freshmen know that it is one of the ultimate clichés. Right up there with good as gold and white as snow and frolicking, rippling brooks.

"Try the piano. Something foreign is on top of the piano."

"Oh yeah. Thanks."

Lugging the Galbraith to the table, he closes his eyes, I count to about eight, he starts to gobble down the casserole. When he's less hurried, he gives twenty-five-count silent prayers on leftover snacks. ("How many times this stuff been blessed already?" Eddie once said, eying a hunk of cold chicken. "At least one, right? Besides I suspect its nourishing and strengthening attributes are directly related to its vitamin and mineral content. I don't recall an Adele Davis chapter on food prayers."

"Adele Davis," I said triumphantly, "is dead."

"Yeah," said Eddie. "She should've asked a blessing on her Virginia Slims.") Ten ten. Here comes Ben now. Friends, Bennion Harris Lockersby.

"Just call me Ben."

"Have a good meeting?"

Take it. I've got to go warm up the casserole.

My hands are knotted around the steering wheel, and the poultry truck in front of me looks sure to lose a crate or two. I plot escape routes for one, two or three crates falling off in one, two lanes. I have a crate beside me too—filled with squawking creatures of another ilk—my creative writing students' work folders. I've got to play Lady God and give out grades.

It's Thursday. Ben will be home to dump on. "I'm exhausted," I say as I lug my crate into the front room.

"Here," he rises gallantly. "Where do you want it?"

"There." I point down.

"Okay. Sit."

I flop onto the floor cushion. "Traffic was awful. I almost brought home a crate of live chickens. Would you have strangled and cleaned them for us?"

"No," he says. "I would have helped you take them back to the rightful owner."

"Get a lot done today? Quiet here?"

"Chapter outline pretty well straightened out. Potter likes it, thinks the rest of the committee will too. You?"

I hold up my hands. "I've been strangling the steering wheel. Want to kill it and clean it for dinner?"

"I've got dinner going."

I don't need to ask what it is. Crazy Ben's sloppy combo—comes out different every time.

"Thought I'd try it with those beets Madeleine gave us."

"The pickled beets? I can imagine what color it is."

"Tastes good. I've been sampling."

What can I say? I've got the perfect man. Even the head of our women's caucus would love him. A genuine independent. Mends his own socks. Better than I could. I'd stick the hole together on the sewing machine. He vacuums. Does the shopping. Gives great back rubs.

"Your Ben," says Madeleine, "is one in a million. He goes to church. You don't even have to drag him there."

"Lots of Mormon men go to church without being dragged," I say.

"And drink," says Madeleine, "he doesn't. Where did you find such a jewel?"

"Lots of Mormon men don't drink," I say.

"And good to you—you're his night and day," says Madeleine.

"Good to me," I say, "he is. But his night and day—I'm more like his mid-afternoon."

Saturday. One batch of final exams down. Two to go. Deadline Tuesday. Spread all over the kitchen table is my Sunday school lesson. It'll probably take the whole day and most of the night. All my favorite resource books are heaped up on the end—stories that high school sophomores might respond to—they like best the struggling-across-the-plains stories, J. Golden Kimball anecdotes, and retold tales from the C. S. Lewis science fiction trilogy. I wish fervently the pioneers had spent another forty years crossing the plains, that J. Golden Kimball could squawk down a few reports from the Celestial Kingdom, that C. S. Lewis hadn't rudely gone and died. Those stories have a kind of sanction that the Sunday school presidency, marching in and out of classes and solemnly nodding—hey, I want to shout, this is not a job I'm seeking tenure for—approve of. I use other stuff too—Mishima's suicide story, Vonnegut's "Harrison Bergeron"—that jiggles them a little. I have to. What's the point without a picture?

Ben is at the stake farm. Left at 5:00. I didn't even open my mouth, just hmmmed when he got up. He'll come back this afternoon, exhausted. He'll shower. Then he'll take his work to school because I like to work aloud. Share I call it. He could do a Sunday school lesson for a pack of fifteen-year-olds in forty-five minutes. And it would be a good lesson. The Sunday school presidency would beam, broadly, as Ben puts it. Some of the kids would even stay awake.

"Sister Lockersby," says Wesley, brother of Ronald incidentally of the fire fame, "another good illustration of what jealousy does to us is Laman and Lemuel. They were so jealous of Nephi that they wouldn't pay any attention to his teachings." Wesley is the kid who'd be on the edge of his Book of Mormon even if Ben were teaching.

"What happened to them that was so bad?" asks Melvin defiantly. "Their descendants outlasted Nephi's descendants."

"But they," says Wesley, stressing *they,* "are probably in hell. Aren't they, Sister Lockersby?"

"Sandra," says Mickey, Mickey and a few other girls call me by my first name, which makes me feel less archaic but more vulnerable, "we don't believe in hell, do we?"

I sigh. What *do* we believe? They won't know what they believe until I tell them? "The Mormon position," I say, "is that very few individuals, probably not Laman and Lemuel, are assigned to the traditional hell. We believe in a sort of graduated afterlife—you get what you earn."

"And that reminds me," I interrupt myself, "of something J. Golden Kimball said." Even Melvin and Wesley drop their weapons. "'So you're going to die!'" I do one of my old world accents, "says someone to a flagging J. Golden Kimball. 'Don't worry. You'll get everything that's coming to you.'

"'That,' says J. Golden Kimball, 'is what I'm afraid of.'"

Mild guffaws.

After, Mickey waits for me. I am uneasy. Mickey is the most draining. I figure, to look at her, she went through puberty when she was about eight. She is very intense. Her father is not a member and, unlike my father, is moderately hostile. "Sandra," she says with a touch of a whine, "can I talk to you for a minute?"

She doesn't, of course, mean a minute. "Just a second," I say, I hope brightly, making a neat pile out of my story books and scriptures. I am giving myself time to pray madly, "Let her ask an easy question this time." I smile now with all my attention.

"What can I tell my father, Sandra? He says that man just made up God and religion and that there isn't anything up there or after this and when I tell him if he would just pray then he would know, he laughs at me and says man can talk himself into anything and can do it better if he gets on his knees and shuts his eyes and concentrates."

I shudder a little. Mickey has started to cry. I should have been forewarned, her voice had become queasy about her second word.

"Let's go talk to the bishop, Mickey," I say.

"Oh, no," says Mickey, and her eyes become instantly dry. "I don't want to talk to the bishop. I hardly know him. I want to talk to you. What do you say when people say that to you?"

I gulp. I tell her what I say. "It feels right to me. I can't make it feel right for anyone else."

(Might as well be a Methodist, said Eddie. We can't even have an intelligent discussion when you fold like that.)

"I'm not very good you see, Mickey, at answering people's questions. Would you like to come over to our place and talk with my husband?"

Mickey considers. "That would be okay. When?"

When, I think, is Ben going to be home. On Sunday it is

absolutely unpredictable. "When I find out when his meetings aren't, I'll call you," I say. "How about that?"

Mickey nods.

"What does your mother do," I say, "when you and your father argue?"

"Nothing. I don't think she even believes it anymore." Mickey pulls my arm. "It is true, isn't it? You know it's true, don't you?"

I look at her. I can't give her what she wants. "It works for me," I say.

Mickey's ride home, the Zimmermans, are leaning against their station wagon. It's too hot to get in. I give her what I hope is a pat not a push and drop my books into our car. I haven't seen Ben all morning. I didn't see Ben all night either—I heard, felt him, but my eyes wouldn't quite open. I could think maybe a stranger had climbed in and out of bed if I didn't know how absurd it would be for anyone else to get up when it is still dark on the longest day of the year, or almost, and leave for a meeting with only a chocolate chip cookie under his belt.

Here he comes. Still talking at people behind him. "Look Sandra," he says, "you take the car on home. I'll have Carl bring me."

"When?"

"About two."

"Stay a while then, okay?"

"Awhile."

Angry at myself for reflexively tugging at my skirt when Sister Jessel looks over at my knees, I mellow in a minute and put a hymnbook over the offending swatch of flesh. Brother Shibler is talking. I am not sure what he is talking about. I started to listen about twenty minutes ago, but Lily's baby in front of me is much nicer to look at than Brother Shibler. Brother Shibler's family, sprawled all over one bench a few rows down, is also nicer to look at than Brother Shibler. Brother Shibler is quite interesting though when you catch him at a basketball game—his son plays, the tall kid propped there against the wall—and he tells you about prosecuting the people who sell apricot pits for cancer cures or about the doting old judge who falls asleep.

The bishop now has fallen asleep. So has Brother Jessel. Even the Shibler twins are tugging at each other's hair. Ben beside me is very awake. When Eddie would come to church, he would bring Wallace Stevens to read. I thought that rather pretentious myself. I really don't understand Wallace Stevens. Eddie hasn't been to church since I got married. That's not why though, he told me. The one time I ran into him, he was all crusty with scorn. I softened all over when I saw him. He is so sad, I said to Ben.

"He wouldn't be so sad if he lived the way he should be living," said Ben.

I haven't mentioned Eddie since.

That makes Ben sound self-righteous. He isn't. Eddie, in fact, is. Or self-wrongtious, he might say.

I feel a nudge at my elbow. "Listen to this," says Ben, who suspects I haven't been.

"They had faith enough," Brother Shibler is saying, "to start a bank without money, without legislative charter, without knowledge of economic principles."

I listen for a few minutes. Lily's temple garments are outlined clearly under her summer blouse. I am always offended by the things showing. My summer blouses are darker than Lily's. I like Lily though. She likes to read the Russians, and she has a splendid baby.

Mickey went away satisfied this afternoon. She had a satisfying lecture from Ben on how everythingwillworkoutforthebest if she is faithful, and she had a satisfying slab of Madeleine's rhubarb pie. Madeleine for the first time looked askance as she saw Ben in earnest conversation with a big-busted fifteen-year-old. "Part of his counselling responsibilities," I said. Madeleine looked unimpressed.

Part of the congregation is laughing, the virtuous part. "What did he say?" I whisper to Ben. Ben looks at me as though I am seven. I consider asking Sister Jessel but decide it's not worth the trouble.

"Wasn't that a great talk?" says Ben as he shakes open the sturdy lock on our front door. I'm always saying "Isn't that a great story?" and am disappointed at less than enthusiastic response, so

I nod my head as vigorously as befits one who missed out on the one good laugh.

"Let's go to bed early," he says.

"I can't," I say. "I've got to get another batch of finals done tonight."

"Sandra," he says, "you were going to try not to do them on Sunday."

"I did the Lord's Sunday school lesson all day and all night Saturday. I can't help it if my ox marched right into the mire."

"You could get up really early."

"I'm going to get up really early. And I'm going to go to bed really late. And that way *maybe* I'll make my deadline."

"Okay," he says, mashes me to him, and takes Nibley's *Joseph Smith Papyri* to bed instead of me.

I fall asleep about fourteen times over Jeremy Herter's exam. Maybe I'll, Ben's vernacular, hit the hay. Besides things are looking up. And if I finish grading too early tomorrow night, I'll have to feel guilty for not putting off till then what I did on the Sabbath (keep it holy) Day.

I slip into bed quietly. I have probably awakened Ben, but he pretends to sleep so as to lessen my guilt feelings. We're maybe the jitteriest sleepers that Sominex would ever hope to meet. As soon as my head hits the pillow, I fall wide awake. I could grade another dozen exams. Except that by getting up I'd wake up Ben. Again. And as soon as I pulled out Jeremy Herter's blotch-inked final, I'd fall asleep. I know me.

Or do I?

The room is almost black. I look at the crack of light coming in from the streetlamp through the rumpled shade. I check both eyes to make sure I am not blind. I am not blind.

Something is rattling around in the room. A moth I think. I look up. Tiny lights flashing wildly across the ceiling. It lasts forever, maybe three minutes. In a Flannery O'Connor short story it would be a symbol of the Holy Ghost. In a Mickey-like Sandra it might be a terrifying suggestion of a heavenly visitation. I yawn. The firefly is gone. I roll over, nuzzle into Ben's back, and call it a Sunday.

EIGHT

Born of the Water

WAYNE JORGENSEN

His mother may have been right, a long time afterward, that he had not been baptized until he was ten because he was afraid of the water. He had been afraid. He must have been four or five, wading in the shallow end of the pool or standing tentative on the steps. Someone—he could not recall even a face—grabbed him, yanked him into deeper water. A bony arm clamped around his ribs, a hard chin bored into his head, he twisted, then the sun and the bright noises were gone and water stung his eyes and roared into his ears, his mouth and throat, warm and heavy and oddly solid, a lump of clay too big to swallow.

The bigger body bore him down, then a hand between his shoulders shoved him deeper till he was loose in the water, floating unsure of bottom or surface, twisting to find a way out. Then he saw the changing sky of light before his eyes torn by a hand that gripped his right arm high near the shoulder and drew him out. His father. He clung with arms and legs to his father's thick body, coughing and crying, and his father loosened him, turned him down across one arm and whacked him between the shoulders so he coughed more water out, then clasped him again to his body. "It's all right, Carlie, I'm here. He's gone. It's all right."

He had been afraid. But there was his father too, not a member because of Grandma Wendell, whose father had been so fanatic, even his mother said, that his children went without shoes and decent clothes so he could give to the church. Grandma had nothing good to say about Mormons, and his father hardly talked about religion at all, unless his mother might say, "Gray, don't you believe in the hereafter, don't you want to be together in heaven?" and he'd answer, "When you're dead you're dead. I've seen a lot of things die and go back to the dirt. They can just stick me in a pine box or tie me in a gunny sack."

The summer he turned eight, the bishop came with his father's friend J. B. to see about him being baptized. He said he didn't want to, not knowing why he said it but sure he didn't, and his mother made one serious nod toward the bishop. Then J. B. said, "Gray, we could take care of you at the same time. You'd make a better Mormon than half the people in the ward. What do you say?" His father just grinned and said, "No thanks, J. B., not this time." And J. B. said, "We'll get you under yet."

Afterward, hunched behind the end of the couch and the living room wall, reading in his place, he heard his mother and father in the kitchen. "Graham, why don't you go with him? He's reached the age now, and you're a good man, better than most of them like J. B. says." "I don't believe in it. They're not putting me under water." "But at least encourage him. You can do that. You don't mind if he does, do you?" His father didn't answer, then the tap turned on, his father getting a drink, and pans rattled in the cupboard, his mother starting supper.

•

He got over being afraid of the water. Bathing he would sink in the full tub till warm water covered him, every part except his nose, and his skin, the boundaries of his body, seemed to blur so he wasn't sure where he ended and water began, and his own blood surging in his ears sounded almost like noises of the house, creaking or popping of beams his father had cut from timber and sawn himself, water running in the pipes his father had plumbed.

And his father and mother had gone on taking him swimming, along with his big brother Jared, who was in high school, and his baby brother Joel. He would watch his father swim, turning into something like a seal or a big fish as if water were another home.

Maybe it was that same summer he was eight, when his father took him into the deep. His father liked to dive, thundering cannonballs or sharp jackknifes slicing into the water straight for the bottom. He'd stand on the springboard, turn to them and say to watch him swim like a rock, then he'd dive, both feet coming down arched on the end of the board, the board bending, straightening, lifting his body into the air to turn in a clean arc, shining, then to fall straight on into the water solid as a brick but cutting so cleanly that when his feet disappeared there was only a little splash like a white wing waving or the quick fin of a fish. He'd watch for his father under water and sometimes lose him, he stayed so deep so long, as if he had turned, hide, hair, meat and bone, to the water's own bluish lucence, invisible as an angel in air. Other times he followed a pale blur streaming snakelike as if without effort along the bottom. Then his father would surface, blowing a spume like a walrus, snorting or barking, black hair streaming with water down his forehead and neck.

"Let me give you a ride, Carlie. Come on. On my shoulders." So he rode his father's wide bristling shoulders while he waded in water up to his chin, sometimes over his head, so Carl felt scared again of going under, down the steep slope into the eight-foot. But his father would turn back up to shallow. "That was o.k., wasn't it. Now sit on my back, wrap your legs around me, just like around a horse, and hold your hands right here on the sides of my neck, and ride while I swim." So he did that too, the water streaming around his elbows and waist as he straddled his father's back, watching his arms in long sweeping strokes, the water sleeking his black hair, feeling his father's back pumping when his legs frogkicked.

Another time his father had him hook the fingers of one hand into the waist string at the back of his swimming trunks while he surface-dived, and scared, Carl let go and thrashed in the water till his father turned and caught him under the chest. "You didn't go down. You were swimming but you didn't know it. Now hang on again and this time go down with me." So Carl did, eyes clamped, nose pinched, lips bitten shut, feeling the water lift him and stream his hair back, finally opening his eyes to the blur of his father's body gliding, a thread of bubbles twinkling up behind his head. After that he started to go on his own, started under water with his breath burning behind his breastbone and finally learned to hold his head out or turn it sideways for air. "Good, Carlie," his father said. "You'll be all right." So the fear was gone without his thinking about it, and the summer he was ten he told his mother he wanted to be baptized, this too without thinking about it, only knowing.

•

It was Saturday morning. His mother had him combed and dressed in a white shirt and borrowed white pants and again asked his father if he'd go down with them to watch. "No, I've got to get supplies for the sheep camp. Too many hypocrites anyway." And his father went out and drove the truck down the street ahead of them, turning toward town while they kept on to the ward. "Hypocrites," his mother said. "Sometimes I think he's as scared of being baptized as you were of swimming." But Carl doubted his father was scared of anything.

Only the lights at the front of the chapel were on, so most of the hall rested in mild, brownish half-gloom, except for flat mid-morning sun on the opaque panes of the east windows. It was like opening exercises for Primary or Sunday school, but with only the second row filled, three or four mothers and one or two fathers with children from other wards, younger, so he didn't know them even from school. He'd taken his shoes off when he first sat down, and he stared at the strangeness of his white socks. They sang a hymn he hadn't heard before, and his mind went over one verse:

> We will be buried in the stream
> In Jesus' blessed name,

And rise while light shall on us beam
The spirit's heavenly flame.

Brother Sharp talked about Jesus being baptized by John to fulfill all righteousness and the Holy Ghost coming down on him in the form of a dove and his father's voice saying, "Thou art my beloved son, in whom I am well pleased." Light flashed off the circles of his glasses as he told how Alma baptized his band of fugitives in the wilderness as a witness that they would serve the Lord and have the Spirit poured out upon them.

In the basement hall, dark double doors had been opened on a little room with a little pool in it, tile steps going down into the water. It must go deeper into the ground, he thought, than the furnace room. A lanky blond man in a white coverall was standing waistdeep in the water. Carl was first, and nudged by Brother Sharp he walked down into the font, the unexpectedly warm water soaking his white clothes to his chest, and stood by the man, who took his left hand and closed it around his right wrist and whispered, "Hold tight there, grab your nose when I say amen, and sit." Then he held Carl's hand and wrist with his own left hand, clapped him once on the back of the neck with his right, and spoke: "Carl David Wendell, having been commissioned of Jesus Christ I baptize you in the name of the Father, and of the Son, and of the Holy Ghost. Amen."

Carl was pinching his nose when the big hand tightened on his hand and wrist, and he felt an instant's wild panic as the other hand came down heavy on his neck, caving his knees under him and thrusting him down. Then the water folded over his head, he floated free of the tile bottom, light and lost, for a second not feeling the hands that held him, and then he was raised up streaming and guided to the steps, blinking to clear his sight. Brother Sharp helped him out, shaking his hand, and his mother led him to the restroom door and handed him his dry clothes and shoes and a towel. His wet white clothes clung to him, a heavy, slow new skin.

When he came out his mother hugged him and straightened his hair and told him how glad she was that he belonged to Heavenly Father's Kingdom now. "I just wish your dad could have been too or done it himself. At least Jared will be down tomorrow to lay hands on you and confirm you." Then they drove home. She offered him lunch, but he said he didn't want any right then, and he walked around the house and yard, wondering if he would feel new, believing and doubting the cool lightness that had still not left his skin entirely. He looked at the green ash tree, leaves on a few branches turning their paler undersides in a shift of noonward air. He walked back of the house and lay down in the shaded arch of the lilac bushes where the grass was sparse. The lavender and white cones of bloom were gone, with their scent that drowned the air in April, but the light under the bushes felt moist, almost tasted of the heartshaped green leaves that he had still not learned to make bleat with the shrill buzzing his father could blow through them. Lying on his back he lifted his arm to look at his birthday watch. The second hand swung in its jerky circle, and close to his ear it made a small steady clanging. But deep as he looked, the sky seemed unturning, the light and shade of earth standing in utter arrest. He said the one word Kingdom to himself, then the one word Lord. A brown sparrow darted from behind his head, low across his sight with one .beat of wings in the bright air, past the bushes and into shade behind the house. He felt then the solid world turn under him, wheeling on its axis like a giant millstone, himself turning evenly with it, and his hands gripped into the thin-bladed grass.

Then he heard his father coming back, tires grinding into the gravel, the whine of downshifting, and turning his head to the side he saw the light green pickup nose into the garage and then his father walk toward the side door of the house. He got up and went in, past the drying sheets his mother had hung near daylight.

"He hasn't had lunch yet," his mother was saying. And his father: "We can eat at the camp. If Knute's there he'll fry us some mutton." She shrugged and put the loaf back in the breadbox. "If you both want to, all right. Do you want to ride up to the sheep camp with Daddy, Carl?"

"Yes," he said, the weight of solemnity on him lightening but still muffling the excitement. His mother knew how much his father liked driving on the twisting roads, eating fresh mutton and potatoes cooked in grease in black iron pans on rusty campstoves, squatting on his heels and talking with herders, and how he, Carl, liked going with and watching all this, his father's pleasure. "Then change your clothes," she said, "and take your hat and jacket. It'll still be cool up there."

"You come too, Leah," his father said.

"Not this time. I've got to get Joel from Maureen's and make his lunch, and there's the wash to finish. You two have a good ride."

•

The pickup climbed between pale cliffs, the road winding even more than the stretch called Rattlesnake in the main canyon where Grampa Swensen's Model A got coasting too fast and Gramma got ready to throw out baby Jed but then Grampa rolled the car up the sidehill and got it stopped. Coming down a south branch of the canyon was a deep dry gully where Great Grampa Swensen's wagon rolled over and killed him and one of his sons and they weren't found for two days. Carl tried to imagine that. He sat in the middle of the seat, next to his father, wishing Tuck were sitting next to the door with his nose stuck out the open window into the wind, ears blown back, but Tuck had been sent to another herd. When his father shifted gears, the lever ground against his knee and his father gripped his leg to move it one side or the other.

Often he dreamed of roads almost like these, only through rust-red clay, and more twisting, more rollercoastering and dizzy: he'd be riding with his father, and sometimes his mother and little brother, not too fast but at a speed that would have made his mother put her hands on the dashboard, up over abrupt hills, around sharp curves with steep slopes above and sheer cliffs below, billowing a caterpillar cloud of pink dust behind them, climbing higher and higher and seeming to go ever slightly faster. Sometimes the dream would just fade midway in the journey, in a strange suspense of peril and safety. Other times it would end with the truck's front wheels over the edge of a deep washout, lurching him awake like being thrown forward in a sudden stop. And sometimes, the worst, it would speed to the top of an impossible hill, go over, and float on nothing, shimmer into nothing itself, and he'd be falling, crying out for his father or mother, the dream spinning him awake, dizzy, gripping the edge of the mattress that was still turning over under him to spill him on the floor, panting, his chest tight, heaving and pounding hard.

Even the first times, when he cried aloud before he could stop himself and his mother came, he could not tell the dream, and he'd never told anyone since. Even the shrillest terror carried its strange comfort that he kept to himself.

Out of the canyon and going through gray basalt hills of scrub juniper and pinion, up the ranch dugway, he could remember riding in the open back of the GMC with its sideracks let down for benches, and how he'd cling to the uphill side, as far from the drop as he could get but not able to stop looking over and down at how the world fell away, huge, bowl-like, widening and deepening and drawing him into its center as if its enlargement made a vacuum that would fill itself with him. He was over that now, could take pleasure like his father's in that opening space, though he still felt the pull of the widening.

Driving, his father sang parts of old songs:

> Oh when I was single oh when oh when,
> Oh when I was single oh then,
> Oh when I was single
> My pockets would jingle,
> I wish I was single again.

At home his father would play an old guitar to sing with, thumb and fingers going one-two or one-two-three, and his mother would join in with different notes, the two of them smiling at each other wishing to be single again. Driving now his father sang, "I'm ridin old Paint, I'm leadin old Dan":

> When I die take my saddle from the wall,
> Put it on my pony and lead him from the stall,

Tie my bones to his back, turn our faces to the west,
And we'll ride the country that we like the best.

His father wasn't a cowboy but a sheepherder for his own father a long time ago and now a sheepman with other men working for him, but he sang those songs. "For the fiery and snuffy are rarin to go." Even when Carl hadn't understood the words, didn't know the words at all, the songs made him happy.

I went to see Saint Peter,
He smiled at me so sweet.
He asked me in to supper, boys,
And this is what we eat:
    Oh corn bread, buttermilk,
    and good old turnip greens,
    Corn bread, buttermilk,
    and good old turnip greens.

He liked how his father's thumb would climb down and then up the low strings for good old turnip greens.

They went through the ranch gate and onto the road that climbed east toward aspen and the high meadows, going slower now as if his father wanted to make it last longer, through the cooler flittering shade on a narrower track with a green humped strip of grass and seedling trees in its center, between whitebarked trunks carved with flourishing names and dates going back to the early twenties, his father's own childhood, when he had ridden here with Grandpa Wendell to haul food and water to the camps and maybe stay a week to help herd. Sheep and the mountain pastures had been so much of his father's life, he knew, that his parents' honeymoon had not really happened until a year and a half after their wedding, when they spent a month in the camp with Jared a six-month-old baby.

•

When they reached the camp, a canvas-covered wagon that always made Carl think of pioneers, except that it had rubber tires and a tin chimney and was like a little cabin inside, Knute was not there, nor were the usual scruffy dogs, yipping and then cowering back under the camp, wagging tucked-down hindquarters to beg and avoid being petted. "Probably chasing strays," his father said. "Let's get this stuff unloaded and fire up the stove for lunch."

Carl helped his father pull out the four bales of hay and stack them behind the wagon. The ten-gallon milk cans of water were too heavy for him, but he carried in a box of groceries and set it on the high lumpy bed built across the back of the wagon. His father stepped up the wagon tongue and into the doorway, tilting his hat back off his forehead to wipe the sweat with his cuff. "He's almost out of mutton, and I see he's got a yearling tied up out here he likely means to slaughter. Let's you and me take care of that."

His father killed a sheep about once every summer out behind the garage and cut and wrapped the meat for their freezer, but Carl mostly stayed away, inside the house, until the carcass was ready to hang, blunt-necked, oddly skinny in its braided lean and fat, the legs chopped short at the hocks, ribs whitely arching inside the body cavity. His arms went watery and his chest hollow, but he said "OK, Dad," and got up and walked out and down the iron tongue, a little surprised his knees carried him.

His father reached through the cab window into the glove compartment, got out his knife and stone, and whetted the blade for a few seconds. The steel rasped against the soft chitter of aspen. Then the man pulled a coil of rope and a short piece of shovel handle from the truck and walked toward the sheep tethered at the edge of the trees, looking indifferently at them with its milky blue eyes, its lower jaw jerkily chewing. "What do you want me to do?" Carl asked.

"Just wait. You help after this first part." His father straddled the sheep, gripped it behind the withers with knees and calves, and untied the length of braided baler twine from its neck. The sheep bucked forward once, couldn't get free, and stood still. The man crooked his left forearm under the sheep's jaw, drew it back sharply so the muzzle strained skyward, the throat taut, then he pulled the knife across once, hard and quick, opening the throat clear to the neckbone. For an instant Carl wondered when the blood would start. Then it pulsed rich and dark, foaming into the grass and black soil. The sheep stamped and bucked, hooves springing and skittering, then its legs buckled under the man's body bearing it to the ground where he held it, now kneeling astride the fat flank and holding the head still farther back while the blood ran in weaker surges and the breath rasped from the severed windpipe. When the kicking stopped, he stood, wiped his knife on the wool, and tilted his hat back to wipe his forehead, hissing through his teeth.

"Well." He looked at Carl. "That's done. Get me a clean pan out of the drawer."

"Yes sir," Carl said and ran to the wagon. What surprised him was his father's face, that it was without revulsion yet without pleasure too, except the satisfaction of having done the thing neatly, the same as when he oiled some kid's squeaky tricycle or got the water regulated in all the furrows of the garden. What surprised him more was himself, that he too felt this a matter of fact, a kind of work, new, but after the first startling slash of the knife just something to see and do. But it was death and it would feed them.

When he came back with the pan, his father had already slit the hide from neck to vent, spilled out the entrails into a coiled, steaming pile already drawing a few lumbering flies, and had a dark-red, fatty knot of heart and the darker, almost purple flared lobes of liver ready to lay in the pan. "If Knute don't want those, we'll take em home. Set the pan by the stove and see if you can find a clean cloth to lay over it."

When Carl came back from doing that, his father was sliding the chunk of shovel-handle through slits in the sheep's peeled legs just above the chopped-off joints and knotting the rope at its center. He stood, tossed the end of the rope over an aspen branch as high as he could reach, pulled the end down, and handed it to Carl. "Let's hoist im. Easier with a block, but we'll manage." They pulled together, hands alternating on the taut rope as if in a game, and the carcass swung free of the ground and swayed in front of the tree. The leaves on the bobbing branch winked like flung coins.

"Now help me peel the hide," the man said, "like this," and

gripping with his left drew the edge of his right hand like a blade between hide and muscle, stripping the skin back an inch or so. Carl stepped beside him and tried the same on the other side, surprised at the heat of the flesh, at how hard he had to grip and pull with his right hand and cut with the bones of his left. He found himself breathing steady and heavy and falling into his father's rhythm, forgetting to keep his shoes from under the slow drip of the neck.

Their hands met at the backbone just as the dogs came up yipping and sniffing at the entrails and the bloodsoaked earth, with Knute behind them walking his little roan. The mare spooked when she caught the scent, and the herder dismounted and tethered her to the far side of the camp wagon. "How's Gray?" he hollered, coming toward them still a bit stiff-legged.

"Just dandy," his father answered. "Got you some groceries."

"Done my chore too." The herder cracked a snaggly grin across his lean, seamed face. "Who's your help?"

"Ah, you remember Carl."

"Sure. Named for your Dad. But don't see him up here much."

"Sometimes he's his mother's. But he's with me today. Just got baptized."

Struck, Carl couldn't look at either of them for a second. He'd forgotten the morning, his lightness, the expectation of his brother's hands on his head tomorrow. He felt now as solid, weighted, as the bone and meat of the hung lamb, unable to locate within himself that earlier feeling, but sensing no absence either.

"Now that's all right," the herder was saying. "He's a good boy." And Carl grinned up at him, almost extended his stained hand for a shake, then felt the formality wouldn't suit.

"He is," his father said, then, "How about cooking us some lunch?"

The herder coughed and said sure, his sourdough was ready and he had taters and onions and some chops if this boy would light the stove. So Carl did that while the herder helped his father finish skinning the sheep and chopping through the neckbone. Then the herder kneaded dough in a square pan for biscuits and slid the pan into the oven, sliced onions and diced potatoes into a greased black frying pan, and laid the chops in with them to sizzle and spit. While the food cooked and the stove heated the wagon, the boy tried to play with the dogs, who would whimper and grin at him and swat their tails in the dust under the wagon but not come out. Then he cut with his pocket knife (his Grampa Swensen's white bone-handled, given him last year after the funeral) a finger-long piece of aspen twig and tried to remember how Jared would make a whistle, but split the bark when he tried to slip it, and gave up. He looked at the hung carcass, wrapped now with a chunk of canvas tied with twine to keep flies off, turning slightly when the wind moved.

He tried to remember Grandpa Wendell whose name he wore: himself on a big man's knee by the tall console radio? Newborn Joel in the broad hands of a gray-haired man whose face was almost like his father's? The memories were black and white and gray like the blurred-edge photograph his parents kept on their dresser. Of the funeral, the thick sweetness of massed flowers in Grandma's front parlor where the radio stood and in the emptied bedroom just off it, where the casket was. He could see himself going up to the gleaming dark-brown side of the casket.

"Everything fell on your father then," his mother had told him this past year, and that was why his father had started drinking. And she'd asked Carl if he didn't remember her and Jared helping Daddy up the stairs and into bed time after time, but he didn't except for maybe noises of feet on the stairs. That was all over now.

The herder called to come and eat it before the dogs grabbed it, and he went into the wagon hot as an oven and ate sitting by his father, enjoying like his father the sweet hot onions, the meat that coated lips and tongue with grease, the potatoes not quite cooked through, the tough sourdough, the clear water from home that washed it all down, the chipped enamel plates and cups.

When they'd finished and put the dishes into the big pan to soak in soapy water, the herder pulled from his pocket by its blue tag dangling on yellow string his Bull Durham pouch. "Roll you a smoke, Gray?"

"No thanks. You know I quit. But you go ahead."

"At's all right." The man grinned again his gapped yellow teeth.

Carl remembered his father coming home from the doctor's and saying he was quitting, and how the last unopened pack of Luckies still lay at the back of the hall shelves, "probably all wormy by now," his mother said. "Might as well have been smoking horse manure from the corral." His father had kept pipes around the house for a while but couldn't get to like them. All that was part of why he might as well be baptized, but he wouldn't.

The herder rolled a lumpy cigarette which he lighted by opening the firebox of the stove and holding it to a coal. He puffed blue rings that wavered to the arched canvas roof and broke. Carl could remember his father doing that, once in a while getting one ring to go right through another.

After a while his father stood and said, "Well, thanks, Knute. Think we'll drive on up over Seven-Mile and back down Lions Trail."

"Sure enough, Gray. At's all right." The herder stood and stepped to the door of the camp as they walked out to the truck. "Now you watch that boy," he grinned and coughed and spat onto the ground.

•

He knew where his father meant to go: the weathered tent-frame set on the foundation of big logs they called the half-house, Grandpa Wendell's summer camp that for years now they had used mostly for picnics on the Twenty-fourth of July. So they climbed steeper and narrower roads through the aspen, past a still lake and on up into big pines where his father had logged timber to build the house before he was born and then onto level road at the pine-shaded edge of the seven-mile-long valley that later this summer would be dotted and clumped white with sheep, one of the places his father had herded as a boy. Where this road bent east, they turned off and climbed up into the edge of the pines and parked next to the frame that looked like a house someone had given up finishing. He had never seen it with canvas stretched and battened on it, though he wished every time they came that they could set it up and stay.

"Let's get a drink," his father said. He doubted his father was thirsty, but none of them would pass here without stopping for a drink, the water was that good, icy cold out of the bones of the mountain and clear as air. His father had told him how he and an old herder had found the spring high under the summit, and how Grandpa Wendell had bargained with the town of Cumorah for some wooden pipe discarded from the town's old supply line and had laid the pipe with his sons' help a quarter-mile down from the spring to the site for the half-house, then cut the big pine trunks to lay the plank floor on and set up the frame.

Back of the frame on the uphill slope, shaded by two big pines, was the end of the pipe, the water spilling into a shallow graveled basin, then overflowing to become one head of a creek that ran all the way to the valley and watered farms before it emptied into the river. His father knelt and put his mouth to the bright arc of water and so did he. It froze the lips, bit into the teeth like chomping on an iron railing in winter, and went down like cold molten metal. When they had drunk, his father held under the spill from the pipe a gallon jug sewed with twine into a salt sack and, when it was full, let it stand in the basin so the burlap would soak and keep the water cold. Even so, Carl knew, when you drank it back in town it would be already warm as tapwater, its sweetness flattening.

"I remember Dad, your Grandpa Wendell, taking his shower here when we camped," his father said. "He'd rigged a piece of one-inch pipe to run up over here, with a shower head on the end of it. He'd run out here first thing, bare-naked, while Grandma was starting the bacon, stand under the damn thing and yank on the chain and then stamp and dance around, hootin and hollerin till he couldn't stand it, and then run back in for breakfast. By God. Said it'd help him live to ninety if it didn't give him his death. Never could get me to try it. He didn't last that long."

The sack was well-soaked now, and his father lifted it out, dripping. "We'd better go. Get another sip if you want it." Carl knelt to drink again. He remembered one other thing of Grandpa Wendell's funeral: Brother Petersen was telling a story about himself, how he'd given a talk in sacrament meeting one time about brotherly love and later in the week had been out riding and been stopped by a big man on a horse. "That was Carl Wendell. He said to me, 'Son, that was a fine talk you gave last Sunday. Now what are you going to do about it?' And the two of us got down off our horses and set and talked an hour or more, and I got to know Carl Wendell." The boy couldn't remember what Brother Petersen got to know, but that was now his clearest image of his grandfather, lost and called up again, the big man on the horse and then sitting in the dirt talking. (He must have gone to church some, been baptized when a boy, so why not his own father?) And now this new clear sight: the man dancing naked in the water cold as stone.

•

They drove north over the divide to head down the switchbacks. Near the steep brow of the mountain, his father stopped again. "Let's take a look off here," he said, and they got out and walked to the ledge. He'd been here often before, after every Twenty-fourth-of-July picnic and almost every drive; he'd always asked to see the lookout, then hung back from the very edge when they got out to it. He went closer today.

From the lookout the world scooped away east and north and northwest in the widest, deepest bowl, one rim maybe in Colorado. His father liked to get to the very edge, stand and just look, and he too liked the wide domain of colors and ridges behind and behind one another, bluegreens and blues that lightened in the farthest distance: it went almost forever, blueing into sky.

He didn't know he would ask until he did. It was like his first dive off the board when he knew his fear was gone but hadn't tried this, doing the thing before he knew he'd decided.

"Dad, do you think you go nowhere when you die?" The words almost cost him his balance, and he felt his father's hand jump to his shoulder to steady him, then let go before speaking.

"Don't know." He looked up, but his father still looked out on the spread ranges. "I've dug my living out of the dirt and out of the hides of sheep and don't want you boys to have to do that, but I don't mind going back to the dirt. It's good country. If there's a God he made it the way he liked it."

His father still did not look at him or touch him again, and Carl did not need to say or ask anything more. Then his father pointed in front of them to a small island of pine in a meadow below a curve of the road. "If I had money and the BLM was selling, I'd buy an acre up there and build me a cabin. Or I'd level off a place to park a house trailer. There's a good spring there—see where the willows are?"

He saw and felt again the slow, centered pull of the widening bowl, like what you feel when ready to dive. The world in its lines and colors sloped out and away like a wave gathering to crest, all one: God's kingdom and his father's good country, and he knew himself in both for life.

NINE

The Christianizing of Coburn Heights

LEVI S. PETERSON

God had blessed Coburn Heights, a suburb on the east bench of Salt Lake City where wealthy Saints shared with their gentile neighbors the pleasures of wide, curving streets, spacious houses, and driveways cluttered with motor homes, power boats, and snowmobiles. The foremost shepherd of the faithful in this prosperous suburb was Sherman Colligan, president of Coburn Heights Stake. On a wintry Saturday morning, Sherman shopped for his wife in Albertson's supermarket, pushing a shopping cart containing a growing mound of beef roast, pickles, muffins, potato chips, Postum, and all kinds of things which make life tolerable. A few feet into the pet food aisle he stopped abruptly. Coming toward him was a tattered, crooked little woman who might have emerged from the cargo bin of a garbage truck. She wore a soiled brown dress, askew at the hem and pinned at the breast. Dark cotton stockings sagged on her bony legs; warped, scuffed shoes slopped on her feet. Staring at her, Sherman realized that she was lopsided because her entire left side was atrophied: her leg was shortened, her arm dwindled, her breast shrunken, her cheek and ear diminished. She listed and leaned, having not two sides, but one and a half.

The woman pulled a yellow wagon in which she had set her wadded coat, four sixpacks of orange soda pop, and a box of macaroni and cheese. Intuitively Sherman knew her. She had to be Rendella Kranpitz, the bizarre newcomer whose bishop had threatened to excommunicate her for contentiousness. Sherman had found the charge incredible. No one was excommunicated these days for contentiousness. The little woman came up against Sherman's shopping cart and stopped. He blinked, looking closer to see whether this woman truly had, as her bishop claimed, a heart for fire and rage, a will for running against the wind, for rupturing barricades, for trampling down the walls of the world.

The woman looked Sherman up and down, then put forth her strong right arm and shook his hand. "You're President Colligan," she said. "If I were you, I wouldn't let that second counselor—what's his name—conduct at stake conference anymore. He isn't up to snuff. No way at all."

"It's certainly nice to meet a new member of my stake," Sherman said pleasantly.

The woman continued to shake his hand. "I would sure spruce up my stake conferences if I were you. When that choir sang last time, you could have laid me out square for being on a goat farm."

"You must be Sister Kranpitz," Sherman said warmly.

She dropped his hand and eyed him suspiciously. "How come you know my name?"

"Bishop Bosen has told me about you."

"So what's he say about me behind my back? That's what I'd like to know!"

"Nothing but the best. He says you're a good, faithful sister." Sherman, whose large frame carried fifty pounds of excess weight, towered over the little woman. He wore galoshes and a checkered overcoat and a narrow-brimmed hat. He tried to amplify the friendly smile which he made it a policy to carry on his round, clean-shaven face.

"Say," Rendella said, "do you have all the Articles of Faith memorized?"

"Not entirely," Sherman said. "I once had."

Rendella fixed her eyes on a shelf of bags filled with dried dog food and began to recite. "First: We believe in God, the Eternal Father, and in his Son Jesus Christ, and in the Holy Ghost. Second: We believe that men will be punished for their own sins, and not for Adam's transgressions. Third: We believe—"

"That's excellent," Sherman interrupted with an admiring exhalation of breath. "It looks like you have every one of them down pat."

Rendella wandered to the side of Sherman's shopping cart. She picked up a bottle of expensive grape juice, shook it, and peered suspiciously at the label.

"That isn't wine," Sherman said. "It's grape juice imported from Germany."

Rendella put the bottle down and picked up a jar of peanut butter. "That peanut butter isn't any good," she said. "There aren't any bits in it." She tried without success to unscrew the lid and then returned the jar to the cart.

"Who's your dad?" she said. "He isn't one of those Colligans from Kanab, is he?"

"Our line never got farther south than Provo. Actually my dad was—"

"That's good," Rendella interrupted. "Those Kanab Colligans aren't worth a bucket of peach pits. Really, you know, you've got to do something about this stake. I never saw a worse one in my life. Some of the sermons that get preached in the Fifth Ward would puke a turkey."

"I don't know about that. It seems to me we've got a pretty good stake. In fact it's one of the best in the entire church."

"I can preach, but nobody ever asks me to," Rendella said. "Maybe you don't think I can preach," she added bitterly.

"I don't doubt you can preach. Why not? The gift of eloquence is given to many."

"People think I'm crazy, but I'm not."

"Why would anybody think that?" Sherman said congenially. "You're just another good, faithful servant of the Lord."

She looked down at her dress. "What do you expect when somebody has to wear rags like these?"

Sherman brightened. "We can fix that in a minute. Bishop Bosen will get you a welfare order and we'll get you some nice dresses."

She stiffened. "Are you trying to tell me I don't dress so good?"

"Golly, no," Sherman said.

"Who did you say your dad was? My dad was Simon B. Kranpitz. He lived in Monroe for seventy-eight years, and he was never anything but a ward clerk. And then they went and made Ranny Jackson second counselor when Chad Hislop got made bishop, and Dad said, 'That's it—when old Ranny Jackson gets made counselor and they pass me by, I quit.' And he never went to church again."

"I'm sorry to hear that."

Rendella put her hand into her pocket and pulled out a candy bar. She looked at it a moment, glanced up at Sherman, and thrust it back into her pocket. "You think I'm not going to pay for that, don't you?" she said angrily. She pulled the bar out and placed it on a sixpack of orange soda pop in her wagon. "Don't ever say I steal anything!"

She smoothed the front of her dress. "Who did you say your folks were? What kind of uppities were they?"

"My folks were just ordinary people."

"How come you got this job then?" she said. "Let's see what you know. Tell me what this scripture means." She drew herself up on her longer leg and said in an oratorical tone: "Lamentations, chapter four, verse twenty-one: 'Rejoice and be glad, O daughter of Edom, that dwellest in the land of Uz; the cup also shall pass through unto thee: thou shalt be drunken, and shalt make thyself naked.'"

Sherman hemmed and looked about uncomfortably.

"So what does it mean?" she insisted. "You're supposed to be the stake president and you don't know anything."

A half-hour later Sherman sat in his car in the Albertson's parking lot, eating a doughnut. He had been wise enough to order thirteen doughnuts at the bakery stand; finding an even dozen, his wife would have no reason to be disappointed with him for breaking his diet. Grey winter clouds lowered over Coburn Heights; the parking lot was icy with the remnants of last week's storm. As Sherman pulled out his handkerchief to wipe away the final crumbs, he saw Rendella Kranpitz emerge from the grocery store. The sleeves of her black coat draped over her hands and the hem hung nearly to her ankles. Pulling her wagon, she lurched erratically across the parking lot. Heedless of speeding cars, she jaywalked across the nearby boulevard and disappeared into a side street. Sherman looked at his watch and decided that he had time to visit Arthur Bosen, bishop of the ward in which Rendella lived.

Arthur was in his backyard dredging out his goldfish pond for the winter. At Sherman's insistence, Arthur went on with his work as they talked. Chunks of ice lay about the perimeter of the pool, from which Arthur scooped bucketsful of water. Sherman admired the look of outdoor competence which Arthur's woolen cap and quilted ski jacket gave him. Arthur Bosen was the best of Sherman's seven bishops. He was punctual in making his reports and successful in turning out his quotas of members for temple work and welfare assignments. Sherman and Arthur had been good friends since high school days and in private had dispensed with the formality of calling one another President Colligan and Bishop Bosen.

"I just met Rendella Kranpitz at Albertson's," Sherman said.

Arthur scrutinized Sherman closely. "You seem to have come out of the experience unscathed."

"Are you still thinking about excommunicating her?"

"You better believe it!" Arthur muttered grimly as he dredged up a shovelful of muck and dumped it into a standing wheelbarrow.

"Is the problem all that bad?"

"It's worse," Arthur declared. Three months of that woman were too much for any ward. Rendella Kranpitz was retarded or insane or, more likely, both. She had come from a small town in Sevier County. Arthur couldn't for the moment remember which one. By an appalling fluke of circumstances, she had inherited a house in Coburn Heights. The trustee of her inherited estate was a gentile lawyer whose office was in downtown Salt Lake. He was a civil liberties crank who resented the way society treated children, prisoners, and idiots, and he protected Rendella in the possession of her house. Rendella had a spirit of deceit and disruption. In any church meeting where there was the slightest possibility that she could take the floor and speak, she usurped time and corrupted purposes. In the monthly testimony meeting she invariably rose and, instead of briefly bearing her testimony, entered upon a lengthy sermon, peeling off in her arrogant voice incessant strings of scriptural passages and quotations from modern prophets and apostles. She exhorted, chided, and berated, and when at last she became silent and sat down, she had brought her fellow worshipers to a seething boil.

"She belongs in an asylum," Arthur concluded vindictively.

"You are exaggerating, of course," Sherman said, chuckling with appreciation for Arthur's ironies.

"You can't exaggerate anything in the case of this woman."

"Well," said Sherman, "we are after all the guardians of the unfortunate."

"I thought maybe I was the unfortunate one."

"Sometimes the Lord gives us a burden that is a blessing in disguise."

"This one is burden all the way through."

"We owe special care to those who can't make distinctions between good and evil."

"She isn't one of that kind. She knows exactly how to go for the jugular every time."

It appeared that Arthur's ironies were not ironies; he really meant to excommunicate Rendella Kranpitz. A pity for this little woman had come over Sherman. Wasn't she, after all, a spirit child of their Father in Heaven? Wasn't she a spirit sister to Sherman himself? And to Arthur? The warrior in Sherman Colligan began to awake. He heard martial trumpets, the hoofbeats of war horses, the clash and clatter of swords. He was proud of his stake. His people tithed with unusual generosity, and they achieved outstanding percentages in home teaching and church attendance. Sherman himself was a model for the members of his stake. He had risen to a vice-presidency in a savings and loan company in the city. He took courses in motivation and management. He had a lust for challenge, resistance, and obstacles. His thick chest and broad shoulders suggested solidity, drive, the ability to move and to make move. Yet his fine face beamed with kindness and good sense. The man-of-arms within him was tamed to Christian purposes; he was tuned entirely to the pastoral services of his calling. He forgave the sinful, comforted the bereaved, sustained the wavering. He prayed for himself and his people a proper testing, a sufficient trial to keep them alert, spiritually fecund, resistant to the softening which comes with abundance and blessings.

"We can't abandon this poor sister," Sherman said. His voice vibrated with compassion. "Excommunicate her! We think a missionary does well to *convert* one person during a two-year mission. Isn't it worth as much to *save* one who is already with us—the one lost sheep strayed from the ninety-nine that are found?"

Arthur leaned disconsolately on his shovel. "It was the other ninety-nine I had in mind when I thought about excommunicating her."

Sherman waved his hand impatiently. "Gosh, man, we owe Heavenly Father some service for all these blessings he has given us. Look at us here, you and me, standing in this two-acre oakbrush lot of yours. This land alone, without your house and improvements, has got to be worth thirty thousand."

"If we have many like Rendella Kranpitz around, it won't be worth two hundred."

"She balances you out, don't you see? She puts you on your mettle. Just think of her as a test. You'll be surprised how quick you get on top of all these problems." Sherman could see that Arthur was wavering. He had never been a match for Sherman in an argument. Sherman slapped him on the back. "Cheer up, brother! This woman was put in your ward for a special reason. Who else could handle her the way you can?"

"Dang it, Sherm, I just don't have the spirit to wrestle with her anymore. You don't know what she's like."

"Of course I know what she's like. I just saw her in the grocery store, didn't I? Are you going to admit you can't outthink that poor disadvantaged creature? Just put yourself into her frame of mind and think ahead of her; anticipate her. You'll come up with some solutions."

Arthur shook his head dolefully. "So far it's been her who outthinks me. Every time."

Sherman put his arm around Arthur. The old technique of loving a subordinate into compliance always worked. "Come on now, Art. No more of that excommunication talk. OK?"

"Well, sure," Arthur said, "if that's what you want, we'll give her another go."

"That's the talk I like to hear! That's what I like about you, Art, and always have. You're Christian all the way through, and you've got drive and guts and energy. Go do'er, man! Keep up your courage, say your prayers, and tear into it. You can't fail!"

Later, thinking about the little matter involving Arthur and Rendella Kranpitz, Sherman had the warm feeling of a duty well done. He didn't doubt for a moment that Arthur would come up with a total solution. Arthur had always underrated his own capacities. As for Rendella, Sherman was happy to have done some small thing in behalf of another of the souls entrusted to his care. That's what made management and leadership rewarding, whether in Sherman's professional life or in the work of the church. He always felt that what he did was vital; it touched lives and helped people.

On a Sunday evening two weeks later, as Sherman sat by the fire working on a church report, his wife escorted into the living room a sober-looking delegation. It was a high-powered group from the Fifth Ward, heavy with rank and distinction even by the standards of Coburn Heights. The three men were a physician, an insurance executive, and the owner of a supermarket; the two women were a state legislator and a hospital trustee. Uttering a hearty welcome, Sherman had an uneasy intuition that he must distract his visitors. He pointed out a painting hanging on the wall. It was a primitive work of Nauvoo, done by one of Sherman's forebears—a priceless heirloom. Harmon Roylance, the physician and the apparent spokesman of the group, scarcely noticed. It was unusual, Brother Roylance admitted in a grim, braced voice, for church members to rise spontaneously like a posse of vigilantes, but they had been driven to it by the excesses of Rendella Kranpitz.

"I believe Bishop Bosen is taking care of that problem," Sherman said.

"Yes," Brother Roylance agreed, "like a man fighting a lion with a toothpick. And he says you say there's nothing to be done about it."

There were items of behavior which the bishop might not have made known to President Colligan, the physician said. Rendella Kranpitz was always abroad. On certain days of the week she ranged beyond the boundaries of the Fifth Ward. People humored her in her claim to be an agent for Deseret Industries. She often dragged her yellow wagon home loaded with old furniture or clothes, which she stockpiled in her house on the pretense of calling in a thrift-store truck. But no truck had ever come, and the interior of her house was sordid with debris. Her yard was kept decent only by the unsolicited efforts of neighbors whom Rendella was more likely to berate for trespassing than to thank for their services. On other days Rendella worked within the Fifth Ward, where she exploited certain timid, selfless sisters. She rang doorbells and asked to come in for visits. Some sisters bluntly refused. Others cowered silently behind their drawn drapes while Rendella repeatedly rang their doorbells. But a few responded and let her in. Once there, she stayed all day and ate lunch and sometimes supper, following the housewife around her home with incessant tales of scandalous behavior among ward members and church authorities.

During the week just past she had delivered a political tract from door to door throughout much of Coburn Heights. Brother Roylance put a copy of the tract on the coffee table before Sherman. On it was the photograph of a frantic-looking man with a receding chin and bulging eyes. The pamphlet announced the candidacy of Alphonse D. Farthingage for president of the United States in an election still a year and a half away. Mr. Farthingage proposed a simple platform: if elected, he promised to open negotiations with the occupants of the numerous UFOs intruding in earth's airspace, in hopes of welding them into a coalition against the Soviet Union. The text of the pamphlet went on to imply that the general authorities of the church supported Mr. Farthingage.

"Can you imagine how much this woman is doing single-handedly to damage the image of the church in Coburn Heights?" Brother Roylance said in a voice which had become increasingly melancholy.

That led him to the most insufferable of her traits—worse than her bizarre body, her unkempt clothes, her predatory raids upon the neighborhood, her obscene house, her constant disruption of church services. It was her arrogance, her desire to insult, her aggressive will to attack, accuse, and provoke.

"There's only one thing to do," Brother Roylance said, chopping the air with an emphatic hand. "Cut her off! Get her out of the church. Even if we can't put her out of the neighborhood, we don't have to associate her with the name of the church."

The other members of the delegation broke into a medley of accusation and protest.

"We're ashamed to be Mormons!"

"She's undercutting the missionary work."

"My kids don't learn disrespect in the streets. They learn it in church."

"We paid for that chapel. I shelled out twenty-five hundred dollars! You'd think I'd get to enjoy it. Either she goes or I go."

The accumulation of angry respectability cowed Sherman. He shook and quivered with the blows. Then his stubbornness resurged, his anger flared up. He resented these unvaliant brothers and sisters. Even more he resented that lurching, off-centered, cunning fraction of a woman who could singlehandedly obstruct the function of one of the most successful stakes in the church. He became determined. Whether she liked it or not, whether they liked it or not, this woman would go forward in the sustaining fellowship and sanctifying ordinances of the Fifth Ward of the Coburn Heights Stake.

Sherman took the offensive. "So," he fulminated, "you can't cope. A ward filled with fifty-thousand-dollars-a-year people—college graduates, professionals, members of Rotary, Kiwanis, and the Exchange—and you can't cope. God Almighty didn't set up wards and stakes to save ninety-nine percent of the members; he set them up to save 100 percent. Are you telling me we aren't a 100 percent stake?"

Sherman glared about scornfully. The members of the delegation appeared crestfallen, confused, ready to search their memories to see what they had failed to understand.

Sherman stood and walked up and down before the delegation. He turned to one of the sisters, thrust out his arm, and fingered the sleeve of his shirt. "That's a forty-dollar shirt—a luxury. Shall I take God's fine gifts without any pity for someone who doesn't have so much as a normal body?"

He turned to the fireplace and put another log in the fire. "Well, go ahead if you've just got to," he said wearily. "Throw her to the Gentiles. We won't try to save anybody in Coburn Heights who isn't rich and beautiful to start with."

Tears welled in the eyes of one woman. The men fidgeted and stared at the floor. In one of those moments of inspiration which sometimes came to Sherman in the heat of tough action, he saw what must be done—a plan, a coordinated program to rehabilitate Rendella Kranpitz. He became intense. His voice varied in pitch, it rang with vision and purpose. "We're going forward. I promise action. I will personally assist Bishop Bosen to devise a plan that will solve this problem. We will energize the entire Fifth Ward. We will not cast off this woman."

Sherman sat again, took up his pen, and while he talked doodled on a pad of paper. Formless, incoherent lines, loops, scratches fell into order. Two words appeared: *firmness, love.* Magic ideas, unfailing principles. In the matter of firmness, the authorities would insist that Rendella conform. No more invasions of private homes, no more slovenliness, no more lengthy, out-of-place speeches. She had to know where the limits were, and she had to respect them, order being a divine commandment, an eternal fact to which the human spirit had to adapt itself. In the matter of love—well, wasn't this a great opportunity, an exciting chance to show how the gospel really worked? Sherman's face glowed. He gestured with open hands. The entire ward must join together in an outpouring of love which would inundate Rendella with reassurance and sweep away her fractiousness like so much debris in a roaring river.

Sherman sensed that he was clear at last. The good people of the delegation were behind him now. The eyes of the women lighted with admiration and the men nodded their assent. Still he had the feeling that he had won by only a millimeter, and after the group had gone he dialed Arthur.

"I just lost a patch of skin, Art," he said unhappily. "That was low of you to turn that delegation loose on me.

"I didn't undercut you," the bishop said after Sherman had told him about the visit. "Those people are smart enough to figure things out for themselves."

"Whip them into line, can't you?"

"Whip them into line! It's that woman who is out of line."

"I hope you're remembering what I told you about outthinking her."

"Heck, I can't catch up with her long enough to outthink her. She's got the ball all the time."

"Look, I've got a solution for you. It came to me when that bunch was here a few minutes ago. You'll get the whole Fifth Ward into this. You'll redo that woman; you'll rehabilitate her; you'll give her a new personality."

Arthur groaned into the telephone. "I'm burned out, Sherm. Why don't you do it?"

"A violation of administrative principle. This is a ward problem. You and your counselors have got to deal with it."

"No way, Sherm."

"What do you mean, no way?"

"I mean I didn't want this bishop's job in the first place. I got nothing against you, Sherm. You're the best. But I resign, right now."

"Look, Art, I didn't mean you had to do it alone. I'll help you with this Rendella Kranpitz thing. OK?"

"I don't know," Arthur said. "It really felt good to say I resign."

"This isn't any time for joking. The first step is for you and me to call on Sister Kranpitz."

A mood of near invincibility had come over Sherman. He was convinced that all would go well, that the disturbance of mind and spirit which afflicted Rendella Kranpitz would be reversed by a bold application of gospel principles. Nonetheless, when Sherman and Arthur called on Rendella on a Tuesday evening, Sherman brought along Celia, his wife, as an added precaution. Rendella's yard, which lay under a mantle of snow, was not so unusual for Coburn Heights, but the interior of the house jolted Sherman. In the living room relics of fine furniture groaned beneath bundles of newspapers and card-board boxes from which cast-off clothing dangled. A disorganized mountain of shoe boxes covered one wall. Some were shut tight; others had spilled out ball bearings, yarn remnants, and aquarium gravel. A broken rocking chair sat upside down in a corner. On the coffee table, as if serving as a centerpiece, was a large broiling pan filled nearly to the brim with rancid cooking grease.

Firmness and love: these were the principles Sherman repeated to himself as he set a small, broken drill press onto the floor and sat down in the chair it had occupied. Disciplining himself to a total candor, Sherman told Rendella that her behavior was unacceptable for a member of the Fifth Ward of the Coburn Heights Stake. He forced himself to speak slowly and emphatically as he explained the offenses she had committed. Then he went on to cheer and entice her by explaining that, using welfare funds, they intended to buy appealing new clothes for her and to arrange for a visit to a hair salon. Several fine sisters of the ward were to be called to help her in grooming and dress. Families would invite her to supper several times a week. Certain couples would call for her on Sunday and take her to meetings—making sure, of course, that she was well dressed and groomed.

Braced by her strong leg, Rendella crowded into the corner of an armchair. Her eyes roamed everywhere in the room. Sherman was disconcerted by the relentless, cross-grained squint of her mouth and the startling disparity of her left side, upon which the limbs and features of a smaller person seemed to have been grafted. She was dressed in a faded green bakery uniform; a rip along the thigh was closed by six brass safety pins. She did not seem at all impressed by what he was saying. She could not help hearing, yet when he was through he saw that she had not heard.

"How come nobody ever asks me to be a Sunday school teacher?" she said peevishly.

"We don't aspire to particular callings in the church," Sherman said. "We do whatever we are asked to do."

"Well, I want to know what my calling is. How come I don't have a calling?"

"Your calling?" Sherman paused a moment, then saw an opening. "Yes, well, your calling is what I've just been telling you about. Your calling is to reform your life a little." Sherman congratulated himself on his ability to seize the moment. He patiently explained again what had been unacceptable about Rendella's behavior and what excellent new things awaited her.

"What kind of bishop do you call him?" she interrupted, pointing at Arthur. "You think he's a good bishop! Word going around is he's playing hankypanky with more than one. I could tell you who with, if you wanted to know."

"What next?" Arthur moaned, rolling his eyes in frustration.

"I absolutely will not tolerate that kind of talk," Sherman roared. "I know for a fact that Bishop Bosen is a righteous man."

Rendella shrank. "Well, I just wanted to know what my calling is. How come nobody ever asks me to pray? Sister Jenson has got asked to pray five times in the past three months."

"Gosh," Arthur said, "I don't keep track of how many times people get asked to pray."

"He won't let me sing in the ward choir," Rendella said to Sherman. "I got all practiced up and now I don't get to sing."

"It was Sister Hanney's decision."

"You backed her up!"

Arthur turned toward Sherman. "Sister Hanney likes the choir to sing a cappella. She let Sister Kranpitz practice with the choir for three weeks. She even let her sing with them in sacrament meeting once." Arthur paused and shook his head in disbelief. "A whole choir off key—thirty of them! Sister Hanney stopped them twice to get back on pitch, but it didn't help."

"Sister Hanney is a third cousin to that Tinford bunch in Salina. That's why she doesn't like me. Ever since Grandfather Kranpitz beat old man Tinford for alderman in Richfield, those Tinfords have been down on the Kranpitzes."

"Maybe it would help if you didn't sing so loud," Arthur said.

"See!" Rendella said to Sherman. "Right there is what is wrong with the music in this ward. They're all afraid of somebody who can sing louder than they can."

The bishop shrugged and slumped into his chair.

Sherman cleared his throat and began again. He gestured emphatically to fix her attention as he explained once more the changes to which she would have to submit. Rendella's eyes wandered. In a moment they came to rest on Celia.

"Why doesn't she say something?" Rendella said. "You're looking peaked, honey." Rendella got up, hobbled into the kitchen, and returned with a bottle and a tablespoon. She poured out a spoonful of dark, gummy liquid and offered it to Celia. "Take this. It'll build your blood."

"Gracious, no, thanks; I just couldn't," Celia protested in a fluttery voice, whereupon Rendella spooned the liquid into her own mouth, gave the spoon an additional lick, and set it and the bottle on the coffee table.

At that moment just as his will was beginning to waver, Sherman was struck by a brilliant idea. He sized it up and recognized it as inspiration. He called Arthur to a whispered conference in the hallway.

"Let's call her to be a Sunday school teacher."

Arthur's eyes bulged incredulously.

"We'll schedule her in one of your classrooms, and we'll call four couples to attend her class for three months. Then we'll rotate."

Arthur still had the appearance of a strangled man.

"It'll work. It'll be the outlet she needs. And it's the bargaining point we need. The people can put up with her because it's a call and won't last forever."

Sherman led Arthur into the living room. "Sister Kranpitz," he said, "we have decided to call you to be a Sunday school teacher in the Fifth Ward."

Rendella's face froze. Then her eyes shifted suspiciously from Sherman to Arthur and again to Sherman. She asked what kind of class it would be. Sherman looked expectantly at Arthur, who had not recovered his speech. Well, that didn't matter, Rendella said, if it was a real Sunday school class. Did he mean a real Sunday school class? Arthur finally spoke, though weakly. It would be a gospel doctrine class—a special course for adults. Rendella relaxed in her chair and beamed with pleasure. She wanted to know if they could go over to the bishop's office right now and get a manual. Arthur said he would drop one by after work the next evening.

Rendella limped into her bedroom and returned with a copy of the Bible. "Some people say I don't know the gospel," she said defiantly. She patted the book and tapped her own forehead with a finger. "I know it, all right. You'll see I can teach."

Then Sherman drove his bargains. The class was conditional upon Rendella's accepting the changes he had been talking about. He knew now that she listened, and point by point he coerced her assent. She must allow some of the sisters to help her dress more nicely; she must call in the truck from Deseret Industries and clear her house of trash; she must stop scouring the neighborhood with her wagon; she must not give lengthy discourses in testimony meeting. In return she would have nice clothes, invitations to supper, friends to take her to meeting. And, of course, her Sunday school class.

The plan was in effect by the following Sunday—another testimony to the efficiency of Sherman Colligan. He followed up every call Arthur made. He stayed on the telephone for hours, assuring the brothers and sisters who had been asked to assume duties in behalf of Sister Kranpitz that their assignment had come from the Lord. The plan, if carried out with enthusiasm and energy, could not fail.

On Sunday night reports of a startling success came in. Brother Horrup, who had been called to attend Rendella's class, telephoned Sherman to express his satisfaction. He and his wife were proud that their little bit had helped. He had a revised opinion of Rendella. Her lesson had followed the manual closely. He was especially impressed with her knowledge of the gospel. She had no need to pause, search for scriptural passages, and read them; she had them already memorized. Wasn't it amazing what a little love and kindness could do for a person whom you had written off as deformed and maybe a little crazy? Later Arthur telephoned to express cautious optimism. He was reluctant to believe anything could go right where that woman was concerned, but it looked as if the plan might work. Unless you saw her, Arthur said, you couldn't believe how good she could look all dressed up and with her hair curled—like Cinderella, a beauty out of the ashes, and so forth. Sherman was charmed. He was already thinking of pushing Rendella toward some kind of simple job—perhaps work at the welfare storehouse or at the Deseret Industries thrift store. Exhilaration came over him and, with it, a sense of gratitude. He always won, but he recognized that he had help far beyond his own abilities.

Early the next Sunday morning Sherman had a telephone call from Arthur. "Things don't look so good," Arthur said in a depressed voice. "I'm afraid maybe it's going to fall to pieces."

"What's going to fall to pieces?"

"It looks like one Sunday is about all Rendella Kranpitz is good for."

"Dang it, Art, you don't have enough faith!"

"I don't know if my faith has anything to do with it. She doesn't look like a person who intends to stick with her bargains."

"For heaven's sake, tell me what's happened."

"She's been on the streets most of the week. And when she disposed of some of that trash, like she promised she would, well, guess what? She called in the opposition."

"The opposition?"

"The Salvation Army truck. You know, instead of calling in the Deseret Industries truck."

"What difference does it make? It all goes to the poor, doesn't it?'"

"It just goes to show you what kind of person she is. If she can figure out a way to dig you, she will."

"That doesn't sound so bad, brother," Sherman said, trying to pitch his voice at an enthusiastic level. "Let's go forward with this plan. A few setbacks don't mean anything."

"It's today I'm worried about."

"You mean she won't teach her Sunday school class?"

"Oh, she won't miss that, not on your life. The problem is that yesterday Sister Melchoir and Sister Jacobs went over to help her do her hair. Can you imagine the sacrifice it is for those ladies, with all their kids, to get dressed up on Saturday afternoon and go over to Rendella's for an hour? And she ran them off. She said, What's the matter. You don't think I look so good the way I am, huh? She called them names you wouldn't believe."

"Shall I go to her class today?"

"Would you do that, Sherman? That would sure be great. If you're there, maybe she'll be decent."

A little before the classes were scheduled to begin, Sherman went up the stairs of the meetinghouse, turned down a corridor, and came to the room assigned to Rendella's class. He took a seat at the back. Within a few minutes three couples filed in—the Smiths, the Dinwoodys, and the Horrups. All of them smiled at Sherman and spoke a respectful greeting. The men came to the back for a moment and shook his hand. They all appeared a little resigned, yet hopeful and full of good will. The rank and file of the church, Sherman thought appreciatively, were excellent people—always willing to meet new challenges.

Rendella Kranpitz came in. Sherman shuddered, closed his eyes, then took a second look. Men's shoes, unlaced, clattered on her feet; a vile bag of a dress fluttered around her bony frame; her hair sprouted from her scalp like Swiss chard or turnip tops. Her arms were filled with books—the scriptures, a lesson manual, sermons by some of the general authorities of the church. She set the books on the table at the front of the room and surveyed the class.

"Where's Brother and Sister Brown?" Rendella asked in a tone of accusation. At that moment the door opened and the couple entered. "There isn't anything so crude and unrefined as busting into a class late," Rendella said. "Can't you come on time?"

The tardy couple murmured an apology as they took seats. Looking up, Sister Brown uttered a gasp of surprise. Rendella advanced threateningly toward her. "Maybe you don't think I dress so good." She glared around the room as if to dare anyone else to disapprove.

"Now the lesson." She returned to the side of the table and stood erect on her good leg, maintaining the other leg at tiptoe in the throat of its unlaced shoe. "Our lesson today is on the gathering of Israel. If you are going to gather Israel, you've got to know who you're gathering. So let's see if you know who Issachar was. Who was Issachar?"

The class members looked blank. Sister Dinwoody thumbed through the pages of her lesson manual.

"You won't find it there," Rendella said. "You're just wasting your time. How come you don't read your scriptures? Issachar is one of the twelve sons of Jacob." She raised her eyes to the ceiling. "Genesis, chapter forty-nine, verse fourteen: 'Issachar is a strong ass couching down between two burdens.'" She looked about triumphantly. "I got you on that one, didn't I?"

Rendella shuffled back and forth, as if undecided. Then, leaning against the table, she directed her eyes toward the light fixture on the ceiling and began to recite: "First Chronicles, chapter two: 'These are the sons of Israel; Reuben, Simeon, Levi, and Judah, Issachar, and Zebulun, Dan, Joseph, and Benjamin, Naphtali, Gad, and Asher. The sons of Judah; Er, and Onan, and Shelah: which three were born unto him of the daughter of Shua the Canaanitess. And Er, the firstborn of Judah, was evil in the sight of the Lord; and he slew him.'" She went on for ten or fifteen minutes, unfolding the genealogies of the sons of Jacob. She spoke in a high, oratorical voice and, without hesitation, as if she read from a prompter projected on the ceiling. Sherman listened intently, trying to appear alert and interested, but the rocking cadence and monotonous sonority of her words lulled him. With winking eyes and slumping shoulders, he teetered toward sleep.

Rendella's hand suddenly slapped down on the tabletop. "Can't you get your sleeping done at home?" she cried out. Sherman's eyes snapped open, but it was not Sherman she had shouted at. Rendella glowered down on Sister Dinwoody in the second row. "You've got the manners of a magpie," Rendella said belligerently. "Now I've forgotten where I was. I'm going to have to go all the way back to the beginning. Our lesson today is on the gathering of Israel. *Israel* is a word that means the people of God. At first it was the name of the twelve tribes descended from . . . ."

Sister Dinwoody rummaged in her purse. Rendella broke off her speech and waited, arms akimbo, with a mock patience until Sister Dinwoody had found her handkerchief. "You just won't listen to anything, will you?" Rendella said. "Well, if you think you know everything, let's see if you know what this scripture means. Amos, chapter two, verse two: 'But I will send a fire upon Moab, and it shall devour the palaces of Kirioth: and Moab shall die with tumult, with shouting, and with the sound of the trumpet.'"

Rendella leaned toward Sister Dinwoody. "So what does that mean?" Sister Dinwoody dabbed at her eyes with her handkerchief. "Sniffling won't help you any," Rendella said. "Maybe you don't think I teach so good."

Tears flowed from Sister Dinwoody's eyes. She got up, crowded past her husband, and made for the door. "No you don't, not on your dingdong tintype!" Rendella shouted. She seized Sister Dinwoody by the arm. "Nobody gets out of this class till the bell rings."

Brother Dinwoody leaped up. "Let loose of my wife, you old catfish!" he cried. He shook Rendella until she released her. Rendella bent over, took off a shoe, and launched an attack upon Brother Dinwoody. With a roar he grappled with her, but the best he could manage was to grip her shoulder with one hand while he used the other to fend off the flailing shoe.

"Run for it!" Brother Dinwoody shouted. His wife darted out the door. The other couples, mouths agape, looked about uncertainly. "Get out of here before she kills me!" he yelled.

"Let her go, for pity's sake," Sherman shouted. "I can handle this."

"Sorry it didn't work out better," Brother Dinwoody said as he made for the door.

Rendella stood panting like an animal at bay. Sherman came forward slowly and deliberately, swollen with a magnificent wrath. Rendella dropped her shoe and with astounding speed lunged through the door and disappeared beyond the turn in the corridor.

Coming down the stairs into the foyer of the meetinghouse, Sherman met Arthur. Arthur eyed Rendella's abandoned shoe, which Sherman held in his hand, and said in awe, "What happened, Sherm? I sure hope Brother and Sister Dinwoody don't apostatize."

"Go after them and cool them off," Sherman snapped.

"I don't think I want to get involved in it," Arthur said, backing away. "Maybe you ought to go talk to them."

"I said go after them and cool them off. You're bishop, aren't you?"

"Well, no," Arthur said. "I resign for sure this time. I've had it up to here with this business."

"You can't resign. You were called by inspiration, and by golly you'll get released by inspiration, which I haven't had any of on the subject of your release."

"Disfellowship me if you want to," Arthur said gloomily. "I can't take any more of this stress."

"Suffering salamanders, Art!" Sherman roared. "Why do you have to turn belly up on me every time I get a crisis?"

"I just wasn't cut out to be a bishop. Especially in a ward with Rendella Kranpitz."

"OK, OK, I get your message. You shut up about resigning, and I take over that woman. She's a stake problem now. We'll declare her house a non-ward territory. Now where is she? I'm going to lean on her so hard she won't know up from down."

Sister Horrup informed Sherman that Rendella was cowering in the ladies' rest room in the back wing of the meetinghouse. Sherman strode down the darkened corridor and pounded on the door with Rendella's shoe.

"Rendella Kranpitz, you come out of there," he commanded. There was no response. He pounded and shouted louder. At last he shouted, "I'm counting to ten and then I'm coming in after you. One. Two. Three. Four. Five. Six. . . ." The door opened a crack, and an eye gleamed in the dim light.

"Well," Sherman said, a little more calmly, "you sure messed things up royally, didn't you?"

"Yes, sir."

"The best chance you ever had to do something decent, and you spit all over it, didn't you?"

"Yes, sir."

"We are going to give you one more chance. The whole works. And if you mess it up this time, you know what I'm going to do?"

"No, sir."

"I'm going to excommunicate you. You won't be able to go to church anymore. And when you die, you'll go to the telestial kingdom. And you'll never get out. Forever and ever." He smacked his palm with the heel of the shoe. "Now you shape up! Got that?"

"Yes, sir."

"And you get this straight, too. Sherman Colligan never quits. If you misbehave, I'll hunt you down personally. And you're going to get rid of the rest of the trash in your house this week. All of it."

"Yes, sir."

"You're going to let the sisters come over and get you lined up with some decent dresses and a nice hairdo. And you're going to teach a class next Sunday. But you're going to do it right. Just like you did last Sunday. Got that?"

"Yes, sir."

"OK. Take this abominable shoe and go home."

Sherman spent the afternoon reorganizing the rehabilitation of Rendella Kranpitz. For hours he was on the telephone in his office in the stake center. Outside a storm had begun. Looking out his office window from time to time, Sherman saw the thick, jostling swirl of snowflakes. Ordinarily he would have watched with tranquil satisfaction, but during this long afternoon he was on edge, still unnerved and disgusted with himself for having spoken abruptly to his good friend Arthur and for having threatened Rendella with such anger. Love and firmness? It seemed rather that the rehabilitation of this woman might degenerate into fire and brimstone. With that thought, fresh determination came to Sherman. He would personally see to it that the loving pattern of the gospel would prevail. He decided to call people from all wards in the stake, with the exception of the Fifth Ward, which could be considered already to have done its duty in this matter. He telephoned a score of people—the individuals who would assist in his project and, of course, their bishops, whose support and approval were vital. When evening had come and Sherman stepped out into the storm, he felt at peace. He could take a moment to appreciate the luminous gyrations of the snowflakes beneath the streetlights. None of the good people he had called seemed half-hearted or doubtful. Once again he felt sure his project would succeed.

Sherman drove home in the snowy darkness, parked in his garage, and tramped along the walk to the front entrance. Celia had turned on the porchlight for him. Its rays created an iridescent aura among the floating snowflakes.

And there, sitting on his doorstep, deposited upon a salad plate a little larger than a saucer, was a human stool—a small, looped mound of fresh human excrement.

For a moment Sherman stood transfixed. Then his eyes fell upon tracks in the snow. Though they were half-obliterated, he knew that shuffling foot could belong only to Rendella Kranpitz. Sherman picked up the plate and hid it beneath the drooping branches of a shrub. He shook the snow from his hat and went into the house.

"Hello, sweetheart," Celia said, giving him a kiss. "Isn't it a fine night?"

"Um, yes, a fine night," Sherman mumbled as she helped him take off his overcoat.

"There are sandwiches and soup in the kitchen," she said. "If you want to hurry and wash your hands, Randy is still at the table. You could eat with him."

"Right, good idea. That would be great. I'll hurry," Sherman said. But when he had gotten into the bedroom and had taken off his suitcoat, he sat on the bed, feeling strangely disoriented and removed from reality. It seemed as if nothing in the world was very important. He wondered how long a man could continue in intensive combat without breaking. He remembered having read that some soldiers held up for years. That cheered him for a moment. He reminded himself that Sherman Colligan never quit. There was no reason why he should lose his nerve because of a frail, demented little woman. There was a godly purpose for the affliction which had come to him and his stake—there had to be. His testimony, his sanity depended upon it. Rendella Kranpitz was obviously not a run-of-the-mill test, an ordinary, everyday trial. She was an epic probe, an examination of heroic proportions. Nonetheless, Sherman took out his wallet and looked at his pocket calendar. When his wife came in, she found him still trying to calculate how long it would be until he had served the normal term of a stake president and might expect to be released.

TEN

I am Buzz Gaulter, Left-hander

DARRELL SPENCER

*W*e live with acts of God. This is the good news I have for François, so I phone him, direct distance dialing to L.A. No answer, only a dull ringing in my ears. I keep the phone to my head. Seeds, black Shetland sheep dog at my feet, lifts her muzzle and shows me the whites of her eyes. I turn down the TV, but can still hear a squirrel-cheeked man outlining the end of the world. He tells us it will come while we sleep. He claims to be Leland Freeborn the Parowan prophet. His last words are: "Say your goodbyes." The ringing in my ears is like a moaning. I hang up and turn the set off, then on again, waiting for the weather.

Less than a mile away, Utah Lake rises in the moonlight, fed daily, engorged nightly, bloated ceaselessly by lunatic rivers. Madcap water escapes its banks and throws fits. It uproots trees and undoes bridges. A reservoir up Sardine Canyon is threatening towns below.

My pacing has Seeds's attention. She hurls herself at my foot, pins it, and takes in sock. I waltz, I reel, and she rides me out. Her instinct is to herd.

When I reach François, there will be a moment of silence while he relights a cigar. He will toy with small change and say, "Relax. Get your feet up. We all know what the world needs more of: frivolity and squalor. All the good things." He is a smart man— friend, writer, and fiddler on the violin.

But the lake encroaches, and the moon waxes, and I say out loud: "Los Angeles is not the end of the world, François. Orem is." This is the bad news. Orem, Utah. Utah's watch-us-grow city. Home of the Osmonds, Donny and Marie.

What François does not know, what I want him to know, is my waking at odd hours, popeyed, a fist of air in my throat, my left or right arm as dead as clotted clothes. He doesn't know my nightly walk through hallways, past closet doors spooks have opened against their hinges. What I want him to see is the hand of God.

I have thrown my wife out. When I did, she spit scripture. She said, "The moon will turn to blood." Now I hear footsteps overhead. I want François to understand they are real.

East of Orem is the Wasatch Fault. It runs the length of the Wasatch Mountains. It waits. Its time will come. The local paper carried a photo of the mountains above and the cities below and a fracture severing them, ripping the God-made from the man-made. Next to it was a drawing of a house of cards and a caption: "Gambling with Seismic Safety." The crack was the grin of a jack-o-lantern.

For now the big story is south of here. Thistle, Utah, is under water. Spring rains saturated the hills and Billy's Mountain came down. Mud outran the highway department. It choked off the road, then dammed up the Spanish Fork River and tore up railroad lines. Behind the slide, the water is sixty feet high and rising. Twenty-two houses have gone under. NewsWatch 2 filmed looters in scuba gear. People are water-skiing. The Texaco at the corner is selling FISH LAKE THISTLE caps and T-shirts.

The paper has begun a series called "Floodwatch." It tells us that the rivers have not yet crested and assures us that the Army Corps of Engineers is on its way. And the governor is coming. We've been told to boil our water.

We made *Time.* I say we, but I am not *we.*

Orem is my wife's town. Lois grew up here, with women named Alma, LeOra, Alvina; among men named Orrin, Manti, Helaman, and Ephraim. She introduced me as her Bernard. She told me, "You can be Bernard now." Then she looked me in the mouth. She took me up to people. "This is my Bernard," she said.

I am not Bernard. I am Buzz, Buzz Gaulter. Buzz at the Bel Air in L.A., where with a wedge I can turn a Titleist into a feather and float it to within three feet of any flagstick, from fairway, rough, or sand. I was Buzz at SC, eighteen years ago, where I started three years at first base, a hot dog, running out walks, dinking singles to left and jerking them into right, laying down a bunt when even God didn't expect one, dropping an occasional double one inch inside the left field foul line.

I am Buzz Gaulter, left-hander, though I swing my woods and irons right-handed. I adapt; I am no spectator. I putt left-handed and dead-eyed.

I won't play golf in Orem. Men in tennis shoes and corduroys wander the fairways. They tow their clubs behind them. No one bets. There is nowhere to get a drink after a round. And cards. Poker is a wet dream here.

It was Lois's brother, LaDell, who got us to Orem. He wrote her and told her the family home was ours if we wanted it. We could steal it for $60,000.

So we did.

The house is old, on the register of the Utah State Historical Society. We get a tax break if we refurbish. The hardwood floors creak and are a comfort. Our address is RFD, and we're on a party line with LaDell.

He and his fat wife, Faye, live behind us, across an open field, half a mile away. This is farm country. There are fence posts and sagging barbed wire, but no real fences. I grew up with cinder block. People knew their place.

I'm sure Lois has gone to LaDell's. Where she'll sleep I don't know. There is no room. Their place is only a basement. Walking in, you feel like you're being sucked into a root cellar. LaDell tells me he gave up. He set out to build a two-story with a basement, but the day he began laying bricks for the ground floor, he quit. He shut off the mixer, knocked down the framing, and tacked on shingling. He trimmed the edges with sheet metal and finished the chimney.

On good days LaDell and Faye sit in their yard. He flips back and forth in a La-Z-Boy while she sews, her work and herself spread out on a moss green vinyl couch. They act like they're in Florida. Utah Lake is their Atlantic.

Lois must be there.

The day I kicked Lois out, she had hacked her way across the kitchen, her robe open, her cardboard-soled slippers like trash in the wind. She was as out of control as whooping cough. She smelled like a soybean baby.

I said, "Out."

She scraped food into Seeds's bowl and piled dishes in the sink. "Out."

Lois went to our bedroom, then on to the bathroom. I heard the door lock. Muttering "Out, out, out," I piled her clothes on the bed. When she came in, I was tossing underwear. I said, "Pack." I hauled out her luggage.

She stood like a floor lamp, robbed of its shade, the bulb off.

I said, "You're out. Strike three."

She pleaded. But her issues were dead. I ignored her questions. They were moot. I felt no urge to explain. I raised my right arm like Moses and with my left hand pointed toward the world. I said, "I pay the bills."

We were on the porch when she said, "The moon will turn to blood." I kicked her overnight case, and it skidded across the cement. She said, "Where to?" I phoned LaDell, which is a tricky thing to do on a party line; you have to dial yourself. He came running. We watched him bob across the fields.

I said, "Seeds stays." To prove this I undid the ribbon Lois had tied to her collar. I gave it to Lois as if I was awarding her something, and I shut the door so I wouldn't have to see LaDell.

I drove to Duff's and bought a McCulloch 510 chain saw on sale. Two hundred forty-five dollars, and worth it. I ripped our king-size bed in two, from baseboard to headboard. Sawdust fell like powder, on me, on the carpet. I left it to be ground in. Cutting the mattress was not what I thought it would be. It was like slicing meat. I used cinder blocks to prop up my side. Hers I carried out to the patio and I dragged out the box springs. I gathered up any chair Lois had sat on, any plate she had eaten off, and her chest of drawers. She had left some clothes. I put a match to it all.

The smoke began white and thready. I settled into a lounge chair, and Seeds hopped to my lap. I thought about the farmers. Utah Lake is robbing them. It will leave a foot of mud. From where I sat, I saw cows huddled on humps of dry land; others stood dumbfounded, water rotting their hooves.

The fire grew. LaDell had told me about the floods of '52. Graves had opened, uncorking bodies and spinning them down city streets. Headlines had asked: "The Second Coming?"

I dumped Seeds to the ground and circled the fire like a primitive. Smoke rose in cartoon clouds. No one would care. Just another farmer burning weeds and limbs. But LaDell and fat Faye and Lois would see and worry. Crazy Buzz is burning the family home. I listened for sirens.

I looked up at an old backboard and hoop bolted to the eaves. The patio had been some kid's court. Lois has six brothers and two sisters. A government study says Orem has the highest birth rate in the nation. I eyed the basket. Pumping energy into my legs, I took one and a half steps, rose as Buzz Gaulter, and slam-dunked Lois. Seeds barked and nipped at my heels.

The furniture burned. The box springs stunk.

All this was three days ago, to be accurate, on the day of the night God came. I want to say he struck. Lois would say struck is more accurate. He came like a thief in the night.

I had gone to the west desert. I needed Vinnie and the Dodgers. Only Vin Scully and his voice clean-as-a-double-up-the-alley could save me. Seeds and I took the back roads, cut left into Lehi, and parked in front of Stubby's Beer and Billiards.

I do love Stubby's.

My first night there, I asked him about the sign above the register. It says, "Gary Gilmore drank here." I said, "Is that true?"

He said, "Often."

He keeps a stack of *The Executioner's Song* on the counter. A big thick book. One day I'll buy one. I asked him if it was true. He said, "It happened."

I gave him my hand. I said, "I am Buzz."

"My name's Pinkie Bender," he said, "but they call me Stubby."

I can't go for a Dodger game without stopping at Stubby's, even if it's only for one beer and a few chips. To hear the Dodgers I have to drive beyond the west mountains. I end up on the Utah-Nevada border near the Goshute Indian Reservation. The road follows the old pony express route. Once I pass Dugway the radio picks up Vinnie and I might as well be in L.A. I know the sun is up in the city, and it is probably low enough to be tough on whoever is playing right field.

What surprised me the evening of the day I threw Lois out was Utah Lake. It got to me as I drove. The water had begun to take over. Trees staggered against its weight. There was no longer a shoreline. The water was beading like quicksilver on the land. The Jordan River picked at the road bed. I parked, to let Seeds out, to measure the damage. She yapped sharply and took bites out of the Hatu wind. A white moon held itself above the Wasatch Mountains. It was veined. It was perfect in its orbit.

I was spooked but put everything behind me. I thought about the Dodgers' Lasorda. He'd have a joke for all this. I pictured a towering shot in the bottom of the ninth and Dodgers merrily circling the bases. What I got, as I sat on the hood of the car, drinking beer and feeding Seeds Twinkies, was a triple play against the Dodgers—a line drive to Schmidt, who stepped on third and fired to first. Bases-loaded wasted. I wept. Seeds sneaked into my lap. In the ninth Virgil singled home two Phillies. In the bottom half, Carlton fanned three Dodgers.

I drove like a madman. I tried to ignore the lake, but the moon had turned night into day. For the first time in my life, I felt its tug.

It bristled the hair on my neck. We got home at 2 AM.

God had come and gone.

The roof had caved in—dead center on the south side. Seeds and I circled the yard. Ashes smoldered on the patio. I said, "Seeds, God has brought his fist down, like Khrushchev and his shoe." We climbed the stairs to the attic, where we walked among timber and shingles. Seeds sniffed for a trail. The moon looked in on us. I faced up to it. I said, "I am Buzz Gaulter, left-hander. What is it?" Seeds went for my foot and I shook her off.

I couldn't sleep, so I drove to the 7-Eleven for a paper and a Big Gulp. Mud slides had wiped out a neighborhood, burying the old and the slow. Survivors were in a high school gym. There was a picture—cots, etc. A dike had broken, and a car had been carried from I-15. "A whole family has gone under," said a state trooper. Polygamists were shooting each other in the head. Obeying a revelation from God, two crazies slit the throats of a twenty-four-year-old mother and her one-year-old daughter.

At 8:00 I drove back and got a morning paper. Same news. Deer were being slaughtered. Driven into the valley by the winter's heavy snows, they were starving and baffled. Men were shooting them with .22s. Blood flowed in orchards. A headline said, "Thistle Could Not Be Saved." The Army Corps of Engineers was retreating.

I phoned a roofer. He parked his Volvo cockeyed to our retaining wall, left it running and shook my hand. "Karl Bowler," he said. I pointed to the hole.

He said, "An attic?"

Seeds and I led him up. He kicked debris. I said, "Can you explain this?"

"Old house," he said. "Rot. Gravity. An act of God."

"Will it all come down?"

He didn't think so. He went to his pocket and came up with a plastic clip. It had a magnet stuck to it. He said, "I invented this. They hold back shower curtains. Do you want to invest $20,000 or $30,000?"

I told him no, and he put it away. He looked like a hero gone to seed. Hair a shade too red. Features more round than chiseled.

Skinny. And short. His mustache a mistake, an idea he should have given up on.

Back on the front lawn, he said, "Want to get in on a running store? Ground floor. Make you rich."

I said, "No. The roof?"

He added figures and quoted me a price. I called around. No one beat his estimate. He said, "I'll need three days and a free hand." I gave him both.

Trucks came and went while a crew hurled trash out the hole. I left. Seeds and I went for a drive. We parked downtown, afraid to go up any canyons or near the lake. We avoided the freeway. There were dikes running the length of Third South. People stood on them while a photographer snapped a picture for fifty cents. We went home.

The second day Seeds barked at a crane as it lowered a skylight toward the roof. I asked no questions. I retreated. A free hand is a free hand. I clipped articles from old newspapers: "Deer Feeding Program Killing More Than It Saves"; "Crack Found in Skyline Dam"; "Two Drown in Thistle Lake." I used a razor blade and cut out quotes from officials: "Jeffrey Dunn, City Engineer, says, 'God only knows when the lake will stop.' The governor says, 'We'll go to the White House if we have to.'" I put it all in envelopes and addressed them to LaDell's.

I knew they were keeping an eye on the work. I saw Lois and fat Faye with their hands on their hips. LaDell was bucking up and down in his La-Z-Boy and studying things through binoculars. I flipped them a bird.

They're wondering what crazy Buzz is up to. What has he done? I have done nothing.

More trucks came, and I stretched out on the sofa. Seeds picked up and put down her head. Things were being moved in. I bit my tongue. I spoke only Spanish to myself. Up the backstairs men carried heavy objects. I recognized the sound of an industrial sander. Seeds curled back her black lips and showed teeth. The sander whirred above us, and dust fell on the room where I lay. Seeds gathered herself in.

The sander came down. Trucks pulled out. It was getting dark when Seeds and I headed for Stubby's. I drank beer. Seeds sat at my feet and ate Twinkies. Stubby doesn't mind her.

I said, "Pinkie, give me your number."

"Here?"

"Anywhere. I may need help."

"Wherever you call, ask for Stubby," he said. He gave me three numbers. He could see I was serious.

I told him about the roofer. *Am I a coward?* I wondered. Stubby didn't think so. I admitted I had driven off without looking back. I confessed to throwing my wife out. He gave me a beer and a package of Twinkies on the house.

I drove out to confront the lake. It was picking at the road. I saw asphalt fall away. I braked and another piece dropped into the water. There was no moon showing. I felt the way you feel when you let the tub overflow—as if you have gone on vacation and left a burner on. Back at Stubby's, I had a beer and phoned the highway department. No answer. There should have been sawhorses and yellow blinkers out there. The road to the west was gone.

And there was this ringing in my ears. Like a moaning. Seeds and I drove home in a thunderstorm. Seventeen thousand lightning bolts hit the ground.

As we turned toward the house, the rain stopped. The clouds cleared like curtains. I saw the skylight lit up, dead center in the roof. The trucks were gone. Only Karl Bowler's Volvo idled where he had parked it that first day. I was sure Lois was staring out of LaDell's place, her eyes six inches above the ground.

On the front lawn, a woman and maybe a dozen children moved in the moonlight. Her hair was wet. She danced an African shag. As I got out of the car, she came at me. I held Seeds and twisted my keys into a weapon. She said, "He's done this before."

I let Seeds into the house.

She said, "Moves in. Practically."

Seeds batted the door behind me. I banged it, and she stopped. The woman backed away, looking up at the skylight. The Volvo spun on. I realized it had been running all this time. It had been there in the back of my mind.

I said, "Mrs. Bowler?"

"My husband. Yes," she said. She seemed to be an immigrant. A bun at the back of her head tucked lines in her face. Her dress hung like a quilt from her clothes-hanger shoulders.

I said, "I've gone days without sleep."

"Tell him to go."

"He's welcome. There must be a reason."

"He'll call himself Gillette."

I turned for the door.

She said, "What do you want?"

"What do I want?" I said.

"I'll stay. I won't leave till he comes around. He'll turn your place into a foundry. Make brass bookends or install a kiln and throw pots and think he's an artist."

I looked at the fresh moon and shut the door in her face.

She yelled, "See." I went to a window. She held up a gas can. She called a boy to her and handed it to him. She gave him money. He ran off, slinging the can. Five minutes later he was back. They met at the Volvo, and the woman poured gas in. She screamed, "Till hell freezes over," and shook the empty can at me.

The moon is out and full. Water drips from the roof. Like unshakable foliage, the woman watches the skylight. Her children sleep around her. The police have not come.

François does not answer. I dial again, thinking I got it wrong. No answer, only the ringing.

Footsteps pass back and forth above me. The hardwood floors creak. Bowler works late.

I turn on the news. Thistle Lake won't hold. It's been declared a disaster area. There is a shot of the governor, on a cliff, beaming through his new beard. Along the freeway, dikes are failing. I-15 is closed north and south. A film crew in a helicopter flies over flooded fields and collapsing barns. Cows look like Stonehenge. A weatherman shakes his head and says, "The ground cannot contain any more water."

Outside, the Volvo engine idles. LaDell and Lois want their home back. It's on their mind, but it's in my name. They sit in their dark hole. As Buzz, I could step outside, tee up six Titleists, address them cleanly, and cut wedge shots onto LaDell's roof: plink, plink, plink. I could send one or two down the chimney, let them rattle around.

But the woman is in the yard, troubling it, troubling me.

The footsteps have stopped. Tomorrow I will ask to see his work. Tomorrow will be the third of the three days Bowler asked for. Now I stare at TV: "Nightmare Theater." Steve McQueen, who is dead, and the Blob.

Still François does not answer. When he does he will say something educated.

My phone rings. A boy says, "Do you have a John there?"

"No John," I say. "Only a Buzz."

"No John?"

"No John," I say.

He says, "What do you do then, pee out the window?"

Seeds turns in a mindboggling circle as she chases her tail, and I dial Wyoming.

"Cheyenne Poison Control," a voice says.

I say, "Dr. Frentheway."

"One minute."

This is childish I know. I set the phone near my stereo and hold the arm over Norman Greenbaum's "Spirit in the Sky." When Frentheway says, "Hello," I lower the needle. My forearms weaken, but what are old college friends for? I say into the phone, "Psycho." I hang up. We called him Psycho. Everyone had names then.

In the predawn light I dial François and let it ring. I have a twenty-five-foot cord and can take the phone into hell if I have to. I picture him on the beach. He has his violin, and he is sending pure notes to beings on other planets. More likely, he is on a pier, studying the pelicans, figuring out how to describe them as they drop into the Pacific.

I carry the phone to the kitchen. It rings on. Utah Lake swells. Seeds, stuck to my foot, drives me from the back door. Suddenly she stops. Things are stock still. I remember Lois saying, "God's ways are not our ways." Dead quiet. Calm. The ringing, the moaning, in my ears has stopped. I look at LaDell's. His chimney shudders. Out back is the shell of the moon, what is left of it. It could be God's fingertip. Neighborhood dogs bark. Seeds gives me her pork eye, and I say out loud, "Orem is the end of the world, François."

Overhead, barefooted Bowler stirs, and behind me the Wasatch Fault grins.

ELEVEN

Windows on the Sea

LINDA SILLITOE

Strange that the world looked reassuringly the same although Lora Starkham would never look the same to the world. From the stocking-lined mask fitted over her face like a cat burglar, her gray-green eyes observed the traffic around the sunny atrium on the hospital's seventh floor. She was newly grateful for her sight, for the fact that her eyes opened easily. She had been afraid for a time that her eyelids had melted, just as she knew the flesh over her cheekbones and chin had—we are, she observed wryly, clay after all.

Pleasant to sit in the sunlight and crochet with the big hook her seared hands could manage well. She idly watched the medical personnel and the patients in the halls, feeling invisible as only someone who is politely ignored can become. The visitors' occasional second looks at her swathed head no longer stung. She didn't blame them, considering herself the opposite of a blind uncle she had liked, whose emotions played on his face, visible to everyone but him. Besides, she was easily as relieved as the squeamish might be for the mask that postponed the day that her burned, refurbished face must meet air and eyes. Now she was between skin grafts, an ideal oasis, given her condition. The pain was manageable, allowing a private mourning.

Since this was a Sunday, her family would drive the 120 miles from Cedar Springs to Salt Lake City for a visit this afternoon. She would hear Brad's heavy heels crescendo down the hall, although Amy would probably appear first, Luci by the hand. Jake and Marcus would be quarreling without bitterness, ignored by Tim, who was used to it. Luci's red hair would flame like a candle, Lora thought; she envisioned that and the baby's face, bobbing over Brad's shoulder when he turned. She wanted Amber's arms around her neck, a longing tactile as hunger. Missing all of them ached at the core of her pain, yet visiting hours would leave her exhausted, worn by hugs. No kisses these days. No place to kiss.

Now noise of a different sort was approaching and Lora recognized it at once. The teenagers from the disturbed adolescents ward again, fierce in black leather, spiked and colored hair, dripping filthy language, calling each other remarkably hateful names with either venom or affection—hard sometimes to tell. As the clot of them rounded the corner of the atrium, Lora applied herself studiously to her crocheting. They appalled her. Their hostility and boisterousness reminded her why she and Brad had moved their family out of Salt Lake City before Amy began junior high school. Even in Cedar Springs, kids got into trouble, but there was not the drug traffic, the counter-culture, the preponderance of children who seemed to be raising themselves with only their fellow travelers in the streets and alleys for comfort.

"He-ey!" she heard one of them exclaim, as they caught sight of her on the couch, then some laughter before their voices and boot heels faded down the hall. Quiet again.

"I like it," a voice said a minute later, not loudly, but Lora jumped and looked up. One of them, a girl with blue and orange hair above black-rimmed blue eyes had held back and was lounging, hip out, behind the couch opposite her.

"Excuse me?" Lora said finally.

"I said I like it. Your head gear."

"Oh." Thank you seemed the wrong response. What did she

mean, she liked it? She waited for the girl to go away.

"You think I could get one?"

"Well, I don't know. Why would you want one?"

The girl sighed suddenly, came around the couch and sat down, thin knees apart in faded jeans. Her black jacket was slashed down one side and matched her short black boots. Lora watched her uneasily, but she seemed harmless, probably not that much older than her daughter Amy. For two months before Lora's accident, Amy had seemed to spend most of her time in front of the bathroom mirror.

"Seriously," the girl said now. "I would like a mask like that. Do you think you could get one for me?"

"I have no idea." A pause. "Are you making fun of me?"

The girl leaped up as if she'd been slapped, whirled, then turned back, her mouth curling downward on one side. "Of course, I could just do what you did to get one. Burns, right?"

"I don't recommend it. There must be an easier way."

"Good." The girl nodded formally, almost as if curtsying. "And thanks for not smiling." Turning gracefully in her motorcycle gang garb, she hurried after her peers.

On Monday Lora wept describing her family's visit, which had gone as usual—too short, too long, the tearing and relief when they left her there alone. Madeleine, the trauma therapist, softened her usual piercing gaze and laughed with Lora when she protested that she couldn't weep properly yet, since her tear ducts didn't work right. She was beginning to anticipate going home, sorting like so much laundry what her children's reactions might be when she wore her strange, new face to PTA meetings, to church, to the park on family outings. The mask first; then the face itself.

"They'd never hate me," she had told Madeleine before losing control, then noticed that Madeleine's eyebrows, always sensitive to nuance, rose.

"What did I say?"

"You said they'd never hate you."

"Oh, hurt me I mean. I meant to say they'd never hurt me."

Madeleine considered. "Hate me is what you said. Maybe you're more deeply concerned than you like to admit."

And that was when she'd started to sob, not at all like the mother she was, but heart-brokenly, as Luci had when her kitten ran into the street.

Lora felt better afterward, all cried out. "Sometimes," she commented, as Madeleine glanced discreetly at the clock on the wall behind her, "I really want to wear this stocking mask forever." That reminded her of the girl in the atrium on Sunday who wanted a mask also, so she told Madeleine about her encounter.

"A thin girl with blue eyes? About five feet tall?"

"Yes. Blue and orange hair."

"The hair changes by the day, sometimes by the hour. She's my client, too. Can you tell me what she said?"

Lora recalled for Madeleine how the girl had pressed her for a mask like her own, developed to apply light pressure to burned tissues and prevent excessive scarring. "A pretty weird request, isn't it."

Madeleine seemed lost in thought. "Maybe." Her hands turned the papers on her desk, then she asked crisply, "Well, do you think you could get one for her?"

"I don't know. Why?"

"Just a hunch. She isn't doing well in therapy, and she's very troubled. If this is something she wants, maybe it will lead somewhere."

"But if you requested it from the staff," Lora began.

"She asked you," Madeleine said, the piercing look back again. "Maybe you can become a friend. She needs one."

So do I, Lora thought, but not a disturbed alien from another planet, a prospect that weighted her steps back to her room where she fell immediately into a sound sleep.

The next afternoon in the atrium Lora gave Pril—that was her name—the soft stocking worn inside the mask next to the skin. Pril fondled it reverently, but her mouth was snarly. "Did you swipe it?"

"I asked for an extra so I could change it myself if I slopped a little food on it." It had taken far more explanation than that, but

Lora didn't elaborate.

Pril nodded. "You didn't say what happened to you."

Lora waved a hand resignedly. "We were up the canyon the week before the Fourth of July. My four-year-old, Luci, came back to where we were toasting marshmallows carrying some fireworks in her hands—Roman candles, giant firecrackers, I've never been sure. Brian and I both yelled at her to stay back, to put them down, but there wasn't time even to slow her down, she was that excited. I felt frozen there by the fire, but I did grab them out of her hands and turned to throw them just as—"

"Pow!" Pril exclaimed.

"Exactly." Lora folded her hands under the pink yarn on her lamp. They hurt and trembled. Pril was silent for perhaps three minutes.

"Sometime," she said shyly, "maybe you could come to my room." Lora was glad the mask hid her surprise and a little annoyance. "I'll perform a meditation for Luci," Pril added, then jumped as a black hand snaked down and flipped a long cigarette butt out of the ash tray. A boy, clad entirely in black except for a red band around his head, smacked his lips at Pril, ignoring Lora. "Hello, Slime-sleaze," Pril said bitterly as he plopped his other broad hand on her small shoulder. She wound an arm around him, and they sauntered toward the elevator, the contraband cigarette entering his back pocket.

"Why Luci?" Lora asked Madeleine later, catching her at the nurse's desk in the burn ward to tell her about Pril's conversation. "Luci didn't get hurt."

"I don't know. Maybe she thinks that Luci assumes blame for your injury or that you blame Luci."

Lora shook her head. Even in her worst hours, she had been grateful that Luci was not the victim. That would have been infinitely harder to bear. "So strange," Lora mused. "She said maybe I could come to her room and that she would perform a meditation for Luci."

She looked up to find Madeleine staring at her. "She said you could come to her room?" Her tone sounded disbelieving.

"Yes. But should I?"

Madeleine shook her head. "Lora, Pril's room has been off limits to everyone, including the hospital staff. If anyone invades it she becomes almost catatonic. She has the only private room in that whole ward, possible because there are only three girls now and two of them room together. If she'll allow you to go to her room, by all means go."

Suddenly Lora wanted to go back to her own room and watch something bland and nonsensical on television with her roommate, who had the set on eighteen hours a day. "You make me feel like a spy."

Madeleine took her arm and walked down the hall a few steps. "It's deceptive," she said, "when you see these kids roaming the halls. They've progressed enough to earn that privilege. But they are disturbed, all of them, certainly Pril. How can you be a spy if you help her in ways none of us have been able to so far?"

"Why me?"

"I've considered that," Madeleine said. "Certainly she doesn't warm up to me. Is it because you're so naturally a mother? Or because she sees you as a victim, maybe a fellow victim? Or maybe it is something about your mask. She isn't afraid of what she'll read on your face."

"Does her family visit?"

"We begin family group therapy at our evening session tomorrow night. Pril hasn't been eager to see them. Most of our kids here aren't. War at home, you know." She patted Lora's sleeve and hurried away. "Got a meeting."

Wednesday evening Lora positioned herself outside the small auditorium where a sign announced a family therapy meeting. She took up her crocheting and prepared to scout out Pril's parents. In her bag between the pastel yarns lay Pril's invitation, penned neatly in schoolgirl cursive. "Please come to my room, Windows on the Sea, tomorrow promptly at 2 PM. My sincere best wishes, Pril." Underneath in very small print between very small parentheses were the numbers 737.

"Why do you call your room, 'Windows on the Sea'?" Lora

asked curiously when she read the invitation. "It's very poetic . . ."

"You'll see tomorrow," Pril had said, the words clinging to the corners of her mouth like cigarettes.

What Lora wanted to see first were the parents of these junior gangsters, Pril's in particular. They arrived in ones and twos, the black boy's parents easy to pick out, then the look-alike mother of a blond, heavy girl who always wore a red leather mini. Lora's heart went out to the mother, who looked both respectable and terrified— and very alone. Divorced? Lora wondered. Busy husband? Never married? What could keep a father away from a counseling session when his teenage daughter was hospitalized? Three other couples, one appearing to be a mother and grandfather, entered the auditorium before Lora saw Pril's parents coming and knew at once who they were. The features that on Pril were soft and pixyish—the cherubic mouth, despite its snarl, the upturned nose and eyes— were, on her father, boyish. A cute man, Lora decided; he looked accustomed to loving care and approval, she thought; maybe his mouth seemed a bit spoiled. Pril's mother was a large woman with a dark brown pageboy, apprehensive dark eyes, and a determined chin. Watching her, Lora could feel her worry and had a swift impression that these people were still shocked at the transformation of their sweet, smart daughter.

Pril's parents appeared to be the last couple, and as they approached the auditorium door, the patients filed past Lora and into the auditorium from the opposite direction without a glance to left or right. Lora saw Pril coming at the end of the line and gasped. The whole row of them looked armed for battle, leather, dye, and boots all in place, but Pril had somehow stuffed or shaped the stocking mask she obtained from Lora to resemble a helmet. Then as Pril smartly turned toward the door, Lora saw where today's paint job had gone. Thick red streamed down the bare backs of her legs, pooling slightly at her shoe tops. Lora's eyes flew to Pril's parents, staring aghast as Pril marched past Lora's line of vision. "Oh my—goodness!" her father breathed, looking to his wife for support. But she was following their daughter, both hands whisking aside tears.

Lora crocheted for some time after the auditorium doors closed, thinking over what she had seen. She felt sick, vulnerable. What children couldn't do to you! Had they no sense of how vulnerable a parent's love is? She imagined the yelling, the stony silence, the defiance or tears, storming behind those doors and had no desire to be in the lobby when the group dispersed. A little shakily she gathered her yarn and pattern and put them in her bag beside Pril's ladylike invitation. Tomorrow. Weary, she crept back to her room thinking that Amy was already fourteen—and Amy's mother was scarred for life.

During that first visit to Windows on the Sea, Lora was thankful she had brought her bag of handwork with her. She stood outside Room 737 for a few minutes contemplating the ceramic sign below the room number, deciding that Pril had created the graceful nomenclature in a craft class. The sign was pale azure with lettering carefully applied in dark pink, deftly outlined in vermillion. Nervously Lora lifted her hand and knocked. The door opened.

The room Lora entered was all white—white walls, white ceiling, white tile floor, two white bunks built into the walls. The pillows and sheets were white, and a small, high window caught the pale summer sunlight and threw it back into Lora's eyes. Pril motioned her to sit down on one bunk, then tiptoed to the far corner of the room and performed a pirouette. Lora sat, her eyes on the apparition in front of her. Pril wore no makeup. Her skin was clean and light pink, her brows and lashes barely visible, soft blond like her hair. She wore a light pink leotard, tights, and ballet shoes. Altogether she was a vision. Lora was speechless, but Pril didn't seem to mind. She hummed as she curled into the corner of the other cot and smiled.

Finally Lora reached into her bag and took out her crocheting, an afghan that was almost finished. "You know," she began, hoping her voice sounded conversational, "you look awfully nice like that."

Pril's eyebrows raised slightly in amusement? scorn? appreciation?

"I've wondered—is Pril short for April?"

Now Pril uncurled like a cat and twirled away from the cot

singing (to the tune of "Frere Jacques"), "Princess Prilla, Princess Prilla, Here's your prince. Here's your prince. Prilla is my sweetheart, Prilla is my sweetheart, I'm her prince, I'm her prince."

She ended poised like a doll on a jewelry box. Lora applauded lightly then added, "Oh, Prilla. What a pretty name."

Pril sighed and sat down. A silence followed.

"Pril, what do you do with your time when you're not in therapy or a workshop?"

"Time for you and time for me," Pril said softly, "And time yet for a hundred indecisions, And for a hundred visions and revisions, Before the taking of a toast and tea."

She wandered restlessly for a minute while Lora tried to place that bit of poetry and wondered what it meant to Pril. She had studied it at some point, she knew, but for Pril it seemed precocious.

"Is that Eliot?" she asked finally. Her college poetry class had been a long time back.

Pril smiled then frowned. "Do I dare disturb the universe? In a minute there is time for decisions and revisions which a minute will reverse."

"I remember that one," Lora said. "At least I think I do. Isn't it Eliot's poem about the cat, the fog? What's the name? The line that's stayed with me is, 'I have measured out my life with coffee spoons.' Except for me, I suppose it would be baby spoons."

Pril was pacing now, a little agitated. "And I have known the eyes already, known them all . . . ," she added, spinning toward Lora accusingly. "The eyes that fix you in a formulated phrase."

The next words popped into Lora's brain and she said them quickly. "And when I am formulated?"

"Sprawling on a pin! When I am pinned and wriggling on the wall, then how should I begin to spit out all the butt ends of my days and ways!"

"Pril," Lora said, rising, "Pril, don't cry." But Pril spun past her to the window and stood staring out.

Lora took up her crochet hook again and waited. As minutes passed it occurred to her that Pril had not said so much as a sentence of her own. Everything had been verse. After a while she said, "Pril, tell me. Are you upset about the family therapy session last night? I imagine that might be pretty tough."

"I should have been a pair of ragged claws," Pril told the window pane, "scuttling across the floors of silent seas."

"She was like a chrysalis," Lora reported to Madeleine late that afternoon, "pink, newly formed, graceful. She spoke poetry, she danced, she almost cried. She's a beautiful girl, not a hoodlum."

Madeleine listened, clearly impressed. She shook her head. "Poor Pril," she said. "She's like a stone in here—and how did you like her getup last night? You know, now that I think of it, she may have quoted something from that same poem to me once. Which one is it?"

"I looked it up in the big literature book I had Brad bring from home. 'The Lovesong of J. Alfred Prufrock.'"

Madeleine turned to the marker, leafed through the poem and nodded. "Yes, here it is." She looked up, her eyes amused. "Last week when we finished what I thought was an unusually probing conversation—at least I thought we got somewhere—Pril flounced to the door, turned, and said, 'That is not it at all, That is not what I meant, at all.'"

They both laughed. "But what is it?" Lora asked. "I saw her parents. They aren't monsters. What's upsetting her so horribly? She's not crazy?"

A shadow crossed Madeleine's eyes then, and she drew back a little. "She's not responding to therapy. She's protecting someone, maybe her whole family. Her being freaky may be the only way for those she loves to survive, or so it seems to her subconsciously."

"But—" Lora began.

Madeleine shook her head and picked up Lora's chart. "So you have skin grafts Monday and then, in a few days, you'll be out of here. We'd better have you ready for that homecoming."

"Yes," Lora said. "I'm trying to get ready."

That night Lora dreamed she was at church with her family. The children were seated all down the pew with Brad at the other end, holding Amber. But no, they weren't all there. Amy was up in front with two other girls her age, who were warbling a hymn. But Amy was belting that song Cindy Lauper had made popular, "Girls Just Wanna Have Fun." Her lank hair had been wound into fancy coils and braids, her glasses hung on a black chain around her neck, her skinny little waist showed between a halter top and shorts that looked so small that even in her dream Lora believed they must be Luci's. Suddenly Lora realized that Luci and the other children were smiling at Amy, cheering her on, to the horror of the other parishioners. "Children!" she whispered, but they turned their faces steadfastly away from her, refused to see, refused to hear. Knowing she was the cause of this uproar, she awoke shivering in her hospital bed.

Lora visited Windows on the Sea again, but this time she did not try so hard to engage Pril in conversation. Lora had a new project, a white quilt top she was edging in blue, this time with a smaller hook—more difficult to wield. Their next-door neighbor's daughter was expecting a baby soon, and Lora wanted to give this former babysitter an unusual and personal gift. Pril seemed at ease, stretching quietly on the other cot, then polishing her nails with clear polish, then simply staring at the ceiling. "I'm going to miss you Pril," she said finally. "Sometime next week, after my skin graft, I'm going home. Will you write?"

Pril said nothing but stood and stared out the window.

Lora began to gather her things. It would soon be time for dinner and she was hungry. "You'll probably go home before too long," she suggested.

"Pril-la come and dance with me," she heard then and straightened to see Pril curtsey to an imaginary partner. "Both my hands I offer thee." Her hands extended, eyes glazed, Pril was facing but not seeing Lora. Her next gesture was sexual, almost obscene. "Right boob first, left one then; Daddy's girl comes home again."

Pril was still crouched in a bow as Lora, trembling, let herself out the door. Tomorrow, Sunday, she would see her family; the next day, surgery. She walked to the nurse's desk and asked if they would page Madeleine to see if she happened to be anywhere in the hospital. She was.

"Incest!" Lora announced to Madeleine. "That's what it is!"

Madeleine shrugged. "Likely. And she has a younger sister to protect, with two brothers in between."

"I've been sitting here putting things together and I'm furious. You really think that's what it is, why Pril's . . . ?"

"Incest is more common than you think," Madeleine said. "Nobody's admitting it yet, and maybe it's never been fully expressed, but I'm meeting with Pril's parents separately this week."

"But I'm going home next week," Lora said numbly.

"And you have your own problems," Madeleine said. "You have to keep Pril in perspective."

"Thanks Doc," Lora said and sank back on to the pillows. She doubted she would sleep.

"So, when do you check out?" Pril drawled out of the corner of her mouth, dropping down on the sofa opposite Lora, who was waiting for her family.

"It depends on how the skin grafts go tomorrow. Will you write to me?"

Pril shrugged and flipped a booted ankle up on one knee. "I'm not much with words."

Lora almost laughed. "I think you do all right."

Pril scowled. "Can you keep your mask?"

"For a while. I don't know how much longer."

Pril blew upward at the bangs on her forehead and sighed. "So I guess you just can't wait to get home, right?"

"Yes and no. In some ways it will be hard."

The scowl stayed, but Pril began nodding slightly. "Yeah. Me too. Like, I know my dad needs me."

"Mmmm," Lora agreed carefully. "And your mom?"

"My mother was always fighting for me," Pril growled, getting up abruptly.

"Good for her."

Pril wheeled. "What? You fight with your kids?"

Lora took a deep breath and tried to sound as level as Madeleine would. "That's not what you said, Pril. You said, 'My mother was always fighting *for* me.' And I saw your mother. I think that's probably true."

Pril arched like an offended cat. "So screw you, Lora. Mothers always stick together, right?" She flounced away.

Lora's family came and went, then the anesthesiologist, the surgeon, Madeleine, and in the morning all of them again. Time drifted, and she with it, in and out of mists and dreams, familiar now from the weeks after her accident and the surgeries that followed. Once or twice she thought Pril drifted through the mist, but words were bright kites with hairlike strings; she could seldom catch one and pull it in before it blew past her.

Wednesday came sharp and clear. Lora showered, ate, talked with the surgeon and Madeleine, walked twice through the halls, then returned and reached for her tote bag. She sorted through it twice before she realized that the white quilt top, now halfway edged with blue, simply wasn't there.

Of course, she knew at once where it had gone. She hurried down the hall toward the disturbed adolescent ward, anger quickening her steps. The anger felt good, a righteous indignation toward all the wrongs of children toward parents, the careless pranks and thoughtless acts that betrayed in an instant years of devotion. Rounding the corner she paused at the drinking fountain, fingers shielding the edges of her mask. She reminded herself as she drank the icy water until her teeth ached that she should not, could not, let what might be her parting incident with Pril be a sour one. She must find some way to let her know that stealing her work was unacceptable but that she was still accepted. Maybe, she thought, her anger lightening, she could find out why Pril did it.

She stood outside the door, admired the ceramic sign again, then tapped lightly.

"Pril, it's Lora."

Cautiously Lora opened the door slightly, then more. She could see Pril's bare leg and foot prone and pale on her cot. Her heart leaped, and she shoved the door open wide, bursting into the room in one motion. But Pril was only asleep, sound asleep, and nude. Draped across her, one corner tucked under her chin, the other in her crotch like a diaper, was Lora's quilt-top, except that now it was lurid with color, defaced as Pril often defaced her body, her hair.

Why? Lora wondered, outraged on behalf of the blue crocheted edging that had been so difficult to accomplish with the small hook and her injured hands. "Pril!" She stepped closer.

Pril was breathing as steadily as a baby. Close up, Lora could see words on the fabric, colored in Pril's neat cursive. Tipping her head, she could read a few. "Always Fighting For Me." So she had taken that sentence Lora had challenged her on back to her room. This sentence didn't rhyme or chime except—maybe—with truth. Beneath it Pril slept like a soldier wrapped in her flag. Markers littered the foot of the bed.

Lora looked up and away as her eyes burned with the tears that still couldn't quite flow. Outside Pril's small window, the sky was a flaming glory, and Lora stood on her toes, knees pressed against the cot for a better look. Purple and gold streaks soared above an improbable peach glow at the horizon. As she watched, the lower rims of the high mauve clouds singed like brimstone, then billow after billow caught and flared. Minutes passed before she realized that the igniting rays flashed upward from the salty lake, a thin, silver streak she hadn't noticed before at this distance. Pril's slight snoring underscored Lora's breaths that drew in color and light, spilling all her eyes couldn't absorb like a blessing on the girl beside her. What if I had lost my sight, she thought, and missed this?

How many evenings, she wondered, had Pril knelt on her bed to watch this long embrace of sun and lake? Often enough to name her room Windows on the Sea; frequently enough to sanctify this cell that beamed scarlet from its vacant walls to poetry and motion. Enough to let the girl within the scaly armor emerge and shine.

Lora considered the quilt-top again. Finally she selected a blue marker from the foot of the bed. She stooped beside the free corner of the quilt. "For Pril," she printed neatly, "with love, because we're both finding our way home."

TWELVE

Woman Talking to a Cow

PAULINE MORTENSEN

I had to leave Judd and Eileen in the house to come out and carry hay. I had to leave them alone and come out. I know you don't mean anything by it because you got to eat, too, everybody does. But I'm just saying. Everybody's got to eat.

And then there's this here manure fork. See it? Only three tines. You think you got problems. See that? See how it takes me so long? Hay falls right through. Don't blame me all the leaves knocked off by the time I get here. It's not my idea of how to do things. And you can just keep your green tongue to yourself.

No, it's not my idea. What we need is a barley fork. But can we have a barley fork? No-o-o-o. We ain't good enough. I said to him, "Alton, when we getting back our barley fork? Ain't we got as much use for it as Harmon and Clive?" And do you think he'd listen? Do you think he'd stand still for me going over there and getting it, when we could use it right here? His head holds onto an idea about as good as this here fork.

Now watch this. See, what did I tell you? But that ain't the half of it. After this I gotta feed those sheep. "Feed my sheep," he says just like that and walks out the door like he was Christ himself.

Going into town to make some miracle happen, he is. And Judd and Eileen in the house while I'm out here.

That Eileen better mind what she's doing, is all I can say, or I'll blister her good. She can get into more trouble, likes to throw the dishes out of my cupboards, my best dishes, Grandma's flur-de-lees. She climbs up the front like it was a ladder. Throws them down to show Judd. I could beat her brains out. And Judd just one year old, getting the biggest kick out of that. My best dishes with the gold leaf. She's a climber, all right. Boy, can she climb. But I'll blister her good if she does it again. And I will too. I got to do it. She has got to learn.

Don't you maw me. I'm doing the best I can. All you gotta do is stand there. I have to keep after her. She's always into something. Like throwing my pictures into the fire. My pictures of down home. Negatives and all. And there them two were sitting in front of the stove watching them pop and crackle. Little shits. I could have skinned her alive for that one. She always goes for exactly what you don't want her into. She was old enough to know better, too. I wanted to skin her alive.

You think *you're* standing in the mud. You don't know much about Karakul sheep, do you? Them are those black curly sheep over there. Each one worth about ten of you. That's 'cause they're special. No everyday sheep for us. No sir. We couldn't put our farm money into anything like potatoes or sugar beets. He doesn't listen to me. No, we had to get Karakul sheep. Going to make a killing with those sheep. We made a killing, all right.

Here chew on this. First he gets this special deal on a herd of fifteen sheep. He puts every cent we got into them. I feed them right here one whole winter. Come spring he finds out something. You know what he finds out? The wool on his sheep ain't no good because they're mixed breed. And to make any money you have to have pure breed. And we got fifteen sheep of Karakul and something else. But does he give up on the Karakul sheep business? You can bet your cow cud he doesn't. No. He trades those fifteen sheep down to six. Those right over there. And he called that a deal. Traded the whole herd for six. But they were purebreds. And I was just a woman and couldn't understand a deal like that, now could I?

Now come spring again, he finds out this: each one of them sheep eats two tons of hay a day for the entire winter, and we can't sell that wool. That's right. Do you know why? We can't sell it because Karakul sheep don't shear like regular sheep. No. To make them curly black coats for all them women back East, those hundreds and thousands of women dying to buy our wool, you gotta get the wool off of the lambs. That's the finest quality, the fine black wool before it gets coarse. That's what you gotta do. Take it off the babies. And that's what he finds out come spring. And he gives me this here manure fork with only three tines. Move your damned head.

You don't seem to understand, do you? They make those women's coats out of their black curly hides. You gotta skin them to get it. And Alton, he don't find that out until he's got all the money spent. They don't want the grown-up coarse wool. They got to skin the lambs. Peel off them hides no bigger than puppies.

But this is the last thing he finds out. Neither one of us has got the stomach for it. Killing the babies. So we got those six sheep over there eating us out of house and home, and we got a fistful of black curly hides drying hard in the barn, and we got two kids in the house breaking everything I got and waiting to be fed, and we haven't got enough of those black curly hides to make one coat.

And he goes off like that to crack one more deal. Listen here, old gal. You got your nerve to lick my leg and want more hay. You're the last thing on this farm that's worth a damn, so you just better look out.

THIRTEEN

Benediction

NEAL CHANDLER

Ardmoore told Carmen Stavely, who'd been away in Idaho visiting family, that what happened that Sunday morning was absolutely confidential. The bishop had instructed all who'd been present to keep the matter strictly to themselves; and he, Ardmoore, did not think (though as usual his optimism was naive) that more than a very few people outside the ward were acquainted with the details. As for himself he had not been present, had not, therefore, been warned or instructed by the bishop, and was reporting only what he could not help learning from the entirely unsolicited accounts of others. If what he told her was not in all respects consistent, Ardmoore would have been the first to confess confusion both at the contradictions and at the ardor with which each teller insisted upon the complete accuracy of his or her own version. Fortunately there was general agreement on the basic sequence of events. The incident had occurred on the fourth of five Sundays in May and thus marked the fourth appearance of Brother Kevin Houston as the new gospel doctrine teacher.

The partitions in the multi-purpose room had been pushed back all the way and propped with metal folding chairs because, unfortunately (or providentially—here the opinions were as sharply as they were unevenly divided), Sister Reeva June Parish, who teaches gospel principles, had been home again with mono, and all her neophyte faithful and her missionary-surrounded investigators had come on over to hear Kevin.

The truth, as Ardmoore well knew, is that most of those people would have been there even if Reeva June, bursting with good health and sound principles, had put in her scheduled appearance. Reeva was sweet, but Kevin Houston put on a truly spectacular show. And in four weeks word-of-mouth had already made gospel doctrine a standing room sellout. With the exception of Ardmoore, who tended the flame in the clerk's office, and of the other bishopric members, whose reliable absence was a matter of form and tradition, almost everyone thinkable had been in that class, including, as is now well known, Damon Boulder himself, who had not set foot in the class nor in the church, for that matter, the entire four weeks since his own formal and unbidden release as gospel doctrine instructor.

Now Damon must have come early because he'd sat in the next to last row near the door. For the most part, people said, he was quiet and uncharacteristically reticent to speak or to take part unless called upon. But perhaps, as some now insist, he was only playing possum, biding his time, waiting. On this hotly contested question of premeditation, however, Ardmoore was himself unwilling to express an opinion, and it is perhaps important, before we go any further, to point out that Ardmoore had always really rather liked Damon Boulder; that he had, in fact, defended Damon at the very ward council meeting in which Bennett Sarvus, practically as his first official act as newly installed Sunday School president, had recommended Damon's release.

Leaning back and pulling lint from the cuff of his blazer, Bennett had mentioned almost offhandedly that Boulder had now been teaching the adult class for over a year. Surely it was time to release him with many thanks and to offer him some new challenge in the ward. There followed several nodding, lip-pushing, "well, why not" seconds from among those present, but practically no one was taken in by this careful show of nonchalance. Bennett and his seconds had just declared war.

Utterly predictable pockets of guerilla resistance quickly formed up and returned fire. In particular the militant and military-looking Marvin Chisolm led the counterattack. Marvin was the ward liberal, an unabashed Democrat rendered respectable by his brahman Utah roots and successful consulting business. He wore his expensive, Ivy League education openly with his mustache, his penny loafers, and his herringbone jackets. In church his schooled reverence for the rigors of academe took the general form of irreverence for the popular accommodations of faith. In a tone of purest acid he declared himself: (1) entirely satisfied with the present teacher and (2) categorically opposed to any change that might, in Marvin's own term, "further abet the already rampant and reprehensible 'Koo-laidization' of Mormon theology." Even Ardmoore said, in a conciliatory tone, that it seemed to him a shame in a New Testament year to let go the only teacher in the stake who read Greek and who had some formal training in ancient scripture.

By this time, however, Bennett Sarvus had come to full attention atop the powder blue sofa on which he was sitting, and he began to speak with a hushed gravity quite beyond his twenty-five and a half years. Precisely this, he explained, was the problem. Brother Boulder had, it was true, a great deal of worldly learning—which was no doubt commendable in its place, but at the same time he openly spurned the authorized lesson plan, and, in fact, when President Sarvus had gone personally to inquire after the manual, Damon, who couldn't even remember its title, had had no idea at all of its whereabouts, except to say that perhaps it might be "somewhere in the car." As everyone well knew—that meant somewhere awash in the ragged sea of books and papers spilling around the back of Damon's wheezing, barnacled, 1963 Plymouth station wagon, a brontosaurial conveyance bizarrely adorned with seraph's wings that Carmen Stavely's own husband Walter and the boys in his Scout troop gleefully referred to as "The Fourth Nephite." It was also common knowledge that Damon's lessons were, in fact, taken largely from whatever obscure, uncorrelated, probably even foreign and idolatrous book he happened to be pouring over at the time. More than a few people, especially established, full-blood Saints who were not afraid to speak out behind his back, complained that he talked over the heads of new members. He loved Latin words and questionable or extreme ideas, and though, yes, Damon Boulder had a great deal of worldly knowledge, Bennett, whose own field was information management, felt compelled to point out that raw, unmanaged, uncorrelated knowledge was not unlike raw weather or raw language or for that matter raw sewage. It posed a serious environmental hazard, in this case to the fragile spiritual ecology of the ward. Hadn't the scholars and intellectuals among the Jews managed with all their learning to befog the very light of Christ? Bennett, for his part, was not anxious to follow their example in the Sunday school for which he was now personally responsible.

He finished on a note of such sincere and impassioned concern that the room fell into a kind of rhetorical arrest. Even Boulder's angry supporters sat as if molded in aspic. And Ardmoore, embarrassed at his earlier comment and obvious shallowness, stared through the carpet at his feet. The bishop, however, shuffled restlessly and then coughed for attention.

"Look Bennett," he said, "I've been through all this before." And indeed, over the years and at the behest of many, he had tried to shift the reluctant Damon Boulder from teaching into nearly every other thinkable kind of position. As a temporary Scout leader Damon had, with the saturnalian hubris of innocence, taken the entire troop skinnydipping in the pond at the stake farm. In the clerk's office he had actually, knowingly subverted certain statistical reports with figures taken, as he later freely admitted, from a table of random numbers. When questioned he explained guilelessly, but without repentance, that though doubtless inaccurate, his impossible numbers were certainly as useful and as significant as those called for in the reports. As ward in-service leader he'd cancelled four consecutive monthly meetings, only to occupy the entire hour and a half of the fifth reading long exhortatory passages from the *Journal of Discourses* with a bright, theatrical enthusiasm comprehensible solely to himself. He refused categorically to deal with the ward finances, insisting loudly that God and common sense forbade him to do so, and when called once, long ago, in a moment of sublimely naive inspiration to serve on the ward building committee, he had, while toiling faithfully and knowledgeably for a better than standard plan building, also written a light-hearted, fun-poking letter of complaint and suggestion to the Church Building Committee in Salt Lake City. Unfortunately, in that higher, thinner, "intermountain" air, every vestige of fun and good nature must have evaporated utterly from the document, for on its account Damon's then brand-new bishop suddenly found himself skewered and roasting painfully over the fire-red carpet in the office of a very angry stake president. It was a lesson he hadn't forgotten.

"I could call Damon to the bishopric." He paused, absently fishing broken animal crackers from the watch pocket in his vest while looks of horror sprouted around him like crabgrass in time-lapse. "But if I did he'd accept reluctantly and then celebrate by growing a full beard and what hair he has left to his shoulders." He looked up with a gesture of conclusion. "If the stake would let me do it, I'd retire and ordain him to teach mysteries to the high priests quorum. But since they seem determined he's going to be the oldest active elder in the church, I'm going keep him right where he is. He likes it, and as long as he's not teaching some open heresy or other, I like it too. A little, hard-core education isn't going to hurt anyone. We're just not used to it. If you think someone is seriously troubled," he added as an afterthought, "well, we have other classes, don't we?"

But the problem was that there were, in fact, no other classes. Reeva June Parish was, for reasons beyond her control, becoming seriously unreliable. And family relations was once again without a teacher, the last one having disappeared quite suddenly and in fact mercifully after the revelation of her imminent divorce. No one new had been called, and the bishopric's own wait-and-see footdragging was to blame. So it was not surprising or even unwarranted when, not many days later, a delegation of appropriately credentialed Saints went privately to the bishop's home.

In an old bathrobe he led them to the cluttered family room where he sat, almost primly for a man of his comfortable dimensions, staring resignedly at the crackled leather of his slippers while Sunday School President Sarvus, after apologizing for the hour, polled his militant companions and then closed with another, even more impassioned appeal for retrenchment in gospel doctrine. When Bennett had finished, the bishop without raising his eyes from his slippers took a deep breath and let it go. Then placing his hands on his knees, he thanked all present for their concern, stood, and left the room. According to Ardmoore, he must have gone straight off to bed without so much as a nodding farewell to his guests. The house beyond the family room remained dark and eerily silent. And when after much too long a time the bishop had not returned, the abandoned and incredulous party of kingdom patriots found its own groping way out of doors, there to caucus one more time in troubled whispers on the moonlit drive before disbanding stealthily into the night. The partisans were puzzled and pessimistically insecure about what their night ride had accomplished. Yet the very next Sunday the bishop himself, ignoring channels, called Damon Boulder in and told him he would soon be released from his teaching job in prospect of a weightier assignment. Ardmoore, who was in the outer office, swears that Damon Boulder laughed out loud. And this is not improbable, for Damon too had heard it all before. It may have seemed to him at first like a private joke between old friends until, of course, the handwriting would not fade from the wall. Then he just sat in glum silence while the bishop performed his rehearsed enthusiasms across the desk.

There is no doubt Damon took it badly. He stayed away four full weeks, reappearing, as everyone now knows, on *that* fateful Sunday. The news of his return could not have spread any more quickly if it had been posted on a billboard in the parking lot. And round Rachael Holbein, one of the midnight riders, made a point of stopping Kevin Houston in the hallway, taking his sleeve, and whispering with all the theatrical subtlety of a silent movie conspirator that Boulder was back. And indeed, since Boulder was not known as a particularly forgiving or deferential man, Kevin might well have been apprehensive; except, of course, that he wasn't.

Kevin Houston had that particular kind of self-assurance which in a secular and sophisticated world is taken as evidence of old money. In Kevin, however, whose prosperity was in fact nearly as green as the bank notes in his wallet, it signalled instead a kind of fore-ordination to the high, blood bureaucracy of Zion. He spoke in the accumulated ecclesiastical jargon of four generations. And his voice, as the cynical Marvin Chisolm delighted in saying, had the "perfect grain and color of simulated walnut formica." Moreover, when he took the stage in Sunday School, he left no doubt at all in any mind, not even Marvin Chisolm's, as to who among those players present commanded top billing.

"So you gotta follow the brethren?" The sentence sliced through the room at a whining pitch and decibel level that stunned the still-conversing class members into silence. Having thus seized attention, Houston, who had not even reached the front of the class, whirled on his heel and backed the rest of the way up the center aisle. "Is that right, Brother Zimmer?" A young man in a short-sleeved white shirt and blue tie came to attention. "Ya gotta follow the brethren?" Again Kevin whined the sentence out in a minor third so nasal and obnoxious that a newborn infant would have recognized it as a taunt.

"Well, I suppose." Zimmer, though reliable, was startled and embarrassed at an answer which, while clearly correct, somehow sounded ludicrous in the face of his interrogator's tone. Once having spoken, however, he immediately regretted his vacillation and as quickly repented. "I mean, yes! Of course!"

Kevin kept silent for a moment surveying the expectant class, then looked back to Elder Zimmer, now with a sardonic cast to his familiar smile. "Why?" he demanded. "You're an educated man, David." Zimmer shrugged. "Now don't be modest, a well-educated man, and you regularly study the scriptures? Does he read the scriptures, Ariel?"

David Zimmer's wife nodded vigorous confirmation. "He certainly does," she said.

"Well, I thought so. Now tell me this, Ariel. Is he a responsible man? Does he exercise good judgment in his work, for his family, in his church assignments?" Again Ariel's affirmation was aggressive. "Then why on earth should David Zimmer, a man of education, preparation, and sound judgment feel compelled to follow anbody's 'brethren'? Why don't those church leaders out there," he made a dismissive gesture in a vaguely westerly direction, "just leave him alone to follow his own gospel-inspired, common-sense course to salvation?"

As Houston turned from Ariel to the rest of his audience, the predictable hands already fluttered aloft. There was round Rachael Holbein; there were the Cutters, Sylvia Potter, Arlon Crisp, who was elders quorum president, and finally there were two of the six missionaries, all telegraphing urgent signals at the ceiling. But Kevin had something else in mind.

"Brother Chisolm, what do you think?" Marvin Chisolm had sat in class for four weeks now nursing a loud silence and an expression of weak nausea. It was time to call his bluff.

"I don't know, Kevin." Chisolm raised his eyebrows and lowered his voice so that the people behind him strained forward to hear. "I'm not even sure I know what 'following the brethren' means. Perhaps you could explain."

"It's obedience!" Rachael Holbein had read the lesson and could no longer wait to be recognized. She dashed in headlong. "It means obeying the commandments and always doing whatever you're asked." She sat back resolutely and folded her hands on the manual in her lap.

"When I do what I am asked," Marvin looked at Kevin and not at Rachael as he spoke, "I am being polite or considerate or accommodating. I am obedient on the other hand when I do what I am told. Perhaps that is what is meant. Perhaps urging us to follow the brethren is simply a euphemistic way of warning us to do what we are—"

"Now Marvin," Houston cut him off decisively at the offending verb, yet his tone remained as smooth and sweet as whipped topping, "do you suppose it is a simple thing to direct the affairs of a world-wide church of several million Saints?"

"Of course not." Marvin didn't see the point.

"We all know, Brother Chisolm, that you have had a good deal of administrative experience yourself. So let me ask you what sort of system, what method you personally would suggest to the brethren for governing the important spiritual and, yes, even temporal affairs of an organization of millions spread all over the world?"

Marvin, who had felt a little cornered by the relentless warmth of Houston's questioning, smiled an air-conditioned smile. "I'd teach them correct principles and then let them govern themselves."

"Well now, I think that's a marvelous answer. In fact I think it's just exactly what the Lord would have each and every one of us do . . . ultimately. But in the meantime, Brother Chisolm, tell me. How do you teach people those correct principles? I mean, how do you *really* teach them? And how do you get people and, believe me I'm including myself here, how do you get them to really govern themselves?"

When Marvin didn't answer immediately, Kevin bored in like a trial lawyer on a scent. "If we just talk to everybody, tell them about it, will that do it? If we just preach at 'em a little on Sundays, will they learn those principles, and will they live by them?" A snicker went through the class. "No one seems to want to say 'yes.' Well, why not then? What, when you get right down to it, is the only truly effective way to teach the gospel?" He turned to the blackboard and took a piece of chalk. "I think we all know that to teach effectively, we've got to teach by—"

"By the Spirit!" Rachael Holbein, the Cutters, and the missionaries, all bleated out in unison.

"Well, of course. Certainly, you've got to teach by the Spirit, now don't you?" And Kevin wrote SPIRIT in block letters on the board. "That's an excellent answer, and we're going to get right back to it too. But before you can teach by the Spirit, you've got to teach by something else first." He wrote again: EXAMPLE. "You've got to teach by example. Isn't that right, Brother Cutter?"

"Sure is," Cutter grinned. "Actions speak a whole lot louder than words."

"They certainly do. And if you've got to be an example in order to lead the people of God, then maybe it's about time we took a good hard look at just what kind of examples our leaders are." Kevin paused and paced slowly across the front of the room in apparent self-absorption, bouncing a piece of bright yellow chalk in the palm of his hand. When he reached the windows banked shoulder high across the mint-green cinder block wall on the far side, he stared out into the sunlit spring morning for a moment and then whirled, as if with sudden inspiration.

"Now take Peter," he announced, "the very first chief executive officer of the church, the George Washington of Christianity, so to speak. Now just what kind of a man was this Peter. Was he an all-American? Ask yourselves! Was he a genuine, all-conference, all-church champion, or was he just some guy off the street looking for a job? I mean," he raised his open palm to a vertical plane in direct line with his nose, "what do we really know about Peter?"

The class was a little stunned. And when no one showed any sign of responding, Kevin called on the elders quorum president. "Arlon?"

Arlon Crisp, who was in the habit of speaking before he thought, always divided his sentences into two distinct parts, a universal or boiler plate introduction and a more specific, though equally formulaic, conclusion joined by varying periods of awkwardly searching silence.

"Well, one thing we can say for certain," he began and then foraged his crowded mind several seconds long for whatever it was that could be so certainly said, "is . . . is that . . . that he was chosen of the Lord." He smiled. But Kevin was not buying.

"Oh no, Arlon, that's too easy. What we have to figure out here today is why the Lord chose Peter in the first place. What did this man have that someone else didn't? Was it prestige? Was it education? What did the guy do for a living?"

"He was a fisherman, wasn't he?" A very pretty young girl, a convert of only a week or two, spoke with soft hesitancy from the third row.

"A what?" Kevin put his hand to his ear.

"A FISHERMAN," the missionary on her right confirmed boldly.

"FISHERMAN?" Kevin's obvious incredulity made both respondents wince as if some terrible and terribly obvious mistake had been made. "You mean he didn't have a Ph.D. in religion? He wasn't an expert on theology? Are you trying to tell me that the man chosen by the Lord to preside over the church didn't have a doctor's degree or a master's degree or even a piddly little old bachelor's degree? Why, next you'll be trying to tell me, he wasn't even an intellectual, that he was some sort of simple, honest working man. Well, well. Well, well. Well, well." He spoke his "wells" in melodic pairs and crossed back to the other side of the room.

"Tell me," he re-addressed the third row in slow, dramatic dismay, "was he just any old fisherman? Do we know anything else about Peter?"

By this point most of the audience was beaming, though a few predictably, smoldered. None, however, was foolhardy enough to take up Kevin's newest invitation to dance. His sure orthodoxy was too subtle, too deceptive, too unorthodox. And though they loved (or loathed) the tune, no one had any further illusions about being able to mind the step. Kevin would have to answer his own question.

"Well, brothers and sisters, we know this much. We know he owned his own boat. Owned it outright. And he hired other men to work for him. This man they called 'the big fisherman' wasn't looking for any handout when the Lord and the church came along. He supported himself, supported his wife, his children. We don't know for sure how many he had, but you can bet your life he had more than two. Why, he even supported his mother-in-law. Now that should tell you something." Kevin paused for the accumulating appreciation to catch up with him.

"Now," he continued, "I'm going to tell you another thing, something not many people have figured out yet. Old Peter was a pretty darn good business man. When the Lord called him in to head up the church organization, he was already worth a considerable amount of money. He had a savings program. Made sound investments. He was a man who'd magnified his 'talents' (and some of you had better look up the real meaning of that old Jewish word in your Bible dictionaries).

"Now," he continued, "do you want me to tell you how I know about this, how I'm absolutely certain of it? Well then," he accepted the rapt silence as assent, "I will. If you'll take your Bibles and look up First Corinthians 9, verse 5, you'll find out that when Peter was called to go out and preside in the mission field, he took his good wife right along with him. Now in my father's family, as some of you know, we've had considerable experience in this area, and let me admonish all those priesthood bearers here today. Brethren, believe you me, you do not take your wife into the mission field unless you've first put more than enough money aside to support her in the manner to which she is bound and determined to remain accustomed. And that is the gospel truth."

When the laughter finally paled, Kevin became serious again. "In those rough, ancient times when thieves and shiftless beggars, when high-paid parasite priests and crooked, Roman tax-collectors were the norm, in those dark times, not unlike our own times today, here was a man who carried his own weight, who took care of his family, who got ahead in business, a man with the stature and with the financial means and know-how to truly serve his church. Now that's something we know how to appreciate even today.

"That man was as solid and reliable as a rock. And, in fact, my brothers and sisters, did you know that 'rock' is the very meaning of the name Peter, a name, by the way, which was not given him by any earthly power. Why, his parents thought his name was Simon." Kevin shook his head in good-natured recognition of human folly. "The Lord himself gave Peter his proper name when he called him to the work. Now, don't you just suppose that the Lord knew exactly what kind of man he was hiring. Don't you just suppose that when he gave old Simon Bar-Jona, that successful, self-reliant, maritime business man from Galilee, the name 'Peter,' he was sending you and me a message, telling us that here was the kind of a man the Lord is looking for, an ensign to the nations, an example to each and every one of us." A wry wrinkle gathered itself on one side of Kevin's forehead. "Or do you suppose he gave him that name just because he had nothing better to do on a Saturday afternoon?"

Kevin waited patiently until the familiar, if now more hesitant, hands began to collect in quantum spurts and flutters and then once again looked beyond them to the back of the room.

"Dr. Boulder, what is your opinion?"

The class froze. Kevin was having it all his own way. Chisolm was long since vanquished, and Damon Boulder's uncharacteristic silence seemed to confirm once and for all the calling and election of the new order in gospel doctrine. So why this? Why taunt the dragon?

Boulder himself seemed surprised. He sat a while thinking before he answered. "The giving of a name in itself is not really very remarkable, Kevin. It was a common practice for Jewish rabbis to give titles to their disciples, usually some word that pointed to promise in a situation or placed an obligation on the bearer. Christ, of course, did this more than once, and there are various examples in the Old Testament."

He paused and looked around. "As to this particular title, well, I really don't think it was a product of financial analysis, Kevin, nor of character analysis for that matter. In fact, it has always seemed to me more like wishful thinking. I, at least, would be hard put to think of a title less descriptive of the man's actual behavior."

"What do you mean by that?" Sunday School President Sarvus was standing in the back of the room where he had been watchfully presiding since shortly after the beginning of the lesson. The clarion annoyance in his voice sent a shiver through the more timid in the room, and attention closed in around the discussion like a crowd around the scene of an accident.

"Well," Boulder continued unperturbed, "he didn't show himself to be much of a rock, now did he? The man was almost fatally impulsive. When, for instance, Jesus called to him on the Sea of Gennesaret, he was all hot to get out and walk on the water, but two or three steps and his self-assurance collapsed. He nearly drowned. More importantly, he was the first and the loudest of the disciples to confess his loyalty to Christ, but we know he was also the first to deny him . . . and the most insistent. He had a temper. He was violent. Threatened people. Even cut off some poor fellow's ear. How often did he have to be slowed down, cooled off, rebuked? Oh, he mellowed as he got older, but he wasn't cured. Even after he'd been called to lead the church, he couldn't stay out of trouble. In fact, he got into so much trouble with the law in Jerusalem, he had to be released from that highly visible, presidential position and sent out into the boondocks to preside over a mission (an expedient by the way which is not unknown to the church in our own day). But in the mission-field, I think, Peter finally hit his stride. He was a great teacher, you know, a baptizer, and because doctrinal purity was far from chief among his passions, inside the church he became a capable politician. Perhaps the best she's ever had."

"Politician?" Kevin Houston, who had been listening intently, arched his eyebrows into pointed interrogatories.

"Certainly. Somebody had to mediate between those pureblood Jewish hardliners up in Jerusalem and Paul and his liberal rabble in Rome. No easy task, you can be sure, and no one to set him apart for it, but he carried it off like a ward politician with consummate pragmatism."

"With what?" Rachael Holbein had been lost for ten minutes. None of this was in the manual.

"Pragmatism, Rachael, consummate political pragmatism. Paul complains in Galatians that his old friend and fellow missionary Peter knows all too well which side his bread is buttered on. Oh, he's an ally of sorts. But when the occasion and the realities of power require, he is not in the least above dissembling and backing down to those starched bureaucrats in Jerusalem, even when doing so violates his own inner convictions. And that, for good or for ill, is political pragmatism."

"I don't understand." Bennett Sarvus broke in again, but this time directed his metallic gaze and his question to Kevin Houston. "Is Brother Boulder insinuating that the Apostle Peter was some sort of cheap political hack?" His measured enunciation and crystal tone made it clear that he was very upset.

"Oh no," Boulder quickly responded before Kevin might intercede, "he was a very fine politician, a very successful one. He did more perhaps than any other to keep an early and sorely divided church together, to prevent schism. And I don't think political successes like that come cheaply either. They are almost always bought at great personal cost. In a way that's Paul's point, isn't it? That too often we pay out again in personal integrity whatever it is we win for the integrity of the community? In any case I was only wondering out loud and at Brother Houston's invitation, of course, if perhaps in retrospect 'Simon Politikos'—Simon the Politician—might not have been a more accurate title and, consequently, higher praise."

Boulder leaned back in his seat with his face carefully blank and with an air of dreadful satisfaction. And indeed the marvelous spell holding the class enthralled before Kevin had so rashly conjured this spirit was gone. The crowd was visibly restless, palpably unsure and disoriented. Yet Kevin stood among the ruins of his Sunday School lesson as calm as a summer's morning. "You know," he said so quietly and with such intense reflectiveness that the class immediately forgot its agitated milling and whispering to listen, "You know, I think Brother Boulder is right."

Even Damon Boulder glanced up.

"I think he's reminding us that though Peter was a good man, a great man, a chosen man, he was not in fact a perfect man. Like you and like me, he was human. Isn't that right, Brother Boulder?"

Surprised at being invited back into the discussion, Damon nodded. "Peter shows us pretty clearly everything that the call to leadership involves in human privilege and weakness."

Pursing his lips, Kevin nodded. "Yup, there is certainly something to what you say. But you are wrong on one point, Damon—the point about the name, because the Lord knew exactly what he was doing when he gave that imperfect fisherman the name Peter. You know," his voice took on a sudden air of confidentiality, "when I was preparing this lesson, I ran into a real puzzle. I looked up that name Peter in a fancy dictionary I have at home. It's an old Greek dictionary. Now the New Testament was written in Greek. Isn't that right, Damon?" Damon nodded. "And in Greek the English name

Peter is spelled P-e-t-r-o-s."

Kevin wrote it on the board, turned, and winked at his audience. "You see, there's a bit of the scholar in some of the rest of us as well. And do you know, when I looked up P-e-t-r-o-s in that dictionary, it didn't mean *rock* at all. The real Greek word for *rock* is P-e-t-r-a." He spelled it out on the board and wrote the translation directly underneath. "So just what do you suppose P-e-t-r-o-s means?" He pointed to the still empty space under the first word on the board. And when everyone including Boulder remained silent, Kevin turned and wrote out the answer. "It means 'stone,' an ordinary stone.

"Now," he whirled and faced his audience with a bolt of new energy, "that might not seem like a very big difference to some of you, but think about it. What is a rock? I mean there's the Rock of Gibraltar and the Rock of Ages. There's the man who built his house upon a rock, and then of course there's the rock of revelation upon which the Lord has built this magnificent church. Surely a rock is something pretty big, pretty darn substantial. But if that's a rock, what then is a stone?"

For a moment or more he scanned the ceiling while he dug in his trouser pocket, then pulled a smooth round chip of shale out into the sunlight and held it up between his thumb and forefinger for all to see. "Now there is a stone, and a stone, my brothers and sisters, is also a rock. It's a little rock, a rock you can put in your pocket or skip across a lake. And so I asked myself, why did the Lord want to go and call that big, strapping, six-foot fisherman and business tycoon 'Mr. Simon Little-Rock'?" It puzzled me all morning long. And then . . . then suddenly, like revelation, it came to me that it was nothing so very remarkable at all, that you and that I, that all of us do the very same thing almost daily."

Kevin advanced to a still open expanse of the bright green blackboard. "Now, take a name, almost any name like Bill or Tom or Jim or even 'Rock.'" He listed the names in a column. "What do we call Bill or Jim or Tom before he's grown up, before he reaches the full stature of a man? Why, we call him Billy or Jimmy or Tommy." He added the diminutive ending to each name as he spoke it. "And we mean 'little Bill' or 'little Jim' or 'little Tom.' He's our 'little man' we say, just as those old Greeks could have told us that 'Petros' meant 'little Rock.' So you see, surely Peter was a rock. He was all rock, nothing but rock! Yet a rock, let's admit it, with a great deal of growing to do before he reached the full, magnificent stature of a perfected, celestial rock. Now doesn't that just make sense? I'll just tell you it does. I'll tell you, the Lord knows just what he's doing, and just exactly what he's saying. Doesn't he?"

Flames of affirming attention that had dimmed and sputtered now burned brightly again all over the room.

"And do you know, brothers and sisters, I pondered that name." He turned to the board and filled in the final "y." Then placing the chalk on its side, he drew a broad, yellow circle around the name. "'Rocky'. . . there's something special about that name, isn't there, something out of the ordinary? We don't just give that name to children. In fact we associate it with tough guys, with fighters, and with a special kind of indomitable spirit.

"Remember, back at the outset of class I said that we would get back to the Spirit. Well, I'm going to keep my promise, because recently I was taught something truly wonderful about spirit, something that has a tremendous bearing on the lesson the Lord wants us to learn here today. Recently I had the privilege of attending with my good wife the final in a series of three remarkable films, all of which, amazingly enough, bear that same name given nearly twenty centuries ago to an enterprising Galilean fisherman with tremendous celestial potential."

While Kevin underlined the crucial name once more on the board, Marvin Chisolm, his nausea and piqued impotence at full mast, twisted around nearly 180 degrees in place to fix Damon Boulder with fierce, "for heaven's sake, do something!" eyes. Damon, however, waved Marvin off with a gesture of hand-washing indifference.

"I'm sure," Kevin continued, "some of you saw those movies as well, but let me tell you about them. Let me tell you about a young man without education or wealth or worldly sophistication, without social position or powerful friends or political influence. Let me tell you how that young man, starting from the absolute bottom-most rung of a corrupt and indifferent sports world with only his vision, his pure heart . . . with hard work and an indomitable spirit to sustain him through setback and suffering, through temptation, trial and travail, when those nearest and dearest forsook him, when none believed in him or in his vision or in the transcending power of his spiritual resolve . . . let me tell you how that young man became a world champion . . . and how he endured to remain a champion, overcoming the fierce enticements of worldly success, overcoming even the brutal, crushing physical onslaught of a veritable angel of hell. Yes, let me tell you about a real man with real spirit."

And Kevin Houston told them. He told them the parable of "Rocky," the difficult core of an ancient story made plain and simple in the bright, allegorical shell of a new one. He showed them the Hebrew fisherman as a secret, inspiring foreshadow of the tenacious Italian Stallion, the triumphant Philadelphian in vivid similitude of the intrepid Galilean. And when he had finished his story, when he was done, somehow . . . somehow it was as if Rocky himself were right there among them, bruised, pummeled, punished, exhausted, and, yes, victorious, as magically, improbably, and inevitably victorious as virtue and goodness and truth.

Then after a moment Kevin Houston stepped forward into the idolizing hush and, like Dan Rather at the last day, drew the sum.

"So you see, brothers and sisters," his full, round baritone contracted to a flesh- and soul-penetrating whisper, "you see, Damon Boulder is right. The Lord cannot supply perfection in those all-too-mortal men he calls to show us the way. But he loves us, and because he loves us, he gives us instead the very best men there are."

Kevin paused and seemed to look every man, woman, and child directly and simultaneously in the eye. "He gives us champions, *world* champions of the spirit, heroes from his very own Righteousness Hall of Fame, to captain the team, to pace us on that straight and narrow course, to set the inspiring, endure-to-the-end example that God's loyal fans all over the world will follow to success, salvation, and celestial glory." He paused again with a fatherly and summarizing smile. "Peter may not have walked upon the water as the Lord did. But among mortals those two or three halting steps still make him the all-time, number-one, water-walking champion of the world. And that, Brother David Zimmer, my dear brothers and sisters, O ye nations of an unregenerate world, that is why we must all gladly, gratefully, humbly follow the brethren."

The ensuing silence was as tight and translucent as Jello, one of those sweet, shimmering moments that are a passionate teacher's only genuine wage. And Kevin Galinghouse Houston let it roll and glide and glitter voluptuously during the few brief seconds that remained before the final bell. When the bell rang, however, it found him alert and ready.

"Brother Boulder," there was honeyed olive branch in his radio voice, "would you please say a closing prayer for us?" The tactic was bold. Like a rabbit surprised in the brush, Damon Boulder seemed to shudder in his seat. Kevin meanwhile fixed him with gentle, "would you please" eyes. The day was won. It lacked only the formalities of concession. "Damon," he entreated, "we'd like your benediction."

Boulder made no move, though he stared back in what some have described as stunned disbelief. The many in the class who understood what was going on began to fidget. Yet Kevin only smiled with the long-suffering beneficence of a Buddha and waited.

After an agonizing silence, Boulder finally arose and made his way to the front of the room. When he arrived he seemed to have found his resolve and to the relief of everyone turned decisively and faced the class. With ritual solemnity he tilted his round face earthward and held it in commanding obeisance until all present fell into a cough-stifling, child-threatening silence. Kevin closed his eyes.

What happened next can be recounted. It cannot be conveyed.

"Give me an R." The words were spoken clearly enough but even so remained wholly unintelligible to a class poised comfortably over a familiar prayer wheel. "Give me an R." This time Boulder said it louder, and several listeners glanced up as a check against their obviously errant hearing. After the third time half the class was looking at him from under its still inclined eyebrows. "Give . . . me . . . an . . . R!" he intoned slowly, this time with pedagogical emphasis. Boulder was staring resolutely back at his timid onlookers with one fist raised to the height of his shoulder in punctuating encouragement.

At some point during the fourth incantation a light flickered, though oh so ephemerally, in the communal confusion. It flickered just enough to catch the attention of Marvin Chisolm, and then for Marvin alone it flashed again brilliantly. His head came up. His eyes cleared, and he came very near to raising his hand. "R," he stammered with experimental insecurity, and when Boulder cocked his head in recognition, he took courage and repeated himself with conviction, "R!"

Damon Boulder smiled. "Give me an O," he inveighed, raising his other fist, and Marvin Chisolm responded in tempo.

"O!"

"Give me a C!"

"C!" came the answer, and this time a second voice chimed in. It was the pretty young girl in the third row, so wide-eyed and freshly baptized that her name was still known only to the missionaries who hovered around her in dense-pack.

"C!" she sang out in a fresh, green soprano that took even Damon Boulder's breath, while the missionary on her right, the carefully combed and Old-Spiced boy who had baptized her, recoiled helplessly. His much younger companion on the left, however, joined with equally helpless enthusiasm in the response to Brother Boulder's subsequent calls for a "K" and then for a "Y."

"Y!" they all sang out, a chorus of three voices now, or as some insist four (though no one will name the fourth accomplice, and none has come forward to confess). But whether three or four, Boulder pushed them relentlessly on into the finale, raising his alternating fists in rhythmic emphasis, if also with the self-conscious awkwardness of a tubby and sedentary older man.

"Give me an 'R . . . O . . . C-K-Y!'"

The room reverberated with the answer, and Damon Boulder

stooped as low as he dared to rise up again with his revelers and with the trombone glide of the triphthong to a dramatic, tiptoe climax.

"YYYEEEEAAAAAA ROCKEEEEEEEEY!"

When it was all over, a matter of seconds, the entire cheering section was on its feet, though at the first poisonous look from his companion, the young missionary dropped back into his seat like a cinder block. Marvin Chisolm meanwhile trotted to the front of the room and grabbed Damon Boulder's hand.

"Now, that's spirit, Damon. That is definitely championship spirit!" He squeezed hard and then turned quickly to Kevin, who was off a little to the side in the strange, semi-crouched position he had assumed at the first words of Damon's benediction and had not abandoned. He looked strangely contracted. Marvin reached down a little and pumped his hand as well. "I think you've really taught us something here today, Kevin. Yes sir, and that is not an every Sunday occurrence." He pumped again and strode out of the room. The young lady meanwhile had disentangled herself from her gaggle of anxious missionaries and was pursuing Damon Boulder, who had already escaped down the hall. No one else had moved. No one.

It was quiet again, but the quiet was no help. The strange silence seemed to demand filling. And Kevin, though Marvin Chisolm seemed to have pumped him upright again, could find no words. He struggled, but the hundred formulae churning up from his mental archives filed back as mutely as they had come, and it was a long overdue release when Rachael Holbein broke for the door and scuttled sideways down the hall toward the bishop's office.

The rest of the story, the official aftermath, is of course sealed up in the records, and the bishop has expressly forbidden everyone, including Ardmoore, to talk about it. But there was one other thing, not a matter of record, which he confided to Carmen Stavely.

When he had entered the bishop's office just moments after the distraught Rachael Holbein had left it, he had found the bishop swaying precariously on his loudly squeaking, vinyl swivel chair, great round tears streaming down his flushed and helpless face. To the alarmed clerk he seemed out of control, as if he were suffering some terrible seizure, some convulsive and almost wanton attack of hysteria.

"Oh my!" gasped Carmen Stavely involuntarily. And when that same afternoon she recounted the entire affair to her closest and most trusted friend and then later, of course, to her family over dinner and at every subsequent retelling, she inaugurated her story with a heartfelt expression of concern for the bishop. "The poor man," she sighed with a grave, sympathetic shake of her head, "the poor, dear man." And then she paused for her listeners to look up expectantly.

FOURTEEN

Lost and Found

MICHAEL FILLERUP

Over the years he had tried all kinds of tricks to outfox it. He had eaten humble pie by candlelight in the dark privacy of his hovel while reading the nativity story from Luke. He had tried to lose himself in anonymous acts of service in the village. Once, in a fit of self-spite, he had driven two hundred miles into Gallup and gotten roaring drunk. Another time he had gone all the way to Flagstaff to sit through midnight Mass at St. Mary's Church—as a novelty and a diversion more so than religious devotion: he had his own church. Sort of.

Tonight he was going to drive to the top of the mesa in a snowstorm to rescue a beautiful young woman in distress.

Actually he did not know if she was beautiful. Nor did he know if she was truly in distress. Her foster mother in Phoenix seemed to think so. Her voice, scratched to obscurity by the crackling static, was controlled hysteria on the phone. "Well, we'd do just about anything to get her back." A telling pause. "Well, just about. I mean, we really want her back. Especially under the circumstances."

Her name was Loretta Yellowhair, and she had been missing from the Indian Placement Program since August. It was a mystery.

No one knew where she had gone, not even her natural parents, or if they did they weren't talking. But a week ago the caseworker had heard a rumor . . . .

"I guess what happened is that last winter was really hard on the family. A lot of sheep didn't make it. Loretta's mother got real desperate and borrowed a thousand dollars from some old fellow with the promise he could marry Loretta in exchange."

Another voice, Brother Myers's, interrupted on another line: "Yeah, if you could, we'd like you to intercept the old coot's pass, so to speak!"

Tom winced at the reference to old coot.

"The caseworker says Loretta can go back on Placement and finish up her senior year," Sister Myers explained, "but she's got to be in Phoenix by Tuesday morning for an interview, absolutely positively."

"Tuesday?" Tom said. "What's so sacred about Tuesday?"

Sister Myers chuckled, almost intimately. "Monday's Christmas, silly!"

"What's so sacred about Christmas?" Tom quipped. And he laughed. Once.

Sister Myers was silent.

"Sorry," Tom said, wondering who had given her his name and number. The missionaries maybe. Or the idiot caseworker. At moments like this he almost wished the Tribe hadn't put in phone lines a year ago. Electricity, yes. Running water, great. Telephones? They reduced his insularity. He could feel the outside world creeping in, tightening its noose.

Tom clasped his hand over the receiver and looked at his cat, an ornery old Siamese-and-something curled up on the rumpled bedspread that drooped to the warped floorboards beneath his metal frame bed. "What do you say, Nashdoi? You up for a little adventure tonight?" The animal didn't stir. Beside the bed was an old chest of drawers. A single light bulb burned in the cramped kitchen where a pine sprig in a glass jar served as Tom's token tribute to the holidays. Normally his quarters seemed warm and cozy, but tonight they felt dark and claustrophobic. Grim.

"I just hate to see it happen," Sister Myers said. "She's just such a wonderful girl—bright, gifted, a valiant testimony. I know it's Christmas Eve, but . . . ."

Tom unclasped the receiver and whispered into it, tentatively, so as not to arouse false hope, "Sister Myers, I'll do my best!"

"Oh, thank you, Bishop! We really do appreciate this!"

Tom winced again. He wasn't really a bishop but a branch president by default: he was the only ordained elder in the area. But he had retired from truly active duty years ago—he thought he'd made that clear.

He fed a couple sticks of juniper into the wood stove, turned the vents down low, and put on his Marlboro Country coat—suede with a sheepskin collar. He was tempted to bring Nashdoi along for company, but he didn't have the heart to awaken him from such a deep, exclusive sleep. He was a little jealous really.

Snow was falling lightly but steadily as his battered blue pickup rumbled past the trading post, a big stone box locked up for the night. The village was abandoned, a ghost town. Winter had pronounced it dead and tossed a white sheet over it. A pregnant mutt, her swollen teats dragging along the snow, plodded towards the rock schoolhouse where Tom earned his daily bread. About the only joyful thing in sight was the play of the snow in the lone security light. The dainty flakes were twisting and tumbling like gleeful little gymnasts. But even here he saw a tragic element in that they could just as easily be butterflies trapped inside a jar of light, trying desperately to break out. He could almost hear their wings beating frantically against the glass. Or was that his heart rap-tap-tapping, or his truck thumping across the cattle guard?

Or his heater? He flicked the switch and the little fan rattled like dice in a cup, spewing out lukewarm air. Up ahead he could see Hosteen's old hogan, a black face with a white helmet. Two years ago he would have asked Hosteen to join him. The old man had just the right touch of craziness for a wild goose chase like this—and it would be a wild goose chase, Mission Double-Impossible, Tom knew that. So why was he going? Well, boredom was a factor. (What else was on his agenda tonight besides huddling by his wood stove feeling sorry for himself?) And duty. (She was a lost sheep. It was his job to find her.) And, yes, there was curiosity too: who was this young beauty who commanded a bride price of a thousand dollars, a phenomenal fifty sheep in Navajo currency? He wanted to know.

Tom smiled recalling the way the old man's eyes used to peer out from under the flat brim of his black felt hat, the dark little orbs floating behind his Coke bottle lenses like jellyfish in formaldehyde. A fringe of silvery whiskers dripped from his gaunt jaw like pieces of clipped fishing line, and calluses doubled the size of his gnarled little hands. Tom had first met him twenty years ago while making home visits with the missionaries. Hosteen was limping out of his outhouse on skinny bow legs, zipping up his fly. One look at the missionaries in their dark suits and white shirts and he had grinned: "What are you folks doing, selling life insurance?" Tom had liked him instantly. Later when the missionaries asked the magic question—"Is there anything we can do for you?"—the wrinkled corners of the old man's mouth had twisted sardonically. He led the threesome back behind his hogan and pointed to a huge mound of piñon and juniper. "You folks can cut all that up for me. About this size," he said, spreading his hands shoulder width. "Better hurry, though. Sun's going fast." Hosteen used to say he didn't exactly believe in the old ways or in the new ways either. "I'm just a horse-teen of a different color," he would chuckle, punning on his Navajo name.

Tom tried not to think about Hosteen; it still saddened him. Somehow that, too, had been his fault. He turned his thoughts elsewhere. Sister Myers. He could still hear her voice crackling in his ear. "Well, they think she might be up to the mesa."

The mesa! Swell! Talk about a needle in a haystack!

"Or they say she might be staying with Louise Yazzie's brother-in-law. Do you know Louise?"

A needle in three haystacks.

Driving the desolate reservation roads on a winter night, Tom could go for miles, light years, without seeing anything but the infinite swirl of snowflakes. He was an astronaut hurtling solo through outer space, and the feeling could be terrifying or exhilarating, depending upon his particular state of mind. At that moment he felt neither terrified nor exhilarated, only a general desolation that always seemed to intensify about this time of year. The simple truth was, he really didn't much care what transpired tonight. He just wanted to get it over with, "it" being this night.

His front tire plunged into a pothole, rattling the truck and sending a shaft of pain into his lower back. Several years ago he had injured it falling off a horse, and now every little bounce or vibration was a voodoo pin in his fifth lumbar. Great, he thought. Swell. I'll be a pin cushion before the night's through.

The pickup crawled past the little trailer where for one hour every Sunday morning Tom went through the holy motions on behalf of old Sister Watchman and a few other faithfuls of the Bitterwater Branch of the Mormon church. Sister Watchman, who had no eyes to see but could weave an intricate rug of many colors, could also read the desperate scribble on his heart: "I feel sad for you, Hastiin T'aa geed 'Asdzani. You feed all these others, who will feed you?"

"My Heavenly Father," he used to say, but each time with a little less conviction.

Straight ahead a giant boulder was sitting comically atop a skinny spire like a giant head with a pencil-thin neck. Striped with snow, it looked like a weird giraffe-zebra hybrid straight out of Dr. Seuss. In the background, the mesa rose up like a great white wall. In the fuzzy snowfall it appeared to be wavering ethereally, as if any moment it might swell up and crumble down upon him like a tidal wave, or simply vanish altogether, like a mirage.

Tom wondered about Loretta Yellowhair. Who was this young Navajo woman in distress? "Yellowhair" would be a misnomer. Black hair, dark eyes. He tried to visualize her in his mind, but she remained as fuzzy and obscure as the falling snow.

"Distress" might be a misnomer as well. His personal feelings about the Indian Placement Program had always been ambivalent. The dark view held that Navajo children were being taken from their natural families so they could be transformed into white and delightsome little Mormons. The "inspired" view said it gave them a shot at a "real" education. Tom had seen both sides of the coin. Placement was a ticket out, but to where? Anything to spare them the boarding schools. Every year when his handful of little sixth graders graduated he felt an overwhelming sadness, as if he were sending them off to war. The girls would end up pregnant, the boys would come back little drunkards and dopers. Placement? Stealing their culture? There were six sides to that story. Ask Celeste Bighorse.

Tom had always been lenient on Placement interviews. If a kid had a shot, he wasn't going to nix it on a minor technicality.

"What church is this?"

A look of stupor. "Uh . . . Catholic?"

"Close enough."

The snow was falling so thickly now he seemed to be submerged in it. The pickup struggled along like a submarine in rough waters. His thoughts drifted back to the little church trailer he had passed a few miles back. A week ago Sunday, opening his official church mail, he was shocked to see his mug shot, albeit a very outdated one, on the MISSING PERSONS BULLETIN. By some computer glitch, perhaps the simple inversion of two digits in his social security number, church headquarters had failed to link one of their anointed local leaders with the black-and-white countenance on the bulletin. It had been sobering to see his face amidst the other Lost Sheep: teenage runaways with pimpled cheeks and hair in their eyes, a watermelon-shaped man who could have been his father, a jolly white-haired woman who reminded him of Mrs. Claus. Tom had always felt depressed when perusing these monthly alerts. Each face was a tragedy in miniature, a despairing tale of loss. He pictured heartbroken parents grieving for their prodigal sons, grown-up children searching desperately for crippled mothers and fathers on the run. Sometimes, studying the photographs, he would invent stories of his own, whole sagas and family histories. And sometimes, in the process, he would mentally rewrite his own. He occasionally wondered who, if anyone, might be grieving for him?

He had noticed a crucial difference between his mug shot and the others. They were accompanied by a brief physical description (height, weight, color eyes, color hair, distinguishing features), the location where the individual had last been seen, their hometown, and a contact person to call. His read, simply: THOMAS DAVID BARLOW 6/24/51. That was all. No contact person, no phone number.

Tom had recognized his high school graduation picture. The blond ponytail was gone now, and the cocky grin. His chiseled cheeks were padded, tanned and leathery, and his jaws were beginning to sag in the sad sack manner of Dick Nixon. Mentally he had updated his description: 5'10", 205 pounds, built like an over-the-hill linebacker. Hair (the surviving patches on top) like sun-singed grass. Hazel eyes—vacant. Twin flashlights with dead batteries.

His hands had trembled while handling the sheet of paper, as if ghosts or spirits had been captured on the page. On the one hand, it had been like reading his own obituary. On the other, it meant that someone, somewhere, was still looking for him. But who? His mother and father had gone AWOL before he could even walk. He had no brothers or sisters, no real family to speak of. . . . His father-in-law, maybe? Tom sneered. "You're a very intelligent young man, Tom. You're very smart. But you've got no heart. You're a taker, not a giver." That was the last thing Bishop Tyler (the *real* bishop) had said to him two days before Tom had eloped with his only daughter. She had liked him because he was a California oddball who was going to set the world on fire, although he wasn't quite sure how. She had liked him because her father hadn't. The bishop had mapped out his daughter's life a little too perfectly: temple marriage, kids, grandkids, death. Sorry, that wasn't Kathy. Of course Tom had had to be baptized and join the fold. Kathy was saucy and spicy and radical for her little Utah town, but she was still Mormon. "I want you forever," she had whispered during an erotic moment, "not just the here and now. Don't you want me forever too?" Sweet persuasion. Failing that: "Look, I'm not a one-life stand!" So he had played the game until it had become almost real to him.

He had promised her the sky but instead had given her Bitter-water, Arizona.

He switched on the radio. It spit and crackled. He should have had it fixed back in October. He fiddled with the knob, searching for a voice, any voice, but found nothing but fuzz and static, an audio version of the falling snow. He noted the permanent film of dust on the dash and the ever-widening cracks across the faded blue vinyl: they were tragic mouths, gaping wounds, sarcastic smiles aimed at him.

He tried to keep his eyes and thoughts on the road, but they kept drifting to Christmases past. One year—he was six or seven, he forgot exactly—but he was living with Aunt Margie in Del Mar and decided to play a joke on his cousins. He made them all joke gifts. They were poems: "Roses are red/ Violets are blue/ Christmas is dumb/ And so are you!" Stupid little ditties. Christmas Eve he placed them under the tree. But when he got in bed, something funny happened. Maybe it was the carolers outside. Or maybe Uncle Max had spiked the eggnog again. Tom wasn't sure. He just felt weird about it. So he sneaked out and took back all the joke gifts, and he trashed them.

Except he didn't get them all. He thought he had, but he missed Sherry's. She wasn't retarded, exactly, but she was . . . well, she was slow. Her present was buried at the bottom of the pile, and before Tom could stop her, she'd unwrapped it. She started jumping up and down, shouting, "A present from Tommy! A present from Tommy!" She gave it to her mother to read because she couldn't. Aunt Margie smiled at first, and then her face turned to mush. She gave Tom a dirty look but smiled at Sherry. And then she read: "Roses are red/ Violets are merry/ Christmas is here/ And I love Sherry!" Tom had never seen his cousin so happy. She threw her arms around him and danced and danced. He couldn't look at his aunt. He couldn't look at anyone after that. He just stood there feeling like absolute dirt.

It was the story of his life: big plans, big screw-ups.

Tom put his hand over the heater vent: still lukewarm. He should have had *that* fixed too. He could feel the cold creeping into his toes, slowly taking over. The steering wheel was turning to ice; his hands were stiffening. Why hadn't he brought his gloves? He always brought gloves—always! He gripped the steering wheel in anger and stamped the accelerator to the floor. The truck lurched forward and hit a slushy spot, shimmying several yards before the tires regripped the road. More Christmases came to mind. This time he was eight, living with his Aunt Winnie (they were never blood relations, but he liked to call them "aunt," "uncle," "cousin," if they allowed it). For Christmas she had given him a little pet hamster. He loved it because it was small and soft and furry and warm and absolutely his. Two days later he woke up and it was dead. He hadn't even named it yet. Charlie. Furry. Toby. He was still trying to decide. It was his fault. He wasn't sure why, but it was. It was the first thing he had ever really truly loved, and he'd killed it.

That night he had a dream. There was a noise, a rattling in the plastic bucket under the bathroom sink. He reached in, thinking it was Hamster. He grabbed—and screamed! Not Hamster, but a giant rat leaped onto his collarbone and bit into his neck. Like a vampire.

Tom clenched his eyes shut a painful moment, trying to clear the white fog in front of him. He tried to think of other things: the Missing Persons Bulletin. He had been tempted to call church headquarters to see if he could find out who had placed him on the bulletin, but why borrow trouble? No news was good news.

A third of the way up the mesa, in the proverbial middle-of-no-where, he saw off to his right a tiny nest of colored lights like a multicolored constellation. You just can't escape it, he thought, not even out here. Then he felt ashamed of his feelings as he turned down a side road and made a silent confession: he didn't like Christmas. Every year, privately, he wished he could drop a black cloth over it. In his head he knew better: Christmas. The birth of Christ, Lord, Savior and Redeemer of the World. The Prince of Peace. But he couldn't feel the occasion, couldn't feel the music or the cheer. He wasn't a Scrooge about it; he always put on a good face and taught his students some carols and encouraged them to decorate their little classroom tree. But he was always glad when it was finally over, yet saddened too.

The pickup squirmed and squiggled down the mushy side road leading to Louise Yazzie's shack. The snow had graciously covered the splintered dwelling with a fresh white coat. Chicken wire covered the lone window. A slender little woman with beautiful almond eyes answered the door. A few threads of gray lined her shiny black hair, which was tied in a traditional Navajo bun.

"Ya'at'eeh, shimayazhi," Tom said, offering his hand. They touched palms, Navajo-style. "I'm looking for Loretta Yellowhair. Do you know where I can find her?"

Louise's lithe frame blocked the narrow doorway. Two little girls poked their black-braided heads around either side of her pleated skirt and giggled.

"No," she said. Short and bittersweet. Although Tom had visited Louise on several occasions, she always treated him like a total stranger. Why did he always have to play these stupid games? He wearied of them. He wearied of frantic foster parents. He wearied of everything. But he knew the rules. Fight fire with fire, ice with ice. He waited, stubbornly.

"She's up on the mesa, I think," Louise said. "I don't think you can get up there tonight."

"I need to talk to her about Placement," Tom said coolly.

Placement! It was like saying abracadabra! Suddenly Louise became cooperative. She knew the score.

"Yes, I think she wants to go on the Placement. I think she's at my brother's house. I'll tell him you came by."

"I need to talk to Loretta tonight," Tom said. "I need to interview her. She has to be in Phoenix by tomorrow."

"Tomorrow?"

"Yes, tomorrow."

"I can go up there and tell her, I guess."

"Maybe I could follow you over . . . since I need to interview her."

Louise didn't like that idea. Tom posed what he knew would be a more agreeable option. "Or I could just drive there myself—if you can tell me where to go."

"Okay," she said, "why don't you just drive over there yourself. It's Sam Bizaholoni. Just follow the road. You'll see a trailer. There's a camper shell out front."

"Okay, I'll try there. I'll drive to the top of the mesa if I have to."

"Well, she might be on the mesa. Or she might be in Sheep Springs, at her mother's. Last weekend she went to Sheep Springs. Her mother lives there."

A needle in six haystacks.

"Thank you," Tom said. "*Ahehee.*"

"*Aoo'.*" she said. And then she reminded him of what night it was. "*Ya'at'eeh Keshmish!*"

Tom flushed, embarrassed. Of course. "Merry Christmas to you too."

He continued up the mesa, the pickup crawling stubbornly through the mud and snow mix. The sky continued falling, swiftly and steadily. The road before him was paved perfectly white; behind, it was a black and white smear, like a child's chocolate finger painting or the tracks of a drunken skier. Scrub pines hunkered on the rock ledges like Cro-Magnon hunters in polar bear skins. Lying in wait, it seemed.

Again he tried to visualize Loretta Yellowhair. Instead he saw the ghost of Celeste Bighorse: small, slender, doe-eyed. A heart-breaking dimpled little smile. Glossy cheeks, glossy black hair in a ponytail that dropped past her waist like a long velvet cord. She must have had a crush on him from the very beginning because she would always stay after class, just sit there with her brown hands clasped on her wooden desk until he would finally ask, "Celeste, would you like to erase the blackboard?" And she would dip her chin shyly and smile—those sweet little dimples! Kathy's smile in miniature. And she had a gift—she could draw horses that leaped right off the paper. Every day after school he would help her with her sketches. She liked it; she liked him. Then one day he told her she had a great future if. . . No. Not that. Something terrible had been misconstrued, hopelessly lost in translation. He had never ever, ever . . . except for maybe an encouraging hand on her shoulder. No! No! Her *shoulder,* just her shoulder. Like this—see? Just like this.

But she was an early bloomer, a sixth grader with incipient little breasts, and he was—well, he was white, and he was alone. And no white man chose to live alone out there. No normal white man. There was talk. Celeste was having bad dreams, her mother said. And she was a big intimidating woman who wore sunglasses and stretch pants and had her hair permed in Albuquerque. "You *bilagaanas* think you can come out here and get away with anything!" She went to a crystal gazer who implicated Tom, then took Celeste out of school for two weeks to have a *yeibichei* ceremony performed over her. Hosteen said Gladys Bighorse had a bug up her rear end, but it was only the protests of Sister Watchman that had saved Tom his job. After that he had always walked on eggshells, careful to avoid even the appearance of idiosyncrasy. He had kept a safe, professional distance from every-one—students, teachers, men, women, missionaries. It was a lonely life. Safe, but lonely.

Celeste graduated from the elementary school that June. She was supposed to go on Placement, but after the incident her mother had withdrawn her application. So little Celeste had left for the boarding school in August, young, pretty, talented. A year later she had returned a mini mom.

Tom found the trailer with the camper shell in front. He left the truck running. No colored lights here: the power lines stopped at Louise Yazzie's place. A paunchy man with oily black hair met him at the door.

"Are you Sam Bizaholoni?"

He eyed Tom tentatively. "Why?"

"I'm looking for Loretta Yellowhair. She wants to go on Placement. Louise said you might know where she is."

His face scrunched up like a sponge. "Louise?"

"Your sister. Do you have a sister named Louise?"

He smiled. Tom counted three teeth in his impoverished mouth. "She's not here," he said shaking his head. He was barefoot in baggy pajama-like pants. Tom relished the heat wafting out from the wood stove. He could hear little children laughing and a woman's voice. She was singing "Jingle Bells" in Navajo. Tom thought it should make him feel happy, but instead it was a rusty nail scratching more sad graffiti on his heart. He heard phantom voices, phantom laughter.

"She's not here," Sam said. "I think she's up on the mesa."

"Or in Sheep Springs maybe?" Tom muttered under his breath.

"What?" He was clever, playing the dumb Indian. "Did you say Sheep Springs? No, I don't think she's in Sheep Springs." He chuckled indulgently. "No, she's up on the mesa." Sam poked his head outside. "Brrrr! Wouldn't go up there tonight. Nas-teee!"

"Can you tell me where to go? It's very important. I need to interview her for Placement."

The magic word again! Tonight it seemed to hold more hope, more promise even than the word "Christmas." "Sure!" he said, flashing his three-fanged smile. "Just follow the road. You go past the cattle guard, the third cattle guard I think. There's a great big rock, it looks like a whale kinda." Then he laughed in that inimitable way of the Navajo. "You can't miss it!"

"Thanks. *Ahehee.*"

"*Aoo'*," he said. "*Ya'at'eeh Keshmish!*"

Tom had to smile. Sam reminded him a little of Hosteen, that same wry humor. But then he was overcome by an old despair. It was not Christmas this time but close enough. Winter. White. Cold. Snow. Icicles hanging like six-foot fangs. He had made a rare trip into Farmington to buy supplies. He still wondered what spirit had prompted him to check into a Motel 6, and for not just one night but two? When he returned late Saturday evening, they said the old man was *adin*—it didn't mean "dead" exactly but gone, not existing. He had died in his sleep, and *chindi,* his ghost spirit, had claimed the hogan, forcing his brittle old wife and two daughters to vacate. The only white man in the village, Tom routinely prepared and buried their dead: the Navajo wanted no contact with *chindi.* In his absence though, they might have simply burned the hogan down— they had done that before. Instead they had wisely waited three days for his return so he could remove his friend's body and prepare it for proper burial, meaning a "proper Christian burial." They had known that he, too, had lines that couldn't be crossed, although Tom had always tried to respect their beliefs and traditions. "We know you don't believe," Hosteen had once said, "but at least you try and understand. You don't laugh behind your sleeve like the others." He had wondered what Hosteen had really meant by that, "the others?"

Although in his head Tom knew better, something still whispered that it had been partly his fault, that if he had not gone to town that day and stayed so long, Hosteen would still be alive. He also knew his logic made as little sense as their childlike fear of Hosteen's ghost, but . . . one man's superstitions were another man's religion. He had learned that much.

Tom was glad to get out of the blowing cold and back into the lukewarm cab. His feet were numb from just that short stint outside. Ice had crusted on the windshield, infringing on the easy sweep of the wiper blades and cataracting all but two hemispheres of glass. He glared at the eternal snow. This is crazy, this is stupid. Why am I doing it?

For Loretta, he thought, or tried to convince himself. For God. Inasmuch as ye have done it unto the least of these . . . Okay, for me then. Me. And how so me?

The tires spun and the rear-end wriggled as the truck struggled up the slick road. Although he couldn't see beyond the hood, he could feel the road growing steeper and narrower. The snowfall thickened; it was pouring down like sugar through a giant sifter. Far to the right he saw a tiny light shining in the white commotion. It was a dark horse chance, but he decided to take it; anything beat driving to the top tonight. He left his truck parked in the road, the emergency flashers spitting blood onto the snow, and plodded several hundred yards until arriving at a homestead: a couple of shacks, a hogan, a corral, an outhouse. Padded with snow, they looked artificial, like stage props or pieces in a diorama. He wondered what he must look like laden with snow—a ghost maybe or the Abominable Snowman.

As he headed for the lighted hogan, three mutts sprang out from under a plywood lean-to, snarling and barking. He cooled them off with a couple of snowballs. A big, stocky woman answered the door, remarkably indifferent, Tom thought, as if this were nothing out of the ordinary, a *bilagaana* appearing at her door in a blizzard on Christmas Eve. She looked about forty-five. A green velveteen blouse covered her broad shoulders and torso, and a pleated skirt dropped to the middle of her pillar-like calves. She had big, bulgy cheeks, as if she were hoarding walnuts in them, and the part down the middle of her gray-streaked hair appeared to be widening as if from some peculiar erosion. She appeared understandably suspicious.

"*Woshdee,*" she said at length, and he stepped inside, ducking his head a bit.

It was a large hogan with a dirt floor. The smell of fried potatoes and mutton tortured Tom's empty belly. Instinctively he gravitated towards the makeshift woodstove, an old oil drum whose sweet heat seemed to reach out and grip his frostbitten parts, pinching them painfully, wonderfully. The stovepipe soared through the square smokehole top-center like a fat periscope. He noted the coats and cowboy hats hanging on nails along the north wall, most noticeably a red Pendleton jacket that appeared brand-new. A Mexican felt painting, wild stallions on the run, and family photographs and certificates of school achievement covered the rest of the wallspace. Three youngsters were cuddled together like bear cubs on sheepskins beside a small piñon tree, laced with strings of popcorn and dripping with tinsel. Little wrapped gifts were loosely stacked around the wooden stand, and the ochre hand of one sleeping boy rested upon a cube-shaped gift as if he were prematurely claiming it. The tin foil star on top of the tree reflected the stingy light from the kerosene lamp on a wooden table where a skinny old woman with arms as dark and tough as greasewood was kneading a mound of dough. An old fellow with a gray mustache that drooped below his chin and a face as deeply seamed as a casava melon was sitting cross-legged nearby the children, keeping vigil. He wore a black felt hat with a flat brim and a silver band reminiscent of Hosteen's. There were two other women, young mothers growing fat in t-shirts and blue jeans. One was casually feeding her brown breast to her baby. Nearby a young man with a thick mop of black hair eyed Tom like a deer smelling trouble. On the other side of the hogan were two middle-aged men, one innocuously big and round, the other austerely cut with the high, chiseled cheek-bones of a warrior. He was wearing a red headband around his silver hair, and his dark eyes were fixed on Tom like bullets waiting to be fired. Tom wondered if this were not the old coot to whom Loretta had been promised. If so he looked quite formidable: a Navajo Clint Eastwood.

The heat was suffocating. Tom quickly regained the feeling in his hands and feet, and his armpits grew soggy with sweat. He wanted to doff his suede coat but chose not to: he didn't want to send the wrong signal. This would be a short visit.

The matron spoke first, surprising him. "She's out there," she said, motioning towards the door. Tom was confused. She? Loretta? "Last night," she explained, "in my sleep, a man in white came and took her away. He said, 'Don't worry. She'll be all right.' He said, 'She's coming with me.' That's how come I knew you were coming."

Tom felt a tingling warmth. He looked at his sleeve: most of the snow coating him had either melted or dropped to the floor, but it had made the point. This was going to be easier than he had thought.

"I need to see Loretta," he said. "Loretta Yellowhair."

"Loretta?" Now the matron looked confused. Tom wasn't sure how to interpret her colossal disappointment.

"Are you her aunt?"

She shook her head. "No," she nodded solemnly. "Loretta's not here. She's on the mesa."

"On the mesa?"

"*Aoo'.*"

Tom gazed up through the smokehole at the wild flurry of snowflakes. They were insects flying too close to a fire, or falling stars melting by myriads. They wanted in, it seemed, but the instant they came too close to the invisible heat—poof! Oblivion. They were the opposite of those white butterflies caught inside the cone of light. Or were they brothers? Cousins maybe? Tom looked at the sleeping children by the tree and thought that maybe he wanted to sit down. Maybe he wanted to stay awhile. He did not want to leave, he knew that.

"*Ahehee,*" he said, and he could feel their eyes upon him as he trudged back into the snow.

An hour later he curved around the great whale-shaped rock only to find himself facing a meadow of knee-deep snow. He pushed in the clutch and jerked the stick into reverse. The gears whined as the truck struggled backwards fifty feet. He shoved the stick forward and bore down on the accelerator, gathering speed down the plowed stretch until the headlights slammed into the snowbank. It was like ramming into a tackling dummy: the snow gave a bit but then held firm. Steam rose from the extinguished headlights. He backed up and took another running start. Again the snowbank relented a few feet and then held fast. He tried again, gunning the engine full-throttle. The snow gave a little more, but not much. This time he did not back up. He pressed the accelerator to the floor. Huge pinwheels of mud and ice flew past the side windows, black and white blurs, as the headlights burrowed deeper and deeper into the snow. He could smell the transmission cooking.

"Damn!" He slammed the cab door and checked in back: no shovel. He must have forgotten to put it back after clearing his walkway. "Dammit to hell!" He knew he shouldn't swear, but right now he didn't care. He didn't care about anything except getting his damn truck out of the damn muck. He glared at the falling snow as if some invisible nemesis were hiding behind it, or within it. He felt like yelling at it, challenging: Come out and show yourself! Come out and fight me face to face! He threw himself on his knees, by the front tires, and began scooping out the snow with his bare hands, madly, angrily. The cold nibbled piranha-like through his fingers and his legs from the knees down. At first he was too angry to feel any pain, but after awhile each time he plunged his hands into the mud it was like sticking them in a fire, or into the jaws of a wolf to be briefly masticated. He buried them over and over, until they were gone, and it was just his arms, sticks with floppy pads on the ends, which he kept stabbing into the muck, muttering and cursing until tears leaked from his eyes—tears of anger and frustration and a pain that cut much deeper than this simple calculable cold. An anger and frustration that had nothing to do with his impossible quest to find Loretta Yellowhair.

He dug, he scooped, he swore, angrily, fanatically. Insanely.

The snow kept falling, relentlessly, invidiously, like a great white plague; like locusts attacking his precious crops. He stood up and waved his arms wildly to chase them away. He felt utterly helpless, like a blindfolded kid trying to break the piñata but his older brother keeps yanking it impossibly out of reach. He turned a circle and saw nothing but white madness. Distress? Who was in distress? That seventeen-year-old kid? Distress! He could tell you all about it! He wondered, bitterly, if anyone was braving the storm to visit him tonight? He whirled around and roared at the omnipresent snow: "Where the hell's *my* shepherd? Who the hell's going to rescue *me*?" So this was his reward! This was his fate, his destiny! His stinking rotten lousy miserable thanks! "Your vessel, your lonely solitary vessel, and what do I get? Shat on, spat on! Well, to hell with them! To hell with You!"

Then he repented. Sort of. He thought the real Jesus would understand his momentary craziness under duress. The real Jesus would accept his intentional lack of Christmas fanfare. The real Jesus wouldn't be dumb enough to be born in the dead of winter either. In a stable, yes. In rags, sure. Winter? Never. The real Jesus would know better. He'd understand about Hosteen and Kathy and Celeste Bighorse and the Missing Persons Bulletin and Loretta Yellowhair and all the rest. Didn't care about colored lights and tinsel. Wasn't sitting by a fireplace opening gifts and getting fat on rice pudding. The real Jesus was probably walking some dirty ghetto street waiting (wondering? hoping?) for some true blue disciple to invite him in out of the cold. To heat him up a can of soup and make him a ham on rye. Wherein saw ye me a stranger? Naked and clothed me? Hungry and fed me? Wherein? Whereout? Where?

He tried to reassure himself. The time his appendix ruptured and Hosteen drove him to the hospital in Farmington and sat by his bed all night in ICU singing ceremonial healing chants. (The nurse had told him this after he came out of anesthesia.) Later Hosteen had brought him a Louis L'Amour paperback—Tom hated Louis L'Amour, but the thought—the thought! When he asked about the healing chants, the corners of the old man's mouth curled in his familiar way: "Hell, I was just singing a bunch of old squaw dance songs—just a lot of Indian mumbo jumbo. It was the only way they'd let me stay in that crazy place with you all night." Hosteen! Five years later he was dead. *Adin.* Removing his body from the hogan, Tom had been startled by its lightness. Hosteen was tiny anyway, but minus his spirit it was like lifting a large piece of balsa wood. Carefully, lovingly, Tom had prepared the corpse for burial, wrestling the purple tunic of velveteen over his stiff little doll-like body, the silver concho belt around his narrow waist. At one point Tom's fingers had searched the old man's face, reading the deep corrugations there. Each wrinkle was a lifeline, an arroyo, a timeless impression in the land Hosteen and his forefathers had claimed by blood and birthright. At that moment Tom had never felt so lonely and displaced, so totally outside the pale. He had wept, and through his tears he had watched the old man's face grow smooth and soft, youthful, but thin as air, like a full-color shadow or a reflection on water. Tom thought if he had pressed down, his hand would have punched right through it. Instead, he held up his own palm like a handmirror only to see his face in similar form: soft, smooth, youthful, a shadow. He made a fist and it had all disappeared. Later, as he was delivering the eulogy, a small miracle had happened. Halfway through, several hands went up. Heads were nodding, shaking. He looked at his interpreter, Sister Watchman's son. What? What? Had he said something, done something *bahadzid*? No, Herbert's expression said. And his gritty little smile formed beneath his black mustache. Just keep talking. You don't need me.

Tom had gazed down at the crowd of wrinkled faces, head-banded and cowboy-hatted men, silver-haired women, packed in rows of folding chairs beneath the red and white-striped revival tent, all nodding, nodding, nodding. And later he would not recall a word of what he had said, only that it was like a beautiful gold scroll rolling out of his head, and all he had to do was read it. He couldn't recall any of the symbols—they were runes, Chinese cuneiform, hapless kid scribble—yet at the time they had made perfect sense to him, to them.

Tom glared at the falling sky as if it were attacking him personally. His teeth were chattering and his shoulders shaking. What was he trying to prove? What was he doing here? Boredom, duty, curiosity. No, no, no! He clenched his teeth and plunged his frozen paws deeper into the muck.

Then a thought: Sticks! Branches! He got up and staggered through the knee-deep snow, flailing his arms like a drunkard or a blind man on the run, until he smacked into a dead piñon tree whose brittle branches he began attacking with Kung Fu kicks and karate chops. Using his numb arms like giant tweezers, he carried the broken branches to his truck and laid them in two narrow trails behind his rear tires. But when he looked back he saw the snow was smothering the sticks faster than he could spread them.

He crawled back into the cab. Most of the interior heat had dissipated, but it was a relief just to get out of the blowing cold. He could feel the voodoo pins everywhere: back, chest, neck, legs. He closed his eyes and groaned mournfully: Dear God, please get me unstuck. But then he felt guilty. It had been so long since he had prayed sincerely, beyond the banal Sunday rote to appease his little congregation. He felt ashamed for waiting until his moment of despair to finally cry out. Or was he admitting something else? Confessing even more: I don't just don't like; I hate. Who? What? Wherein? Whereout?

He tried to turn on the ignition, but his hands were gone. It was like trying to thread a needle wearing boxing gloves. He swore, he laughed, and then he stuffed his hands down his pants, between his legs, and waited as his body warmth slowly carved out of the two cold clods fingers, knuckles, creases, hair.

He tried again. The starter whirred, the engine grabbed, the wheels churned, and he went nowhere.

"Dammit all!" He slammed the door again. His whole frame was shaking now, and for the first time he thought he might be in authentic danger. He thought he ought to start a fire, but he had no matches, no lighter. And even if he did—how with these worthless hands? Idiot! Stooge! Moron! Had he set himself up for this or what? He knew better—he knew! Suppose he couldn't get out now and the snow kept falling? He looked around to get his bearings and saw nothing but a white blur. His truck was gone, its tracks were covered. He was next. He imagined the snow building, rising like flood waters: it was at his knees, his waist, his chest, his neck. He was under. Buried. Gone. *Adin.* He imagined his body stiff at attention, like an arctic sentry, frozen on duty. Who would know, until the spring thaw? And who would care? Nashdoi maybe? Would his cat notice the difference, as long as someone—anyone—filled his plastic bowl with table scraps? And who would feed old Nashdoi? Who would come looking? Sister Watchman perhaps?

He wondered about his spirit passing through the veil. His mother and father had disclaimed him in life. Would they do likewise in death? How would Kathy receive him? With open, loving arms? Had he fought the good fight? Or would she turn her head in shame, embarrassed by the way he had squandered his life, his whole damn life, among this people? Oh, he had married them and buried them, had taught their children to read and write, had wiped their runny little noses on cold winter mornings. But would she embrace him for that, or merely out of marital duty? Or deny him altogether? Would she, too, condemn him for Celeste Bighorse? Or had she died for his sins? Then where was the real man in white? Where was the real Jesus? Or was he the white veil with a zillion fluttering parts, waiting to smack or lovingly smother you?

Then another possibility came to mind: suppose the Mormons were wrong, the Navajos right? Suppose the hereafter was a nebulous netherworld, an eternity of falling snow?

Tom calmly sat down and waited as the cold consumed him cell by cell. It had taken his legs and belly and was moving into his chest now. Soon it was a blanket covering him with motherly warmth. He lay back, closed his eyes, and succumbed at last to the Christmas memory he had been trying to evade all night: their first Christmas Eve together as man and wife, their first on the rez. They were still strangers in the village. She was eight months pregnant, very vulnerable, atypically weepy. Sitting in their dark little kitchen staring glumly at the little scrub pine he had cut down and which she had dressed with her construction paper decorations, he did something very stupid. He made a little joke: "How about some eggnog?" And right there her spirit snapped. He thought he could actually hear it. "Eggnog? *Eggnog?* Very funny! What eggnog? What anything in this lousy rotten hell-hole? Drunks and dead dogs, that's all you ever see. Eggnog? All anyone ever wants around here is a big fat handout! They come to church for handouts, they come to the school for handouts! If they're so broke, how come everyone's driving a new pickup? We can't even afford a tuneup for our lousy rotten VW Rabbit! And these people act like you owe it to them. They look at you with their hatchet faces: gimme gimme gimme gimme. I'm sick of it, Tom! I'm fed up! Every time it rains or snows this place turns into a chocolate swamp. And if it's not the rain, it's the damn wind blowing so thick you can't see your nose in front of your face. I hate it, Tom! The water's orange. God knows what creepy critters inhabit that stuff. And this lousy rotten trailer. This stupid tin can. We freeze all winter, fry all summer. I'm sick of it. There's no one, absolutely no one, here for me to talk to. You go to work, sure, to your little rock schoolhouse where you're treated like the Great White God, but I'm stuck here in this tin can. Stuck! No telephone, no TV. I carry water in a bucket. I practically cook over an open fire. I hate it! I'm not a damned pioneer. I said whither thou goest, but this is the end of the road for me! I mean it, Tom. This is it! My father was right: you're a loser and you'll always be a loser! Misery's your middle name!"

Later she apologized: "This volleyball in my belly. It does weird things to you. It really messes up your mind." But when he told her to forget it, he understood, she unleashed again: "How could *you* understand? You had nothing to lose. I had everything!" And then she fled into the bedroom and slammed the door: "Merry Christmas!"

It was close to midnight when he was awakened by a knock. He had fallen asleep on their ragged little sofa. It was Rose Tsinijinnie, the secretary at the elementary school. A tall, slender cowgirl, she was out of breath. "Come to the school," she panted. "Hurry!" And ran off.

Tom put on his snow boots and coat and trudged over to the rock schoolhouse. Rose met him at the door. "Where's your wife?"

"My wife? You didn't say anything about—"

"Go get your wife!" she ordered. Then laughed in that delightfully free manner of Navajo women. "Go get your wife or we'll have to find one for you!"

He trudged back to the trailer and asked—begged, really—her to come.

"I was almost asleep."

"We can't say no. You know how they are."

Grumbling, she threw on a maternity smock, boots, and a coat. "I feel like an Eskimo," she muttered.

"A very beautiful one," he said.

"Don't placate me."

"Okay, ugly as an Eskimo. Fat as an Eskimo. Ornery as an Eskimo. Snotty as an—"

"All right, all right. I get the picture."

When they arrived at the schoolhouse, the lights were out and Rose was gone.

"Swell," Kathy muttered.

They were wet, cold, and the snow was falling. As they turned back towards the trailer, Rose appeared around the corner, waving them to the side door. "Hey! Psst! Come on!" As they stepped inside, the lights came on. And the most incredible thing: the whole community was there—parents, students, babies in cradleboards, grandpas in cowboy hats, grandmas in pleated skirts. Two hundred plus crammed into that little room, and they were all smiling while the children sang "We Wish You a Merry Christmas," which Tom had taught them the week before in school. There was a pine tree in the corner with presents piled up underneath—baby clothes, boxes of disposable diapers, Navajo rugs, turquoise jewelry, a cradleboard of varnished cedarwood. He and Kathy stood there, stunned, silent, and wept.

Afterwards they trudged through the mud and snow back to their dingy little trailer with the wood stove and the foot-long cockroaches and the scrawny little Christmas tree, and they made the wildest wickedest love they ever had. Tom remembered lying in bed afterwards, listening to the snow like gentle fingers tapping on the glass. Her head was on his shoulder and she was curling his chest hairs around her finger as she whispered, "I'm so happy!" And at that moment so was he. It was the first time she had ever really said that. She had said "I Love You" often enough, but never that. And for the first time he really honestly truly thought they were going to make it.

A week later as they were driving home from a New Year's Day shopping spree in Farmington, he fell asleep at the wheel. When the VW Rabbit veered onto the shoulder, jerking him awake, he overcompensated and the little car hit the gravelly shoulder and became a flying missile. And that was it: two in one blow. Why he had survived and not her still angered and puzzled him. Maybe God leaves behind the one with the most rough edges. (But he could hear her counter from the other side: "Don't placate me!") Besides, he knew better: he was doing penance.

Hosteen used to tell him it was bad luck to speak about dying or the dead: to even think the act would increase its likelihood of happening. Tom always wondered if there wasn't some truth to that, or if Kathy had just had a premonition. A month or so before, she had instructed him—no, ordered him was more accurate: "If anything ever happens to me, I want you to remarry!"

"But who would ever be stupid enough to marry the likes of me?" he protested.

"I don't know. But look hard. You'll find some sweet little sucker. But just make sure you do! I don't want a horny husband meeting me on the other side of the veil! Understand, rubber band?"

He had had no intention of staying. In fact, his plan was to leave immediately. Just go. But where? To whom? One year ran into two, two to three, and before he knew it he was stuck there, stuck up to his axles. He was like the snowflakes swirling around in the cone of light: white butterflies trapped in glass.

He jackknifed to attention, brushing the snow from his body as if it were some kind of white vermin. The snow had stopped and the skies had cleared except for a small patch where the moon was peering through a crack like an eavesdropping eye. Stars appeared

like tiny ornaments. Moonlit, the snow-covered expanse looked like
a weird florescent icing: cold, clean, beautifully barren. A glittering
wasteland. Radioactive. Out of this world. Tom closed his eyes and
took a deep, cleansing breath. He saw a light shining at the foot of
a white cliff far ahead. As he trudged towards it, the snow started
up again. The sky was perfectly clear but flakes were falling, as if
the whole Milky Way were fluttering down. Soon he was the man
in white again. Hands, feet, legs, head. His body was numb but his
heart was on fire. He trudged: left foot, right foot, left foot.

It was a homestead almost identical to the one he had stopped
at down the road—the corral, the outhouse, the shacks, the hogan.
Three pair of eyes glowed orange underneath a plywood lean-to.
The same matron answered the door. Clint Eastwood was there
too, glaring at him but sadly this time, as if his bullet eyes had
prematurely misfired. The old woman with the greasewood arms
was kneading her dough, and her black-hatted old mate was keeping
vigil over the sleeping children by the tree. The young mothers and
the young man with the black bangs watched.

This time the matron spoke sternly to him. "She's in *there!*"
she said, and her finger steered his eye across the corral towards
a little hogan on a hill. "This morning, we dug a hole for you.
There's a pick and a shovel too. Last night in my sleep, a man
in white came . . ."

And then he understood.

She belonged to the Salt Clan and was born in the year the
cottonwoods greened early, which made her a little over ninety but
under one hundred, and that was all he would know, all they would
tell him. But as he trekked across the white field towards the hogan
on the hill, all the rest would become quite clear. He would wonder,
since the year the cottonwoods greened early, how many hundreds
of sheep had she shorn, how many thousands of pieces of fry bread
had she made, how many rugs had she woven, how many winters,
snows, how many Christmases had passed? He tried to picture her
in his mind. Instead he saw the dimpled smile of Celeste Bighorse.
He looked back only once, and saw the others watching on the far
side of the corral: the bell-shaped matron, a young woman in a

screaming yellow windbreaker, and the sketchy silhouette of the old man as he touched his forefinger to the brim of his black felt hat, and with that simple gesture thanked him across the white eternities of the omnipresent snow.

FIFTEEN

Family Attractions

JUDITH FREEMAN

Evelyn sat in the kitchen, trying to figure out what to do for the twins' birthday. She was going through the "Family Attractions" column in the newspaper.

"How does Magic Mountain sound?"

"Bor-innng," Lois said. Linda didn't respond. She was lost to the music coming through her headphones.

"Hollywood Wax Museum . . . ?"

Lois shook her head. "Why don't we get George in here? He might have an idea."

"Don't ask George what he wants to do because he won't have an answer," Evelyn said. George wasn't the father of the girls, although he'd accepted that role as well as he could, given the fact he was a lifelong bachelor and over sixty when he met and married their mother, several months ago. The girls' real father had died in a fiery collision near Barstow.

"Cabrillo Marine Museum?"

"Dead fish," Lois said. "I can open a can of tuna if I want to see that." She stuck her thumb in her mouth.

"What's that thumb doing in your mouth?"

"I can't answer, I've got a thumb in my mouth," Lois said.

"And you're turning nine tomorrow." Evelyn shook her head. "I rue the day I gave you binkies."

Linda took her headphones off. "Are we going to have lunch or what?"

"Or what," said Evelyn. "It's not even noon."

"We could go to McDonald's."

"Wait till George finishes what he's doing and we'll eat. But we're not going to McDonald's. There's leftover meatloaf from last night. We'll make sandwiches."

Linda put her finger in her mouth and bent over the table, pretending to gag. Evelyn looked hard at her.

"You know, there are lots of starving kids in the world who would be very happy to get meatloaf."

"Name two," Linda said.

"Very funny. I don't know why I'm going to all this trouble here. You two are ingrates."

When George came in from the yard, they were still sitting at the table.

"Ugh," Evelyn said. "You're tracking something here."

George looked at his shoes, then tiptoed back through the door and reentered moments later.

"I hope that wasn't what I think it was," Evelyn said, looking up from her newspaper.

"Just mud," George said.

"The girls haven't been picking up after the dog this week. In fact, they've been very lazy about their chores. I don't know what we're going to do about it." She looked at her daughters severely.

"How about we string them up by their toes and put goose feathers under their noses?" George laid a finger lightly on the end of Lois's nose. She squealed happily.

"George!" she yelled, twisting away from him.

From the beginning, during those first awkward days after the wedding when tests of various kinds were common and the twins saw to it that George remained unassimilated, everyone had agreed that the girls should call him George, and not Dad, as a means of letting them guard their familial territory until such time when they could accept him naturally. For weeks, they kept him outside their circle, sometimes refusing to talk to him at all, other times being intentionally rude. Unkind reminders of his age were used to distance themselves from him: "George is old enough to be our grandfather," Lois said one day in front of him. "George is older than our grandfather," Linda added. Quite recently, however, something had happened. The tide had turned. More and more they warmed up to him, sensing, old or not, George was the kind of person who, without striving for it, was a source of marvelous fun.

"So how are the plans coming?" George asked.

"Mom doesn't know what we're going to do," Lois said wearily.

"There's the Stuntman Hall of Fame," Evelyn said, still reading from the newspaper. "Or the Museum of World Wars, Sea World, the Pasadena Flea Market. Hey, how about the flea market? That might be fun."

"Fun for you," Lois said.

George spoke up from the sink where he was scrubbing his hands.

"When I was a boy," he said, "I took my mother rowing on Lake Larson every year for her birthday. Lake Larson is in Minnesota," he added.

Evelyn, who harbored a low opinion of George's athletic abilities, said, "I didn't know you could row, George."

"They had the prettiest little boats that you could rent," George said. "That was Mom's idea of heaven." He was about to tell them what color the boats were, a bright blue, and how his mother liked to row to a monastery on the far side of the lake where, near a statue of Christ, they sat on a marble bench and ate their picnic lunch, but Evelyn spoke up first.

"Why don't we take a picnic to Lake Sherwood tomorrow and George can row us around the lake?"

"I don't know this Lake Sherwood," George said. "Is it near?"

Lois, taking her thumb out of her mouth, brightened and said, "Can Barky go?"

"I'm sure they don't allow dogs," Evelyn said. She wanted to slap her daughter's hand away from her mouth. Ignore it, the shrink said, but it was easier said than done. Evelyn turned to her other daughter. "What do you think, Linda?"

Linda held up her hand to indicate that her mother should not, at this crucial moment, interrupt her musical concentration.

"I'm talking to you," Evelyn said.

"She can't hear you," George explained, pointing to his ears.

Evelyn yelled, "I'm trying to plan something here!"

"Sounds good to me," George said happily. "Rowing, a picnic. Great. I could use a day in the sun. Sometimes I think this job is killing me. It's bad enough during an ordinary week, but when it's hot people get crazy and they'd like to kill you. You go into people's houses and they're filthy, especially under the sinks. I had to crawl under a house yesterday because a rat died between a wall and the bathtub and the smell was coming up through the pipes. There wasn't anything I could do to get that rat out of there. 'You're going to just have to wait until Mother Nature does her work,' I said. 'Dust to dust.' But the woman didn't want to hear that. They don't want to pay you if you can't fix everything, but you've got to charge them for trying."

"What about Barky?" Lois said.

"Take that thumb out of your mouth, you're nine years old."

"Technically, I'm still eight," Lois said.

"I think Barky could go," George said. He stood behind Evelyn and put his hands on her shoulders. As he spoke he softly kneaded her flesh. "We'll sneak him in."

Evelyn felt a sudden annoyance. Everything was working against her. The whole family was like a wave shoving her back to shore when she was trying to make a little headway here. She waved a hand in front of Linda's face. "Hey you," she said. She waved again.

Linda took her headphones off and stared at her mother. "You just interrupted the best part of 'Material Girl.' Like the very part I've been waiting for."

"What the hell have I done wrong," Evelyn said, and walked out of the kitchen.

George and the girls were watching TV when Evelyn came down later and apologized for being short-tempered. "I'm getting my period," she whispered to George, settling down beside him on the couch. "I haven't actually started bleeding yet but I feel awful. Edgy, you know."

"Oh," George said. He was still unused to a woman confiding in him about her cycles.

They were watching a program on vampire bats on the public television station. The bats were shown flying through the air in slow motion, undulating like swimmers, and although their faces were terrifying, Evelyn thought their bodies quite beautiful. Lit from behind they had a human shape—legs and arms—with wings of the thinnest membranes, translucent as fine pink silk, stretching from the arms to the body like some sort of see-through garment.

The narrator said that in a small town in Mexico, bats were posing a problem for livestock raisers who annually lost hundreds of animals to anemia as a result of bats preying on them.

In the next scene two bats were shown sneaking up on a tethered horse that was so gaunt its bones protruded like the spikes of a broken umbrella pushing against the fabric. The bats moved along the ground, hopping like quick little monkeys.

"How do they get these pictures at night?" Evelyn asked.

"Infrared photography, I guess," George replied.

"Ssshhh, you guys," Lois said.

A bat hopped onto the horse's hind leg and bit it just above the hock. The horse stamped its foot and the bat scurried away. But it was too late, the narrator said. The bat had already done its work, injecting a numbing agent, secreted in its saliva, into the horse's leg. Now the bat would wait until it could return to the site and feed without the horse feeling anything. The bats hopped around the horse like mischievous fairies. A few moments later, one of the bats jumped onto the horse's leg and began drawing blood. Afterward the bats returned to their cave and were shown feeding regurgitated blood to their babies and mates, who hung upside down from the cave's ceiling.

"I just don't see how they get these close-up shots in a cave," Evelyn said. "How come the bats let somebody in there to take pictures?"

"They're using a hidden camera," George said.

"God," Linda said in disgust. "Look at those things."

"I've told you not to use God like that."

"You do."

"You're not old enough. Can it."

Since the farmers were losing livestock, the narrator said, it was decided the bats must be controlled. The same gaunt horse that had appeared in previous scenes was injected with a slow-working poison. When the bats returned to attack it that night, they filled up on poisoned blood and returned and fed it to the others. In the last scene, helmeted men with flashlights were examining a cave littered with bat corpses.

"I don't know how we can eat dinner after that," Evelyn said when the program was over. She puckered her mouth and squinted at George.

George laughed. "It's just nature, Evelyn."

"We could go to Chuck E. Cheese," Lois said. She stretched, yawned sleepily, and rolled over onto her stomach, lying on the carpet in front of the TV. Linda put her feet on Lois's back.

"Get your dirty socks off me," Lois said, and twisted away from her, rolling over and over across the floor.

"That stuff in the fridge is going to spoil if we don't eat it."

"What are these?" Lois said. She was looking at George's hand.

"Age spots," George said.

"Oooo," Lois said, and fell back on the floor in a slump as if she'd just fainted. "How disgusting."

Linda took off her socks and stuffed them into one big ball and lobbed it across the room at Lois. Lois ducked, then picked up the sock-ball and threw it back.

"Tell you what," George said. "Since you only turn nine once in your life, we'll go out tonight. How does that sound?"

In five minutes, they were ready to leave. But as they stood at the door, Evelyn looked wistfully back toward the kitchen and said, "I just hate to waste food." She sighed. "All that stuff rotting in the refrigerator."

That night George said, "You have so many nice nightgowns, why don't you ever wear them?" Evelyn, wearing a gray sweatshirt, had just gotten into bed.

"I'm cold," she said. "I just want to be warm."

George slipped his arm under her neck and tried to roll her closer to him.

"It's all right, George."

"I thought I'd get you warm."

He smiled. Evelyn looked closely at his mouth and thought, If he went to a hygienist now, it would be a big, unpleasant job to clean his teeth. He had let it go too long.

She turned out the light. Cars sped past the house, the sound building and fading, like waves. A motorcycle roared by, followed by a car with rock and roll blaring from its radio. It was silent for a while; then because the light up the street changed, more cars went by.

George said, "What time should we plan on leaving tomorrow?"

"Oh, whenever we get away."

George imagined rowing his family over the water, pulling the boat across the smooth surface of a lake, balancing the weight of his passengers, shifting to counter their movements.

Evelyn, feeling his hips move beside her on the mattress said, "It's the wrong time for that, George."

At first he didn't understand what she meant, and then he did, and he wanted to say something, how he was thinking about something else. Sometimes he didn't know where things came from, why they didn't understand each other better. How could she think he had wanted that, when he had only been thinking about rowing and steadying the load of his passengers?

"It's lunchtime at McDonald's," Lois said as they were loading blankets and food into the back of the truck, which had the name of George's company, LAYTON HEATING AND PLUMBING, painted on the doors.

Evelyn frowned at the picnic basket she held. Catsup had oozed from the bottle and soiled a napkin. She tightened the lid.

"Ooo, bat blood!" Linda said, staring at the thin line of catsup on Evelyn's hand.

"Bat blood!" the girls shrieked, feigning horror, and backing away from their mother. Evelyn held her hands up to scare them and the girls grabbed for each other and ran behind the *Pittosporum* bush.

"Help us, George," they squealed, "save us please!"

"Coming to get you," Evelyn said. She held her hands up and pulled a face.

"Ha ha ha," she said gruffly and chased the twins around the bush and back to the truck, where George stood ready to catch them and lift them up into the truck bed. They all stood looking at one another, the girls excited and still acting like they were frightened, Evelyn flushed from running, George calmly smiling.

"Now promise me you won't stand up or move around if I let you ride back here," he said to them.

As they pulled away from the house and drove down the street lined with flowering acacia, George checked the rearview mirror to be certain the children were safe and still in their places.

Under a sky that was gray, they drove west on the Ventura Freeway. By the time they reached Calabasas, openings appeared in the clouds and big holes of blue showed through. As they were passing the pet cemetery, Evelyn said, "I wonder where we'll bury Barky when he dies."

This upset George. It seemed unnecessarily morbid since Barky was only three and a vigorous, happy animal.

"Don't think about it," he said.

"I'm trying to think about something other than the damned thumb sucking," she said.

George looked in the rearview mirror. The girls were waving at an older couple in a Cadillac who were following them. The couple weren't waving back.

"Marla tells me to ignore it and I try, Lord, I try, but every time one of them sticks a thumb in her mouth I think, where have I failed here? It's like a picture of my failure. I didn't give them something. I didn't do something right."

George could not think of who Marla was. The counselor at school? The psychiatrist Evelyn went to before the one she had now?

He said, "How do you know those twins wouldn't have sucked their thumbs if they'd been born to somebody else?"

"Well, you can't ever know something like that."

"Everybody does the best they can," George said. "If they could do better, they would."

"Maybe this is over your head. Or out of your ballpark or something."

"What do you mean?"

"Maybe you've got to have kids to know what I'm talking about."

"I've got kids now," he said. He waited for her to say something but she didn't.

The Cadillac pulled into the next lane and began passing. As it went by the girls waved again. He could see their fluttering hands and wished the people would wave back, but they kept their eyes straight ahead, ignoring the girls.

"I wouldn't let them keep their binkies so long," Evelyn said, "if I had it to do over again."

"Binkies?"

"You know, pacifiers."

"That's where they filmed *M*A*S*H*," Evelyn said later, lifting her aviator sunglasses. "That's supposed to be Korea."

They were inland from Malibu on a two-lane road climbing through the dry hills that separate the ocean from the valley. George slowed down to look at the *M*A*S*H* buildings, set back off the road in a narrow canyon. Hawks circled above the ridge, riding a hot wind.

"Look at the hawks," he said.

"I see them," she said.

A few miles later, they came to the Lake Sherwood turnoff. A man sat on a folding chair at the end of a dirt road, cleaning his fingernails with a pocketknife. They paid him two dollars. He made them promise to leave the dog in the truck once they got to the lake. Dogs weren't allowed. He was willing to make an exception, as long as the dog stayed in the truck.

Barky jumped out as soon as the truck came to a stop under a eucalyptus tree, and the twins followed.

"Everybody carry something," Evelyn yelled to the twins. "You take the Playmate," she said to George, meaning the plastic cooler with the drinks inside. George was looking out over the lake. It was a fine spot. Steep green hills rose from the edge of the water. The sun glinted on the water's surface, breaking up into sharp points of dancing light, and George thought it a wonderful sight. The lake seemed to be quite large, and L-shaped, although part of it wasn't visible from where he stood. Next to the truck, a field of orange poppies bloomed, and beyond that stood two small white buildings, the cafe and bait shop.

The children swirled around on the dusty path, trying to grab Barky by the collar.

"I know we shouldn't have the dog," Evelyn said. She walked lopsidedly, weighed down by the picnic basket.

The girls ran on ahead. A wind came up suddenly and lifted their dresses, and George looked away, shy and embarrassed before their youthful shapes.

"I know we're going to get busted," Evelyn said.

"Wait by the dock," George told her. Inside the little store he rented a boat for three hours. He bought KitKat bars for the girls and stuck them into his pocket. He saw some fishing lures on a cardboard display that he thought he could make into a pair of earrings for Evelyn, and he bought two of them. They were beautiful metal ovals, speckled purple and yellow, and he could imagine them flashing from Evelyn's earlobes, catching light and casting pale hues of color onto her neck.

Once outside he waved to his family from the porch and started walking toward the dock. It still surprised him that he had this family, that the identical girls in blue dresses and the woman in a full yellow skirt and black sweater, who were all now waving back at him, their arms raised up into pale and fragile arcs, were actually his own.

"They're fishing, George," Lois said, pointing to some kids standing on the end of the dock. "Linda and I want to fish."

"Ah, fishing," George said. "We'll have to do that." He looked over the row of wooden boats bobbing on either side of the dock.

"Hurry up, honey," Evelyn said. "Pick a boat, any boat, and let's get going before somebody stops us."

The boats were white and in need of a fresh coat of paint. George frowned at them. Finally he picked out one with an extra oar and helped his family climb in, then coaxed Barky aboard.

"George, is this a good idea?" Evelyn said, trying to steady the boat with one hand and pushing on Barky's haunches with the other, in an effort to get him to sit. She held onto the dock while George stepped over the edge, and the boat lowered deeper into the water. Someone appeared on the porch of the bait shop and yelled at them. George with a firm push sent the wavering boat gliding away from the dock.

"It's a very good idea," he said. "Just sit still. Pretend you don't hear him. Don't look at him."

Evelyn put her sweater over Barky's head and tied the sleeves around his neck like a scarf. She put her sunglasses on his nose.

"He looks very human," George said. "One of us."

George had met Evelyn on a Sierra Club bird-watching trip to Point Mugu Naval Station where, in marshes set among the test-firing ranges, they observed blue-crested mallards, willets, leggy egrets, and the rare clapper rail. Nearer the ocean, tide pools were also examined.

"We're here to observe what's above and what's below," Puff McGruder, the outing leader, said to the Sierra Clubbers as they disembarked from the bus. Since they all belonged to the West Side

Singles Chapter, they were also there to observe what was next to them.

During a restroom stop at the golf course clubhouse, a long line formed in front of the facilities. George, who was standing near Evelyn, noticed the flower printed on the front of her t-shirt and asked the name of it.

"That's a giant *Coreopsis,*" Evelyn said.

"How large are they?" George asked.

"Oh, about a thirty-six D," Evelyn said, and they both laughed.

George bought her coffee, served in cups with plastic missiles for stirrers, and they sat together on the bus during the rest of the trip. Soon they were dating regularly.

In many ways they made an unlikely couple. He was sixty-three, she just thirty-eight. He stood six feet four, she was just over five feet. The first time he hugged her, he felt the sharp point of her nose pressing against the bottom of his sternum.

He had never planned to marry, let alone marry a woman twenty-five years younger and one with two energetic children. But Evelyn, in so many ways, was the perfect match for him. She was the only woman with whom he'd ever seen a future. It surprised him. It came late in life, when he'd adjusted to things going another way.

"If you'll have me," he said to her a few months after the Point Mugu trip, "I'm yours."

The lake was smooth and George found rowing easy. He faced his family and contemplated his luck. What would he have, twenty years with them? Fifteen? Life insurance should guarantee educations for the girls if he should go sooner. Recently, the heavyset black woman who was the dispatcher at work said to him, "I bought me an alarm clock, but you know, that thing runs backward. Now, I don't need that." But that's precisely what George wished he had, a clock that ran backward for a while.

He felt for the lures in his pocket and drew them out to show Evelyn, but she was looking through the binoculars, studying some birds feeding close to shore. He put them back and remembered the KitKat bars.

"Want some chocolate?" he said to Lois, who was holding her Barbie doll over the edge of the boat, dragging the permanently arched feet across the surface of the water.

"Yeah," Lois said.

"Say thank you."

"Thanks, George."

"Want a candy bar, Linda?"

"Thanks a lot, Georgio," Linda said.

George decided to row to the small island in the middle of the lake. It was farther than it looked. Progress was slow in the small boat, loaded down as it was, but he felt he could row like this all day. About halfway to the island, however, he began to feel a tiredness in his arms that progressed to an overall fatigue he was embarrassed to admit. He stopped for a moment, pretending to enjoy the scenery, and they drifted, borne by a wind that moved them toward another boat where people were quietly fishing.

"Hallooo," he called, and the fishermen gave a friendly wave.

By the time they reached the island, George felt he needed a rest and suggested they go ashore for their picnic.

"But it says no trespassing." Evelyn pointed to a sign posted by the Department of Water and Power, that threatened trespassers with fines and prosecution.

"Who's the wiser?" George said, and put the boat ashore on a sandy strip between two rocks. He was the first out, stepping into shallow water in his chunky shoes and black socks, claiming the island as the sovereign territory of the Laytons.

The island was so small it took only a few minutes to climb to the summit where they had a view of the whole lake. Lois, Linda, and Barky ran down to a grove of oak trees while Evelyn spread the blanket and set out brightly colored containers of food. George felt out of breath and lay down close to her. He closed his eyes. Spirochete-shaped objects floated before him, rising and falling fluidly against the pinkness of his eyelids, illumined by the sun. He felt a little nauseated, his back ached, and his wet shoes were uncomfortable.

He looked up at his wife, who was spreading pimento cheese on crackers, her breasts full and free under her dress. Reaching out, he touched her, while Evelyn continued making sandwiches. He didn't fondle her breast, but held it still and firmly in his hand, enjoying its weight. It made him immensely happy that Evelyn allowed him to do this. From a distance, he heard the children's voices, singing in unison: "We are the thumb suckers of the thumb-sucking club," and the giggling that followed.

Evelyn frowned.

"Evelyn," he said, and when she looked at him, he smiled. "It's OK."

After they ate, the kids cracked rocks and examined their interiors.

"This one looks like an M&M, doesn't it?" Lois said, and held up a white rock with a black interior.

"This one is even prettier," Linda said, exhibiting a plain rock that wasn't very pretty at all.

Evelyn and George lay on the blanket and dozed, thinly aware of the world, the motorboat in the distance, the flies above their heads, the dog digging a hole, the girls hammering on their finds.

When he awoke, George called to the girls and together they climbed a large boulder at the very summit of the hill. He took two balloons from his pocket and blew them up and gave one to each girl, telling them to make a wish and let the balloons go. The balloons, a red one and a blue one, were carried by the wind out over the low trees, over the island's shore and beyond the boat, floating far out over the lake before they descended and skittered across the surface of the water.

"You will live long lives," George said, assuming an erect posture befitting his role as mock fortune-teller. "You, Lois, will marry a whale," he predicted, "and live happily in the sea. You, Linda, will marry a bear and be queen of the forest."

"George," Evelyn called. "We ought to get going. What are you guys doing up there? It's getting late."

The children ran down the hill, dodging clumps of cacti and the prickly bushes, racing toward the boat. Evelyn and George followed at a slower pace.

"George," she said just before they reached the spot where the boat was tied, "would you like to have a baby?"

George laughed. "That's a new one." He felt his heart beat faster.

"I've been thinking we could have a child together if we do it soon. Lots of women have kids when they're my age."

"I don't know," George said, but he did know, and he would tell Evelyn later, when he had thought it through and knew exactly how he wanted to say it.

Rowing back across the lake, the sun was low and their skin glowed a golden apricot color in the light. George pulled at the oars, but his arms felt heavy and he was very tired. Frequently, he looked over his shoulder to check the distance to the docks, which never seemed to change. Lois hung over the side, dangling her doll, moving its legs so that sometimes Barbie swam, and sometimes she walked on the water. Linda slept, her head on her mother's lap. Each time he looked at Evelyn, she smiled at him so kindly that she appeared beatific to him. As they rounded the rocky point where the water eddied into a cave at the shoreline, something swooped out of the sky and darted past so quickly that for a moment George wasn't certain he'd actually seen anything. He thought some trick of the eye had fooled him. But then a second time the thing dove in front of him, and this time he saw it for what it was, a bat, moving out at dusk from some dank and darkened dwelling.

SIXTEEN

At the Talent Show

PHYLLIS BARBER

Act I. The Soloists

*W*hen I was nine years old, the bishop of the Boulder City Ward, who happened to be my father, asked me to be the organist for Primary. Mormon children met together at Primary on Wednesday afternoons to study the restored gospel and sing such things as "The Handcart Song," about pioneers who walked across the plains singing "Some must push and some must pull."

"It's time to share the talent God gave you," my father said.

I said yes. I went to work. And of course I thought I sounded good. The teachers in Primary told me so. At the time I didn't understand how adults manipulated children, praising anything that wasn't total disaster.

Week after week I listened for word filtering through the ward at large, hoping to hear about the new virtuoso rising up from under the desert sand, bubbling like a spring into the ward consciousness.

One Sunday afternoon at sacrament meeting, my father, in his position as bishop, made an announcement: "Two weeks from this

Friday night, we're having a ward talent show. Dust off your banjos and ukeleles, warm up your vocal cords, mend that costume at the back of your closet. This is for the whole ward, not just for the few pros we love, but always hear from."

During the week, the verification I'd been waiting for came. I received three phone calls.

"Hello, dear. This is Sister Floyd. I've heard you're a fine little pianist. Could you accompany me for the talent show? I'd like to sing again."

Sister Floyd had six children who never sat still at church. The youngest threw themselves onto the floor in tantrums when they couldn't drink every cup in the sacrament tray. They grabbed handfuls of bread when they were only supposed to take one piece of the Saviour's flesh. Sister Floyd was the woman I studied after my father told me about sex during a Sunday afternoon dinner when I asked the question he couldn't avoid answering. "She does that?" I asked myself later at sacrament meeting when I saw her with a baby on her lap. "Him too?" Her husband seemed so much smaller than she was.

Second phone call: "Hello. This is Brother Frost. I come out to the ward once in a while. Maybe you remember me, maybe not. I used to play trumpet in a combo. Do you think we could practice together for this talent show?"

I remembered Brother Frost. He didn't come to church much, and I'd heard whispers about how he was a Jack Mormon and how he'd fallen. He scared me, a shadow at the edge of the ward activities while I'd been taught to hold my candle high and bright and in the middle of things. He looked like a frost giant—a tower of a man with blonde wavy hair, a red-veined nose, and midnight blue eyes with snowflake spokes around his irises. But I'd been given my talent by God, my parents reminded me often. It wasn't mine to hoard, and I should be generous with it, like Jesus holding out his hands to the lame and the diseased.

"I'd be happy to play for you," I said.

Brother Higginson sounded like Methusaleh when he called. "It's time to get my violin out. Polish up something for the show."

He'd been retired from the railroad for twenty years and lived with his son, the town barber.

I was flattered. Nine years old, and three adults called me to accompany them. I was surprised they hadn't called Sister Doyle, the ward chorister, organist, choir director, and all around leader of music.

Brother Higginson started our first rehearsal by sinking into the big cushions on our sofa and telling me about his railroad days in Washington state—how he used to tend coal and clean cows off catchers. He unlatched his worn case that was more cardboard than cover, put the violin under his chin, and began tuning the strings. "Give me an A," he kept saying as though I hadn't heard him. He struggled out of his seat and hobbled across the space between the sofa and the piano while I played more As.

He shook when he walked; he shook when he handed me the piano music. He also shook when he played. His solo was a blur. "Darn strings," he kept saying as he played a vague rendition of "The Hot Canary." "Slips right out from under my fingers."

He tried for a while but finally said he'd had enough. "You're a fine little sight-reader, Julia." He patted my head. "You've got something we talk a lot about in the business. It's called promise."

His fingers trembled as he laid the violin to rest. "My beautiful friend." He stroked the varnished wood with one finger. "Sleep tight," he said as he closed the case.

Brother Frost came over next. "He's trying to make a comeback," Mother told me when she saw his car pull up in front of the house. She shook her head like she was in a world where things went slowly. "I hope this'll be good for him. Your dad's trying to help him back on his feet."

"When I used to play this tune, the girls'd line up for a city block." Brother Frost handed me the brand-new sheet music to "Cherry Pink and Apple Blossom White." "I had to drive in to Vegas to buy this." But we didn't get through the piece. He kept stopping and apologizing for his lip, never passing "It's cherry pink . . ." without strangling the tone. "Out of shape," he said. "Flabby. Sometimes I wish I'd a been smarter about a few things." He blurted a B flat into my living room. "Let's try it again."

Once he passed the "pink," he had trouble on the falling note, which wouldn't land in tune.

"Damn, damn, damn," he said while his cheeks purpled. I could hear the distorted curses coming out of the bell end of his trumpet while I struggled to modulate to a new key.

"I'll get this if it's the last thing I do," he said, opening the spit valve and shaking his trumpet dry. "I'm gonna do it. Damn right, I'm gonna do it." He pulled out the mouthpiece, dried it with green felt, and placed the pieces of his instrument in the gold velvet interior of his trumpet case.

"I like your rhumba rhythm," he said. "And the way you sight-read! I bet you'll play Carnegie Hall some day."

"What's that?"

"The place of all places in New York City. If you play Carnegie Hall, you've made it big time."

"Did you play there?" I asked.

He laughed. "I've never seen the front doors, child."

"I was a lead in *H.M.S. Pinafore*," Sister Floyd said when she came over to my house after school, "Parowan High School's musical. You should have heard the audience when I sang 'Little Buttercup.'" She tucked her hands under her breasts and asked me to play up and down a five-note scale. "AH, ah, ah, ah, AH, ah, ah, ah, AH." We slid up a half step and repeated it again, up and again, up and again, until her voice disintegrated. "Sore throat," she said.

Then she handed me the battered sheet music of "Little Butter-cup," the one she'd used in high school. I sight-read the introduction successfully, glided into the first few bars of her song, and then she stopped me with both hands waving. "This is too high for my mature voice. Do you think you could transpose it to a lower key?"

Suddenly my ascending curve toward musical fame seemed threatened. I didn't know what transpose meant, let alone know how to do it. Ground shifted under the piano bench and my feet. My vision of Carnegie Hall had been growing larger ever since Brother Frost came to practice. The Grecian columns, its brass doors with floral ornamentation, its thousand steps leading to the entry guarded by stone lions. This picture which had been vast in my young fantasies diminished to tiny doll-house dimensions in one flash of a second. One question. One word I didn't understand. Tiny Carnegie.

"Oh," she said after the protracted silence, "if it's too hard for you, we'll just get by."

"I'm sure it's not too hard," I protested. "It's just that . . ."

"No, no, never mind." She dismissed the subject with finality while one of her children slid down her leg like it was a firepole. I wanted to tell her I'd learn to transpose. I could do whatever I set my mind to if she'd just give me time. I could do music. I knew how to figure things out. But she was swamped by four of her children, their running noses and untied shoelaces, before I could plead my case.

"I'll sing all the verses," she said as she buttoned a child's sweater. "And don't forget the *ritardando* at the end. We need a dramatic ending, like my high school coach taught me."

The night of the talent show, I dressed in a homemade green dress with plaid trim. My big sister Ellen pinned a matching plaid bow in my hair and told me I might be pretty someday. "Maybe," she said, ". . . if the earth's axis shifts."

Mother showed me how to make the toes of my brown shoes shine with a torn piece of my old baby blanket—a flannel strip of faded stars and moons. "Rub circles on the toe until you can see yourself smiling back."

"So, you're going to be in the talent show tonight," my dad said through a veil of steam rising from the breaded pork chops. "Fancy that. My little nine-year-old playing up a storm for the ward."

"Four times she's going to be in the talent show." Mother filled her glass with grape juice. "Singing in a trio with her girlfriends and accompanying several members of the ward. Ray Frost included," she said in a different tone of voice. "Was that your idea, Vern?"

"Shh," my father said. A quick, short "Shh" meant for her ears, not ours.

"Three people asked me to accompany them, Dad," I said proudly. "And they didn't ask Sister Doyle."

"Oh really?" my dad said quietly.

"Sister Floyd, Brother Frost, and Brother Higginson."

"Big deal," my sister Ellen said.

"You might consider," my dad unfolded the paper napkin onto his lap, "that Sister Doyle was too busy. Did you think of that?"

"Vernon!" my mother said sharply. "Why did you have to say that?"

"'Pride goeth before the fall,' you know that."

"Well, that's true," my mother acquiesced, passing green peas and pearl onions flecked with dill. "But Julia's a fine accompanist, and I'm sure the people who called her recognize her ability."

I put my elbows on the table and stabbed my fork into a baked potato just unwrapped from its foil. Always right, father, mother, always right to stop trains in their tracks, trains chugging to somewhere, stop them quickly, suddenly, unavoidably, to remind them to be humble and not chug with too much bravado, not to make too much of any accomplishment lest the Lord take it away, lest the Lord frown, lest, lest, lest.

"I don't mean to take anything away," he said again, "but you know how easy it is to be puffed up with pride. It's not an attractive thing to see, Julia."

Bloated fish. I'd seen them. Dead. Floating on top of the rank water at the edge of Lake Mead. Smelling for miles. Full of maggots and flies and death. It wasn't attractive. My father was right about that.

When they announced Brother Higginson's name, the first to perform, I walked up the stage stairs with care. I didn't want to fall after what my father had said. I promised myself not to puff up with self-importance. I promised to float on top of God's gifts to me, not pretending to any superiority because of them, to remember I was only a lucky wayfarer who'd been given presents to carry to God's house, not to keep for myself.

Brother Higginson quivered like a butterfly wing all the way from his chair in the audience to his place on the stage. Everyone clapped when he arrived safely. Then he rested the violin against his chest and asked me for an A. Five, six, eleven times I played an A until he was satisfied. Slowly and shakily he lifted the violin into playing position, the chin rest snug, his left arm extended uncertainly. His tremulous bow bounced lightly on top of the strings and made imprints of music on the silence. He nodded for me to begin the introduction, which I did. Pregnant silence as his bow hovered over the strings. Finally he stabbed at the high E which was supposed to sound like a canary whistling, but he hadn't aimed right. We started over three times, and finally he stepped out of playing position and said to the audience: "Do you remember the one about the train conductor in Walla Walla?"

After that, no one paid much attention to his "Hot Canary." They thought it was just another joke. I heard myself laughing with them, laughing so breezily at this man, God's butterfly. Yet the sound of my laughter burned my ears, and I worried about pride even though Brother Higginson was genuinely funny as he stood there laughing at himself and shaking like he was without a coat in the Arctic.

Sister Floyd was dressed in a yellow checked pinafore over a white lacy blouse. She'd painted two bonbons of pink on her cheeks and tied a yellow satin bow around her neck. Her youngest children slid off their wooden folding chairs and wandered in the aisle until several of the sisters in the audience coaxed them into their laps and secured them with their arms.

Sister Floyd had told me to wait until she gave me the go-ahead. She needed to take a few deep breaths and find the most comfortable place to stand. She swayed where she stood, back and forth like she was rocking a baby to sleep, and she closed her eyes to concentrate on the words and music that would soon be coming out of her mouth. Finally she looked at me and mouthed the word, "Okay."

"I'm called Little Buttercup, dear Little Buttercup." First, she leaned toward the audience on her right side, then on her left. When she sang "Sailors should never be shy," she wagged her finger like a coquette, turned her back to the audience, and peeked over her shoulder to flutter her eyelashes. Everybody laughed and cheered. "Mommy, Mommy," her smallest boy shouted.

"I've snuff and tobaccky, and excellent jacky." Everybody joined in the fun, and there was so much noise that nobody heard her shrill notes that were out of tune. Nobody but me noticed when she started singing an octave lower.

"Yeah, Sister Floyd," everybody cheered when she curtsied at the end. "Yeah," like she'd hit a home run.

As he came to the stage, I noticed that Brother Frost wore a too-starched, short-sleeved shirt, a light blue tie and slacks that matched his eyes. He was so tall he had to stoop under the valance that fell in graceful pleats from the top of the stage. His trumpet looked small under his arm, like a plastic toy for boys. He looked more like an uncomfortable giant than a trumpet player, and I wondered how he ever picked up his first horn and decided to make music.

When this great hulking man put this instrument to his lips, everyone in the audience looked at him curiously. Who was he? Where had he come from? But then I spotted my father beaming from his place in the audience and remembered he had something to do with Brother Frost standing on the stage with a brass horn in front of the congregation of the Boulder City Ward.

Brother Frost took a huge gulp of air, like Jacob at the bottom of his ladder, deciding whether or not to begin the ascent to heaven. Then came the notes: "It's cherry pink," almost in tune until he slid off the highest one. But he didn't stop to apologize like he had in rehearsal. Not then. Not later when he came to the same hurdle in the piece. He was perspiring, great large blotches of wet diluting the starch in his shirt, trickles of water down his temples. He pushed the notes through the brass as if he were making a bid for a new chance.

When he finished, the audience clapped with polite warmth, but my father stood up and cheered, clapped his hands hard, even whistled between his teeth, and time stretched until all I could hear was the sound of one man clapping. I wanted to close my eyes and ears to my father, embarrassing me as he stood there by himself, clapping for Brother Frost who wasn't all that good on the trumpet, clapping even though the rest of the audience had stopped.

Brother Frost shrugged his shoulders, rubbed the top of my head, and whispered, "Doesn't matter about every note. We made it all the way through, didn't we?"

He was smiling, but his lips were blue, his nose red. The frost giant's hand on my head was freezing cold even though he was covered with perspiration. The chill filtered through my curls and into my skull.

I felt two sensations as I walked off the stage: an indiscriminate one related to the harsh tones in Sister Floyd's voice, the liver-spotted hand curving around the neck of Brother Higginson's violin, Brother Frost's cold hands, my father standing alone in the audience, and his words about pride. The other was a sense of rare coldness in the Boulder City Ward in the desert in Nevada. Like words and snow falling on our heads as we tried to sing and play. Little people in a giant snow storm, walking through white, hidden by a thick curtain of flakes. Potential stars trying to shine in the broad daylight and in the snow. The snow piling high, lulling everyone to sleep beneath its blanket. When we open our mouths in our dreams to sing pure high notes, to purse our lips on a brass mouthpiece, or to steady our bow hand, more snow falls. Our tongues and our mouths and my hands slow in the cold. The sound freezes.

Act II. The Three Chiquitas

I scanned the audience to find my two best friends, Rose and Sheila, but the chairs next to them were taken. I'd been up on the stage too long. Choosing the next best alternative, I headed to the row where my family was sitting. My father wasn't there though. Neither was my mother. But Ellen and Ed were. I scooted in next to them.

"Where'd Mom and Dad go?" I asked Ellen.

"They're helping one of the performers," she said, cracking her chewing gum between her molars.

"Can I have some gum?"

"Most certainly not," she said like she always did, like she was the Queen of Something while I was but a serf.

"Don't sit so close to me." She pushed me away with her elbow. I wanted to ask her if she thought I'd played the piano well or if she thought I'd go to Carnegie Hall someday, but I knew the answer before I asked the question.

"Come here, Ed," I said to my four-year-old brother. "Come sit with me." I herded him into my lap and held him tightly while Brother Hamlin played a polka on his clarinet. I needed somebody close to me. I needed Ed's heartbeat under my hand.

"Do you love me?" I whispered in his ear.

He nodded yes, my faithful brother.

"Did you like how I played the piano?"

He nodded yes again.

"Are you always going to be my best friend? Through thick and thin and cold and dark and dreary?"

"Yes," he whispered back. I squeezed him and kissed his rubbery cheek.

Then I felt a finger tapping my shoulder blade. It was Rose. "Julia, it's time. We have three performers until we're on."

"Already?"

At Sister Doyle's urging, Rose, Sheila, and I had decided to form a trio and sing "Chiquita Banana." We hadn't practised all that much, spending more of our time buying plastic bananas, grapes with rubber stems, and strawberry pincushions at the dime store; testing ways to tie scarves on our heads—knots low on our foreheads, knots above our bangs, knots over the right and left ear, under the chin, at the back of our necks; experimenting with make-up—corals, reds, pinks on our cheeks and lips, blues, greens, grays on our eyes—what would look best on stage, what would make us glow; figuring out a way to make the bananas, grapes, and strawberries stay securely on our heads—giant safety pins, glue, tape, needle and thread, ear muff headpieces without the muffs; deciding on the look-alike white blouses and orange squaw skirts that we were supposed to wash, put on a broom handle while wet and fasten with rubber bands to dry, the latest fashion in town. Last of all we practiced our song.

"Come on," said Rose.

Even though we'd been preparing for weeks, I didn't feel like singing yet. I wasn't feeling warm enough to sing about bananas and the equator and still needed Ed against my chest and my arms tight around him. But when Rose and Sheila started backstage without me, I slipped Ed off my lap, told him to go back to his seat. "This will be *uno* great act," I told him in my best senorita imitation.

"Sure," Ellen said. One last elbow in my rib. "Don't buy her propaganda, Ed."

In the girls' bathroom Rose unlatched her mother's brown vinyl cosmetic case and placed bottles and tubes in a row on the sink. She opened a plastic square of rouge and spread large red balls on her cheeks, bright unnatural spots that seemed to keep growing even after her fingers had gone to other tasks. Sheila opened a Baroque Pink lipstick, its tip sculpted into a fragile peak from much use. I unscrewed the lid of Peacock Blue eye shadow and smudged my eyelids. This was the real thing, our first official time to wear make-up for public display. I was shivering as if caught in the uncertain sails of Columbus's ship as he set off for the edge of the world.

Rose manifested some natural artistic ability as she painted a new face on her old one, but Sheila knew the territory like she was born with make-up in her hand. She looked more beautiful than possible as she lined her eyes with black pencil and made her lips stand up in peaks.

I pressed a tube of lipstick against my mouth, dark red, bold red, a gash on my face because I couldn't follow the outline of my slippery lips, not enough experience in my wrist. Dark blue on the eyelids, smeared heavily from brow to lashes, me peering through two holes in a deep blue sea, eyes blinking slowly under the painted heaviness of the lids. Red on my cheeks—wide circles of paint. Egg-colored powder on my nose and forehead. The bandana tied in place, knot on top of my head. Bananas, grapes, and strawberries dangling over my ear. Giggling all the way to the stage in our white blouses and orange squaw skirts. Rose Red, Sheila Shimmer, Julie Jewel, we'd named ourselves.

Sister Doyle smiled as she sat down on the piano bench where I'd been a few minutes ago, probably suspecting what was to follow. Nevertheless, she thumped out the bright calypso rhythm on the piano. We placed our hands on our hips as we'd planned, then bounced with the rhythm.

"I'm Chiquita Banana," we started out strongly, "And I've come to say." Laughter from the audience, then a titter from Rose. We all looked straight ahead, steeling ourselves against the inevitable.

"Bananas have to ripen in a certain way." More laughter from the audience. Because I never had been able to keep a straight face when anybody laughed at one of my jokes, I was the next to go, and the entire house of cards went with me. Laughter engulfed us, took us for a ride, wouldn't let us stay at the talent show. Soon we were bending over, our hands on our knees, our mouths wrenched out of shape with laughter, our sides being pressed by the sides of our arms in an attempt at quiet, at peace, at containment, the show must go on.

Between us we popped out a few words here and there, sometimes completing an entire phrase. "Chiquita, Chiquita," somebody called out of the audience. "Ariba," plus a high trill on someone's tongue. Everyone seemed to be having a good time, laughing along with us, no investment in perfection. Perfection was whatever happened at the Boulder City Ward Talent Show. Somehow, we rallied at the end, just soon enough to lend credibility to the fact we'd come on stage to sing a song. "So, you should never put bananas . . ." We climbed the scale up to the high point of "nas." We hit the high D together, bravely suppressing our laughter. Together we held the final high note in a triumph of unity, clarity, and song. Rose Red, Sheila Shimmer, Julie Jewel—flourishing our arms in front of the ward, bobbing the fake fruit on our heads, flaunting our innocence, our pre-adolescence, our tight buds of femininity soon to blossom. The Three Chiquitas.

After the high D we finished off with the sermon from the United Fruit Company: (Where should you never put bananas?) "In the refrigerator. No, no, no, no." We shook our hips and fingers in a scolding fashion and then hissed the words "cha, cha, cha" like sassy Latinas. The applause was wide and large and plentiful.

We were a hit. We'd laughed, sung a little, blushed much, paraded ourselves in front of the audience.

And I stood there and bought their applause, swallowed it. I stood there in the swell, my body growing taller, smarter, brighter, nourished by the sound, swelling with the helium of praise, and warming my toes, my heels, my knees, thighs, and chest. They loved us. They loved me. This was much more fun than being an accompanist or playing a piano solo while everyone squirmed and coughed and wished I'd hurry up and finish. This was the applause that spoke to me.

I knew I was destined for something larger. The lights out there somewhere were waiting for my particular beauty, talent, elan. Waiting for all of us—Sheila Shimmer, Rose Red, Julie Jewel. But especially Julie Jewel who played the piano too and could sight-read like lightning.

Act III. Lovely Hula Hands

When Rose, Sheila, and I descended the stairs on our way to the bathroom to change out of our costumes, I saw something I wasn't sure I saw. Someone who looked like my father climbing up the stairs, climbing up to the stage, passing us as we climbed down.

He was dressed in a grass skirt, two half coconuts connected by a string hanging around his neck and covering his nipples, a few straggling hairs at the center of his chest, a sultry black wig on his head, red on his cheeks and lips, blue eye shadow like the blue on my eyes. My mother stood at the bottom of the stairs laughing, her hand over her mouth, the hem of her red and white jersey dress bouncing from her laughter. She had a handful of make-up—lipstick, rouge, eye pencils. She must have been the artist who painted the man who just brushed my side. My father.

"Let's go sit out front," Mother said. "Hurry." She pushed me along. "You don't want to miss this."

"What's happening?" I said.

"Stop asking questions."

She put her arm around my shoulders, and we walked through the room that usually served as a classroom, now doubling as a dressing room, prop room, all purpose throw-everything-in-there room. Music cases against the wall; Maori sticks that had been tossed back and forth by a former New Zealand missionary and his wife while they chanted a Maori song; Brother Jeppson's magic act—a top hat, a cane, a white rabbit in a small cage; a pair of stilts; a Spanish dancing costume hanging from a nail where a picture of Joseph Smith receiving his vision hung on Sundays. We walked around the obstacles and opened the door onto the large room where everyone was watching my father, who usually appeared before them in a suit and tie on Sundays.

The music was beginning. Ukeleles. The sound of the Pacific. Water crashing into shores, rolling out. Mother and I stood against the wall because our seats had been taken by someone's children. Mother could hardly contain herself, wrapping herself with her arms, hugging them tightly around her so her bursting insides wouldn't fall out in front of everyone.

I'd seen my father at home. He loved to dance, and it often seemed to me that some part of him could only be released when music played. And now he was swiveling his hips, paddling air with his arms on one side of his body and then the other.

Without his eyeglasses his eyes were soft blue and inviting like movie star eyes. Bedroom eyes, like Ellen told me she had. Pretty face. Soft skin on his chest. Delicate fingers. His lustrous lashes that mother had mascaraed black fanned out against the backdrop of his painted blue eyelids. He had long black hair in place of a long blank forehead. He wore a flower in his hair and colored leis piled over his shoulders. And I wondered where he learned to make his hands swim like fish through the water and his fingers scoop for poi.

A scratchy version of "A Little Grass Shack in Hawaii" played on the ward's record player as he threw kisses to the audience, tossed his long tresses with one hand, shimmied the coconuts on his chest. My mother was laughing so hard tears were running down her cheeks.

I was not laughing yet because I was still too curious. My father maintained a solid deadpan: a disdainful island princess ignoring her suitors. He held his chin high as if to snub us and puckered his lips as if to say, "Kiss me, if you dare." And he arced the wrists of his "Lovely Hula Hands" more gracefully than a bird in motion. Wrists bending in and out, swan's neck hands. And then he started jutting his hips out faster, holding his arms wide, come-a, come-a.

Laughter raged like fire through the audience and swept over me. I couldn't hold back any longer. I laughed until tears rolled out of my eyes and my legs felt weak. My father, the dancer, the joker, the bishop of the ward.

Finally the music ended and he curtsied, his foot crossing in front of his bent leg rather than in back like in a proper curtsy, showing off the plastic leis around his ankles one last time.

A standing ovation. Two people standing up on their chairs and cheering. Whistles. Clapping hands, stamping feet sounding through the cracks of the ward windows into the night, passersby probably wondering what was happening inside.

"That's the funniest thing I've ever seen," I heard Sister Palmer telling my mother. "I swear it's the funniest."

"How'd you get your husband to do that?" someone asked.

"It was his idea," my mother said.

"Bishop Moore should be a stand-up comedian," all these voices over my head, talking to my mother, spewing words about my father. "He's as good as any comic I ever saw." And I could hear their voices as they turned away from my mother, still talking. "He really looked pretty, didn't he? Even beautiful."

And I ran back through the room with the costumes and props. I ran onto the stage to hug my father and squeeze him with pride before he changed into his suit. Everybody loved my father.

As I hugged his hips covered with the grass skirt and as he stroked my cheek and everyone crowded around him to tell him he was sensational, I sensed I was hugging a mystery, even a trickster like Loki in the Norse myths my teacher read to us at school. Loki could change into anything, even a mare who birthed an eight-legged pony. I liked that my father was a surprise, but I needed to hold onto him for now.

"I love you, Daddy," I said while people pressed close to us.

"Did you like that?" he asked, beaming through the blue eye shadow, his powder, his rouge.

I looked up to tell him yes, yes, yes.

He wasn't talking to me. He was tossing words in the air over my head. Catching Sister Doyle's words in return. "Definitely yes," she was saying.

"You really liked it?" he asked again.

I watched his face. His mouth was open in anticipation of her words. He was smiling, waiting, yet I could see him attempting to mask his eagerness. He didn't want Sister Doyle to know it mattered; he didn't want himself to know it mattered. He was preening, tail feathers alive. He was puffing up before my eyes.

"Terrific. Just terrific," Sister Doyle was saying. "Never saw anything so funny. I swear, Vernon, you ought to get a job in Vegas."

He patted my head as he smiled with satisfaction. Then, as if I were something he wished were in another room, he whispered, "Don't hang on so tight, Julia," he said. "I'm sweating like a dog."

Sister Doyle overheard. "Ladies don't sweat," she said. "They perspire."

"Guess I'm still a man, then." He laughed.

"You're one heck of a great guy." Sister Doyle patted his shoulder, straightened his loops of leis, and kissed him on the cheek. My father shone like noon sun; he stood tall like the wooden Indian in front of the town drugstore. No war bonnet but a high, proud chest and a black wig.

Then Sister Doyle bent down and held my chin with two fingers. "Julia," she said. "Your dad was right. You do a great job accompanying. Glad I recommended you." Then she went over to the piano to close it up for the night.

Suddenly, I felt the weight of the bananas, grapes, and strawberries on my head.

"Let's go, Julia," my father said absentmindedly as if his cup wasn't full yet, looking around to see if anyone else waited to say something.

"Not yet, Dad," I said, still hanging onto his hips. "I need to ask you something."

"Come on, come on," he said, pulling me apart from him. "I've got to get out of this itchy skirt. Driving me bananas."

"I'm Chiquita Banana," I started to sing as we walked toward the stairs. "And I've come to say. . . . "

"How'd your song go?"

"We laughed too much."

"You can never laugh too much," he said as he pulled a flower out of his wig.

"Or dance too much?" I asked him.

"Right. By the way, you did a fine job helping out Brother Frost tonight. Appreciate your helping him out, getting him over the rough spots."

Suddenly, I summoned my courage and blocked the doorway to the stairs and the dressing room. "Do adults rule the world?"

"What do you mean?" He pulled the wig off his head and bent down on his haunches, his coconuts knocking against each other, until we were eye to eye. His blue eye shadow looked severe at close range.

"Sister Doyle told all those people to call me, didn't she?"

"If you have to know, yes, she did."

"Nobody called me just because they thought I was good, did they?"

"That's extreme."

"And you told Sister Doyle to tell them, didn't you?"

"You got to perform didn't you?"

"It's not the same." I stomped the stage with one foot. "Now I feel stupid, stupid, stupid! I wish I'd never learned to play the dumb piano."

"Come on, Julia. Settle down."

"And don't start preaching pride to me. You liked how everyone told you how great you were tonight. I watched you. You like being a star for yourself, not just for God. You can't fool me."

His grass skirt rustled in a draft that seeped through the wood frame of the Boulder City Ward house into the room where everyone's props were waiting to be taken home and put back in closets. And it seeped into me and my father's suddenly sad eyes as he excused himself. "I've got to change clothes," he said. "Wait for me."

SEVENTEEN

The Fringe

ORSON SCOTT CARD

*L*aVon's book report was drivel, of course. Carpenter knew it would be from the moment he called on the boy. After Carpenter's warning last week, he knew LaVon would have a book report—LaVon's father would never let the boy be suspended. But LaVon was too stubborn, too cocky, too much the leader of the other sixth-graders' constant rebellion against authority to let Carpenter have a complete victory.

"I really, truly loved *Little Men*," said LaVon. "It just gave me goose bumps."

The class laughed. Excellent comic timing, Carpenter said silently. But the only place that comedy is useful here in the New Soil country is with the gypsy pageant wagons. That's what you're preparing yourself for, LaVon, a career as a wandering parasite who lives by sucking laughter out of weary farmers.

"Everybody nice in this book has a name that starts with *d*. Demi is a sweet little boy who never does anything wrong. Daisy is so good that she could have seven children and still be a virgin."

He was pushing the limits now. A lot of people didn't like mention of sexual matters in the school, and if some pin-headed child decided to report this, the story could be twisted into something that could be used against Carpenter. Out here near the fringe, people were desperate for entertainment. A crusade to drive out a teacher for corrupting the morals of youth would be more fun than a traveling show, because everybody could feel righteous and safe when he was gone. Carpenter had seen it before. Not that he was afraid of it, the way most teachers were. He had a career no matter what. The university would take him back, eagerly; they thought he was crazy to go out and teach in the low schools. I'm safe, absolutely safe, he thought. They can't wreck my career. And I'm not going to get prissy about a perfectly good word like *virgin*.

"Dan looks like a big bad boy, but he has a heart of gold, even though he does say real bad words like *devil* sometimes." LaVon paused, waiting for Carpenter to react. So Carpenter did not react.

"The saddest thing is poor Nat, the street fiddler's boy. He tries hard to fit in, but he can never amount to anything in the book, because his name doesn't start with *d*."

The end. LaVon put the single paper on Carpenter's desk, then went back to his seat. He walked with the careful elegance of a spider, each long leg moving as if it were unconnected to the rest of his body, so that even walking did not disturb the perfect calm. The boy rides on his body the way I ride in my wheelchair, thought Carpenter. Smooth, unmoved by his own motion. But *he* is graceful and beautiful, fifteen years old and already a master at winning the devotion of the weak-hearted children around him. *He* is the enemy, the torturer, the strong and beautiful man who must confirm his beauty by preying on the weak. I am not as weak as you think.

LaVon's book report was arrogant, far too short, and flagrantly rebellious. That much was deliberate, calculated to annoy Carpenter. Therefore Carpenter would not show the slightest trace of annoyance. The book report had also been clever, ironic, and funny. The boy, for all his mask of languor and stupidity, had brains. He was better than this farming town; he could do something that mattered in the world besides driving a tractor in endless contour patterns around the fields. But the way he always had the

Fisher girl hanging on him, he'd no doubt have a baby and a wife and stay here forever. Become a big shot like his father, maybe, but never leave a mark in the world to show he'd been there. Tragic, stupid waste.

But don't show the anger. The children will misunderstand, they'll think I'm angry because of LaVon's rebelliousness, and it will only make this boy more of a hero in their eyes. Children choose their heroes with unerring stupidity. Fourteen, fifteen, sixteen years old, all they know of life is cold and bookless classrooms interrupted now and then by a year or two of wrestling with this stony earth, always hating whatever adult it is who keeps them at their work, always adoring whatever fool gives them the illusion of being free. You children have no practice in surviving among the ruins of your own mistakes. We adults who knew the world before it fell, we feel the weight of the rubble on our backs.

They were waiting for Carpenter's answer. He reached out to the computer keyboard attached to his wheelchair. His hands struck like paws at the oversized keys. His fingers were too stupid for him to use them individually. They clenched when he tried to work them, tightened into a fist, a little hammer with which to strike, to break, to attack; he could not use them to grasp or even hold. Half the verbs of the world are impossible to me, he thought as he often thought. I learn them the way the blind learn words of seeing—by rote, with no hope of ever knowing truly what they mean.

The speech synthesizer droned out the words he keyed. "Brilliant essay, Mr. Jensen. The irony was powerful, the savagery was refreshing. Unfortunately, it also revealed the poverty of your soul. Alcott's title was ironic, for she wanted to show that despite their small size, the boys in her book were great-hearted. You, however, despite your large size, are very small of heart indeed."

LaVon looked at him through heavy-lidded eyes. Hatred? Yes, it was there. Do hate me, child. Loathe me enough to show me that you can do anything I ask you to do. Then I'll own you, then I can get something decent out of you, and finally give you back to yourself as a human being who is worthy to be alive.

Carpenter pushed outward on both levers, and his wheelchair

backed up. The day was nearly over, and tonight he knew some things would change, painfully, in the life of the town of Reefrock. And because in a way the arrests would be his fault, and because the imprisonment of a father would cause upheaval in some of these children's families, he felt it his duty to prepare them as best he could to understand why it had to happen, why, in the larger view, it was good. It was too much to expect that they would actually understand, today; but they might remember, might forgive him someday for what they would soon find out that he had done to them.

So he pawed at the keys again. "Economics," said the computer. "Since Mr. Jensen has made an end of literature for the day." A few more keys, and the lecture began. Carpenter entered all his lectures and stored them in memory, so that he could sit still as ice in his chair, making eye contact with each student in turn, daring them to be inattentive. There were advantages in letting a machine speak for him; he learned many years ago that it frightened people to have a mechanical voice speak his words, while his lips were motionless. It was monstrous, it made him seem dangerous and strange. Which he far preferred to the way he looked, weak as a worm, his skinny, twisted, palsied body rigid in his chair; his body looked strange, but pathetic. Only when the synthesizer spoke his acid words did he earn respect from the people who always, always looked downward at him.

"Here in the settlements just behind the fringe," his voice went on, "we do not have the luxury of a free economy. The rains sweep onto this ancient desert and find nothing here but a few plants growing in the sand. Thirty years ago, nothing lived here; even the lizards had to stay where there was something for insects to eat, where there was water to drink. Then the fires we lit put a curtain in the sky, and the ice moved south, and the rains that had always passed north of us now raked and scoured the desert. It was opportunity."

LaVon smirked as Kippie made a great show of dozing off. Carpenter keyed an interruption in the lecture. "Kippie, how well will you sleep if I send you home now for an afternoon nap?"

Kippie sat bolt upright, pretending terrible fear. But the pretense was also a pretense; he *was* afraid, and so to conceal it he pretended to be pretending to be afraid. Very complex, the inner life of children, thought Carpenter.

"Even as the old settlements were slowly drowned under the rising Great Salt Lake, your fathers and mothers began to move out into the desert, to reclaim it. But not alone. We can do nothing alone here. The fringers plant their grass. The grass feeds the herds and puts roots into the sand. The roots become humus, rich in nitrogen. In three years the fringe has a thin lace of soil across it. If at any point a fringer fails to plant, if at any point the soil is broken, then the rains eat channels under it, and tear away the fringe on either side, and eat back into farmland behind it. So every fringer is responsible to every other fringer, and to us. How would you feel about a fringer who failed?"

"The way I feel about a fringer who succeeds," said Pope. He was the youngest of the sixth-graders, only thirteen years old, and he sucked up to LaVon disgracefully.

Carpenter punched four codes. "And how is that?" asked Carpenter's metal voice.

Pope's courage fled. "Sorry."

Carpenter did not let go. "What is it you call fringers?" he asked. He looked from one child to the next, and they would not meet his gaze. Except LaVon.

"What do you call them?" he asked again.

"If I say it, I'll get kicked out of school," said LaVon. "You want me kicked out of school?"

"You accuse them of fornicating with cattle, yes?"

A few giggles.

"Yes sir," said LaVon. "We call them cow-fornicators, sir."

Carpenter keyed in his response while they laughed. When the room was silent, he played it back. "The bread you eat grows in the soil they created, and the manure of their cattle is the strength of your bodies. Without fringers you would be eking out a miserable life on the shores of the Mormon Sea, eating fish and drinking sage tea, and don't forget it." He set the volume of the synthesizer steadily lower during the speech, so that at the end they were straining to hear.

Then he resumed his lecture. "After the fringers came your mothers and fathers, planting crops in a scientifically planned order: two rows of apple trees, then six meters of wheat, then six meters of corn, then six meters of cucumbers, and so on, year after year, moving six more meters out, following the fringers, making more land, more food. If you didn't plant what you were told, and harvest it on the right day, and work shoulder to shoulder in the fields whenever the need came, then the plants would die, the rain would wash them away. What do you think of the farmer who does not do his labor or take his work turn?"

"Scum," one child said. And another: "He's a wallow, that's what he is."

"If this land is to be truly alive, it must be planted in a careful plan for eighteen years. Only then will your family have the luxury of deciding what crop to plant. Only then will you be able to be lazy if you want to, or work extra hard and profit from it. Then some of you can get rich, and others can become poor. But now, today, we do everything together, equally, and so we share equally in the rewards of our work."

LaVon murmured something.

"Yes, LaVon?" asked Carpenter. He made the computer speak very loudly. It startled the children.

"Nothing," said LaVon.

"You said: Except teachers."

"What if I did?"

"You are correct," said Carpenter. "Teachers do not plow and plant in the fields with your parents. Teachers are given much more barren soil to work in, and most of the time the few seeds we plant are washed away with the first spring shower. You are living proof of the futility of our labor. But we try, Mr. Jensen, foolish as the effort is. May we continue?"

LaVon nodded. His face was flushed. Carpenter was satisfied. The boy was not hopeless—he could still feel shame at having attacked a man's livelihood.

"There are some among us," said the lecture, "who believe they should benefit more than others from the work of all. These are the ones who steal from the common storehouse and sell the crops that were raised by everyone's labor. The black market pays high prices for the stolen grain, and the thieves get rich. When they get rich enough, they move away from the fringe, back to the cities of the high valleys. Their wives will wear fine clothing, their sons will have watches, their daughters will own land and marry well. And in the meantime, their friends and neighbors, who trusted them, will have nothing, will stay on the fringe, growing the food that feeds the thieves. Tell me, what do you think of a black marketeer?"

He watched their faces. Yes, they knew. He could see how they glanced surreptitiously at Dick's new shoes, at Kippie's wristwatch. At Yutonna's new city-bought blouse. At LaVon's jeans. They knew, but out of fear they had said nothing. Or perhaps it wasn't fear. Perhaps it was the hope that their own father would be clever enough to steal from the harvest, so they could move away instead of earning out their eighteen years.

"Some people think these thieves are clever. But I tell you they are exactly like the mobbers of the plains. They are the enemies of civilization."

"*This* is civilization?" asked LaVon.

"Yes." Carpenter keyed an answer. "We live in peace here, and you know that today's work brings tomorrow's bread. Out on the prairie, they don't know that. Tomorrow a mobber will be eating their bread, if they haven't been killed. There's no trust in the world, except here. And the black marketeers feed on trust. Their neighbors' trust. When they've eaten it all, children, what will you live on then?"

They didn't understand, of course. When it was story problems about one truck approaching another truck at sixty kleeters and it takes an hour to meet, how far away were they?—the children could handle that, could figure it out laboriously with pencil and paper and prayers and curses. But the questions that mattered sailed past them like little dust devils, noticed but untouched by their feeble, self-centered little minds.

He tormented them with a pop quiz on history and thirty spelling words for their homework, then sent them out the door.

LaVon did not leave. He stood by the door, closed it, spoke. "It was a stupid book," he said.

Carpenter clicked the keyboard. "That explains why you wrote a stupid book report."

"It wasn't stupid. It was funny. I read the damn book, didn't I?"

"And I gave you a B."

LaVon was silent a moment, then said, "Do me no favors."

"I never will."

"And shut up with that goddam machine voice. You can make a voice yourself. My cousin's got palsy and she howls to the moon."

"You may leave now, Mr. Jensen."

"I'm gonna hear you talk in your natural voice someday, Mr. Machine."

"You had better go home now, Mr. Jensen."

LaVon opened the door to leave, then turned abruptly and strode the dozen steps to the head of the class. His legs now were tight and powerful as horses' legs, and his arms were light and strong. Carpenter watched him and felt the same old fear rise within him. If God was going to let him be born like this, he could at least keep him safe from the torturers.

"What do you want, Mr. Jensen?" But before the computer had finished speaking Carpenter's words, LaVon reached out and took Carpenter's wrists, held them tightly. Carpenter did not try to resist; if he did, he might go tight and twist around on the chair like a slug on a hot shovel. That would be more humiliation than he could bear, to have this boy see him writhe. His hands hung limp from LaVon's powerful fists.

"You just mind your business," LaVon said. "You only been here two years, you don't know nothin, you understand? You don't see nothin, you don't say nothin, you understand?"

So it wasn't the book report at all. LaVon had actually understood the lecture about civilization and the black market. And knew that it was LaVon's own father, more than anyone else in town, who was guilty. Nephi Delos Jensen, bigshot foreman of Reefrock

Farms. Have the marshals already taken your father? Best get home and see.

"Do you understand me?"

But Carpenter would not speak. Not without his computer. This boy would never hear how Carpenter's own voice sounded, the whining, baying sound, like a dog trying to curl its tongue into human speech. You'll never hear my voice, boy.

"Just try to expel me for this, Mr. Carpenter. I'll say it never happened. I'll say you had it in for me."

Then he let go of Carpenter's hands and stalked from the room. Only then did Carpenter's legs go rigid, lifting him on the chair so that only the computer over his lap kept him from sliding off. His arms pressed outward, his neck twisted, his jaw opened wide. It was what his body did with fear and rage; it was why he did his best never to feel those emotions. Or any others, for that matter. Dispassionate, that's what he was. He lived the life of the mind, since the life of the body was beyond him. He stretched across his wheelchair like a mocking crucifix, hating his body and pretending that he was merely waiting for it to calm, to relax.

And it did, of course. As soon as he had control of his hands again, he took the computer out of speech mode and called up the data he had sent on to Zarahemla yesterday morning. The crop estimates for three years, and the final weight of the harvested wheat and corn, cukes and berries, apples and beans. For the first two years, the estimates were within two percent of the final total. The third year, the estimates were higher, but the harvest stayed the same. It was suspicious. Then the bishop's accounting records. It was a sick community. When the bishop was also seduced into this sort of thing, it meant the rottenness touched every corner of village life. Reefrock Farms looked no different from the hundred other villages just this side of the fringe, but it was diseased. Did Kippie know that even his father was in on the black marketeering? If you couldn't trust the bishop, who was left?

The words of his own thoughts tasted sour in his mouth. Diseased. They aren't so sick, Carpenter, he told himself. Civilization has always had its parasites, and survived. But it survived because it rooted them out from time to time, cast them away and cleansed the body. Yet they made heroes out of the thieves and despised those who reported them. There's no thanks in what I've done. It isn't love I'm earning. It isn't love I feel. Can I pretend that I'm not just a sick and twisted body taking vengeance on those healthy enough to have families, healthy enough to want to get every possible advantage for them?

He pushed the levers inward and the chair rolled forward. He skillfully maneuvered between the chairs, but it still took nearly a full minute to get to the door. I'm a snail. A worm living in a metal carapace, a water snail creeping along the edge of the aquarium glass, trying to keep it clean from the filth of the fish. I'm the loathsome one; they're the golden ones that shine in the sparkling water. They're the ones whose death is mourned. But without me they'd die. I'm as responsible for their beauty as they are. More, because I work to sustain it, and they simply—are.

It came out this way whenever he tried to reason out an excuse for his own life. He rolled down the corridor to the front door of the school. He knew, intellectually, that his work in crop rotation and timing had been the key to opening up the vast New Soil Lands here in the eastern Utah desert. Hadn't they invented a civilian medal for him, and then, for good measure, given him the same medal they gave to the freedom riders who went out and brought immigrant trains safely into the mountains? I was a hero, they said, this worm in his wheelchair house. But Governor Monson had looked at him with those distant, pitying eyes. He, too, saw the worm; Carpenter might be a hero, but he was still Carpenter.

They had built a concrete ramp for his chair after the second time the students knocked over the wooden ramp and forced him to summon help through the computer airlink network. He remembered sitting on the lip of the porch, looking out toward the cabins of the village. If anyone saw him, then they consented to his imprisonment, because they didn't come to help him. But Carpenter understood. Fear of the strange, the unknown. It wasn't *comfortable* for them, to be near Mr. Carpenter with the mechanical voice and the electric rolling chair. He understood, he really did, he was human too, wasn't he? He even agreed with them. Pretend Carpenter isn't there, and maybe he'll go away.

The helicopter came as he rolled out onto the asphalt of the street. It landed in the Circle, between the storehouse and the chapel. Four marshals came out of the gash in its side and spread out through the town.

It happened that Carpenter was rolling in front of Bishop Anderson's house when the marshal knocked on the door. He hadn't expected them to make the arrests while he was still going down the street. His first impulse was to speed up, to get away from the arrest. He didn't want to see. He liked Bishop Anderson. Used to, anyway. He didn't wish him ill. If the bishop had kept his hands out of the harvest, if he hadn't betrayed his trust, he wouldn't have been afraid to hear the knock on the door and see the badge in the marshal's hand.

Carpenter could hear Sister Anderson crying as they led her husband away. Was Kippie there, watching? Did he notice Mr. Carpenter passing by on the road? Carpenter knew what it would cost these families. Not just the shame, though it would be intense. Far worse would be the loss of their father for years, the extra labor for the children. To break up a family was a terrible thing to do, for the innocent would pay as great a cost as their guilty father, and it wasn't fair, for they had done no wrong. But it was the stern necessity, if civilization was to survive.

Carpenter slowed down his wheelchair, forcing himself to hear the weeping from the bishop's house, to let them look at him with hatred if they knew what he had done. And they would know: he had specifically refused to be anonymous. If I can inflict stern necessity on them, then I must not run from the consequences of my own actions. I will bear what I must bear, as well—the grief, the resentment, and the rage of the few families I have harmed for the sake of all the rest.

The helicopter had taken off again before Carpenter's chair took him home. It sputtered overhead and disappeared into the low clouds. Rain again tomorrow, of course. Three days dry, three days wet, it had been the weather pattern all spring. The rain would come pounding tonight. Four hours till dark. Maybe the rain wouldn't come until dark.

He looked up from his book. He *had* heard footsteps outside his house. And whispers. He rolled to the window and looked out. The sky was a little darker. The computer said it was four-thirty. The wind was coming up. But the sounds he heard hadn't been the wind. It was three-thirty when the marshals came. Four-thirty now, and footsteps and whispers outside his house. He felt the stiffening in his arms and legs. Wait, he told himself. There's nothing to fear. Relax. Quiet. Yes. His body eased. His heart pounded, but it was slowing down.

The door crashed open. He was rigid at once. He couldn't even bring his hands down to touch the levers so he could turn to see who it was. He just spread there helplessly in his chair as the heavy footfalls came closer.

"There he is." The voice was Kippie's.

Hands seized his arms, pulled on him; the chair rocked as they tugged him to one side. He could not relax. "Son of a bitch is stiff as a statue." Pope's voice. Get out of here, little boy, said Carpenter, you're in something too deep for you, too deep for any of you. But of course they did not hear him, since his fingers couldn't reach the keyboard where he kept his voice.

"Maybe this is what he does when he isn't at school. Just sits here and makes statues at the window." Kippie laughed.

"He's scared stiff, that's what he is."

"Just bring him out, and fast." LaVon's voice carried authority.

They tried to lift him out of the chair, but his body was too rigid; they hurt him, though, trying, for his thighs pressed up against the computer with cruel force, and they wrung at his arms.

"Just carry the whole chair," said LaVon.

They picked up the chair and pulled him toward the door. His arms smacked against the corners and the doorframe. "It's like he's dead or something," said Kippie. "He don't say nothin."

He was shouting at them in his mind, however. What are you doing here? Getting some sort of vengeance? Do you think punishing me will bring your fathers back, you fools?

They pulled and pushed the chair into the van they had parked in front. The bishop's van—Kippie wouldn't have the use of *that* much longer. How much of the stolen grain was carried in here?

"He's going to roll around back here," said Kippie.

"Tip him over," said LaVon.

Carpenter felt the chair fly under him; by chance he landed in such a way that his left arm was not caught behind the chair. It would have broken then. As it was, the impact with the floor bent his arm forcibly against the strength of his spasmed muscles; he felt something tear, and his throat made a sound in spite of his effort to bear it silently.

"Did you hear that?" said Pope. "He's got a voice."

"Not for much longer," said LaVon.

For the first time, Carpenter realized that it wasn't just pain that he had to fear. Now, only an hour after their fathers had been taken, long before time could cool their rage, these boys had murder in their hearts.

The road was smooth enough in town, but soon it became rough and painful. From that, Carpenter knew they were headed toward the fringe. He could feel the cold metal of the van's corrugated floor against his face; the pain in his arm was settling down to a steady throb. Relax, quiet, calm, he told himself. How many times in your life have you wished to die? Death means nothing to you, fool, you decided that years ago. Death is nothing but a release from this corpse. So what are you afraid of? Calm, quiet. His arms bent, his legs relaxed.

"He's getting soft again," reported Pope. From the front of the van Kippie guffawed. "Little and squirmy. Mr. Bug. We always call you that, you hear me, Mr. Bug? There was always two of you. Mr. Machine and Mr. Bug. Mr. Machine was mean and tough and smart, but Mr. Bug was weak and squishy and gross, with wiggly legs. Made us want to puke, looking at Mr. Bug."

I've been tormented by master torturers in my childhood, Pope Griffith. You are only a pathetic echo of their talent. Carpenter's words were silent, until his hands found the keys. His left hand was almost too weak to use, after the fall, so he coded the words clumsily with his right hand alone. "If I disappear the day of your father's arrest, Mr. Griffith, don't you think they'll guess who took me?"

"Keep his hands away from the keys!" shouted LaVon. "Don't let him touch the computer."

Almost immediately, the van lurched and took a savage bounce as it left the roadway. Now it was clattering over rough, unfinished ground. Carpenter's head banged against the metal floor, again and again. The pain of it made him go rigid; fortunately, spasms always carried his head upward to the right, so that his rigidity kept him from having his head beaten to unconsciousness.

Soon the bouncing stopped. The engine died. Carpenter could hear the wind whispering over the open desert land. They were beyond the fields and orchards, out past the grassland of the fringe. The van doors opened. LaVon and Kippie reached in and pulled him out, chair and all. They dragged the chair to the top of a wash. There was no water in it yet.

"Let's just throw him down," said Kippie. "Break his spastic little neck." Carpenter had not guessed that anger could burn so hot in these languid, mocking boys.

But LaVon showed no fire. He was cold and smooth as snow. "I don't want to kill him yet. I want to hear him talk first."

Carpenter reached out to code an answer. LaVon slapped his hands away, gripped the computer, braced a foot on the wheelchair, and tore the computer off its mounting. He threw it across the arroyo; it smacked against the far side and tumbled down into the dry wash. Probably it wasn't damaged, but it wasn't the computer Carpenter was frightened for. Until now Carpenter could cling to a hope that they just meant to frighten him. But it was unthinkable to treat precious electronic equipment that way, not if civilization still had any hold on LaVon.

"With your *voice*, Mr. Carpenter. Not the machine, your own voice."

Not for you, Mr. Jensen. I don't humiliate myself for you.

"Come on," said Pope. "You know what we said. We just take him down into the wash and leave him there."

"We'll send him down the quick way," said Kippie. He shoved at the wheelchair, teetering it toward the brink.

"We'll *take* him down!" shouted Pope. "We aren't going to kill him! You promised!"

"Lot of difference it makes," said Kippie. "As soon as it rains in the mountains, this sucker's gonna fill up with water and give him the swim of his life."

"We won't kill him," insisted Pope.

"Come on," said LaVon. "Let's get him down into the wash."

Carpenter concentrated on not going rigid as they wrestled the chair down the slope. The walls of the wash weren't sheer, but they were steep enough that the climb down wasn't easy. Carpenter tried to concentrate on mathematics problems so he wouldn't panic and writhe for them again. Finally the chair came to rest at the bottom of the wash.

"You think you can come here and decide who's good and who's bad, right?" said LaVon. "You think you can sit on your little throne and decide whose father's going to jail, is that it?"

Carpenter's hands rested on the twisted mountings that used to hold his computer. He felt naked, defenseless without his stinging, frightening voice to whip them into line. LaVon was smart to take away his voice. LaVon knew what Carpenter could do with words.

"Everybody does it," said Kippie. "You're the only one who doesn't black the harvest, and that's only because you can't."

"It's easy to be straight when you can't get anything on the side anyway," said Pope.

Nothing's easy, Mr. Griffith. Not even virtue.

"My father's a good man!" shouted Kippie. "He's the bishop, for Christ's sake! And you sent him to jail!"

"If he ain't shot," said Pope.

"They don't shoot you for blacking anymore," said LaVon. "That was in the old days."

The old days. Only five years ago. But those were the old days for these children. Children are innocent in the eyes of God, Carpenter reminded himself. He tried to believe that these boys didn't know what they were doing to him.

Kippie and Pope started up the side of the wash. "Come on," said Pope. "Come on, LaVon."

"Minute," said LaVon. He leaned close to Carpenter and spoke softly, intensely, his breath hot and foul, his spittle like sparks from a cookfire on Carpenter's face. "Just ask me," he said. "Just open your mouth and beg me, little man, and I'll carry you back up to the van. They'll let you live if I tell them to, you know that."

He knew it. But he also knew that LaVon would never tell them to spare his life.

"Beg me, Mr. Carpenter. Ask me please to let you live, and you'll live. Look. I'll even save your little talkbox for you." He scooped up the computer from the sandy bottom and heaved it up out of the wash. It sailed over Kippie's head just as he was emerging from the arroyo.

"What the hell was that, you trying to kill me?"

LaVon whispered again. "You know how many times you made me crawl? And now I gotta crawl forever, my father's a jailbird thanks to you, I got little brothers and sisters, even if you hate me, what've you got against them, huh?"

A drop of rain struck Carpenter in the face. There were a few more drops.

"Feel that?" said LaVon. "The rain in the mountains makes this wash flood every time. You crawl for me, Carpenter, and I'll take you up."

Carpenter didn't feel particularly brave as he kept his mouth shut and made no sound. If he actually believed LaVon might keep his promise, he would swallow his pride and beg. But LaVon was lying. He couldn't afford to save Carpenter's life now, even if he wanted to. It had gone too far, the consequences would be too great. Carpenter had to die, accidently drowned, no witnesses, such a sad thing, such a great man, and no one the wiser about the three boys who carried him to his dying place.

If he begged and whined in his hound voice, his cat voice, his bestial monster voice, then LaVon would smirk at him in triumph and whisper, "Sucker." Carpenter knew the boy too well. Tomorrow LaVon would have second thoughts, of course, but right now there'd be no softening. He only wanted his triumph to be complete, that's why he held out a hope. He wanted to watch Carpenter twist like a worm and bay like a hound before he died. It was a victory, then, to keep silence. Let him remember me in his nightmares of guilt, let him remember I had courage enough not to whimper.

LaVon spat at him; the spittle struck him in the chest. "I can't even get it in your ugly little worm face," he said. Then he shoved the wheelchair and scrambled up the bank of the wash.

For a moment the chair hung in balance; then it tipped over. This time Carpenter relaxed during the fall and rolled out of the chair without further injury. His back was to the side of the wash they had climbed; he couldn't see if they were watching him or not. So he held still, except for a slight twitching of his hurt left arm. After a while the van drove away.

Only then did he begin to reach out his arms and paw at the sand of the arroyo bottom. His legs were completely useless, dragging behind him. But he was not totally helpless without his chair. He could control his arms, and by reaching them out and then pulling his body onto his elbows he could make good progress across the sand. How did they think he got from his wheelchair to bed, or to the toilet? Hadn't they seen him use his hands and arms? Of course they saw, but they assumed that because his arms were weak, they were useless.

Then he got to the arroyo wall and realized that they *were* useless. As soon as there was any slope to climb, his left arm began to hurt badly. And the bank was steep. Without being able to use his fingers to clutch at one of the sagebrushes or tree starts, there was no hope he could climb out.

The lightning was flashing in the distance, and he could hear the thunder. The rain here was a steady plick plick plick on the sand, a tiny slapping sound on the few leaves. It would already be raining heavily in the mountains. Soon the water would be here.

He dragged himself another meter up the slope despite the pain. The sand scraped his elbows as he dug with them to pull himself along. The rain fell steadily now, many large drops, but still not a downpour. It was little comfort to Carpenter. Water was beginning to dribble down the sides of the wash and form puddles in the streambed.

With bitter humor he imagined himself telling Dean Wintz, "On second thought, I don't want to go out and teach sixth grade. I'll just go right on teaching them here, when they come off the farm. Just the few who want to learn something beyond sixth grade, who want a university education. The ones who love books and numbers and languages, the ones who understand civilization and want to keep it alive. Give me the children who *want* to learn, instead of these poor sandscrapers who only go to school because the law commands that six years out of their first fifteen years have to be spent as captives in the prison of learning."

Why do the fire-eaters go out searching for the old missile sites and risk their lives disarming them? To preserve civilization. Why do the freedom riders leave their safe homes and go out to bring the frightened, lonely refugees in to the safety of the mountains? To preserve civilization.

And why had Timothy Carpenter informed the marshals about the black marketeering he had discovered in Reefrock Farms? Was it, truly, to preserve civilization?

Yes, he insisted to himself.

The water was flowing now along the bottom of the wash. His feet were near the flow. He painfully pulled himself up another meter. He had to keep his body pointed straight toward the side of the wash, or he would not be able to stop himself from rolling to one side or the other. He found that by kicking his legs in his spastic, uncontrolled fashion, he could root the toes of his shoes into the sand just enough that he could take some pressure off his arms, just for a moment.

No, he told himself. It was not just to preserve civilization. It was because of the swaggering way their children walked, in their stolen clothing, with their full bellies and healthy skin and hair, cocky as only security can make a child feel. Enough and to spare, that's what they had, while the poor suckers around them worried whether there'd be food enough for the winter, and if their mother was getting enough so the nursing baby wouldn't lack, and whether their shoes could last another summer. The thieves could take a wagon up the long road to Price or even to Zarahemla, the shining city on the Mormon Sea, while the children of honest men never saw anything but the dust and sand and ruddy mountains of the fringe.

Carpenter hated them for that, for all the differences in the world, for the children who had legs and walked nowhere that mattered, for the children who had voices and used them to speak stupidity, who had deft and clever fingers and used them to frighten and compel the weak. For all the inequalities in the world, he hated them and wanted them to pay for it. They couldn't go to jail for having obedient arms and legs and tongues, but they could damn well go for stealing the hard-earned harvest of trusting men and women. Whatever his own motives might be, that was reason enough to call it justice.

The water was rising many centimeters every minute. The current was tugging at his feet now. He released his elbows to reach them up for another, higher purchase on the bank, but no sooner had he reached out his arms than he slid downward and the current pulled harder at him. It took great effort just to return to where he started, and his left arm was on fire with the tearing muscles. Still, it was life, wasn't it? His left elbow rooted him in place while he reached with his right arm and climbed higher still, and again higher. He even tried to use his fingers to cling to the soil, to a branch, to a rock, but his fists stayed closed and hammered uselessly against the ground.

Am I vengeful, bitter, spiteful? Maybe I am. But whatever my motive was, they were thieves, and had no business remaining among the people they betrayed. It was hard on the children, of course, cruelly hard on them, to have their fathers stripped away from them by the authorities. But how much worse would it be for the fathers to stay, and the children to learn that trust was for the stupid and honor for the weak? What kind of people would we be then, if the children could do their numbers and letters but couldn't hold someone else's plate and leave the food on it untouched?

The water was up to his waist. The current was rocking him slightly, pulling him downstream. His legs were floating behind him now, and water was trickling down the bank, making the earth looser under his elbows. So the children wanted him dead now, in their fury. He would die in a good cause, wouldn't he?

With the water rising faster, the current swifter, he decided that martyrdom was not all it was cracked up to be. Nor was life, when he came right down to it, something to be given up lightly because of a few inconveniences. He managed to squirm up a few more centimeters, but now a shelf of earth blocked him. Someone with hands could have reached over it easily and grabbed hold of the sagebrush just above it.

He clenched his mouth tight and lifted his arm up onto the shelf of dirt. He tried to scrape some purchase for his forearm, but the soil was slick. When he tried to place some weight on the arm, he slid down again.

This was it, this was his death, he could feel it, and in the sudden rush of fear his body went rigid. Almost at once his feet caught on the rocky bed of the river and stopped him from sliding farther. Spastic, his legs were of some use to him. He swung his right arm up, scraped his fist on the sagebrush stem, trying to pry his clenched fingers open.

And, with agonizing effort, he did it. All but the smallest finger opened enough to hook the stem. Now the clenching was some help to him. He used his left arm mercilessly, ignoring the pain, to pull him up a little farther, onto the shelf; his feet were still in the water, but his waist wasn't, and the current wasn't strong against him now.

It was a victory, but not much of one. The water wasn't even a meter deep yet, and the current wasn't yet strong enough to have carried away his wheelchair. But it was enough to kill him, if he hadn't come this far. Still, what was he really accomplishing? In storms like this, the water came up near the top; he'd have been dead for an hour before the water began to come down again.

He could hear, in the distance, a vehicle approaching on the road. Had they come back to watch him die? They couldn't be that stupid. How far was this wash from the highway? Not far—they hadn't driven that long on the rough ground to get here. But it meant nothing. No one would see him, or even the computer that lay among the tumbleweeds and sagebrush at the arroyo's edge.

They might hear him. It was possible. If their window was open—in a rainstorm? If their engine was quiet—but loud enough that he could hear them? Impossible, impossible. And it might be the boys again, come to hear him scream and whine for life; I'm not going to cry out now, after so many years of silence—

But the will to live, he discovered, was stronger than shame; his voice came unbidden to his throat. His lips and tongue and teeth that in childhood had so painstakingly practiced words that only his family could ever understand now formed a word again: "Help!" It was a difficult word; it almost closed his mouth, it made him too quiet to hear. So at last he simply howled, saying nothing except the terrible sound of his voice.

The brake squealed, long and loud, and the vehicle rattled to a stop. The engine died. Carpenter howled again. Car doors slammed.

"I tell you it's just a dog somewhere, somebody's old dog—"

Carpenter howled again.

"Dog or not, it's alive, isn't it?"

They ran along the edge of the arroyo, and someone saw him.

"A little kid!"

"What's he doing down there!"

"Come on, kid, you can climb up from there!"

I nearly killed myself climbing this far, you fool, if I *could* climb, don't you think I *would* have? Help me! He cried out again.

"It's not a little boy. He's got a beard—"

"Come on, hold on, we're coming down!"

"There's a wheelchair in the water—"

"He must be a cripple."

There were several voices, some of them women, but it was two strong men who reached him, splashing their feet in the water. They hooked him under the arms and carried him to the top.

"Can you stand up? Are you all right? Can you stand?"

Carpenter strained to squeeze out the word: "No."

The older woman took command. "He's got palsy, as any fool can see. Go back down there and get his wheelchair, Tom, no sense in making him wait till they can get him another one, go on down! It's not that bad down there, the flood isn't here yet!" Her voice was crisp and clear, perfect speech, almost foreign it was so precise. She and the young woman carried him to the truck. It was a big old flatbed truck from the old days, and on its back was a canvas-covered heap of odd shapes. On the canvas Carpenter read the words SWEETWATER'S MIRACLE PAGEANT. Traveling show people, then, racing for town to get out of the rain, and through some miracle they had heard his call.

"Your poor arms," said the young woman, wiping off grit and sand that had sliced his elbows. "Did you climb that far out of there with just your arms?"

The young men came out of the arroyo muddy and cursing, but they had the wheelchair. They tied it quickly to the back of the truck; one of the men found the computer, too, and took it inside the cab. It was designed to be rugged, and to Carpenter's relief it still worked.

"Thank you," said his mechanical voice.

"I told them I heard something and they said I was crazy," said the old woman. "You live in Reefrock?"

"Yes," said his voice.

"Amazing what those old machines can still do, even after being dumped there in the rain," said the old woman. "Well, you came close to death, there, but you're all right, it's the best we can ask for. We'll take you to the doctor."

"Just take me home. Please."

So they did, but insisted on helping him bathe and fixing him dinner. The rain was coming down in sheets when they were done. "All I have is a floor," he said, "but you can stay."

"Better than trying to pitch the tents in this." So they stayed the night.

Carpenter's arms ached too badly for him to sleep, even though he was exhausted. He lay awake thinking of the current pulling him, imagining what would have happened to him, how far he might have gone downstream before drowning, where his body might have ended up. Caught in a snag somewhere, dangling on some branch or rock as the water went down and left his slack body to dry in the sun. Far out in the desert somewhere, maybe. Or perhaps the floodwater might have carried him all the way to the Colorado and tumbled him head over heels down the rapids, through the canyons, past the ruins of the old dams, and finally into the Gulf of California. He'd pass through Navaho territory then, and the Hopi Protectorate, and into areas that Chihuahua claimed and threatened to go to war to keep. He'd see more of the world than he had seen in his life.

I saw more of the world tonight, he thought, than I ever thought to see. I saw death and how much I feared it.

And he looked into himself, wondering how much he had changed.

Late in the morning, when he finally awoke, the pageant people were gone. They had a show, of course, and had to do some kind of parade to let people know. School would let out early so they could put on the show without having to waste power on lights. There'd be no school this afternoon. But what about his morning classes? There must have been some question when he didn't show up; someone would have called, and if he didn't answer the phone someone would have come by. Maybe the show people had still been here when they came. The word would have spread through school that he was still alive.

He tried to imagine LaVon and Kippie and Pope hearing that Mr. Machine, Mr. Bug, Mr. Carpenter was still alive. They'd be afraid, of course. Maybe defiant. Maybe they had even confessed. No, not that. LaVon would keep them quiet. Try to think of a way out. Maybe even plan an escape, though finding a place to go that wasn't under Utah authority would be a problem.

What am I doing? Trying to plan how my enemies can escape retribution? I should call the marshals again, tell them what happened. If someone hasn't called them already.

His wheelchair waited by his bed. The show people had shined it up for him, got rid of all the muck. Even straightened the computer mounts and tied it on, jury-rigged it but it would do. Would the motor run, after being under water? He saw that they had even changed batteries and had the old one set aside. They were good people.

Not at all what the stories said about show gypsies. Though there was no natural law that people who help cripples can't also seduce all the young girls in the village.

His arms hurt and his left arm was weak and trembly, but he managed to get into the chair. The pain brought back yesterday. I'm alive today, and yet today doesn't feel any different from last week, when I was also alive. Being on the brink of death wasn't enough; the only transformation is to die.

He ate lunch because it was nearly noon. Eldon Finch came by to see him, along with the sheriff. "I'm the new bishop," said Eldon.

"Didn't waste any time," said Carpenter.

"I gotta tell you, Brother Carpenter, things are in a tizzy today. Yesterday, too, of course, what with avenging angels dropping out of the sky and taking away people we all trusted. There's some says you shouldn't've told, and some says you did right, and some ain't sayin nothin cause they're afraid somethin'll get told on *them*. Ugly times, ugly times, when folks steal from their neighbors."

Sheriff Budd finally spoke up. "Almost as ugly as tryin to drownd em."

The Bishop nodded. "Course you know the reason we come, Sheriff Budd and me, we come to find out who done it."

"Done what?"

"Plunked you down that wash. You aren't gonna tell me you drove that little wheelie chair of yours out there past the fringe. What, was you speedin so fast you lost control and spun out? Give me peace of heart, Brother Carpenter, give me trust." The bishop and the sheriff both laughed at that. Quite a joke.

Now's the time, thought Carpenter. Name the names. The motive will be clear, justice will be done. They put you through the worst hell of your life, they made you cry out for help, they taught you the taste of death. Now even things up.

But he didn't key their names into the computer. He thought of Kippie's mother crying at the door. When the crying stopped, there'd be years ahead. They were a long way from proving out their land. Kippie was through with school, he'd never go on, never get out. The adult burden was on those boys now, years too young.

Should their families suffer even more, with another generation gone to prison? Carpenter had nothing to gain, and many who were guiltless stood to lose too much.

"Brother Carpenter," said Sheriff Budd. "Who was it?"

He keyed in his answer. "I didn't get a look at them."

"Their voices, didn't you know them?"

"No."

The Bishop looked steadily at him. "They tried to kill you, Brother Carpenter. That's no joke. You like to have died, if those show people hadn't happened by. And I have my own ideas who it was, seein who had reason to hate you unto death yesterday."

"As you said, a lot of people think an outsider like me should have kept his nose out of Reefrock's business."

The bishop frowned at him. "You scared they'll try again?"

"No."

"Nothin I can do," said the sheriff. "I think you're a damn fool, Brother Carpenter, but nothin I can do if you don't even care."

"Thanks for coming by."

He didn't go to church Sunday. But on Monday he went to school, same time as usual. And there were LaVon and Kippie and Pope, right in their places. But not the same as usual. The wisecracks were over. When he called on them, they answered if they could and didn't if they couldn't. When he looked at them, they looked away.

He didn't know if it was shame or fear that he might someday tell; he didn't care. The mark was on them. They would marry someday, go out into even newer lands just behind the ever-advancing fringe, have babies, work until their bodies were exhausted, and then drop into a grave. But they'd remember that one day they left a cripple to die. He had no idea what it would mean to them, but they would remember.

Within a few weeks LaVon and Kippie were out of school; with their fathers gone, there was too much fieldwork and school was a luxury their families couldn't afford for them. Pope had an older brother still at home, so he stayed out the year.

One time Pope almost talked to him. It was a windy day that

spattered sand against the classroom window, and the storm coming out of the south looked to be a nasty one. When class was over, most of the kids ducked their heads and rushed outside, hurrying to get home before the downpour began. A few stayed, though, to talk with Carpenter about this and that. When the last one left, Carpenter saw that Pope was still there. His pencil was hovering over a piece of paper. He looked up at Carpenter, then set the pencil down, picked up his books, started for the door. He paused for a moment with his hand on the doorknob. Carpenter waited for him to speak. But the boy only opened the door and went on out.

Carpenter rolled over to the door and watched him as he walked away. The wind caught at his jacket. Like a kite, thought Carpenter, it's lifting him along.

But it wasn't true. The boy didn't rise and fly. And now Carpenter saw the wind like a current down the village street, sweeping Pope away. All the bodies in the world, caught in that same current, that same wind, blown down the same rivers, the same streets, and finally coming to rest on some snag, through some door, in some grave, God knows where or why.

EIGHTEEN

Dry Niger

M . S H A Y N E   B E L L

That spring the Niger had gone dry. Ahmid, my castrato driver, careened our jeep down the riverbank and sped northwest up the dusty riverbed. "All the roads out of Niamey are blown in with sand," he said. "We will make better time here."

I had read the night before in *Le Sahel* of a military caravan that found a jeep, just like the one I was in, stuck in a sand dune that had blown over the main road to Tahoua. No one was in the jeep or near the jeep, and the soldiers found no sign of driver or occupants. The wind had blown sand over all their tracks and eventually, no doubt, them. "Maybe they saw the mirage of an oasis within walking distance," one of the soldiers theorized. It was a terrible story. I was glad to be driving up the riverbed.

We passed under the Kennedy Bridge, and in the brief moment we were in its shadow I felt cold. "You will not shiver again today," Ahmid said, very serious.

I looked back at the bridge and saw a thin man start across it from the south, driving three goats before him. Behind him came a woman carrying on her head a bundle of the black cloth favored by the Tuareg. We were getting a late start. But the jeep wouldn't start in the night, and though the minister of mines herself, Aissa Seibou, had come with the mechanic and waited with me and Ahmid in the shed while we watched the mechanic work, it took time to change a fuel pump, then the water pump just in case, then to put on the new belt I insisted on. "I will follow you in two days," the minister had said. "By then you will have seen and studied these uranium fields as I have, and you will agree with me."

Such confidence. But I was prepared to believe her because I had read URANIGER's reports on the potential of these mines, and the World Bank was prepared to believe me and back my recommendation when I gave it. The bank had money to fund only one project that year in West Africa. The directors had narrowed their choices to two projects: one, a loan to help develop uranium mines in Niger's Zermaganda province eighty kilometers northeast of Sinder; the other, a reforestation project in the highlands of Guinea around the source of the Niger so that rainfall might increase and in forty years the river might flow again to the sea, not dry up at Lake Debo in Mali. The reforestation project offered enormous long-term benefits decades after its start. But exploitable uranium lay waiting in the desert now. West Africa needed help now. Aissa Seibou was probably justified in feeling confident.

I turned back around and watched the riverbed ahead of us. "How often do you get flash floods?" I asked.

"That Allah should send us rain," Ahmid said with almost a laugh. But after maybe ten minutes, he looked hard at me. "If you see any cloud, however small, tell me," he said.

Ah, I thought. So we *would* have to get out of the riverbed. Fast.

We careened around a bend, and there were four women ahead of us digging in the dirt. Ahmid sped past them, blowing them with dust, but I looked in the hole they were digging and could see a fifth woman in it scooping dirt into a bucket and lifting it up to those above her.

"Have you found any water?" I yelled in French.

But the women just waved.

"They will not find water," Ahmid said.

We drove through all the heat of that day and toward evening were approaching Sansanne-Hausa, where they were building a camp for the Tuareg. The Tuareg were finally coming into camps, driven this time by a famine that would not end. Ahead of us I could see great mounds of dirt piled up in the riverbed and maybe twenty Zerma women. "Stop the jeep," I told Ahmid.

He stopped it. I climbed out and pushed through the women that rushed up around us, left Ahmid to keep them away from our water, and climbed up a mound of dirt twice as tall as me. At the top I could look down into a great hole maybe forty feet deep. Three women were digging down there, tying their buckets to ropes. I pulled one up for them. "Have you found any water?" I yelled down, first in French, then in Hausa, which they could understand.

"No," one of them yelled back.

That night I dreamt I was walking in the Gaoueyé district of Niamey, though I had never gone with African whores, not after geneticists in Lagos won the Water War for the coastal dictatorships by spraying the Sahelian troops with mutated viruses that had since spread among whores all over the continent, some of whom could live for fifteen years with the viruses in their bodies. Those viruses could kill a European like me before a doctor could diagnose which virus had attacked me and get the antidote.

But I let a woman lead me up rickety stairs to her tiny room that looked out over the banks of the dry Niger. Her room was filled with plants and flowers that must have cost her a fortune to water. The room smelled clean, and she smelled clean, and I wanted to keep touching her but she pulled back and told me that if I held this certain cloth over my eyes I would see the Niger with water in it. It was the blue cloth she wadded on the floor to keep sand from blowing in under the door. She played these games with me. I knew that. I suddenly knew it was not the first time I had been with her, that I knew her well.

I put the cloth over my eyes. Nothing happened of course. I thought she would kiss me after a minute, but she didn't so I took the cloth away.

"No. Put it back," she said.

She looked so serious. No smile. This was an odd game. I put the cloth back, then felt her small hands press down over my eyes to hold the cloth there, tight.

So I relaxed and lay back on her bed that smelled of her and thought I would play this game out, whatever happened, whatever she wanted.

And gradually heard water flowing by outside in the Niger, lapping the riverbank. I pulled her hands away and the cloth and looked out the window at water.

"I didn't know if you could see it," she said, and she smiled, happy that I could see the water.

She had sprinkled some drug onto the cloth and I was hallucinating, I thought, but the hallucination was lovely. She led me back down the stairs that were somehow sturdier now, and we walked to the river. The water was cold and clean. I drank it.

"You will not get sick," she said, and she drank some water herself, then gave me water to drink out of her hands, then more water, then more. I drank it all.

And woke sweating in my hot room in Sansanne-Hausa. I got up and drank real water from the flask I'd carried in from the jeep, then walked to the window and looked out. The Tuareg camp lay black outside the city, a sea of tents, no fires among them. That sedentary camp marked the death of nomadic Tuareg civilization.

We got another late start that morning because Mai Maïgana, mayor of Sansanne-Hausa, insisted on feeding me breakfast. It really was very good: a mango imported from Brasil, dates, goatsmilk cheese, water. "You can tell the messieurs of the World Bank that Sansanne-Hausa will meet its population quota," he said.

I murmured something polite.

"All of Niger will," he said. "When we began this, when the Bank gave us our quotas, some said, 'How can a country drop from sixteen million people to four hundred thousand in two generations,' but we are doing it and without massacres like those in Mali."

The Mali had massacred their Tuareg who would not submit to population control.

"But the Tuareg do worry me," he went on.

I looked up at him.

"They do not believe in a neverending famine until they walk to the Niger and see that it is dry. They believe the camps are set up to castrate their men."

"Aren't they?"

"Only if they father unlicensed children. But it is dangerous to go out there to abort babies and castrate men or to castrate the illegal male babies that somehow get born. A doctor was murdered in that camp just last month. I have to send the doctors in with troops."

Castrati troops, no doubt, who like my driver had been illegal babies themselves. Such men were supposedly the most efficient at that sort of work.

"We will meet our population quota," Mai Maïgana said.

We drove all day, but the riverbed past Sansanne-Hausa seemed to wind more, and it was rocky and difficult to drive over. Once we drove up what had been a long oxbow that dead-ended, so we had to backtrack. By night, when even with the weak headlights we could not see well enough to drive, we were still maybe forty kilometers from Sinder. So we stopped and slept in the jeep. "We can be in Sinder tomorrow by noon," Ahmid said. If we were delayed much beyond that, I knew, someone would come driving down the Niger looking for us. We built no fire. The day had been hot, and now the night was hot. Ahmid took the first watch.

Sometime later he shook me awake. "You had better wake up," he said. I thought it was my turn to watch, but I looked at my wristwatch and saw that it was just after midnight.

"Get up," he said again.

I sat up and saw that veiled Tuareg men were standing around our jeep. Some had guns pointed at us, others had drawn knives. One started talking to me, fast, commanding, repeating one word over and over: *attini, attini.*

"What does he want?" I asked Ahmid, hoping he could understand Tamasheq.

"Our water," he said. "And your boots and your shirt and our food, the blankets, my belt, our extra clothes."

Then I remembered what *attini* meant in Tamasheq: *give me*.

"Do you speak French?" I asked the Tuareg, thinking I could reason with them, tell them I was here to help them, but not one of them would talk to me in French. I tried Hausa and the little Yoruba I knew, but they would speak only Tamasheq, and I knew only a few words in that language. I could not speak it. Ahmid had to translate for me.

One of the Tuareg reached in the back of the jeep and took out our water. I let him.

"They want your boots and shirt," Ahmid said.

I took off my boots and handed them to the man who had spoken Tamasheq at me. I handed him my shirt. They took the other things they wanted and walked away behind us, tall, regal. It was as if we were a caravan and had paid them tribute to pass through their lands.

"Why didn't they take the jeep?" I asked.

"The army would find that," Ahmid said.

I looked back at the Tuareg, but in their black robes they were already indistinguishable from the shadows of the riverbanks. I suddenly felt sorry for them. They had taken tribute from us, but they had no future outside of the government camps.

Ahmid slept fitfully while I watched. We both wondered if the Tuareg would come back or if others would come along and rob us a second time. Ahmid finally gave up trying to sleep, and we started off for Sinder long before dawn, driving very slowly, creeping around the rocks and holes in the riverbed till it grew light enough to see to drive faster. We had nothing for breakfast, and no water to drink. Once the sun was up, I could not stay awake. I dreamed again of my whore in Niamey. She pressed the blue cloth to my eyes, and when I could see the river we went walking along its banks.

She had brought a picnic of melons, clean, juicy, and bright green. We ate on the grassy riverbank in cool shade under a great tree, and I marveled at the beautiful greenery all around me. I no longer believed I was drugged.

"Is this what was, or what might have been?" I asked.

She just smiled at me, and when she smiled I wanted to love her, there, on the banks of a watery Niger. I took her in my arms and held her, tight.

"Love me," she said.

"I do," I said.

"Love me for a long time, not just today," she said.

"I will."

She broke away from me, picked a leaf from the tree above us, and pressed it into my palm.

"Love me," she said again.

And I did.

I woke sweating and sunburned. The Tuareg had taken everything I could have put over me to keep off the sun.

"We are soon at Sinder," Ahmid said. "They will have creams for your skin there and a shirt."

I sat up straight and rubbed the sweat off my face—but regretted that. My face was so sunburned it hurt to touch it.

"Were you dreaming?" Ahmid asked.

I nodded. "Of a beautiful woman."

He looked concerned. "A woman, you say?"

"Yes, Ahmid." I regretted mentioning women to him, a castrato. He could never know the things I knew. I did not want to hurt him.

"You do not understand what such a dream could mean," he said. "The Djenoun blow about on winds across these empty lands till they find a man's mind to inhabit. If one troubles you, tell me and I will pray to Allah for your protection. Allah can protect you, even in your dreams."

I could not believe that he believed what he was telling me about the Djenoun. Yet for one moment I wondered if Tuareg superstitions could be true, and if a Djenoun were haunting my mind. If she were I would not ask Ahmid to pray to have her taken from me.

I looked at the palm of my hand, but there was no leaf in it. I looked at the dry riverbanks above us on either side and wondered what they would look like wooded. Then I realized I had come on this trip with my mind made up. I was going to recommend the uranium mines to the World Bank. I had never seriously considered the trees.

We passed four Tuareg women in the streets of Sinder. One looked like the woman in my dreams, then I thought all four did, then I thought every woman I saw—Songhai, Hausa, Fulani, Tuareg—all looked like that woman. The old French nurse who doctored my sunburn at the clinic looked like that whore. They were all beautiful. I thought that I had never looked at women like this before, that I had never realized that all women were beautiful. I loved them all. We got water, food, gas, clothes, and struck out across the erg to the Zermaganda uranium fields.

And they were everything I had been promised. URANIGER had set off one thousand seismic charges which proved the deposits greater than those at Arlit, the mines that made Niger the world's fifth-largest uranium producer. The Zermaganda mines would make them the largest. I spent two days studying the ore and the results of the seismic charges, talking with the geologists and walking with them over flat-topped gara and down dry wadis to the best sites. But I spent my nights studying the reports on reforestation. I realized that plan was too modest. The source of the Niger needed to be reforested, yes, but so did the sources of five of the major tributaries. If that happened and if the rainfall increased as might be expected, the river might flow.

Aissa Seibou arrived late that second day, and though tired from the journey from Niamey, I could see the enthusiasm in her eyes. She looked beautiful to me, like my whore.

"What do you think?" she asked.

I smiled. "I think this deposit will be everything you dream of," I said.

"You will help us, then. You will recommend us?"

That was the question.

"Money from these mines would give us money to import water from the sea," she said. "The coastal dictatorships are killing us for water."

It was what the Water War had been fought over. By international law every nation had rights to water from the sea, including landlocked nations like Niger, Mali, Burkina Fasso. But the coastal nations were reluctant to give them land for desalination plants— they wanted to sell them water. Taxes for road repairs on the roads used to truck water inland, charges from the trucking firms, tariffs were not enough. International law was not enough. And the Sahelian nations had lost their war and now had no choice but to pay for water trucked in from the coast.

"You have seen what this country has become," she said. "If even four hundred thousand people can live here we need money. We need these mines."

"Have you studied the reforestation proposals?" I asked.

"You can't be serious," she said. "There is nothing to reforest in Niger."

"But there is in Guinea, Burkina Fasso, Mali. If it works you would have the Niger again and be freed of the stranglehold of the coast."

"In forty years," she said, incredulous.

I dreamed that night of my whore in Niamey, and she was big with child. "You fathered her," she said. "She will be your daughter."

This was an unlicensed child, and I was horrified to think that it would be aborted.

"Only if you tell the authorities will it be aborted," she said. "Otherwise all people will love her when they see her."

"You can look in the blue cloth and go to the Niger with water," I said, "and stay there."

"And wait for you to come," she said.

Then I understood that the blue cloth did not show what was or what might have been. It showed what could be and, I hoped, what would be.

"Name your daughter *Fecund,*" she said.

I thought that name more beautiful than any I had ever heard. "I will come to you," I said. "Down this river when it flows again, to these trees."

She smiled, and behind her I saw the desert greening.

I made my recommendation to the World Bank, and they accepted it. But Aissa Seibou did not leave me in anger. I agreed to stay on with her in Niamey through the summer to help her find outside funding to develop the Zermaganda mines. Ahmid and I followed her jeep back to Niamey, down the dry Niger. We stayed maybe half a kilometer behind her, out of her dust.

Once we rounded a bend and ahead of us, against the bank, I could see the whitened bones of some great animal.

"Hippopotamus," Ahmid said. "Extinct here now forever."

"Maybe not," I said.

"Ah, that Allah should send us hippopotamus again," Ahmid said.

I had him stop by the bones, and we walked over to them. The skull was gone. "It is worth money in the markets of Niamey," Ahmid explained.

All that was left were the ribs and leg bones, a few neck vertebrae. Dry leaves had blown in under the hips. I pulled out a handful of leaves and crumpled it.

"We should go," Ahmid said. "Aissa Seibou will be far ahead of us."

I picked up one dry leaf to take with me. We walked to the jeep and started driving again for Niamey. I held the leaf in my fingers, but it crumbled away piece by piece and blew off into the dust billowing behind us.

NINETEEN

Dust

JOHN BENNION

Dry Springs, Utah: My Father's Property. Since morning my eye has inclined toward the road below my cabin, perhaps because today marks the second anniversary of my removal to the desert. I'm expecting no one in particular, but the wavering, ground-heated air gives the alkali flat the appearance of movement, as if a cloud of white dust billows from its surface. Such a cloud could signify either an approaching vehicle or a misdirected shell, a gift from the chemical weapons testing facility north of here. My polygamist neighbors to the south might read the coil of dust as a sign of the Apocalypse. Leaving my window, I walk three hundred steps to the butte behind my cabin, halfway between Salt Lake City and Ely, Nevada.

Like the uncertain cloud, the butte presents diverse aspects: breast-shaped but with a column of lava on top, an igneous plug which my eye reads as either the thick phallus of the volcano's last thrust or as a hardened black nipple. From this vantage I inspect for any change in the size or direction of the potential cloud. The white blotch shimmers in the heat, dust motes whirling, as real as the pillar of fire in De Mille's *Ten Commandments*.

Rockwood, Utah: forty miles north-east. From my position I can see the range of mountains around my former home. My wife Sylvia and our five children—Benjamin, Abigail, Joshua, Ruth, and Heather—live there with my mother in the town named after my violent great-grandfather, James Darren Rockwood, who was once a body-guard to the prophet Joseph Smith. Anti-Mormon historians claim that Great-grandpa shot the mayor of Carthage, Illinois, Frederick Diggs, because Diggs harassed the People of God. Grandpa J. D.'s violence is genetic: my brother poisoned his boss after being fired and I experienced a sigh of religious fulfillment after completing the chemical blueprint for the nerve gas that killed the sheep.

In Rockwood, when I changed my daughter's diapers, she raised her arms above her head so I could tickle her. "Doat," she said. "Doat, Daddy." Her laugh comes from her belly, a gurgle of mirth. The faces of my wife and older son were identically solemn when I left them two years ago.

Alone on my inherited section of desert, I try to isolate my fear of the Apocalypse (predicted by the Book of Revelations, Jeanne Dixon, and anti-nuclear activists), but the core of my fear is as various as the cloud of dust.

Skull Valley Testing Grounds: The Limits of Non-radioactive Gas. Formerly I worked thirty miles to the northwest of here, where the government designs, tests, and stores lesser tools of the Apocalypse. To approach my bunker I passed through three barriers— woven wire, chain link, brick—presenting my I.D. to three sets of guards. My fingerprints were taken daily to insure that the guards, who saw me daily, hadn't mistaken my face.

As head chemist my duty was to create equations on a blackboard. Two second-level chemists transferred the numbers and letters to paper, a committee ordered the batch, and technicians, dozens of them, manipulated the stuff with long-armed machinery from behind thick glass windows. Working over my abstractions, I was elevated to a pure sphere, like a high priest delineating the mind of God.

Once on my way home from work, a great ball of orange gas

flung outward from one of the army's testing bunkers, boiling toward my car past the boundary fence. I shit myself, understanding that the mind of God held subtleties I hadn't yet grasped. I didn't breathe while I bounced across the desert road for three miles. Behind me the wind gathered the potent molecules, dissipating them upward toward the bench land of the nearby mountains.

The newspapers soon discovered that five thousand head of Hyrum Jorgenson's sheep had died. Government veterinarians explained that the animals were undernourished and had eaten loco weed. Within a year two movies were made about the event: *Rage,* starring George C. Scott, whose son was killed by the descending gas, and *Whiffs,* a spoof which showed tendrils of white drifting through nearby Tooele, Utah. The excitement of seeing their children as extras caused all my friends to forget the dead sheep. After viewing both movies I had the recurring dream that a technician found a way to disseminate my gas using an atomic warhead.

The summer of our first wedding anniversary, my water turn came between one and three in the morning. Several times Sylvia crept down through the cedars above our horse pasture, wrapped only in a blanket, and seduced me before I could remove my irrigation boots.

Lot's Wife: Does Flesh Turn to Sodium Inside Ground Zero? The morning after my bolt of terror, a Saturday, Sylvia and I lay in bed late. The children played in the next room, waiting for breakfast. "That's Daddy's briefcase," Benjamin said. "He won't like you playing with it."

"He won't mind," Ruth said. "He won't mind at all."

"He will."

"Daddy, Daddy, Daddy," the baby said into the shut door. Sylvia smiled but I couldn't: the word didn't seem to apply to me. We heard struggling and a shower of papers. Then I smiled. I didn't go to work the next Monday.

After the third month without a paycheck, Sylvia began to think my fears were silly. "You've got to face it that accidents happen." She shouted arguments at me. I shouted my fear back. Abigail started taking long walks. The baby crawled into our bed every night, unable to sleep alone. Finally, insecure myself, I spanked her to make her stay in her own bed. Joshua wet his pants three days out of five at school. "I try to make it to the toilet, but I can't get there in time," he said. Their troubles, poignant as they were, had little to do with me. I told Sylvia I was going to live on my father's property in the desert.

"Dramatic," she said. "It's really just Andrea, isn't it? You're going to pretend you're pioneering with her." Hungry for land, my father had homesteaded farther and farther west. He finally abandoned my mother, who wouldn't leave Salt Lake to live in the desert with him. I couldn't understand either my father's motivating dream or the adulterous one Sylvia supplied for me.

When she plays the guitar, Sylvia sits in her rocking chair, eyes closed. Her fingers ripple on the strings, moving according to laws of clarity, grace, and intuition, marked by the rhythm of the moving chair.

An Acolyte's Guide to Androgynous Thinking. On this, the second anniversary of leaving my job, my town, and my family, I don't trust my eye's interest in the cloud of dust. My mental/emotional apparatus will take any non-event today and say, "This is what you were waiting for. The reverberation of the coming event impinged on your neurons, causing the condition you call anticipation." I say to my neurons, "Parascience." I deny that my brain picks up invisible signals and creates an impossible tension between me and some other object in time or space. Despite my lack of faith in my own nervous system, my flesh still organizes itself for someone's possible arrival. And I'm double minded again, split between rationality and mysticism, unable to be either a scientist or a saint, as if the bolt of fear at the swarming gas traumatized my corpus callosum, the bridge in my brain.

Coriantumr, Utah: Five miles south of my cabin lives a community of apostates from the Mormon church, two hundred strong, who have returned to the practices of the nineteenth-century pioneers—living in polygamy with all things in common. In preparation for the last day, they have hoarded wheat, honey, and rifles. To satisfy present needs they have a Montessori school and a dairy.

They sent a group of their brethren to Switzerland to purchase a strain of bacteria for culturing milk into cheese which they trade in Paradise, Utah, farther south. They want to pipe the water from my spring to their alfalfa fields so they can grow feed for another fifty cows, but they never mention that. A hundred miles southwest of them lies Ely, where madames and casino owners also live with everything in common.

A Star Named Kolob. My father, the former owner of this property, is in heaven, which the polygamists have determined to be on a planet near the star Kolob, a hundred trillion miles past our sun. God lives there, they believe, with all the spirits who are waiting to come to earth. My sixth through twelfth children are presently on Kolob also, they say. I doubt that my wife's rhythm and my own will coincide seven more times, but that doesn't concern the polygamists.

A Six-by-four Patch of Floor Under My Chalkboard: Vive Vas Deferens. During lunch in my bunker at Skull Valley Testing Grounds, I ate tomato sandwiches, the juice running down my fingers onto the floor. My co-chemist, Andrea Armstrong, looked at me across my red and dripping hands. Suddenly we were tumbling on the floor in the chalk dust and sandwich remains. Upon confessing this to my bishop, I was disfellowshipped. My lack of guilt disgusted him. My emotional incontinence worried me.

Salt Lake City, Utah: A Hundred Miles North-east of Rockwood. On the highest spire of the temple the gold statue of Moroni, his horn to his lips, prepares to signal the rolling together of the scroll. Sometimes in my dreams I hear his trump then sense the stealthy movement of the quivering gas.

My Journal: The Tao of Listing. Like Robinson Crusoe, I have a "certain Stupidity of Soul" and like him I trust lists, not of provisions, but of anchors in space and time. Lists are beautiful— they don't whine. They require no explanation, are non-ardent, non-causal, calm, static, unpretentious, a periodic table of my own elements. However I'm wary of listing *toward,* as in "Our ship listed toward starboard after it struck the rock" or "Since morning my eye has listed toward the junction."

A selection from Robinson Crusoe's list:
>small Ropes and Rope-twine
>a Piece of spare Canvass
>a barrel of wet Gunpowder
>a great Hogshead of Bread
>three large Runlets of Rum or Spirits
>a Box of Sugar

My list:
>the black ridge extending between here and Ely, Nevada,
>>looking like God's darkening brow
>the bank of the spring my father cleared out twenty-five
>>years ago
>the pattern of tomato seeds on Andrea's back
>my son skipping rocks across a green pond
>the harmony of equations across the blackboard, the
>>purer image of the orange gas
>the Rorschach blots created in a mobile cloud

Andrea, Kolob, and I: The Physics of Attraction between Bodies. Sitting on the butte with the border of Nevada a wall behind me, I can sense the faint reverberations of these places and events. Closing my eyes, I sense here the great salt sea, here the mounds of stored bombs and gasses, here my wife and children, my friends, Kolob, the potential cloud, the polygamists. I feel the lines of tension—physical, disinterested—between myself and them.

The Angle of the Cloud: Playing the Futures. If the dust materializes from the north today, it may be Sergeant Mertzke, Recreation Administrator for the Officers' Club at Skull Valley Testing Grounds. He was once a hunting buddy of my father and me, but when I see his dust, I'll compose myself, adopting a persona which will fit into his consciousness—the cautious, land-loving son of my father or the chemist who strained after one too many formulae.

"Have they left?" he says, referring to the deer he wants to shoot by spotlight from the back of his jeep.

"A five-point, two spikes, six doe." I count on my fingers.

"Where're you going to get a better offer?" And he explains

again the idea of the R&R Area. He looks over this desert property, barren except for the fifty square yards around the spring, and sees officers and women of the New Army frolicking through the sagebrush.

"I don't know," I say. "Land's stable, money's mobile."

"But gauge the possibilities."

I won't disturb his vision of my father's property, but before he gets to the part about the raw hunters returning to the tents of their women, I will recast myself as the religious ascetic—a desert saint. I motion for silence, bowing my head. "I will ask." Holding him with my silence for five, maybe ten minutes. "No. My father on Kolob says no. He warns you that God is as displeased with you as he was with the people of Sodom and Gomorrah. His wrath is kindled."

"The hell it is," he says. He comes in the evening despite my warning, the fever for killing heavy in him. I flash the spotlight on this doe, that buck. He shoots and I hear the thud as his hollow-points hit muscle and bone. Even the shower of blood creates no motion inside of me. I could be butcher, conservationist, harvester, accomplice. Any of these could explain my relationship to the event: the spurting blood. Nothing moves.

On winter mornings my son built elaborate houses out of chairs, blankets, boards, and cushions. Once he and his siblings decided that the structure was a houseboat and that I was the shark. My baby lifted her body onto her toes, pumping her legs in place as she tried to escape. I ate her squealing body four times.

The Ark: How Many Roentgens Will Kill a Dove? If the dust arrives from the south, it will come slowly: three of the brethren from the polygamous camp navigating the ruts and rocks in their decrepit pickup.

"Brother Rockwood," the Elders say. "Toward the end of the world, wars and pestilence will be poured out upon the land. The moon will turn red like blood, and lightning will flash from the east to the west as the Son of Man approaches. Only the righteous—those who have entered the new order—will be spared."

I lead them along. "Vanity, vanity," I say. "The work of man's own hands will destroy the world. The only thing that will spare any of us is your buried vault."

"The mind of God moves in mysterious ways."

They have a stainless steel and cement ark buried fifty feet under the desert. Its walls are six feet thick. They plan to go down there and emerge two by two, or rather one by seven, into the millennium. I could believe their myth that the Pentagon, public education, and the mind of Satan move in collusion toward the Apocalypse, but I don't let myself trust major abstractions anymore. At this point I profane the name of their God and deny their pragmatic mysticism. "I am a rational, enlightened humanist," I say. "A member of a powerful conspiracy." And they leave saddened because I can't comprehend their God or their milk barn.

Masters and Johnson on Solitude: Why Crusoe Kept Goats. Through a pleasant inversion of perspective, for a moment the potential dust is my own as I drive my white Ford Fairlane southward to Ely for the weekly venting of my seminal vesicles. In the back are stacks of *Chemical Review,* a weight which keeps me from getting stuck when it's winter. As I drive I call myself adulterer, hedonist, lecher, fallen saint: but all the fragments crumble before I can build them into a consistent foundation. I drive quickly past the polygamist town, made of two-story houses large as dormitories. Beyond their community the volcanic ridge resurfaces, connecting me with Ely.

I park my car in the city and shuffle toward a casino under the swirl of lights. For the girls and the card dealers, I am the rich and eccentric desert rat, dusty, hunch-shouldered. I engage the first prostitute I see, a sad-eyed woman with long black hair. In our room she takes off her clothing slowly, teasing my expectation. The absurdity of our puny climax drains the life from my penis, and I feel disconnected even from it. However she is an efficient woman, improvising with clever lips and tongue, and she makes my body perform. I spend the rest of the evening flipping the lever of a slot machine, anticipating a windfall.

The Prodigal Father. A northern originating dust could also signify my friend, Jonathan Boone, driving from Rockwood. "Howard, your wife is pining," he says. "She's got no money. She's getting food and clothing from the Bishop's Storehouse and that makes her ashamed. What can I tell her? Is what you're doing worth the problems you're causing?"

"I'm making no stand," I say to him.

"Why do you stay here?"

"I've got no reform in mind," I say.

"Just come back with me."

"Please don't talk anymore," I ask him. He doesn't understand the ways his questions strain my introspective faculty. For an hour we walk in the cool of the evening. The breeze has died and, bending low, we smell the mint growing on the banks of my spring.

Options on My Father's Property. If I wait long enough, my back against the butte, someone comes. Last week a friend who was a Democratic Socialist in college drove through. Still an idealist after twenty years, he looked around and his vision was powerful enough to transform the dead soil.

"This is like paradise," he said.

"No, that's twenty miles farther on."

"Can you picture a community here, all friends, lovers, family? People who have repudiated hate." His voice nearly revived my own dreams of Zion, a place where people live in peace. "We could cast off the dead husk of society," he said, and I understood he wanted to build a nudist retreat.

"I won't sell."

"I don't want you to sell." He was eager, running through the greasewood and shadscale, blinded by his narrow optimism, believing that, along with their socks and underwear, people can discard their impulse to aggression.

For him I was the sharp agribusinessman. "My god. This land can produce seven maybe eight tons of prime alfalfa to the acre, and you talk to me about a damn spa. That artesian spring brings up two or three feet of water per second, and all you can think of is some kind of orgy." He left in his jeep, driving with only a centimeter of metal between him and the sky.

The Penultimate Human. Once a man drove through looking for the road to Topaz Mountain. He had his wife and children with him—a family man on an outing. He showed me a sample of a geode he'd found. "We cut and polish these nippers. A real fine hobby for the kids, and it teaches them something. Might as well kill two birds with one stone." He laughed, watching for my response. "Every second they're polishing, they're learning geology. And then we sell them. Isn't it something? A real tidy income." The pleasant wife and children smiled and nodded.

His soft-bellied words irritated me, violated my integrity. I told him the blacktop began twenty miles farther. If the heat is great enough when the lightning flashes from east to west, his stones will melt to glass. For him my eyes became hard and clear, glistening with intensity. "Gog and Magog are gathering for battle: the Apocalypse draws near," I said. "I-Am-That-I-Am says 'Beware the wrath of the Lamb.'" Wide-eyed, he left me alone to ruminate on my father's property.

Personal History: An Escape from My True Self Before God. I can establish no relationship with any point or person secondary to myself in space which is as important as my fear. No end depends from a middle in my life, no new and glorious future grows organically out of my past, as Aristotle, Alexander Hamilton, Walt Whitman, Brigham Young, Horatio Alger, and Karl Marx promised.

When my son was two, he backed into a kettle we had set for scalding chickens. I tore off his diaper and turned the hose full across him. His back and buttocks peeled white wherever the water touched. Later he clawed the healing skin, biting my hands when I held his. I slapped his mouth, hard, and the print faded slowly.

When he was three he helped me harvest corn from our garden, pulling the sheath downward from the silk, breaking out the yellow ears. We filled ten buckets with corn for bottling.

When I was four I walked across this property, following my father as he planned where the fences would go on his new homestead—640 acres of desert land. He bought a faded red diesel engine to pump water from the slow-flowing spring.

I was six. My father sent me to this cabin from the fields a mile eastward, where he was working. "You start dinner," he said. "I'll be along." The road I watched back over became dark through the window. The coyotes yelping made the loneliest sound I have ever heard. He didn't come until an hour after the food was cold.

For years from behind our kitchen door in Rockwood, I heard my mother and father arguing religion: evolution, modern revelation, Christ's miracles, Joseph Smith talking to God. "If the prophet in Salt Lake told you to walk off a cliff, you would do it, wouldn't you?" my father said.

"But he wouldn't ask," said my mother.

"But if he did?"

"But he won't."

Once I fell asleep while listening, and my father discovered me, from my snoring he said, and carried me to my bed.

When I was nine I cut out the heart of a newly dead rattlesnake and watched it beat eighty-three times in the palm of my hand. During my seventeenth summer, as my friend and I irrigated the farm, we grew a potato plant which we watered with only our urine.

When I was twenty-two and Sylvia wouldn't see me any more, my father rode on horseback with me over the mountains surrounding Rockwood and down into the desert toward this homestead. Each night he talked to me about his life, telling me stories, singing songs to me his mother had sung to him—administering to my pain with his voice. Sometimes now I hear him murmuring to me out of the rocks above my cabin.

In 1973 when diesel prices started rising with gasoline prices and he couldn't afford to pump water from the spring anymore, my father sold the ranch on mortgage and repossessed it four times: from some dairy farmers out of central Utah, from a group of Salt Lake bankers, from a machinist who wanted to live in the desert with his family, and from a sheepman who wanted to build sheds for his herds. None of them could make the property produce.

One year before my father died, the day we finished hauling our second crop of hay, I drove him to the shack someone built over a mineral pool ten miles west of here. His mind was already partly in the next world, and he howled and swore as I lugged him into the water, which was heavy as amniotic fluid. I guess he thought I would scald him. I only wanted to ease his joints, but I howled with him as we floated.

When I was thirty my father imagined that the sighing of the wind through the boulders was Marilyn Monroe and her sirens, who had inhabited the butte. He renamed it Whorehouse Rock in her honor. One night he climbed naked through the snow to visit her. When we found him, near where I'm sitting, coyotes had gnawed his nose, ears, and penis.

In the genealogical library in Salt Lake, I tried to trace my ancestry back to Adam. Once I discovered their names and dates of birth, temple officiators could seal each family member to me by ordinance, soul by soul creating an eternal indivisible unity. As I worked I felt a completeness-in-others: I was the epiphany toward which all those souls had been living. In my research I only made it back to 1698 to a man who had to run away from Wales because he murdered his landlord.

When Abigail was small she squirted steaming sauce on the back of her hand while eating a Sloppy Joe. I placed a leaf of iceberg lettuce on the burn to draw the heat out. She ate the rest of the meal with one hand, balancing the green leaf on her other fist.

The Broken Flask. I have more fragments of my own history, but if I add them point by point, measuring the degree of gravity between each one, what is their sum?—a minute and irrepressible motion of my chromosomes toward the Apocalypse. From whom can I learn how to think about this singular and revolutionary inclination?

Can I sacrifice my wife and children to warn the people as Abraham and Tolstoy did? Can I like Moses carry myself and my children toward a new world after the fire storms and plagues? Like Einstein or Newton can I invent a new mathematics, a tool for analyzing my inscrutable impulse toward destruction? The prophet of the polygamists and a Navaho Indian I once knew both believed that they could make it rain by thinking. Can I like Kierkegaard concentrate so fully, a Knight of Vital Faith, that mental impulses become corporeal, and I purge this violence from my blood? I can find no myth, no introspective process through which I can reconnect myself to my father, to my wife, or my children: a double-minded man is uncertain in all his ways. I am here, not farming my father's property, while my autobiography unravels itself.

On good days, after someone leaves, it is only me independent—no frustrated motion. No pointing finger or angle of apprehension. During those minutes I float in benevolent stasis, a calm which is always violated by my anticipation. As of this moment I repudiate the road from which dust does not yet rise. The iron-gray igneous rocks dribbled out over the land in confusion, the ashen alkali desert: these are the emblems of my new world, the world which waits for the cloud.

As I leave the butte behind my cabin, I make an oath that I will hold myself firm against returning to watch again. I will not picture her face and the firm line along her jaw as she drives across the desert—four children in the back of the car, one in the front. The children sit with their hands on their knees, and they say nothing though the air inside the car is stifling.

TWENTY

Outsiders

MARGARET BLAIR YOUNG

My friend Junie and I were Utah Mormons. We knew no blacks till we were teenagers. But the summer I was sixteen and she eighteen, the Peace Corps hired Dad to train volunteers, and Junie and I were initiated into a larger world.

The PCVs, as we called the trainees, would go to Brazil—provided they got through Dad's program at Alta, Utah. They would have to show basic emotional stability and some mastery of Portuguese—or an aptitude to learn it—before the government would pay their ticket to Rio. For now the government had paid their room and board at the Wintergreen Hotel, where program directors had covered the walls with pictures of Brazil. In the lobby were posters of Sugar Loaf. At every landing in the stairwell were scenes from Carnival: devils, angels, dancers in sheer yellow gowns; fat black women with turbans around their heads and bananas hanging over their faces; floats that looked like orchards. In the cafeteria was a huge image of the *Cristo*—Jesus beckoning, arms outstretched against the sea, unrecovered from crucifixion. "Come on in," he seemed to say. "To my arms. To Brazil." The picture took up half the wall.

I worked around the *Cristo*. Dad had got me a job bussing dishes. The work fit me because I was fat. Junie, my glamorous friend Junie, got the artsy job. She drew pictures for the language classes.

We had a room to ourselves between two newlywed couples, one white, one black. Above us was the lounge. We could feel the drumbeats of In-na-god-da-da-vida and Fresh Garbage when some PCV put a quarter in the jukebox. There was someone who played "Heard It Through the Grapevine" every night, sometimes two or three times. Someone else loved "The Age of Acquarius."

My tastes were not so advanced. On the lamp table, I had a picture of Bobby Sherman, the deliciously blue-eyed star of "Here Come the Brides," sassy singer of "Hey Little Woman, Please Make Up Your Mind." I would put Bobby face down when I undressed for bed. Other times, when Junie was using the bathroom or wandering outside, I would kiss Bobby's shiny, back-cover lips. Sometimes, when the PCVs were attending culture classes, I would give the jukebox a quarter for Bobby's song: "Hey, little woman,/ Please make up your mind;/ You got to/ Come into my world/ And leave your world behind."

I imagined swaying hips.

I had never been kissed. Junie had been kissed many times. She said she couldn't possibly count how many, though I begged her to try, and she tried, remembering details of smell and taste and setting. She said the boy who escorted her to the junior prom had tried to unbutton her blouse. "He wanted inside," she said.

"Inside?"

"My pants."

I made voodoo lips. "I might like kissing," I said. "But sex sounds icky."

"I wouldn't know," shrugged Junie.

But she seemed to know a man's body all right. She drew a dozen naked men before she liked one enough to write in the Portuguese names for the body parts. She sat on the bed, surrounded by her nudes, labeling everything in a language neither of us understood. *Cabello. Brazo.* Her hair was golden, hip-length. It touched the bed. It touched the naked bodies of her men.

Later she drew naked women, one for each of her male failures, and matched them up, the best with the best, the worst with the worst. She put my face on one of the women and paired me with a guy whose biceps had turned out square.

"Is that how you picture me?" I said. "With Mr. Robot-arms?"

"It's not you," she insisted, but the likeness was too strong.

"Are you going to save these things or what?" I asked, averting my eyes from their privates.

"Sure. Could be worth money someday. I'm going to autograph them," she said. "Everyone who's kicked out of the corps will get a pair. Consolation prize, you know? My best work I'm giving to those guys there." She pointed to the wall. On the other side was the black couple.

At night sometimes we would listen to them. We put a glass to the wall and took turns pressing our ears against it. We heard them laughing.

Laughing. Silence. Laughing.

Once I said, "Icky!" loud enough that Junie clapped her hand over my mouth and whispered, "Shut up!"

The black man had put a sign on their door, which is the only Portuguese phrase I've retained: "*Terra de nunca nunca.*" Never Never Land.

The PCVs were mostly recent graduates of mostly radical universities. They drank beer. They had vats of pungent wine at the Saturday night dances. When Nixon shook Neil Armstrong's hand on the lounge television, the PCVs hissed.

My favorite was David Marx, a gentle, bearded intellectual with wire-rimmed glasses. I heard him tell my father one day that this business of not letting blacks into our Mormon temples was "rather shitty." "You let them join," David said, "but not go to your shrines. It's sort of like not consummating a marriage, isn't it?"

Dad made some response, and David went on, talking about the alleged curse of Cain. He spoke softly. Dad spoke softly. There was love and resistance in their arguing.

Did I mention that I worshipped my father? I did. He was my

revered commander, my gentle, omniscient patriarch. When he prayed he talked to God. Sometimes I felt as if the ceiling would open and angels descend to grant his desires. He prayed for the poor and prayed that his children would grow to empathize with them, to love all nations of the world, to never lose themselves in wealth or lust. He prayed for our prophet, for our missionaries, for the leaders of the nations. He prayed that Russia would open its doors and let the gospel in. He prayed for the PCVs.

Junie worshipped David Marx. On Saturdays, or after Portuguese lessons and dinner, he took her up the hills that in winter would be ski slopes but in summer were covered with sego lilies and bluebells and sunflowers. He showed her a waterfall. He kissed her, she told me, the way no one ever had. She did a chalk picture of the waterfall, made it look lacy, surrounded it with dots of pastel that were wildflowers, arched two barely visible rainbows over it. On the grass beside the fall, blurred by its mists, lay a man and a woman, their skin gleaming like chocolate.

"For them?" I asked Junie. I pointed to the wall that divided us from *Terra de Nunca Nunca*.

She shrugged.

The black woman's name was Giselle. Her husband was Adam. Sometimes Giselle talked to me. When I picked up her dishes, she said, "How's my Moh-mon gal?" or "When you joinin' up to the Corps?" She told me once, when we were both in the hall and her husband was using the men's room, about her sunburn.

"Too much time in the pool," she said, pulling her tank top so I could see the rosy-gold line on her shoulder. "Had to sleep unclothed," she said. Her lips were full and burnished. They curved around "unclothed" as though it were a note of music. Her head wagged to some rhythm I could not hear, and I saw that she was testing my innocence. From the lounge, faintly, came croons of betrayal from Marvin Gaye. ("Doncha know, I heard it through the grapevine. Honey, honey, yeeeah.")

"I didn't know you could burn," I said to Giselle.

"Honey," said Giselle—at the same instant Marvin Gaye said

it—"Honey, ooh, you Moh-mons, you don't know shit 'bout us. Do ya." She winked playfully, and her hips began to move. Adam came out of the men's room still zipping up. He left his hand near his crotch as his wife moved to him, slowly, full of music, full of desire.

She laughed the laugh I knew. She said, "My old man didn't mind me naked. Not much. Didja, old man." Giselle winked at me again. "*Ciao,* Moh-mon," she said. "You sweet li'l thing, you." They moved away from me down the hall, their motion slow, luxurious, painful. They had afros I wanted to touch.

Junie stayed out late with David, later every night. I listened to Giselle and Adam. I kissed Bobby Sherman's slick mouth.

Then, half-way through training, Ernie Kann was hired as a dishwasher, and I fell in love.

Ernie was Mormon too, working to finance his upcoming mission. He owned a red convertible, which he hoped he wouldn't have to sell for his mission but was afraid he might. He had eyes as blue as Bobby Sherman's. And at a Saturday night dance in the lounge, Ernie Kann asked me to "boogie."

I looked at Junie, who was holding David's hand near the wine vat. Junie was mad at me because I hated what she was wearing: a curtain, draped over her right shoulder. I had told her the truth about how she looked—that she was pretending to be Venus. Junie waved to let me know she had seen me with this boy, but she was mad.

After two dances Ernie asked if I wanted to jump on the trampoline outside. "It's like flying to heaven," he said and took my hand before I could answer.

The trampoline was barely visible. Its coils glistened in the moonlight.

"Let me jump a minute first," Ernie said. "After all that dancing and stuff, I need to settle down. This settles me down. Maybe it's just the exercise does it."

His shirt was white, ghostly. He sprang up, arms overhead. "Can you see me?" he said.

"Yes!" I shouted.

"I'm reaching!"

"I see you!"

"God!" he screamed. "GOD!" And again, "GOD!" Leaping up, flying, a rocket—a glorious impotent rocket, launching again and again and again. He was laughing, screaming, dancing in space, then slowing his jumps to little springs. He fell to his stomach and bounced there until he was still. "You probably can't do that," he said. "I mean fall on your—you know—your bosom. At least maybe you shouldn't. You don't want to damage them, right?" Laughing again, he reached out to me. "Come up," he said.

We started small, bouncing. Ernie's hands came around my waist. "Bigger," he said, and I did. I jumped, leapt, soared, higher, higher. We were in sync, Ernie and I, flying together beyond the earth, beyond the support of black canvas. We were dancing to the rythmn of space, the drumbeat of gravity. We were making love to the whole sky. "Hold me," he shouted, and I did that too, then heard him just above my ear, and cried out with him:

"GOD!

"GOD!

"GOD!"

The air was cold, the stars a cyclone of glitter. I could almost imagine an answer.

Junie, when she came back to our room, was wearing the curtain around her left shoulder. It was near midnight.

"So," she said, sitting on my bed. "Can Ernie Kann?"

"Shut up," I answered.

I felt her hand on my forehead, smoothing my virginal nerves. "Don't hate me," she cooed. "Please."

Ernie kissed me a week later. "You don't know how to do this stuff, do you," he said afterwards.

"Not really," I said.

"I'll bet your roommate does."

"Junie? Yeah, Junie knows about kissing."

"How many boys has she kissed?"

"Maybe a million."

He wasn't surprised. He had never seen a girl as good-looking as Junie, he told me, and kissed me again, licking my lips open, pronouncing me "not bad."

I hated him then and never got over it. I knew what he was doing. He wanted me because I was as close as he could come to her. He kissed me with his eyes closed. Both of us pretended I was Junie.

We rarely mentioned her, though once he asked if she was nice.

"Nice enough," I said.

"Will you tell me something," he said, "and not get mad at me for asking?"

"Depends."

"Does she wear falsies?"

I laughed my child's laugh and said Junie didn't need padding there.

"No padding?"

"She's big enough."

"How big?"

"I've never measured," I said, hating him more for this new, this misguided, intimacy.

I remember the conversation so well because that night turned out to be traumatic: Junie never came home. She was in the cafeteria the next morning, avoiding my eyes. I told her I wasn't a virgin anymore. I lied this way to make her think it was her fault. She didn't believe me. She said if I ever talked that way again, she would tell my dad.

"All right," I said. "I'm a virgin."

"No kidding."

"No kidding," I said. "Are you?"

"Oh shut up."

"Junie?"

"What."

"I want you to not do it anymore."

"Just shut up."

"Please."

She started to cry. I cried too.

Dinner the next night was greasy beef strogonoff over greasier noodles. Carrots for the vegetable. Chocolate cake for desert.

Dad was talking to Giselle and Adam. Junie and David were at the same table, so I joined them. They were all laughing. David was telling a joke about a Jewish nurse, a joke I didn't understand.

"I was raised Baptist," said Adam. "A P.K. Preacher's Kid, you know? So every morning my daddy sang God's praises in the shower."

"Hallelujah," said Giselle and then again, making it bluesy. "Halle-looo-jeh." She moved her fingers beside her face. I could imagine them tinkling. "Praise the Lo'd and shake yo' body," she said, fingers moving, rings shimmering.

Adam laughed. "My old man. Loved God. Loved people. Loved dogs 'n cats."

"Rats and mice," put in Giselle. "Cockroaches 'n ants." She was finishing her song. "Dat preacher man," she said. "Lived in a gah-bage can. Coon't bear to kill the bugs." She clapped once.

"One time," said Adam, "one time an old junkie took my daddy's wallet, and my daddy chased him two blocks, caught him, took him home to supper, and three months later, what do you think, that old junkie's decided to preach the word himself. Far as I know he is singing God's hymns now."

"That's beautiful," said Dad.

"Another time, this skinny ole' granma, she knocks on our door, says if she could just have a sip of broth she'll live till tomorrow. Daddy gave her soup and bread and two strips of bacon and you know, that granny is living at my house to this day and raising Cain."

"Could be why you left, y'ole buzzard, huh?" said Giselle.

"Could be. Plus that I want to make a difference. Go places I'm needed, right? Wanted."

"So you come to Salt Lake, Utah," laughed Giselle. Everyone at the table joined her laughing.

"Here first," said Adam. "Here first."

Giselle turned to my dad. "We went," she said, "to Temple Square the other day? You shoulda seen the looks we got. I could almost hear the Mormon people locking doors on us. Click. Click. I had to laugh then too. I had to say, 'Hey, y'all, we jes' visitin'! We not goin' try nothin'! Hey, we let you be! You jes' stay right there in yo' temple, now.'" She laughed again.

Adam didn't laugh with her this time. Adam watched my father. "Must be hard on you," he said. "Cause I know—I KNOW—you can't think it's right to keep up walls like that. You can't feel good about a church that locks its doors to someone."

Dad explained that we let blacks join the church, it was just the priesthood they couldn't have, just the temple they couldn't enter.

"But you can't support that policy," said Adam.

Dad sat up very straight. His eyes were full of compassion but deadly serious too. You didn't question my father's faith. "I support that policy," he said.

Adam chewed his lip, nodding slowly. Giselle watched him, watched Dad, watched me.

"Why," said Adam, "why do you hate my people?"

"Now listen," said Dad, but Adam slapped the table.

"Who do you think God is?" he demanded, his voice getting full. All the PCVs were watching now. "Who you think he is—some maitre'd of some club?"

"If it were my church—"

"It is your church."

"No, Adam. Not for me it's not. It's God's church for me. God has for some unseen reason ordained this trial of faith. Don't you understand how it is for us? For me? I promise you, it is a trial of my faith to be restrained from giving the priesthood to your people."

"Trial of your faith?" Adam mimicked. "Your faith? Hell, man, you're IN."

"I'm not in charge."

"Come on, Doc."

"When I was a missionary in Brazil," Dad said, "I had three black converts, and Adam, I loved them. Loved them like my kids. Do you know how that felt to tell them—"

"How it felt! You're asking me if I know how it felt? Let me ask you, Mister Sir, what do you know about how it feels?" He stood. "You never been a slave," he whispered, then shouted it for the whole cafeteria to hear: "YOU NEVER BEEN A SLAVE!" He picked up his chocolate cake with both hands and held it ready to throw at my dad. Giselle yelled, "Hey!" and then quietly, "Lover, calm down." Adam squished the cake in his fists. It came out between his fingers as though it were his pigment. He shook off what was left, then raised both his arms until they were positioned like Christ's, whose huge image was a shadow behind him. He howled, "FEEL!" and ran for the stairs, Giselle after him. When she caught him he screamed like he was dying, and she hugged him hard, saying, "Lover, lover, lover, lover."

David pulled Junie close, held her with both arms just as Giselle was holding Adam.

"Lover, lover," Giselle was saying. It looked like she was suckling him.

Dad handed me his dishes, then Adam's and Giselle's. The chocolate cake was glopped on the floor.

"Someone ought to get that up," Dad said softly. "Before a person slips on it." His eyes moved back to the stairs. I thought he might cry.

I wiped the cake with a napkin. When I looked up, Ernie was watching me from the kitchen. He kissed the air as though there were no distance between us and moved his head to sign a rendezvous at the trampoline. I looked away. I did not want to jump for God that night. Not with him, not with him.

Adam and Giselle were going to their room. I knew that when I finished bussing, I could hear them love. They would find that private rhythm, the music only they could hear, that was part anger, part betrayal, part love, part need. Adam would go inside her, groaning, and she would kiss him, touch him, accept him, call him precious names. They would do mysterious, invisible things.

TWENTY-ONE

Iris Holmes

SIBYL JOHNSTON

My mother, who is an artist, decided once to capture a spiderweb she found on our back porch: a huge, hexagonal, nearly symmetrical one. She wanted to make a painting out of it. She stained a board black, carefully knocked the spider out of its web, and succeeded in trapping the web on the board. Then she sprayed the whole thing to fix it and the web vanished, melted.

Notebook, August 24, 1982. I'm writing out on the patio today, watching Iris while Carolyn bicycles up the canyon to the lake and back.

It rained last night. Damp air swells the cottonwoods like a long breath, fills them with movement. The trees are breathing; the sounds—of them bending in their highest parts, three times taller than our cabins' roofs, of the wing-shaped leaves touching one another—are like rain. And out on the river there is the visual silence, the motion and stillness of dragonflies over the water, their gray reflections coiling on its surface. (I think they shed their wings sometimes; I find broken ones, like small tear-shaped windowpanes, all over the ground.) Deeper, the river darkens

into vague colors that seem to be more than an effect of light. I
can smell and nearly taste the water, leaves, soil, and now and
then a rank breath or two: Carolyn and Robert's goat or the Jerseys from the Madsens' farm down the road.

Iris is propped across the table from me in a lawn chair, just
sitting there. She's wearing her pink topsiders today, her cords,
and the rose-colored T-shirt Robert printed for her—"I Wear This
Shirt, Therefore I Am"—and she's wrapped in one of Carolyn's
hand-stitched quilts to ward off the canyon breeze, the river, and
a relapse of pneumonia. My notebook, extra pens, and Diet
Pepsi are on top of the table; from its round edge, between Iris
and me, a spider dangles. It dropped several inches a minute
ago—an almost freefall, an elastic pause like a yo-yo about to
ascend. Now it twirls slowly, legs flexing like signing fingers.

Carolyn and Robert built this patio themselves from rocks
they gathered farther up the canyon. The broken edges are fitted
to other broken edges; the surface is uneven, and I wonder if
Iris's chair would tip if she slid to one side. Carolyn has wedged
her in pretty tightly with the quilt and left me three phone numbers in case anything happens. Iris is easier to watch than most
one-year-olds—she doesn't run away, break things, or fall in the
river—but then she's also more difficult. She just sits. There's a
scar by her eye where one of the chickens ran over her once, just
about the only time Carolyn ever left her on the ground.

The spider is building a web between the table's top and leg.
It's one of many translucent orange spiders, the kind with round
bellies like glass eyes, that make their webs in our windows and
across our open door frames. The Puritans used spiders as meta-
phors for God. I'm a little afraid of them. When I moved out here
I had my cabin fumigated—pointless. The next morning I found
the first of many typed spider poems from Robert stuck on my
front door:

> What but design of darkness to appall?—
> If design govern in a thing so small?
> —Robert Frost

Now I brush their webs away with my fingers or let them stay.

The spider gropes across the surface of the table like a blind hand.

Once, a year ago, Robert said he thought God was sur-rounded with paradox to keep us from approaching in any way but by faith.

The day Robert said that was in August of 1981, about a month after Iris's birth. It was in the university bookstore, a modern flat building in which the shapes and proportions of things are noncommittal: neutral colors that leave no memory, fluorescent lighting that casts no shadows, a pale tile floor. And, behind the random noise of several hundred students buying fall textbooks, bland, aimless Muzak.

Across the room Robert was leafing through last week's *New Yorker*. He saw me and began walking toward me. Robert is sturdy and angular, with wiry auburn hair, slate-blue eyes, and a pink-and-white face he doesn't move much. He always speaks precisely, lingering a little on the consonants, which makes each sentence sound simple and self-evident.

We talked about our summers: I had visited home in Illinois; Robert and Carolyn had bought a goat; I had almost cut my hair; Carolyn had had her baby a month early and in a hospital rather than at home as they had planned. "How did it go?" I asked him. I hadn't seen them since she was seven months pregnant.

The morning before I'd left for Illinois we'd sat together under the trees, Carolyn laughing, dangling a stick in the water with one hand, the other hand returning now and then near to her middle. I leaned toward her and placed my palm on her; through her flesh I felt pressure, an independent lump. I pulled my hand away. Carolyn smiled. "You're funny, Sibyl." We talked about names, labor, the advantages of natural childbirth. We watched the trees; the river; the dragonflies dipping suddenly, violently, over the water, halting, then dipping and swinging again into motion. Carolyn yawned, stretching, her arms strong and dark, the color and sheen of pecans, the edges of her hair shining white for an instant in the sunlight. The trees slanted out over the river, their bark twisted like elephant's skin around the heartwood. Shadows of the bright new leaves blurred and gently changed the light on Carolyn's arms, her face and hair. She took a deep breath and sighed. The baby had begun to press against her lungs, she said, making her short of breath. Carolyn and Robert had not planned on a honeymoon baby; Robert was unemployed and they had no medical insurance. "I don't know, Sibyl," she said that morning. "I yell and yell at him about getting a job and he just sits there and takes it and then I'm even madder. I've decided to stop worrying about it. We're getting by, I guess. We'll just have to keep getting by after the baby comes." She leaned back in her chair, looking up at the trees and the Kodak-blue Utah sky, one hand shading her eyes.

From inside we heard the sounds of Robert fixing breakfast. Carolyn smiled, leaning back in her chair. "Robert's a good cook," she said softly, her fingers caressing her belly. "And you get him between the sheets and he is the best."

The screen door slammed; it was Robert with the breakfast tray. He placed it on the table between us, then pulled out a chair. "I have been remembering, Sibyl, the first time that Carolyn and I visited our midwife. The midwife put an electronic stethoscope on Carolyn's abdomen, and we listened to our baby's heartbeat." He poured Carolyn some goat's milk. "At first we heard only Carolyn's body, but soon we heard a small sound that reminded me of a train. And this was our child's heart." He was silent for a moment, the white pitcher tipped in the air above his glass. "I could feel it in my soul. I think Carolyn had hoped I would react more visibly, and she might have felt disappointed."

"Well," Robert said now, slowly, "the birth was rather difficult." He stopped, swallowed, glanced down at the floor. Then he continued. "Well, it seems the umbilical cord was wrapped around the baby's neck and she nearly asphyxiated. In fact, when she was born she had turned blue and her heart was not beating. Her Apgar scores were one and four." He paused, looked at me. "Do you know what an Apgar score is?"

"What?" I felt a dull chill. "Did—is she all right?"

"Oh, she lived. In fact, we took her out of the incubator today. She was in a coma for two weeks. Our doctor didn't think she would survive. The nurses asked us whether we wanted to change Iris's name so we could save it for our next baby. But Carolyn kept seeing her move. And now she's breathing on her own." Robert took a breath. "One of Iris's doctors told us earlier this week that it looks like Iris's brain was damaged during the birth. So we think she will probably be mentally retarded." Robert cocked his head to one side, tapped two fingers against the wooden stair rail.

"But—Robert, that's awful."

Robert nodded. The skin around his lips and nose was white. Behind him, someone pushing a dolly of books was trying to get past us. Robert turned and we started down the stairs together.

Notebook, April 30, 1982, nine months later. Carolyn, Robert, Iris, and I are sitting by the river on the patio. We are drinking lemonade and I'm taking notes. I have permission to write about Iris: Carolyn said, "Just tell the truth. Tell it so Iris will say it's the truth." She believes we'll all have to face Iris someday.

Robert's garden is beginning to bloom: clover and herbs between the patio's stones, patches of ferns, forget-me-nots, pink impatiens. Fuchsias in hanging baskets and begonias in two cut-off wooden barrels; marigolds and snapdragons around the house; creeping jennie, basket-of-gold. He's built a roof on the chicken coop to protect his garden (and Iris) from the chickens—but now Carolyn's dogs and my cats are warring through the ferns. Carolyn picks up the hose and squirts them, accidentally spraying Robert and me. "Carolyn!" Robert says. He's next to her, holding Iris. Iris flushes, moves her hands, and arches her back. Carolyn turns off the water and bends over them. "I'm sorry, Iris." Then she glances up at us. "See, she knows." Iris is wearing the little bikini Carolyn tells me she surfs in, and the soft terry jacket Robert got her for an early first birthday present.

A bluegill hovers in the shallow water near the bank. The

river is full of fish—mostly carp, though. Carolyn is fishing now, trying to catch us breakfast. She can't cast out very far because the trees hang too low over the water and the lines get tangled in them. She wears a loose Mexican dress, bright white with red, blue, and yellow flowers embroidered on the yoke. She's gotten overweight since the birth. Her face is heart-shaped and freckled, her eyes sage green, her lashes invisibly blond. Her hair is straight and short and blond.

The bluegill flickers in shallow water, seeming to wait, now and then flicking to a different angle. Its shadow wavers on the sand. Robert drops a pebble into the water; the fish vanishes. Robert talks about planting anemones next year, about making a rock garden. He bounces Iris gently on his knee—an exercise designed to teach Iris how to hold up her head, or that she has a head. "Iris is a very strange child," Robert remarks—although, since last summer, Rob-ert and Carolyn have learned more about her: she is blind, her doctors informed them soon after the birth. She is quadriplegic and cerebral-palsied. She now receives Dilantin and phenobarbital several times a day to control otherwise nearly continuous epileptic seizures. Carolyn puts it in the food that she Osterizes and then, four times a day, pours into a plastic syringe with a long, thin tube attached. She carefully slides the tube down Iris's throat and into her stomach—since Iris can't swallow, she doesn't gag—and slowly, bit by bit, pumps the food into her.

And one day last fall Carolyn said, "Iris is deaf," and clanged together an iron skillet and a Revere Ware pan till the windowpanes rattled against the sills; Iris didn't move. And—though there may never be a way to test this—all of Iris's doctors now believe that her develpomental delay is much more than moderate, that only her brain stem functions. Robert and Carolyn have to control her body temperature, covering or uncovering her to keep it stable.

I closed my notebook as Carolyn began reeling in her fishing line. The water wrinkled into a V, which jerked toward us. "I still can't get a picture in my mind of how she's going to be ten years from now, or twenty years from now, if she lives that long," Carolyn said. The red-and-white bob swung in a shortening arc, flinging water on all of us. Carolyn's hand followed it back and forth, then grasped it and moved along the line down to the hook. She leaned over to pick up a worm from the can by her feet. "Iris's first neonatalogist just asked us how much she'd changed in the three months since she'd been born, and we said not at all, and he said, 'Well, that's the kind of thing you can expect from her—how she's grown in the last three months is a reflection of how she's going to grow.'" She put the worm on the hook. "Iris's neonatalogist just said, 'It's all a question of time, how much time will pass before you find out for sure.'" Carolyn cast out again. The fishing line gleamed, a long, silver bow like the strands of spiderweb that float by randomly sometimes when the sun is out.

"Well, I think we've found out for sure," Robert said, shifting position. The aluminum chair squeaked.

"We don't think she'll progress now," agreed Carolyn. Supporting the fishing rod between her knees and leaning her free arm on Robert's shoulder, she played with Iris's hair, flattening a lock between two fingers and pulling gently. The sunlight turned it silvery-white. Carolyn looked up, her voice quickening. "But you just never know; you just never know how much control she's going to get with her hands or with her swallowing, or with anything, because it's just all time. That's the hard part." She raised her eyebrows apologetically. "Iris is just Iris and that's how she's going to be, I guess." Her hand followed the curve of Iris's cheek, gently, to her delicate chin. "The first months we were always looking for things to show that she was going to come out of it—for her all of a sudden to respond a little to sound, or to us visually. . . ." She smiled quickly, touched a fingertip to Iris's wrist. "She does respond tactilely, though—if you touch her she knows, and she wakes up." She trailed the finger up the inside of Iris's arm; Iris's expression changed: she blinked slowly, her mouth moved a little—almost a suck—and her arms flailed toward her face. Carolyn straightened and picked up the fishing rod again. "That's the hardest part—parents always try to get answers and doctors don't give answers. They just say, 'Well, you have to give her a little time, just give her a little time.'"

She stared steadily at the plastic ball on the water, her face still, and rested the fishing rod on her knees. Robert shifted Iris on his lap and put a hand on the back of Carolyn's chair. She turned away from him to tell me about the specialist they had visited the day before. Her voice was a little uneven. "Sibyl, a perfect Apgar score is ten and ten. That doctor said a score of one and four is no accident."

Robert and I looked at her. "What do you mean?" I said.

"I mean, twenty minutes before Iris was born the nurse couldn't find a heartbeat. . . ." Now her voice was slipping, falling across sharp edges, diminishing. She paused, then said quietly, "She was born in secondary apnea—no pulse, no heartbeat, no breathing. . . ." She ticked it all off on her fingers. "The cord was asphyxiating her all that time. Now why didn't somebody do something?" She sat still for a minute, then leaned back in her chair. "That doctor says he doesn't believe in the 'brotherhood of doctors.' He says he thinks we ought to sue."

Robert jiggled Iris some more, looking out over the river, his face expressionless. Iris sat like a thin Buddha cradled on her father's lap, blond brows gleaming in the sunlight. Her pupils seemed to focus, then slid over to one side; doctors had said she could perceive some light. She grasped Robert's fingers—a reflex.

Maybe they just want to blame someone, I wrote in the margin of my notebook. "Well, I guess you're lucky she didn't die," I said.

Carolyn and Robert looked at me for a moment, like they hadn't heard me. "She did die," Carolyn said.

Maybe they need to blame someone.

I spent much of that spring with Carolyn and Iris, lying across Robert and Carolyn's bed, eating creetchies (Carolyn's name for Rice Krispies Treats, on which she and I binged every week or so), looking up through the windows at the trees and the changing sky, talking, putting off other things, taking notes for my book.

The bedroom walls needed replastering; this was the unfinished, usually unseen part of the Holmeses' house. The walls were lined with cardboard boxes full of books, stored foods, and back issues of the underground Mormon newsletter Robert edited.

"I had a dream about Iris," I said one day. A water spider moved on the wall behind Carolyn and Iris, and another up in one of the corners. Carolyn had moved the canary in his three-storied bamboo cage over near the window. I pulled off a piece of creetchie, twisting it to sever the gooey strands of marshmallow. "I dreamed she learned to talk. And I remember, I thought, who would ever have expected her to do that?"

Carolyn shifted from her stomach to her side, leaning her head on her arm and stroking Iris's hand. "People dream about Iris," she said. The pitch of her voice drifted down as she spoke, like a sigh or a sound dying out or something falling. "One time Robert dreamed Iris smiled at him." She propped herself up on one elbow and her face and voice became animated, as if her words were weapons against something: Iris's newest physical therapist, she said, told her Iris's arching her back and stretching when she was uncomfortable was not a cortical brain function—not any kind of communication after all, "Because as far as we know, Iris's cortex doesn't send out any signals"—but a reflex that should have come and gone and come again by now.

"So maybe she doesn't know we're out here after all?"

Carolyn shrugged, shook her head, smiled a little. "And the latest theory is that this reflex will block her from developing other reflexes—like swallowing—and it will overbuild her back muscles so sooner or later, if we can't stop her, she'll be stuck that way."

Like the older C.P. victims you see in wheelchairs, their backs curved the wrong way like bows, I thought. That would be bad for Iris: her prettiness was an asset. Any person, therapist or not, would be warmer and more patient with a blue-and-silver baby like Iris than with others, who looked as bad off as they were.

Outside, the cottonwoods stirred and glittered. The sky was white. A few raindrops hit the windowpanes. I got up and closed the windows; the canary hopped from one perch to another. Carolyn sat up, leaned back against the headboard. She took Iris under the arms, supporting her head so it wouldn't loll and arranging her in her lap, talking to her in a lilting, penetrating voice. Iris's hearing aid whistled; Carolyn adjusted it. The canary began to sing, an intense, quivering coloratura. Carolyn watched it absentmindedly. "I'm supposed to hold her like this to keep her from extending, for as long as I can every day." She smiled and shook her head again. "Poor Iris. But I feel guilty whenever I'm not doing it. . . ." She folded Iris's legs up tailor style, holding the ankles with one hand, then gently pushed Iris's head forward with the other hand. Carolyn's fingers were long and straight, her palms wide. Her hands looked delicate and strong. Her wrists were fleshy. She had gained about forty pounds in the year or so since Iris's birth; now she moved like a pregnant woman again, aware of extra flesh that in some way was not part of her. I could see the outlines of bones in the back of her hand as Iris tensed and strained against her palm. Iris's neck reddened. Her arms came up and flailed slightly. Carolyn grabbed them, then hugged her close. "See? She hates it!" She sighed and leaned back against the headboard, still holding Iris like that, trying to hide her hopefulness. We watched the rain as it washed over the window, bending the landscape. "I think when I go visit my mom this summer I'll get a permanent," Carolyn said. "You know—curly all over?" She laughed. "Robert says I'll look like Harpo." She tilted her head a little to one side and smiled at me again. I thought of Robert smiling across the table at the humanities banquet this past March, discussing Camus's *The Stranger* over lime meringue pie and twirly vanilla cookies: "The meaning of the cliff is in not jumping," he had said. Meticulously, he had scraped the meringue off the lime jello with his fork.

Carolyn continued: she was not happy with what I'd written so far, she said. "You make it sound like I don't love Iris." She handed her to me, showed me how to hold her, then talked about her dying, watching me. "I just can't think of Iris's body being without her. Can you?"

Can I? I thought. "I don't know."

"You should spend some time with retarded children—do some volunteer work or something. It would help your book a lot." I smiled. She reached over and took Iris back, then laughed. "Boy,

Sibyl, it's a good thing we're friends."

I agreed politely. "I guess it's hard for me to really feel a lot of these things," I said. At home I had three books of index cards filled with details and ideas about Iris. I had been putting off sorting them because every time I tried, I wound up overwhelmed, in tears. Now the thought crossed my mind again that maybe I had better just toss them all. This isn't fiction, I thought.

Carolyn reached over to the old trunk beside the bed and picked up a glass picture frame containing photographs of Iris right after she was born. "You might be interested in these," she said. Irony? I looked down at the pictures anyway as she handed them to me. I wrote in my notebook: *Iris in intensive care, lying in a small white plastic box—isolette—ventilator taped over mouth, feeding tube up nose, pins in either side of chest to monitor heart, umbilical catheter in navel for testing oxygen in blood directly from heart. That must have hurt. And did anyone know if it hurt? Name-plate on isolette: Iris Holmes; 7/20/81, 4:29 a.m.; Reg. No. 1020127; Weight: 5 1/2; Feeding: B; pink-and-blue cartoon of stork with baby sliding down one leg. Carolyn holding Iris; Robert masked and holding Iris for the first time. Iris's eyelids are lavender. Her fingernails are transparent, like little bits of waxed paper. Carolyn and Robert touching Iris through an opening in the isolette; Carolyn's father holding Iris.*

When I looked up Carolyn was still staring at me. "It wasn't easy holding her, because of all those tubes," she said. "She was hard to hold."

Carolyn leaned to one side and looked out the window at the river, which was fifteen feet from the house and rising. "If this rain doesn't stop, our landlord says the river is going to overflow its banks and wash us right out of the canyon." Behind her the spider minced delicately along the top of the headboard. The landlord had advised all of us to get some sandbags for that spring.

Carolyn talked on: a box of fifty unreusable plastic tubes for feeding Iris cost $75. Robert had a job interview with Mervyn's that week—a promotional writing job that could take them anywhere in the country, but probably to Texas. Carolyn didn't want to go to

Texas—"But honestly, I don't know how we're going to put food on the table." She's asking for something, I thought: what? Robert had been job hunting off and on since before Iris was born. Carolyn, Robert, and Iris lived off the Social Security checks Iris got because she was blind. And nearly every week someone—an acquaintance from church or a friend of the family—left groceries on their doorstep. Carolyn was grateful. "When Iris is not alive we'll be able to do anything we want, but right now we have to find a job with a good insurance policy." She tilted her head, touched her forehead lightly with one finger, then stroked Iris's hair again.

Everything was blurred green through the wet glass. Crocuses were shooting up in the lawn. We both hoped Peg, the Holmeses' German shepherd, wouldn't destroy them before they bloomed. Carolyn jiggled Iris, who was breathing hoarsely, then pulled a plastic tube out of Iris's diaper bag and slid it down her throat. I imagined the pain of something hard and foreign in my throat, my chest. The tube was attached to a plastic vial, from which protruded another tube, which Carolyn put in her mouth and sucked. There was a sound like the dregs of a milkshake, and the vial began to fill with mucus. Carolyn held the vial carefully upright to avoid getting a mouthful. The mucus trap was one way of preventing pneumonia or strangulation. But I still couldn't use it; the last time I'd tried I'd gagged because of the way the air tasted. Carolyn had smiled: "You're not much help, Sibyl."

"You know," she said now, looking up from the tube, "before, whenever something really bad happened, I just figured it would work out, you know, it would get better." She carefully pulled the tube out of Iris's throat and stuck it back in the pink canvas diaper bag. "Iris is a bad thing that didn't get better."

She touched the thin strands of white linen thread in the bedspread, tracing their small repeating square pattern with one finger. "A friend of Robert's mom crocheted this as a wedding present."

"It must have taken her years."

Carolyn leaned forward to look at the pattern. "You know what, though?" she said. "It seems to me more and more that I'm not a normal person." She looked up. "Iris is my salvation from normalcy." Suddenly the spider dropped from the headboard onto her hand. She jerked, shook it off, releasing Iris, who began to arch backward. Carolyn turned her onto her stomach, folding her arms so her face wouldn't press into the bedspread, then took a magazine from the trunk that sat by the bed, aimed, and smashed the spider. "They bite Iris," she said, replacing the magazine. "I pick her up in the morning and she's got red marks all over her and I feel awful."

There was not much anyone who lived near the river could do about the spiders, though; in my cabin one crouched permanently in the corner above my typewriter—every time I got rid of him, he came back again. I usually picked them up in a glass and took them outdoors; Robert left them; and Carolyn smashed them. And at night when I turned out my lights I would usually see three or four more silhouetted at my bedroom window, spinning. Their webs were always empty in the morning and by afternoon had been blown apart by the breezes.

Carolyn got up to go mix Iris's dinner.

Notebook, July, 1982, a few months later. Carolyn bathing Iris, Iris's body long, her limbs long and soft and undeveloped. The muscles in her back and abdomen hard, defined. Her feet new, pink and white, never walked on, their soles soft and puffy like little pin cushions. I take hold of one and it feels like a hand.

Carolyn lays her naked on the kitchen counter with a folded towel for a pillow, rests one hand on Iris's chest, and turns to close the window. Carolyn wears one of Robert's flannel shirts. Her hair, which is longer now, is tied back with a scarf. Iris's arms are bent at the elbow, her hands in fists moving a little in the air around her head. Her legs are crossed at the ankle, her long toes clenched like fingers. (With her clenched toes, Iris can wear thongs better than a lot of one-year-olds, and she owns several pairs, which she often wears with her bikini.) I try to imagine cool ceramic tiles on my back, no sight, no sound. No consciousness? Not sounds or colors or shapes, certainly.

Tastes? Smells, sensations—and a little light. And does she know she perceives that much? Carolyn says blind people are not more sensitive in other ways—they just learn to do without. Iris's eyes, cloudy, impenetrable, slate-blue, are fixed—focused?—and half open. Carolyn strokes Iris's palm with her finger, gently calls her name. Then, slowly, she caresses each limb and Iris's chest, first with burlap, then with a piece of rabbit skin, then with ice. She hopes to teach Iris that she has legs, arms, a face. Iris pulls away from the ice, but with her whole body—possibly a reflex. Her face reddens and contorts. Both arms stiffen and she seems to look slowly around. "Oh . . . !" says Carolyn, her hand in the air near her cheek. "Is she going to do it?" She waves her hand. "Robert!" Iris's mouth opens and she cries—a short exhalation that sounds like a backward gasp. We all applaud her in the morning sunlight. This could become a problem for Iris: everyone loves it so much when she's displeased.

Carolyn squeezes her, touches her cheek to her belly, kisses her on the navel. "You are Ms. Cute!" She picks her up. "Oooh"—through clenched teeth—"what a chunk!" Iris tenses at the water, her back rigidly curved, and Carolyn continues talking softly to her.

Carolyn's kitchen faces east, so now, at ten in the morning, it's filled with light. The water shines on Iris's body and in the air, where it falls like another form of light when Carolyn lifts her hands out of the sink. She lathers up each of Iris's legs, then turns her over. "Look at this," she says. "Iris has the best bum." She squeezes it, rubs the soap over the soft pink skin. Iris tenses, then relaxes. Carolyn turns her around again and sits her back in the water, cradling her head with one arm. Iris's face reddens. She scowls.

After the bath Carolyn pours olive oil on her hands and rubs it into Iris's skin. It works better than lotion, she says, because it's not clammy. "Besides, I really believe the body can absorb things through the skin. It makes sense, doesn't it? This has got to be good for her!" She holds Iris's arm up by the hand, wraps

*her oily fingers around it and massages it. She bends the arm
at the elbow, the wrist, the finger joints—an exercise to keep
Iris's muscles from atrophying. The doctors say Iris is beginning
to get contractures in her elbows, her wrists, her hips; Carolyn
must exercise her to prevent her limbs from folding up like little
birds' wings. "See? She loves it! Look how loose she is!" Again
she leans over her. "Mmm, smell her now!"*

"Give the girl a pimiento," says Robert.

Robert pushed open my screen door one night that August,
letting in several big moths and—I hoped—no spiders. "Carolyn has
just returned from her visit home and we were thinking, wouldn't a
Reuben sandwich be nice? And I said, well we must get Sibyl. She'll
never forgive us if we go for Reuben sandwiches without her. Want
to come?"

Wells Drive Inn was looped in cursive on a pink-and-aqua
aluminum sign outside the restaurant, *Reuben Sandwich* printed
in black beneath it. Wells's was a loose arrangement of brown-and-
black obtuse angles. Inside, the walls were pine, stained to look like
cedar and hung with macrame owls and planters.

"Diefenbachia," Robert observed.

We ordered our sandwiches and picked up our Cokes from Mr.
Wells, and Carolyn, taking Iris, made for the Ms. Pac Man machine
in the corner near our table. She placed Iris in her carrier on the
floor, then turned to the machine, deposited a quarter, and began
jerking the lever up and down, back and forth, guiding Ms. Pac Man
through the iridescent maze on the black screen. "So what kind of
a job are you looking for?" I asked Robert, snapping the plastic lid
off my Coke. A thin woman in an orange coat pushed open the
door behind him, followed by two little boys.

"Well," Robert said, watching them as they crossed to the
counter, "I interviewed with a company the other day who wanted
to hire an advertising copywriter."

The thin woman leaned across the counter, talking to the cook
as he grilled our sandwiches. Her children twisted the knobs on the
Rubik's Cube machine near Carolyn.

"M-m-my name's not Mike!" said one. "W-we changed names."

"Okay."

"He's sixty pounds now," the woman told the cook. "I don't think either one of us wants to carry that around—"

"M-my name's Matt, y-your n-n-name's—"

The woman looked around. "Matthew. Michael." She glanced down at Iris.

One boy leaned away from the other, arching his back to look upside down at his mother. "When I grow up I'm going to change my name to Stan-ley." Robert watched the little boy, almost smiling.

Carolyn's postcard the week before had asked me whether Robert had found a job yet. That was the deal—he was supposed to be working by the time she and Iris returned from visiting Carolyn's parents. I had never relayed the question. Robert had spent the week gardening, fishing, taking Peg for runs and the little boys from church for swimming lessons, visiting me, closing all the doors and windows, and listening to classical music full blast. In a way, I didn't blame him—with a resume that included a B.A. in humanities, two years of assisting in the university's international film program, five years of raising orchids, and the additional skill of goat milking, the only jobs he could get were the ones that would make him most miserable. And Iris's bills were insurmountable anyway unless he found a job with insurance—again, the kind of job he didn't want. He had swum up to my back porch the day before and hung there, talking about Carolyn's visit home, writer's block, the English department, his hair glossed flat and burgundy-gold in the streaks of light that fell through spaces in the trees and made shadowy light places on the river, places where you could see into the water. The sharp, pale little freckles on his arms and shoulders looked like they were being washed away, and the skin on his nose and his shoulders was turning pink. "One redhead to another," I had said, "you're going to burn."

After a while the porch had gotten all wet where he hung on, there were goose bumps on his arms, and his lips looked purplish. He pushed off from the porch, treading water. His chest looked whitish-green under the water and seemed to bend off at an odd angle before disappearing into the river.

Peg had gotten twisted up in her leash by the back door and started to whine. "Margaret, are you grieving?" said Robert, and began a sidestroke toward the shore to save her.

Ms. Pac Man bleeped and blurped. The freckled woman walked over to look in Iris's carrier. "Pretty baby," she said to Carolyn's back.

Carolyn glanced over her shoulder, then returned quickly to the machine. "Damn! He got me!"

"When I grow up I'm going to change my name to Stan-ley."

"So you'd be writing newspaper ads and stuff?" I asked.

"Well, yes, and probably composing letters and working on ad campaigns, that sort of. . . ." After a moment, the rest of his breath came out in a sigh. Robert looked around the room. "Oh, hell," he said. "I'm not looking for a job."

"About four months?" the woman persisted, her finger in Iris's hand.

Carolyn let go of the lever and shifted to the other foot. She looked up but did not turn around. "She's a year."

"Oh. . . ."

Carolyn didn't wait for the inevitable next question. She turned sharply from the machine and told the woman, whose face was now slack, as if waiting for a punch line or the end of an unfinishable sentence, "Cerebral palsy."

Robert smiled calmly, his lips closed and his eyes wide open, looking at the woman and at Carolyn, who looked back at him. Mr. Wells called out our number, and Carolyn picked up Iris and went to get the sandwiches.

"Robert tell you we're moving south?" she said after she put Iris down on the empty chair, distributed the sandwiches, and sat down herself. "Our lawyer says the case will be stronger if we can get it into a federal court, but the only way to do that is for one party to be living out of state. So we have to go by March first."

"If we decide to move," said Robert.

"Robert doesn't want to leave the old homestead."

My sandwich was oily, tangy. Rye vapors rose in my throat and nose. I moved my straw around in the ice of my drink. "Why would federal court be better, Carolyn?"

"Oh, you know, he just thinks it'll be more professional and quicker. And the county where the federal cases are tried is more liberal than this one, and he thinks a liberal jury'll be in our favor. Besides, if we file here we'll be attacking one of the city's main employers and one of their most prominent doctors, and a good lawyer would use that against us. That's why we have to move, basically."

And because here, Carolyn never wanted to take Iris out alone, she wanted a vacation from church and other people's questions, she wanted to leave. In addition to the strangers who asked what was wrong with her baby, there were old friends she couldn't face without breaking down; the Welfare representative who wanted to see Iris because—we could only assume—she suspected Carolyn of child abuse; Carolyn's obstetrician, who interpreted Iris's problems and their causes differently than Carolyn did; and a long line of well-meaning visitors who almost invariably told Carolyn and Robert what special people they must be to have been given such a responsibility—to which Carolyn had begun responding as she had to me: "You can be special too. Why don't you go volunteer to hold some little retarded babies for an hour a week?" There was Iris's doctor, "the meanest pediatrician in the state," who took one look at Iris and told Carolyn, "That kid's brain is rotten." Carolyn had had to find a place to pull over and cry on her way home from his office. There was Robert's younger brother, just home from being a missionary in Argentina, who asked in complete innocence, "Well, why haven't you healed her?" And there was the day Robert, in a sentimental mood, asked Carolyn, "But would you really want her any different?" Carolyn stopped what she was doing, stared at him, and then gasped, "Yes!" and started crying and couldn't stop for half an hour. "I thought I'd finished that," she apologized afterward.

On the other hand, there was the pharmacist who filled Iris's prescriptions: "She just looked at me—like she knew everything about Iris—and said, 'You take good care of that baby.' I guess she might have known a lot by what drugs we needed. But I don't know—I wouldn't be surprised if she had a baby like Iris." And there was Carolyn and Robert's attorney, "the toughest, most ruthless lawyer around—that's why we got him," whom Carolyn had disliked until once, when she couldn't answer a question about the birth, he had said, "There's no hurry. I lost a son last year in a plane crash." There was Carolyn's childbirth instructor, who had taken herbs and seen doctors and prayed throughout her pregnancy because— again—she was hemorrhaging, and whose baby had been born, brain-damaged, the same day as Iris, and then died. She had buried him where she could see the grave from her house, and now brought Carolyn a big bag of groceries once a month—always "anony-mously." There was Carolyn's bishop, who had handed her a check for $1,600 to cover Iris's latest hospital bill. And there was the fact that when all Iris's other doctors had given up, her insensitive, unsympathetic pediatrician had pulled her through six bouts of pneumonia and never billed Carolyn.

My Coke left watery brown circles on the gold-flecked Formica table. "So you think for sure you want to leave?"

Carolyn glanced at Robert, who said nothing. "We're not sure." She pushed her chair back suddenly and walked toward the ladies' room. "Back in a second."

Robert placed both hands flat on the table and closed his eyes. "I would like to write a story," he said, "about a couple who have a baby, and the baby is retarded, and so the parents wonder why, if God is omniscient and omnipotent, did that happen? But then they come to realize that it was the doctor's fault. So they start believing in God again and attending church and praying that they will win their malpractice suit so they'll be rich the rest of their lives." He opened his eyes and looked at me. Behind him, on the plate-glass window across the room, we were reflected in faint, colorless lines and planes, like ghosts on the night outside. *Break-fast Is Coming,* said the sign on the Hi-Spot across the street. *Entrance* was painted backwards on the door. Don't bother, Robert, I thought; I'm already writing it.

Carolyn was back. "Rob, does Iris have dreams?" Robert moved his eyes to look up at her. "No, really—what do you think she dreams about?"

"Angels," said Robert.

Notebook, August 30, 1982. Carolyn has returned from her bike ride. She bends over, shakes her head and arms out, reaches for her toes. "Ohh," she says, straightening. She pushes her hair back from her face, twisting it up off her neck, then lets it fall. The permanent is starting to grow out now; her hair is smooth and brown on top. Her face and neck are flushed, her freckles invisible. Her skin is damp, silvery at the edges in the late summer light. She picks Iris up, carrying her with one arm, and I follow her up the bank and through her back door. Inside, the air is still, warm, human-smelling. The phone is ringing. Carolyn's Adidases scweech on the gray-painted floor as she turns on the cold water. "Don't answer it," she reminds me. She has been too exhausted lately to want to talk much. It keeps ringing. The water splatters on the porcelain, glassing around her fingers. When it is cold enough she fills two pewter mugs and hands me one. Then she walks into the living room to get Iris's wheelchair—a fancy, $1,200 model with seat belts, a back that adjusts to her shoulder height and leg length, a footrest to keep her legs bent, pads to hold her back and head straight, restraints to keep her legs from scissoring. Two of its parts were especially made for Iris. The wheelchair was paid for by Welfare, is described by Robert as "the most expensive thing we own, practically," and is rarely used because Carolyn is embarrassed by it: "I feel like putting a sign on the back: 'Yes, she's retarded.'" But the chair does hold Iris in the right position so Carolyn doesn't have to, and she will be able to use it for years—maybe all her life.

Carolyn wheels Iris into the kitchen, then sits down across the square oak table from me. Its surface, waxed and unvarnished, is cool and smooth as skin. It absorbs and diffuses light rather than reflecting it. The phone stops ringing and Carolyn unplugs it. "Some woman from the Children's Hospital called last week to ask for a donation," she tells me. They got to talking and the woman told Carolyn that her little boy was born with spina bifida. "She was so . . . cold," Carolyn says. "She just rattled on and on about how her son would learn to control his bowels. And I'll never forget—just before she hangs up she puts on this testimony-meeting voice and she says, 'Carolyn, God doesn't make mistakes.'"

Carolyn leans her elbows on the table for a moment. Then she whispers, "I wish somebody knew how I feel." I think of Robert reading aloud by the river: "Behold, I cry out of wrong but I am not heard; I cry aloud, but there is no judgment."

It is beginning to get dark. Fragments of the sunset float on the water, amorphous but stationary. Dark, vivid twigs, leaves, branches tangle against the sky. A heron passes, flying low along the water, slow-winged in the way that very large things are slow, legato, wing feathers gilded with sun. It follows the river, bending with it into the trees away from the road. Half of Iris's face is in the light. Her mouth is a small curved shadow; her brow, her cheekbone, her chin cast shadows. Her legs, slender and swollen at the knee, are bent; she sits like a grown person in her chair, and for a moment I feel time passing; I can see Iris five, ten, twenty years from now—in this room, in this chair. She is nearly silent, her eyes half open and glaring sideways. We can hear her breathing. "People don't see Iris," I realize suddenly. "They only see what she means to them."

Carolyn's face doesn't change. "What does she mean to you?" she asks. She leans forward, rocking back and forth on her elbows. On the window behind her the spiders are beginning to spin.

Robert has said that Iris more than anyone is a prisoner of her body. Sitting in the darkening kitchen, I think, What does Iris mean? Her image on my retina? The bite she takes out of my vision of things? What should I make of her? "I guess Iris . . . embodies questions I can't answer."

Carolyn glances up at me, then takes a quick breath and looks around the room and down at the table, running her fingers gently over the cool pewter mug. "Embodies questions?" she whispers.

I look at her hands, white on the rough metal cup in the last sunlight. "Carolyn, we're just trying to protect ourselves—that's really all."

"But I can't protect myself—I live with her." She looks at me. "Have you ever tried to know?"

It is nearly dark in the kitchen. There is only the faint gleaming of Iris's wheelchair, the mugs, the windows.

Carolyn pushes herself up from the table and turns away from me to fix Iris's dinner.

TWENTY-TWO

Whole Other Bodies

W A L T E R   K I R N

I remember the time of my family's conversion, that couple of months before He saved our souls forever. The nights I stayed awake too late in bed, playing my radio under the covers, one of those midnight talk shows with people calling from every state, a plumber from Utah with cancer saying, "Hi, this is Don, I'm a first-time caller, and in response to that doctor from Boston—" And hearing my parents' bedroom sounds, their noisy bathroom trips night after night, toilet flushes at five in the morning and someone slamming the cabinet, coughing, spilled pills and my father cursing, kicking the wall as they rolled behind the tub. I remember it as a time of no food, nothing in the fridge, and then, the next day, too much food and all the same kind, cheese, say, pounds of it, but not any bread to put it on, my mother lit up in the fridge door, saying, "Cheese is the one thing you can't have enough of. This family *lives* on cheese." And how she would leave all the windows open and blame it on me or my brother Randy until we went over and closed them, but then in the morning those same windows, open again. Satan was with us then, I think, his spirit of confusion. Inside the house you could feel it.

My friends stopped coming over after school, I stopped letting them. What they might see. My father talking back to the newscasts, making fun of the president, or standing out on the porch with his drink, screaming out at the empty yard, "Of course no one listens! I've lost my voice!" And whenever the mailman came to the door with a box that wouldn't fit through the slot, I'd have to open it only partway, blocking his view of how dirty our house was, of dying plants that never got watered because my mother was always in bed. And sometimes I'd be mowing on weekends, cutting up close to the wall of the house, and I'd look through the window at everyone in there, sitting around the table after lunch, wiping their mouths with paper towels and not knowing what to do next, and I'd think: Too bad for them. Too bad for those sad people. But after my mowing I'd go back in and what I'd said outside would hurt me, I wouldn't like myself then, so I'd just watch cartoons or something, not thinking.

My father wasn't going to his job. He'd eat a big breakfast with Randy and me like he was about to go, he'd have on his watch and his best red tie, but the school bus would come and he would still be there, pouring new coffee maybe, and when we'd run out to the bus he'd wave good-bye, though he was supposed to be gone by then. Except that something was holding him back, making him lazy.

Only God could have saved how we were then. We had everything modern, sure, a phone in every important room, a new French blender, tilt-back armchairs with three positions, and no matter where you went in the house, even down in the basement, there was always some money lying around, all these extra dimes and quarters that you could just steal and spend on anything. But none of that was helping, nothing we had or owned. We were pretty helpless.

Then the missionaries came. They were there one day when I got home from school, two young men in tight dark suits drinking strawberry Kool-Aid my mother had served them. The living room chairs were grouped in a circle, so Randy and I sat down and joined in, a long conversation about Our Lord and his plan for the

American family. The missionaries had short blond hair and slow western voices, their fingernails were pink and all squared off. They said they didn't mean to put us out, just wanted to make us aware of some things, and my mother and father smiled and nodded with wide, shining looks in their eyes, though their faces still seemed tired around the edges from so many months of trouble. The missionaries asked questions from a book, hard ones about the soul and where we hoped to go after death, then waited quietly with their hands folded while we all gave our answers.

The change was slow in our house and took a while to notice, our soft new way of doing things, with less bumping into each other, less noise. After their four o'clock visits, the missionaries left pamphlets and books, and my mother would open them up before dinner, asking if she could turn off the set because TV wasn't important now, its news had nothing to do with us—she'd rather go over the truths of the gospel to calm our spirits before we ate. And my brother would do a thing he'd never done and kindly offer to get us all drinks when we finally sat down at the table. And I would pop up and help him, like magic, not feeling lazy at all, as though it was fun to pitch in and a very nice thing to remember afterwards, how I'd pleased my parents.

The missionaries came twice a week on old beat-up bikes with baskets in front, and one time they brought a movie projector and set it up in the living room, shining its beam on the dark wall where we'd taken down a painting of some dancers. In the movie they showed us, a panel of experts talked about decay, the decay of the nuclear family unit, just like we'd been going through, and it was a wonderful thing to learn that decay was happening everywhere, all over the country and all over the world, not just in our house. The missionaries were proud of the movie and kept leaning forward, pointing their fingers, saying how much we'd enjoy the next part because of its special message, and when the movie was over and Randy turned on the lights, the missionaries rubbed their knees and grinned because they knew how deeply we were learning.

One Saturday morning they took us to a park, me and my brother, no grown-ups. We had a picnic. The missionaries had made the food themselves: peanut butter and honey on white bread, celery sticks and pink lemonade, which they drank even more of than we did. The plan was just to sit under a tree and soak up the peace of sun and fresh air, and before we talked about God that day, they asked us about the sports we played, baseball and soccer and hockey, which were their favorite sports too, and they promised to give us tips sometime. Then the tall missionary with the blonder hair told us about when he'd been a kid, that he came from a ranch with dozens of horses and one time a rattlesnake got in the stalls and he used a twelve-gauge shotgun to kill it. The other missionary talked less, just lay on his side sucking celery sticks, and every few minutes he'd pick up a stone and chuck it sidearm and hit the swing set where no one was playing that day.

My brother got sleepy from reading the Bible, but tried not to show it, being polite. The blonder missionary told him not to worry, to curl up and sleep as long as he wanted, we weren't going to leave the park without him. And while my brother napped on the grass, moving his legs in his sleep, we talked about whether the Holy Ghost could visit a person in dreams, taking the shape of an animal, say, or of a stranger, teaching truths that the person would wake up knowing. And we agreed that this was possible and might even happen someday to one of us.

I started to love the missionaries and so did my mother. She found out when their birthdays were, that they were both in June, and instead of having our lesson one night we drank chocolate milk and played a game where everyone had to wear blindfolds, which fit right in with my mother's plan to sneak outside and wheel in two new bikes, singing "Happy Birthday." The missionaries kissed her on the cheek, then on the back of her hand as a joke, while my father rocked in his chair and smiled. He was at peace like I'd never seen him, his face was smooth where it used to have lines, and I dropped my head to give a prayer of thanks, everyone getting down on their knees and my mother crying but not sad, a beautiful woman with wet cheeks when I secretly opened my eyes before "Amen."

Then it was time for us all to be baptized, a total immersion baptism in deep blue water. We wore white gowns like karate outfits with loose cloth belts. The missionaries gave sermons first and everyone was there, the whole church, a hundred people from different towns who'd set up a table of cold cuts and cheese to eat at the party afterwards. And the sermons spoke of that perfect love which hovers around us always, in the sky, and of how some people ignored this love by always looking straight ahead with pinched, busy faces. But my family hadn't done that, we'd looked up.

One by one we went under the water. First my father, my tall father, clean and pale as he held his breath and let himself fall backwards, braced against the missionary's arm. For a time his hair spread out on the water, then it disappeared, and that was the moment when God took him in entirely. It happened to all of us that day.

Other Notable Mormon Stories and Collections

ABBREVIATIONS

AML Prize Annual award in short story of the Association for Mormon Letters.

BYU Studies *Brigham Young University Studies*

Christian Values Winner Writing contest sponsored by the Center for Christian Values in Literature at Brigham Young University.

Christmas *Christmas for the World: A Gift to the Children* Edited by Curtis Taylor and Stan Zenk Salt Lake City: Aspen Books, 1991.

Dialogue *Dialogue: A Journal of Mormon Thought*

Dialogue Award Annual *Dialogue* Writing Award in fiction.

Greening Wheat *Greening Wheat: Fifteen Mormon Short Stories.* Edited by Levi S. Peterson. Midvale, UT: Orion Books, 1983.

RMR *Rocky Mountain Review*

Rocky Mountain Reader	*Rocky Mountain Reader.* Edited by Ray B. West, Jr. New York: E. P. Dutton, 1946.
Sunstone Contest	Annual *Sunstone* Fiction Contest, sponsored by the children of D. K. and Brookie Brown.
Twenty-two	*Twenty-two Young Mormon Writers.* Edited by Neal E. Lambert and Richard H. Cracroft. Provo, UT: Communications Workshop, 1975.
Utah Arts Council	Annual prize in short story of the Original Writing Contest of the Utah Arts Council.
Washed by a Wave	*Washed by a Wave of the Wind: Stories from the Corridor.* Edited by M. Shayne Bell. Salt Lake City: Signature Books, 1993.

Allen, Penny. "Dandelions." *Ensign,* Mar. 1978.

————. "Representation." *Sunstone,* Nov. 1991.

Allen, Rex. "Grandpa." *Mountainwest,* Nov. 1977.

Anderson, Paris. "You: A Missionary Story." *Sunstone,* Sept. 1987.

Anderson, Tory C. "After Dad Died." *New Era,* Apr. 1991.

Arrington, Chris Rigby. "Wheat Is for Man." *Exponent II,* Dec. 1976.

Bailey, Alice Morrey. "Until Death Only." *RMR,* Fall 1939.

Baker, Virginia Ellen. "Rachel's Wedding." First place in L. Ron Hubbard Writers of the Future Contest (1989, 3d quarter), published in *Writers of the Future,* Vol. 5 (Bridge Publications, 1989).

————. "On the Last Day, God Created." Forthcoming in *Isaac Asimov's Science Fiction Magazine* and in *Washed by a Wave.*

Ballif, Arta Romney. "A Wedding Night." A Christian Values Winner; *Literature and Belief,* 1982.

Barnhurst, Kevin. "A Mormon Fairy Tale: The Elder and the Convert Lady." *Exponent II,* Spring 1981.

Bell, Elouise. "The Meeting." *Only When I Laugh* (Signature Books, 1990).

————. "A Generous Heart." *Christmas*, 1991.

Bezzant, Pat. "Finale." Forthcoming in *Washed by a Wave*.

Black, Nancy. "A Marshmallow Santa for the New Born King." *Christmas*, 1991.

Brown, Marilyn. "The Happiness Bird." *Dialogue*, Summer 1967.

Cannon, Ann Edwards. "Separate Prayers." Honorable Mention, Sunstone Contest, 1981; *Sunstone*, Nov.-Dec. 1981.

————. "The Quilt." *Dialogue*, Spring 1982.

Cannon, Blanche. "The Promise." *RMR*, Summer 1945.

Carver, Wayne. "A Man of Fortune Greeting Heirs." *Furioso*, Summer 1950.

————. "The Country Behind." *Furioso*, Spring 1953.

————. "The Price of Deer." *Carleton Miscellany*, Summer 1960.

————. "Heroes Are Born." *Esquire*, Nov. 1961.

————. "Benvenuto ad Anzio." *Carleton Miscellany*, Fall 1963.

————. "With Voice of Joy and Praise." *Western Humanities Review*, Fall 1964; reprinted in *Greening Wheat*.

————. "A Child's Christmas in Utah." *Carleton Miscellany*, Winter 1966; reprinted in *Dialogue*, Autumn 1972.

Cassity, Kevin. "The Age-Old Problem of Who." *Greening Wheat*.

Christmas, R. A. "I Want a Prayer, Dad." *Stories Southwest*, edited by A. Wilber Stevens (Prescott College Press, 1973).

————. "Another Angel." *Dialogue*, Summer 1981; AML Prize in 1981 and reprinted in *Greening Wheat*.

Clark, Dennis. "Answer to Prayer." *Greening Wheat*, 1983.

Clark, Marden J. *Morgan Triumphs* (Orion Books, 1984).

Coles, Christie Lund. "Victory Girl." *RMR*, Fall 1944.

————. "The Tumbleweed." *Mountainwest*, Mar. 1976.

————. "The Tomato Cure." *Mountainwest*, Apr. 1979.

Doty, Ann. "I Just Don't Think Anymore that It's Such a Big Deal—A Story about Clayboy and Jeanie." *Twenty-two*, 1975.

England, Karin Anderson. "Miscarriage." *Dialogue*, Fall 1992.

Evenson, Brian. "Amparo." *Inscape*, 1989.

Farmer, Gladys Clark. *Elders and Sisters* (Seagull Books, 1977).

Farnsworth, Kent A. "Counterpoint. *Greening Wheat*, 1983.

————."A Season and a Time." *Twenty-two*, 1975.

Fisher, Vardis. "Charivari." *RMR*, Spring-Summer 1939; reprinted in Ray B. West, Jr., ed., *Rocky Mountain Stories* (Sage Books, 1941).

Geary, Edward A. "Jack-Mormons." *Dialogue*, Spring 1989.

Hafen, Lyman. "Epsom Salts." First prize, Utah Arts Council, 1991.

Harker, Herbert. "Mr. Gregory." *Christmas*, 1991.

Hawkins, Lisa Bolin. "Muddy, Rising Waters." First place, Sunstone Contest, 1991; forthcoming in *Sunstone*.

Hawkinson, Sharon M. *Only Strangers Travel* (Bookcraft, 1984).

Howe, Susan. "Getting to Disneyland." First place, Sunstone Contest, 1988; *Sunstone*, Aug. 1990.

Hughes, Dean. "Sun on the Snow." *Christmas*, 1991.

Hurd, Jerrie. "Aunt Betsy." *Dialogue*, Autumn 1984.

Jolley, Clifton Holt. "Feeding the Fox: A Parable." *Dialogue*, Winter 1983.

Jones, Helen Walker. "Hot Leather and Chains." *Mountainwest*, July 1979.

————. "The Snowdrift, the Swan." *Dialogue*, Autumn 1983.

————. "After the Harvest." First prize, Utah Arts Council, 1984.

————. "As Winter Comes On. *Dialogue*, Winter 1985.

————. "Going Through the List." *Sunstone*, Apr. 1989.

————. "The Six-Buck Fortune." First place, Dialogue Award, 1990; *Dialogue*, Fall 1990.

Kalpakian, Laura. *Dark Continent and Other Stories* (Penguin Books, 1989).

Kidd, Kathryn H. "Voucher and the Christmas Wars. *Christmas*, 1991.

Knowles, Mary. "Rosalie the Italian Bast." *Mountainwest*, June 1978.

Lake, Claudette. "Peculiar Ways." A Christian Values Winner; *Literature and Belief*, 1982.

Lane, Elizabeth. "The Pretending Place." *Mountainwest*, Mar. 1978.

Larson, Lance. "Sleeping Out." *Inscape*, Winter 1987.

Larson, Lynne. "Liberty Bolt!" *Mountainwest*, Jul. 1976.

————. "The Bishop." *Mountainwest*, Aug. 1977.

————. "Original Sin." *Mountainwest*, May 1978; reprinted in *Greening Wheat*, 1983.

————. "Bawdy and Soul." Second place, Sunstone Contest, 1982; *Sunstone*, Mar.-Apr. 1982.

Littke, Lael. "The Chastity Gum." *Dialogue*, Fall 1990.

McDaniel, Mary Catherine. "A Little of What You Fancy." Third place (4th quarter, 1986) in the L. Ron Hubbard contest and published in *Writers of the Future*, Vol. 3, ed. Algis Budrys (Bridge Publication, 1987).

Miller, Rob Hollis. "The Morns are Meeker Than they Were."
    Exponent II, 1988.

[Molen], Patricia Hart. "A Ride in the Dark." *Exponent II*, Spring 1976.

————. "The Growler and Sandra House." *Sunstone*, Mar.-Apr.
    1981.

————. "At the Heart of the Labyrinth." *BYU Studies*, Summer
    1981.

————. "The Black Door." *Dialogue*, Fall 1985.

Moon, Harold K. "They Is Gold in Them Hills." *Mountainwest*, Apr.
    1976.

————. "From the Cypress Grove." *Mountainwest*, Feb. 1979.

————. *Possible Dreams* (Brigham Young University, 1982).

Morris, Larry. "The Rock Crusher." *Sunstone*, Mar.-Apr. 1979.

Munk, Margaret R. "Searching," *Dialogue*, Winter 1981.

————. "A Proposal." Honorable mention, Sunstone Contest,
    1984; *Sunstone*, Sept. 1985.

Nichols, Julie. "Pennyroyal, Cohosh, Rue." *Sunstone*, May 1988.

Nicita, Carolyn. "Mechanical Assistance" and "Recycling." Both
    forthcoming in *Tomorrow: Speculative Fiction Magazine*.

Peterson, Joseph. "Yellow Dust." *Sunstone*, Sep.-Oct. 1979;
    reprinted in *Greening Wheat*, 1983.

————. "A Ford Mustang." *Dialogue*, Summer 1980.

————. "The Genealogy of Della B. Paulsen." First place, Sunstone
    Contest, 1982; *Sunstone*, Jan.-Feb. 1982.

————. "The Sure Word." *Sunstone*, Jan.- Feb. 1984.

Petsco, Béla. "The Mustard Seed." *Twenty-two, 1975*.

————. *Nothing Very Important and Other Stories* (Meservydale
    Publishing Co., 1979).

Rogers, Kristin Smart. "Looking for God." Second place, Sunstone
    Contest, 1990; *Sunstone*, Nov. 1991.

Rogers, Thomas F. "Heart of the Fathers." *Dialogue*, Summer 1991.

Rozema, Mark. "Eye of the Beholder." *Literature and Belief*, 1992.

Rubilar, Lisa Madsen de. "Pure Thin Bones." *Dialogue*, Winter 1989.

————. "Songs." *Dialogue*, Fall 1990.

Russell, Marla Zollinger. "What Wondering Brings." Second place,
    Sunstone Contest, 1981; *Sunstone*, Jan.-Feb. 1981.

Saderup, Dian. "A Blessing of Duty." *Sunstone*, May-Jun. 1979.

————. "Out There." First place, Sunstone Contest, 1983;
    Sunstone, Jan.-Apr. 1983.

————. "Turning." *Dialogue,* Spring 1987.

————. "Earl." *The New Era,* Oct. 1989.

Sealy, Shirley. *Beauty in Being* (Butterfly Publishing, 1980).

Shelline, Stewart A. "When the Rains Came Down the River." First place, Sunstone Contest, 1986; *Sunstone,* Jan. 1988.

————. "The Stream Winner." First prize, Utah Arts Council, 1986.

Smallwood, Susan Dean. "Gifts." *Christmas,* 1991.

Snell, George. "Young Love." *RMR,* Winter 1940.

————. "Letter to Elsie." Ray B. West, Jr., ed., *Rocky Mountain Stories* (Sage Books, 1941).

————. "Smoke in the Snow." *RMR,* Autumn 1945; reprinted in *Rocky Mountain Reader,* 1946.

Solomon, Michael. "The Sheet of Our True Lord Jesus." First place, Sunstone Contest, 1984; *Sunstone,* Jan. 1985.

Stewart, Ora Pate. "The Tramp," *Texas Quarterly,* Summer 1968.

Thornley, Diann. "A Distant Legacy." *The Leading Edge: Magazine of Science Fiction and Fantasy,* no. 6 (Fall 1983).

————. "Thunderbird's Egg." Forthcoming in *Washed by a Wave.*

Thurman, Richard Young. "The Credit Line." *Prize Stories of 1957: The O. Henry Awards.*

————. "Not Another Word." *New Yorker,* 25 May 1957; reprinted in *Best American Short Stories, 1958* and in Ken Macrorie, *Telling Writing* (Hayden Books, 1970).

Thurston, Jarvis. "The One and Only Appearance of Jeez Christ on Sun Mountain." *RMR,* Spring 1945; reprinted in *Rocky Mountain Reader,* 1946.

————. "The Cross," *Western Review,* Winter 1959; reprinted in J. Golden Taylor, ed., *Great Short Stories of the West,* Vol. 2 (Ballantine Books, 1971).

West, Ray B., Jr. "The Blue Spring." *Interim,* 1946; reprinted in *Rocky Mountain Reader,* 1946.

————. "The Ascent." *Prize Stories, 1948: The O. Henry Awards.*

————. "The Last of the Grizzly Bears," *Epoch,* Fall 1950; reprinted in Baxter Hathaway, ed., *Stories from Epoch* (Cornell University Press, 1966), and in J. Golden Taylor, ed., *Great Short Stories of the West,* Vol. 2 (Ballantine Books, 1971).

Weyland, Jack. *First Day of Forever, and Other Stories of LDS Youth* (Horizon Publishing, 1981).

————. *Punch and Cookies Forever* (Horizon Publishers, 1981).

————. "Dallas will Still Be There on Thursday." *Ensign*, June 1987.

————. *A Small Light in the Darkness* (Deseret Book, 1987).

————. "The Three Wise Guys." *Christmas*, 1991.

Witham, Craig. "Love Daddy Love." Second place, Sunstone Contest, 1985; *Sunstone*, Apr. 1987.

Wolverton, Dave. "On My Way to Paradise." First place (4th quarter, 1986) and winner of the Grand Prize in the L. Ron Hubbard Contest, published in *Writers of the Future*, vol. 3, ed. Algis Budrys (Bridge Publications, 1987).

————. "Skyfish." *Inscape*, Fall 1986.

————. "The Smiling Man." *Inscape*, Winter 1987.

————. "Wheatfields, Beyond." *Tomorrow: Speculative Fiction Magazine*, Dec. 1992; forthcoming in *Washed by a Wave*.

Wright, David L. "Speak Ye Tenderly of Kings." *Inland*, Spring 1960.

————. "A Measure of Contentment." *The Humanist*, Jul.-Aug. 1960.

————. "A Summer in the Country." *Mutiny*, Fall 1960; reprinted in *Best Articles and Stories*, Mar. 1961, and in *Sunstone*, Fall 1976.

————. "The Hawk." *Arizona Quarterly*, Winter 1960; reprinted in *Greening Wheat*, 1983.

————. "Mice Men and Principles." *Mutiny*, Fall-Winter 1961-62.

————. "Of Pleasures and Palaces" (1961). *Dialogue*, Winter 1990.

Notes on the Authors and Acknowledgments

PHYLLIS BARBER teaches in the Vermont College M.F.A. Writing Program. She won Utah Arts Council first prizes in both the novel and the short story in 1988; won the Associated Writing Programs Award Series in Creative Nonfiction in 1991; and has served as a panelist choosing literary fellowships for the National Endowment for the Arts. Her books include a collection of stories, *The School of Love* (University of Utah Press, 1990); a novel, *And the Desert Shall Blossom* (University of Utah Press, 1991; Signature Books, 1993); *How I Got Cultured: A Nevada Memoir* (University of Georgia Press, 1992); and two books for children. She lives in Colorado with her husband, David H. Barber, has three sons, and is a professional musician. "At the Talent Show" first appeared in *The Missouri Review* (Winter 1991).

M. SHAYNE BELL won first place in the L. Ron Hubbard Writers of the Future Contest (second quarter, 1986); a Creative Writing Fellowship from the National Endowment for the Arts for 1991; and second prize for his short story, "The King's Kiss," in the Utah Arts Council Contest for 1992. He has published a novel, *Nicoji* (Baen Books, 1991), and is currently living in Salt Lake City, Utah, writing and editing a collection of Mormon science fiction to be called *Washed by a Wave of the Wind: Stories from the Corridor* (Signature Books, forthcoming). "Dry Niger" was originally published in *Asimov's Science Fiction Magazine* (August 1990); was voted an honorable mention in *The Year's Best Science Fiction: Eighth Annual Collection* (1991); and will be reprinted in an anthology of current science fiction, *Future Earths: Under African Skies.*

JOHN BENNION teaches writing at Brigham Young University and lives in Springville, Utah, with his wife, Karla, and their four children. He won the Utah Arts Council first prize in the short story in 1987 and the Association for Mormon Letters short story prize in 1988. His story "Burial Pool" was included in *Christmas for the World* (Aspen Books, 1991). "Dust" first appeared in *Best of the West* (1989) and was reprinted in his first collection, *Breeding Leah and Other Stories* (Signature Books, 1991).

ORSON SCOTT CARD lives in Greensboro, North Carolina, and is the owner of Hatrack River Publications, which publishes LDS fiction. His novels include *Ender's Game* and *Speaker for the Dead,* both of which won Hugo and Nebula awards, as well as the Mormon novels, *Saints* (Tom Doherty Associates, 1988) and *Lost Boys* (HarperCollins, 1992). He is the author of two series in progress: "The Tales of Alvin Maker" (latest *Prentice Alvin,* TOR, 1989) and "Homecoming" (the first, *The Memory of Earth,* TOR, 1992). He is also the author of *Saintspeak: The Mormon Dictionary* (Orion Books, 1981). "The Fringe" is from *The Folk of the Fringe* (Phantasia Press, 1989), his collection of Mormon science fiction stories.

NEAL CHANDLER "shuffles papers and sometimes teaches writing at Cleveland State University in Ohio" (where he is actually director of Creative Writing). He is the author of a play, *Appeal to a Lower Court,* published in *Sunstone*

(December 1990). "Benediction" won the *Dialogue* Award in fiction for 1984 and is the title story of his first collection, published by the University of Utah Press in 1989. Permission to reprint the story here is granted by the publisher.

*M*ICHAEL FILLERUP lives with his wife Rebecca and their four children in Flagstaff, Arizona, where he is director of ESL/Bilingual Education for the public school system. He has published *Visions and Other Stories* (Signature Books, 1990) and is working on a novel, "The River, The Rock." "Lost and Found" was cited by the Association for Mormon Letters as the best Mormon short story for 1991 and appeared in *Christmas for the World* (Aspen Books, 1991).

*J*UDITH FREEMAN has published two novels, *The Chinchilla Farm* (W. W. Norton, 1989) and *Set For Life* (W. W. Norton, 1991). She is at work, with photographer Tina Burney, on a book about India, based on a recent trip funded by the Guggenheim Foundation. "Family Attractions" is from *Family Attractions, Stories,* © 1988 by Judith Freeman, and is used here by permission of Viking Penguin, a division of Penguin Books, USA, Inc.

*L*EWIS HORNE teaches in the department of English at the University of Saskatchewan, is a widely published poet, and has had stories reprinted in *Best American Short Stories, 1974* and *Prize Stories, 1987: The O. Henry Awards.* His first collection, "The Scorpion Fire," will be published by Signature Books in 1993. "The People Who Were Not There" first appeared in *Kansas Quarterly* (Summer 1973).

*S*IBYL JOHNSTON holds an M.A. in creative writing from Boston University and was a 1990-91 Fellow in Literature at Radcliffe's Bunting Institute. She grew up in Illinois, now lives in Cambridge, Massachusetts, but considers Utah her home. Her story, "Jessie and Louise," was included in *Greening*

Wheat: Fifteen Mormon Stories (Orion Books, 1983). "Iris Holmes" was published in the Macmillan anthology, *Hot Type,* in 1988 and forms part of a forthcoming novel.

WAYNE JORGENSEN writes poetry as well as fiction. Under the alias Bruce W. Jorgensen he teaches creative writing at Brigham Young University and writes criticism. He is now at work on a book on Reynolds Price. His story, "A Song for One Still Voice," was published in the *Ensign* (March 1979) and also appeared in *Greening Wheat: Fifteen Mormon Stories* (Orion Books, 1983). "Born of the Water" won a first place in the Sunstone Fiction Contest, 1980, and was published by *Sunstone* (January-February 1980).

WALTER KIRN grew up in the midwest and Arizona and is now a full-time writer living in Montana. His first novel, *She Needed Me,* was published by Simon and Schuster in 1992. "Whole Other Bodies" is from his first collection of stories, *My Hard Bargain* (Knopf, 1990), which won the Association for Mormon Letters short story award in 1990 and was published in paperback by Washington Square Press in 1992.

EILEEN GIBBONS KUMP lives in St. Joseph, Missouri. Her story "Everncere" was first published in the *Ensign* (August 1979) and then in *Greening Wheat: Fifteen Mormon Stories* (Orion Books, 1983). "The Ladder" won the Sunstone Fiction Contest in 1981 and was published in *Sunstone* (January-February 1981). "Sayso or Sense," included here, first appeared in *Brigham Young University Studies* (Fall 1974), and was included in her collection *Bread and Milk* (Brigham Young University Press, 1979).

DONALD R. MARSHALL, professor of humanities at Brigham Young University, has won awards in painting, photography, composing, directing, and set design; his most recent writing awards were first place in the 1988 Utah Arts

Council Contest and first place in the 1989 Deseret Book Children's Book Contest. His story, "Lavender Blue," was published in *Sunstone* (March-April 1981) and in *Greening Wheat: Fifteen Mormon Stories* (Orion Books, 1983). He has published a collection of stories, *Frost in the Orchard* (Brigham Young University Press, 1977; Deseret Book, 1985); a novel, *Zinnie Stokes, Zinnie Stokes* (Deseret Book, 1984); and a children's book, *Enchantress of Crumbledown* (Deseret Book, 1990). "The Week-end," which was also included in *A Believing People* (Brigham Young University Press, 1974), is from his first collection, *The Rummage Sale* (Heirloom Publications, 1972; republished by Peregrine Smith in 1975 and by Deseret Book in 1985).

PAULINE MORTENSEN holds a Ph.D. in writing from the University of Utah and is a professional technical writer in Orem, Utah. "Woman Talking to a Cow" is from her collection, *Back Before the World Turned Nasty* (University of Arkansas Press, 1989), which won the Utah Arts Council first prize for short stories in 1987, its Publication Prize the following year, and the Association for Mormon Letters short story award in 1989. The story is reprinted here by permission of the publisher, © 1989.

LEVI S. PETERSON is professor of English at Weber State University in Ogden, Utah. He has published a novel, *The Backslider* (Signature Books, 1986); a biography, *Juanita Brooks, Mormon Woman Historian* (University of Utah Press, 1988); and a second collection of stories, *Night Soil* (Signature Books, 1990). He is at work on a second novel and a collection of "wilderness essays." "The Christianizing of Coburn Heights" is from his first collection, *The Canyons of Grace,* which won the Illinois Short Fiction Award, was published by the University of Illinois Press in 1982, and was published in paperback by Signature Books in 1985.

KAREN ROSENBAUM received an M.A. in creative writing from Stanford University and has been teaching

English at Ohlone Community College in Fremont, California. She lives in Kensington, California, with her husband, Ben McClinton. Her story, "Low Tide" was published in *Sunstone* (September-October 1980) and chosen for *Greening Wheat* (Orion Books, 1983). She won first place in *Dialogue*'s short story contest in 1987. "Hit the Frolicking, Rippling Brooks" was published in *Dialogue: A Journal of Mormon Thought* (Fall 1978).

*L*INDA SILLITOE is a professional writer and editor living in Salt Lake City. She has published a novel, *Sideways to the Sun* (Signature Books, 1987) and co-authored *Salamander: The Story of the Mormon Forgery Murders* (Signature Books, 1988). Her story, "Four Walls and An Empty Door," was published in *Greening Wheat: Fifteen Mormon Stories* (Orion Books, 1983). Her first collection of poems, "Crazy For Living," will be published by Signature Books, and her ethnobiography of Clifford Duncan, "One Voice Rising," by the University of Utah Press. "Windows on the Sea" is the title story of her collection published by Signature Books in 1989.

*V*IRGINIA SORENSEN's eight adult novels and seven children's books include the Newberry Medal winner, *Miracles on Maple Hill* (Harcourt Brace, 1957); a Child Study Award winner, *Plain Girl* (Harcourt Brace, 1955); and two Mormon novels, *A Little Lower than the Angels* (Knopf, 1942) and *The Evening and the Morning* (Harcourt, Brace & Co., 1949). Her story, "The Talking Stick" was chosen for the *Prize Stories, 1948: The O. Henry Awards,* and she was awarded two Guggenheim Fellowships. She was working on an autobiography when she died in December 1991. "Where Nothing Is Long Ago" is from her collection *Where Nothing Is Long Ago: Memories of a Utah Childhood* (Harcourt, Brace, and World, 1963).

*D*ARRELL SPENCER teaches writing at Brigham Young University. His story, "Song and Dance," won second prize in the 1990 Utah Arts Council Contest, and "Union

Business" won the 1991 Lawrence Foundation Award for the Short Story. "I Am Buzz Gaulter, Left-hander," is from his first collection, *Woman Packing a Pistol* (Dragon Gate, 1987), which won the Association for Mormon Letters award. He has finished a second collection, "Our Secret's Out," being considered for publication, and is at work on a novel, "Nasty Town."

DOUGLAS THAYER lives in Provo, Utah, with his wife, Donlu, and teaches creative writing at Brigham Young University. He has published a novel, *Summer Fire* (Orion Books, 1983); two collections of stories, *Under the Cottonwoods and Other Mormon Stories* (Frankson Books, 1977; Signature Books, 1984), and *Mr. Wahlquist in Yellowstone and Other Stories* (Gibbs Smith, Publisher, 1989); and is at work on a collection of personal essays and a novel. His story, "The Redtail Hawk," published in *Dialogue: A Journal of Mormon Thought* (Summer 1970) and in *Under the Cottonwoods,* also appeared in *Christmas for the World* (Aspen Books, 1991). "Opening Day," which won the Dialogue Award in fiction for 1969, was first published in *Dialogue* (Spring, 1990) and then in *Under the Cottonwoods.*

MAURINE WHIPPLE won the Houghton Mifflin Literary Prize for 1938 to help her complete her novel *The Giant Joshua,* which appeared in 1941. In the 1940s she published a number of essays and stories about Mormon country and a visitor's guide to the state, *This Is the Place: Utah* (Knopf, 1945). She died in St. George, Utah, in March 1992. "They Did Go Forth," discovered in Whipple's papers, was first published in *Dialogue: A Journal of Mormon Thought* (Winter 1991), and will appear in *Maurine Whipple: The Lost Works,* eds. Veda Tebbs Hale and Lavina Fielding Anderson (Aspen Books, forthcoming). Used here by permission.

MARGARET BLAIR YOUNG is a writing instructor at Brigham Young University and has published two novels, *House without Walls* (Deseret Book, 1991) and *Salvador*

(Aspen Books, 1992). She won first prizes in both the short story and book sections of the Utah Arts Council Contest in 1989 and its Publication Prize in 1990 for her collection of stories, *Elegies and Lovesongs* (University of Idaho Press, 1992). She is married to Bruce Young and has four children. "Outsiders" first appeared in *Dialogue: A Journal of Mormon Thought* (Spring 1991).